WIDOW *of* GETTYSBURG

Center Point
Large Print

Also by Jocelyn Green and available from Center Point Large Print:

The Heroines Behind the Lines Series
Wedded to War

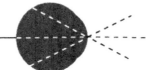

This Large Print Book carries the Seal of Approval of N.A.V.H.

WIDOW *of* GETTYSBURG

Heroines Behind the Lines

Jocelyn Green

CENTER POINT LARGE PRINT
THORNDIKE, MAINE

This Center Point Large Print edition
is published in the year 2015 by arrangement with
Moody Publishers.

Copyright © 2013 by Jocelyn Green.
Map of Gettysburg: Rob Green Design.

Though many of the events in this story are
based on true incidents, characters are either
fictional or depicted fictitiously.

The text of this Large Print edition is unabridged.
In other aspects, this book may vary
from the original edition.
Printed in the United States of America
on permanent paper.
Set in 16-point Times New Roman type.

ISBN: 978-1-62899-688-3

Library of Congress Cataloging-in-Publication Data

Green, Jocelyn.
  Widow of Gettysburg : heroines behind the lines / Jocelyn Green. —
Center Point Large Print edition.
    pages cm. — (Civil War ; book 2)
  Summary: "The farm of Union widow Liberty Holloway is confiscated
and converted into a Confederate field hospital, bringing Liberty face-to-
face with unspeakable suffering. In the wake of shattered homes and
broken bodies, Liberty and Bella, her hired help and a former slave,
struggle to pick up the fragments the battle has left behind"
  —Provided by publisher.
  ISBN 978-1-62899-688-3 (alk. paper)
  1. United States—History—Civil War, 1861–1865—Women—Fiction.
    2. Gettysburg, Battle of, Gettysburg, Pa., 1863—Fiction.
    3. Large type books. I. Title.
  PS3607.R4329255W53 2015
  813′.6—dc23
                                                        2015020457

For those who have suffered loss, and for those who have sacrificed without recognition.
It may be dark now, but dawn is on the way.

Weeping may endure for a night,
but joy comes in the morning.
Psalm 30:5

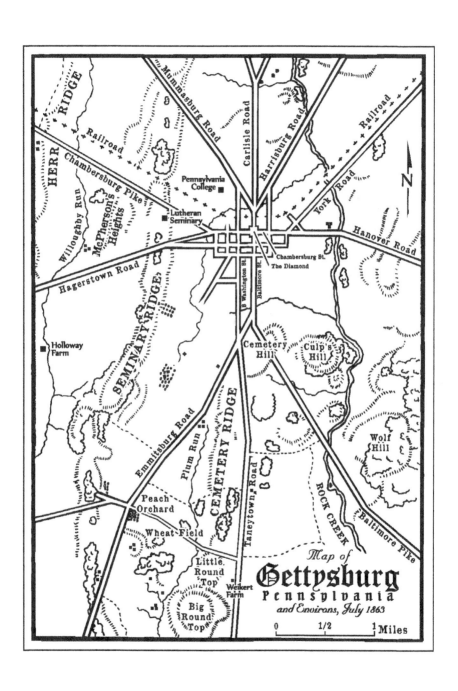

Contents

A Note on the Battle of Gettysburg

Mention the word "Gettysburg" and most people will immediately think of the epic battle that took place in rural Pennsylvania July 1–3, 1863, or of the Gettysburg Address that President Abraham Lincoln delivered four months later. Scores of books have been written about the armies that fought, the military strategy, the details of the battles, and how it might have ended differently if other decisions had been made. In comparison, very few books have been written about Gettysburg itself. But before "Gettysburg" was a battle, it was a town full of ordinary people, people like you and me.

Twenty-four hundred residents inhabited the borough of Gettysburg in 1863 when 163,000 men and 15,000 animals converged upon it for the three-day battle in July. Some fled to protect themselves and their property, while many—most of them women and children—were caught in the crossfire. Surviving the battle was only the beginning. While most history books follow the armies on their journeys away from Gettysburg when the battle receded, *Widow of Gettysburg* keeps the focus on the aftermath being played out in the town. When the armies withdrew, 21,000 wounded were left in their wake, with only 106 Union medical officers and far fewer Confederate doctors. Women and children were drafted into hospital service, whether they felt confident in their ability or not. Days after the battle's end, thousands more invaded the already overtaxed town in the form of relief workers, sightseers, and those looking for their loved ones. The quiet life Gettysburg had known was gone.

Women of Gettysburg did not ask for the distinction, but many became heroines behind the lines just the same. *Widow of Gettysburg* is the story of their resilience. In the words of Gettysburg housewife Sarah Broadhead, "We do not know until tried what we are capable of."

Act One
THE GATHERING STORM

"WE WERE SO USED TO the cry, 'the Rebels are coming,' when they did not come, were not even in sight, that we paid little or no attention to the daily, even hourly reports, that came to our ears and we even laughed and joked among ourselves, little dreaming they were really so near."

—FANNIE BUEHLER,
Gettysburg housewife

"BUSINESS OF ALL KINDS was paralyzed, and the daily reports of the coming of the rebels kept us in a constant fever of excitement. On June 26, they came, spent the night and passed through toward Harrisburg, burning bridges and spreading consternation everywhere. Little we dreamed of the far greater horrors that were in store for us."

—ELIZABETH SALOME "SALLIE" MYERS,
public school teacher in Gettysburg, age 21

Chapter One

The Holloway Farm,
Adams County, Pennsylvania
Friday, June 26, 1863

"Shhhh. Someone's coming." Liberty Holloway cocked her head toward the window as the muffled rhythm of hoofbeats rose above the drumming rain. "Rebels?" The word sat, bitter, on her tongue as her fists sank deeper into the bread dough she'd been kneading. They had taken enough from her already, long before a single Confederate soldier had set foot in the North. Were they now here to raid her property as well?

"Traveler, looks like." Bella Jamison wiped her hands on her flour-dusted apron and peered between the curtains without parting them. "Wet and hungry, I'll wager. You know Black Horse Tavern and Inn down the road are full up right now, and you just hung that sign out by the road last week."

Libbie exhaled, her pulse matching her fear. Though she was a grown woman of nineteen years, she had yet to tame her runaway imagination. But perhaps her hired help was right, and a traveler would be welcome, provided he could pay in greenbacks.

"Then again, we just can't know for sure." Bella backed away from the window, her coffee-with-cream complexion darkening in the shadows. "Rebels don't always have proper uniforms, you know. I only see one on the road, but there could be more coming."

Serves me right for not heeding Governor Curtin's proclamation. Libbie pulled her hands from the sticky dough and went to the window herself. "If he doesn't break into a gallop, we'll have just enough time."

Before the words had left her mouth, Bella had already moved the worktable away from the bricked-in fireplace and slid out several loose bricks. The cast-iron stove and oven served for their baking and cooking, but the summer kitchen's walk-in fireplace still had its purpose. Together, they hurriedly filled the space to keep their stores out of sight: jars of molasses, peach and strawberry preserves, applesauce, tomatoes, and sacks of potatoes, onions, flour, and oats.

Drip. Drip. Drip. The leak in the corner marked time like a metronome as water dropped into a tin pie plate on the floor. Soon, all that was left was the freshly baked rye bread cooling on the sideboard, the abandoned lump of dough, and bunches of parsley and oregano hanging from the rafters to dry.

After replacing the bricks and the table in front of it, Liberty stole another glance out the window.

"We can still hide the horses. Make haste." Resolve pierced through her anxiety as she hung her apron on a wooden peg and stepped out into the rain with Bella close on her heels.

Hurrying into the barn, Libbie swished her skirts to scatter the clucking chickens in their path. The horses, Daisy and Romeo, twitched their tails as the women bridled them, then led them past the summer kitchen and into the great hall of the two-story stone farmhouse.

"We'll be fine here." Bella stroked Romeo's withers to calm him. "Remember, you are the lady of this house. Stand your ground."

"If it's a Rebel—"

"I can take care of myself. Go."

The hoofbeats grew louder outside. Liberty patted the thick, black braid that circled her head and hurried over to Major, the 140-pound Newfoundland sprawled on the rug inside the front door.

"Wake up, boy. Time to look menacing," she said as she buried her hand in the scruff of his massive neck. Not that he could hear anything. "Come on, Major." She hooked a finger under his collar and tugged. Groaning, he lumbered to his feet, yawned, and turned his head slightly to wink at her with his one good eye.

"Come, he's almost here," she whispered, and immediately regretted her choice of words. *I could swear that dog can read lips!* Major perked up and jumped at the door. "No, Major, not Levi." She shook her head. "No Levi."

Liberty led Major out onto the porch and pointed to the splitting wooden floorboards beside her. "Sit." He obeyed. Wild roses the color of lemonade hugged the porch from all sides, lifting their faces to catch their drink. Their heady fragrance infused the air as a man on a gaunt horse rode up the lane to Libbie's dooryard in no particular hurry, as if it weren't raining at all, as if the shelter of a covered porch didn't stand right in front of him. Feeling a pull on her skirt, she glanced down to find Major sitting sideways on one of his haunches, leaning against her leg. *So much for my canine protector.*

The stranger drew rein and dismounted his horse with graceful ease. A rain-soaked denim shirt and brown woolen trousers revealed a lean, muscular body, the kind that was used to work. A farmer perhaps? Carpenter? *Or a soldier.*

"You don't look like a Rebel." The words escaped her without thought.

So did Major. Before she could stop him, he ambled down the steps to the dooryard and slammed right into the man, stumbled back a little, then nuzzled his big furry black head under the man's hand. Liberty sighed. Major's sense of balance was lacking since he'd lost his eye.

The man bent to scratch Major behind the ears and on the white patch on his chest. "I take that as a compliment, ma'am." His accent was Northern, a blessed relief. Straightening again, he doffed his felt hat and bowed slightly before appraising her with moss green eyes. Rain darkened his hair to the color of polished oak and coursed down his stubbled cheeks. He took a step forward. "Miss Liberty?"

"How did you—"

"The sign by the road. Liberty Inn." He rubbed his horse's nose before glancing up at her again. "I'm guessing you might be Miss Liberty?"

Liberty spun the thin gold band around her finger. "Yes." She hoped he would not also guess how very new this venture was. She had three rooms ready for guests on the first floor of the farmhouse, each complete with quilts stitched by her own hand, but not one had yet been used.

"You've lost someone." His voice was quiet, tentative, but for all the world, Liberty could not think why. Two years into the war, women in mourning were a common sight. She crossed her arms across the pleated waist of her faded black dress and wished she had at least worn her hoops under her skirt this morning. She never did while doing chores, they got in the way so much. But now, the way he looked at her, she felt practically naked without them. "You'll forgive me if I ask you to kindly state your business, sir." She caught Major's eye and stabbed her finger at the porch floor again until the dog returned to her side.

He cleared his throat and offered a smile. "I'm a long way from home, and I sure could use a little hospitality."

"Do you mean to say that you need a room?"

"I have neither time nor money for a room, but my bread basket's been empty for quite a spell." He laid a hand on his stomach. "Could you spare anything for me to eat?"

She sighed. Times were tight at Holloway Farm, but she'd never been very good at saying no, to anyone. "Your mount looks as though he could eat something too." She led them both to the barn where the horse could eat hay and oats, then took the stranger into the summer kitchen. Twenty feet behind the house, this was the small outbuilding where she did most cooking, baking, preserving, and laundry during the hottest season of the year. It would serve to feed a stranger without allowing him into the house.

"Sit there." She pointed to the rough-hewn table butting up against the old fireplace and crossed the room to slice a loaf cooling on the sideboard. Major spread himself out to dry on the floor in front of the warm stove, the smells of wet dog and fresh bread thickening the air.

When Libbie turned back to the table, she found the man still standing. He shrugged, his hat still in his hands. "I never sit when a lady still stands. Won't you join me? Or do you mean to make me stand while I eat alone, like a common beggar?"

His smile dissolved any argument on the tip of her tongue, and she allowed him to seat her at the worktable, her face flooding with warmth that did not come from the oven. Even Levi's manners had not gone this far. But to be fair, Libbie had not expected it. Aunt Helen had raised her to believe that manners were not meant to be wasted on the likes of her. Liberty swallowed. She should not think anything uncharitable of the dead. Either of them.

The man's stomach growled as she set the loaf of rye on the table, yet he made no move for it. "Are you waiting for me to serve you?" The question sounded more prickly than she intended.

"Ladies first." He nodded at the bread. "You baked it. You should be the first to enjoy it."

"Well, you certainly don't act like a beggar," Libbie admitted as she helped herself to a steaming piece.

"Wouldn't Mama be proud." He laughed, but a shadow passed over his face. He took a slice for himself then, but before taking a bite, bowed his head for a moment.

Then he ate. And ate—until the loaf was gone.

Finally, when the last crumb had disappeared, he leaned back in his chair and raked a hand through his hair. "I haven't been full in a very long time. Thank you, ma'am."

She nodded and stood, and so did he.

"It doesn't suit me to take something for

nothing, though." He flicked a glance at the water dimpling in the pie plate. "I can fix that for you."

"You needn't trouble yourself."

"Your husband certainly didn't." He dropped his gaze to the ring she twisted on her finger. "Perhaps he is away."

"Quite. He's dead." Libbie bit her tongue in punishment for its bluntness.

His eyes softened. "I do beg your pardon. I meant no disrespect."

"I can get along just fine by myself." Liberty dropped her voice. "This is my property, and—"

"Yours?"

Libbie blinked. Most likely, he thought her too young to own property. "Yes, mine. So I should manage it myself. It wouldn't do to let you spoil me."

One eyebrow hitched up as he looked down at her. "Every woman deserves to be taken care of every now and then, no matter how capable you are." An easy smile curved his lips. "I'd consider it a pleasure to help."

"That isn't necessary." To be alone with a man, even for this long—it was almost indecent. Liberty hoped the warmth she felt in her face did not color her cheeks.

"Necessary? Neither was your sharing your bread with me. But courtesy, kindness, and good manners are all necessary now more than ever."

"Thank you kindly, but I'm sure you have some

place to be. Godspeed on your journey." She waited for him to take his leave. But, rolling the brim of his hat in his hands, he remained planted in the doorway. Rain fell on the ground behind him, speckling his trousers with tiny flecks of mud.

"I am sorry for your loss, truly." His eyes probed her face, and she wondered if she looked sorry for her loss, too. Or just guilty. "How long's it been? Since your husband died."

She swallowed. "Since the Battle of Bull Run. The first."

"Almost two years. You should be out of mourning soon."

Liberty stiffened. "If I so choose. Some widows wear black for the rest of their lives." *Will I forever be told what to do?*

"And bury yourself with the dead? I can't imagine that kind of life for you."

Liberty stared at him. "I can't imagine why in heaven's name you—a perfect stranger—feel compelled to even comment on such a private matter! It's not your place to judge." She turned her back and pummeled the bread dough she'd left on the sideboard earlier that morning.

"There's enough death in this war as it is, ma'am." His tone was tender, not spiteful. As hers had been. "Just when do you plan to come on back to the land of the living? There's so much more to life than death, you know. Sure would hate for you to miss out on it."

An unwelcome tingle ran down her spine. "It's not your concern." She pounded the dough again.

"Just remember what I said. There is more to life than death. Whatever happens. There is more."

"You speak in riddles."

"You'll see soon enough." He stepped outside, and Liberty followed, her doughy fingers gumming together in the rain. "If I were you, I'd go visit kinfolk somewhere else. And don't come back for a few weeks." As if she had family to visit. As if she had anyone at all, aside from her hired hands and her horse.

Her mouth went dry. "What do you know?"

"There's trouble brewing."

"We've been hearing that for months." But her pulse quickened at the intensity of his gaze. "You're crying wolf along with the rest of them."

He looked down at her for a moment, as if testing his reply in his mind before speaking. "Don't you remember? In the end, the wolf actually came."

"It will take more than a wolf to scare me off my farm."

The mysterious stranger shook his head and sighed. "Good day to you. Be well." He held her in his gaze for a heartbeat before tipping his hat and fading back into the rain.

Liberty's heart thundered as she entered the farmhouse, still dripping with rain. *It could have been worse.* She told herself. *It could have been a raiding party.*

But it wasn't. It was just a man passing through. Now if only his words weren't still echoing in her mind.

As she passed her bedroom on the way to the great hall, she caught a glimpse of herself in the looking glass on her bureau, and paused to weave an errant curl back into her braid.

She walked closer to the mirror. At a mere five feet two inches short, if it wasn't for the gentle curve of her waist and the way her corset filled out her bodice, she could pass for a tall child. She ventured a smile, and dimples popped into her cheeks. No one would guess she was old enough to be married, let alone widowed. But her sapphire blue eyes were shadowed by the valley of death the war had carved into her life.

When do you plan to come on back to the land of the living?

The question was, when would her conscience allow it?

She picked up a framed daguerreotype of Levi in his new uniform and studied it. She was sure he had been told not to smile while they captured his image, but he couldn't help it. He was so happy to fight for the Union, even though it meant taking a break from his studies at the Lutheran Theological Seminary in Gettysburg to do it. *I want to fight while I have the chance,* he had told her. *The war will be over before you know it, Libbie, and I have to do my part.* They married first, right after she had come out of mourning for Aunt Helen. It had seemed like perfect timing, and a dream come true for the orphan girl. A family of her own. A new beginning.

But I barely knew him. She was seventeen when they married, a mere child. They knew nothing, absolutely nothing. They believed he would be fine, would come back and finish his schooling and take over the Holloway Farm, and they'd have the rest of their lives to discover exactly what it was they loved about each other. The thought of his possible death was only fleeting. The idea that he may be wounded—wounded beyond recognition and yet still alive—never occurred to either one of them. Her mind reeled back to the day she learned the news.

She had not responded well.

Struggling to bridle her memories so they would not run away with her again, Libbie sat on the edge of her bed and absentmindedly traced with her finger the pattern of the colorful patchwork quilt that covered it. Her first. She smiled wistfully as the last two years flashed through her mind. When other girls her age were having fun together and being courted by their beaus, Liberty Holloway was home, forced into the social isolation of widowhood, learning to quilt and preserve the harvest she grew with her hired hand.

Not that it was that different from before . . .
As an orphan living with a spinster in a community of large families, Libbie had always been an oddity, a curiosity, but never really a friend. Levi's death had merely changed the reason for her solitude. She went from being Libbie the Orphan to Libbie the Widowed Bride.

But that was two years ago. *There's so much more to life than death.* Levi would have agreed. He had told her, in his one passing moment of gravity, that if he died, he would be happy knowing he had died in the service of his country. That he wanted her to find a way to be happy, too.

Maybe it was time, at long last, to try.

Kneeling on the rag rug at the end of her bed, Libbie pried up a loose floorboard, dug out the key she placed there nearly two years ago, and unlocked the cedar chest in front of her. The smell of a sunbaked forest greeted her as she lifted the lid, and she inhaled deeply. Slowly at first, and then like a child on Christmas morning, she lifted out dress after dress that she hadn't seen since those first bewildering months of the war. They were simple, practical, made by her own hand. But they weren't black, and some of them were even pretty.

Liberty's eyes misted over, and suddenly, she couldn't get her black crepe off fast enough. After unfastening the fabric-covered buttons she could reach, she cast her mourning into a rusty black puddle on the floor and stepped into the blue muslin, perfect for a summer day.

"What are you doing?"

Libbie jumped at the sound of Bella's voice from the hallway. Nervous laughter trickled from her lips at the sight of her standing there with two horses in tow, smelling of damp earth and hay. "I'm so sorry to keep you waiting. I was on my way to get you. The danger has passed, we're alone again."

Bella's velvety brown eyes widened as she looked at the discarded mourning dress and back to Liberty. "Those mourning clothes were your protection, Miss Liberty. No man, no matter how roguish, would try to take advantage of a woman in mourning."

Liberty set her lips in a thin line. For hired help, Bella certainly could be outspoken. "Am I not free to make my own decision?" She shook the ring off her finger and into the jewelry box on her bureau. "It's been long enough. Now fasten me up, please."

Bella's brow creased, but she obeyed. "I don't think your mama would approve." It was barely a whisper.

Libbie caught Bella's eye in the looking glass, and with uncharacteristic sharpness, said, "My mother? You know she's not around. She never was."

Guilt trickled over Silas Ford as he rode east on Hagerstown Road, away from the Holloway

Farm. He hated what he had become. And there was no place like Gettysburg to remind him of just how far he had fallen.

The Lutheran Theological Seminary loomed ahead on Seminary Ridge, its cupola white against the pewter grey sky. Silas thought he'd never see it again—not after what happened before his final year as a student there. Yet here he was, near enough to see that the brick building remained unchanged, while he was so far from being the pastor the seminary had trained him to be that the contrast nearly choked him. *Hope deferred maketh the heart sick.*

But regret accomplished nothing. Silas swallowed the lump in his throat and clucked his tongue, urging Bullet up the hill. It was an odd name for a horse whose owner refused to carry a gun. Named before it had come into Silas's possession, Silas had tried to change it, but the horse only responded to "Bullet." As a Lutheran, Silas wasn't supposed to believe in penance, but that's what it felt like. Not that he needed such an ever-present reminder of the sin that had changed more than just his life.

Mud sucked at Bullet's hooves as he carried Silas over the ridge and down the other side, toward town. With Holloway Farm out of sight behind Seminary Ridge, Silas breathed easier.

At least Liberty hadn't recognized him. He almost gave himself away back there, calling her by name like that. It was pure luck that he remembered the wooden sign by the road, the U.S. flag unfurling behind the lettering. If he hadn't known better, he would have thought "Liberty" was some reference to a Northern ideal, and not the name of a girl.

"Woman," he muttered, correcting himself. She was not the girl of fourteen summers he remembered, wilting beneath the scrutiny of the spinster who had hired him to repair her fences. No, Liberty had grown into a woman.

"And I've grown into an old man." The soft body of a student had been chiseled into muscular leanness. The fair skin and butter-blonde hair he'd brought with him to seminary were now darker. The last time he'd seen a looking glass, he'd seen grey hair sprouting at his temples, and lines framing his eyes, though he was only twenty-eight. It should not have surprised him, not after what he'd seen. He doubted that anyone in Gettysburg would recognize him. It would be far easier if they didn't.

Thoughts of Silas's past scattered as he entered Gettysburg, carefully riding slow enough to appear casual, but fast enough that he did not look aimless. He had a purpose, indeed. He was oath-bound. The fact that it had been against his will had no bearing on his situation now.

"Whoa, Bullet." Though this stop was not part of his assignment, Silas drew rein and dismounted in front of Christ Lutheran Church on Chambersburg Street. Removing his hat out of habit, he relished the gentle shower streaming over his body. Oh, how he wanted to be clean.

After tying Bullet to the hitching post in the street, he climbed the stone stairs, passed through the white columns under the portico, and slipped inside the arched door.

And waited. And hoped. Maybe here, in this church, he would feel closer to God than he did in his saddle. Silas did not bother to sit down, knowing his rain-soaked trousers would dampen the oak pews. And if God could meet him on a bench, He could just as well meet him standing in the back. He had met him here before. This was where Silas had worshiped alongside his fellow seminary students. That pew—fourth from the front on the left side—that was where he sat when Rev. Samuel Schmucker had fanned into flame the fire that had been kindling in his belly for the freedom of all men, regardless of color. When Schmucker's wife brought slaves into their marriage years ago, he taught and trained them to live as free men and women, then freed them. The reverend was the seminary founder, Silas's professor, and his role model. *What must he think of me now?* Silas shuddered. With any luck, he'd forgotten him all together.

Rolling the brim of his hat in his hands, he surveyed the narrow stained-glass windows. If the sun were shining, mosaics of vibrant color would depict inspiring stories from the Bible.

But the sun was not shining. So he closed his eyes, listening for God to speak to him anyway, and heard—nothing. Felt nothing. He sighed. *If I were God, would I want to talk to Silas Ford?* His mama had called times like these dry spells. "But the important thing," she had said, "is to keep talking to God anyway, even if He isn't talking back."

Forgive me, Silas prayed. *Show me the way out.* And he left the church feeling as much like a hypocrite as he ever had.

Chambersburg Street was springing to life as he reached Bullet and untied him, with women and children and a handful of men all headed toward the center of town.

"Excuse me," he called down to a young lady carrying a tray of bread down the sidewalk. "Is there a parade somewhere?"

The girl beamed up at him. "Better," she chirped. "Our soldiers are back!"

He raised his eyebrows. "Did they take a holiday? You must forgive me, I'm not from around here."

"I know." She laughed. "I'm sure I'd remember you if I'd seen you before." She flashed a smile that made his skin creep, but he waited for more information. Girls were always ready to talk. "Last week, after President Lincoln called for a hundred thousand more volunteers to defend us from the Rebels, Governor Curtin issued a call asking for fifty thousand of those men to come from Pennsylvania."

Silas swallowed his surprise. Fifty thousand? One hundred thousand? Did they have that many men to spare?

"So about sixty—or was it seventy?—of our boys from the college and seminary here signed up and went to Harrisburg. They are part of Company A, of the 26th Pennsylvania Emergency Infantry regiment. And now the 26th has just arrived by train!"

"Is that so?" Silas's gaze followed the people now streaming past them into the square. College and seminary recruits? They'd be as green as the apples he'd eaten yesterday, and softer, too.

"Yes indeed!" The woman's chipper voice grated on him. "They were supposed to arrive last night, but their train hit a cow on the track and it derailed them." She giggled. "Let's not bring that up to them. I'm just glad they're here to protect us now."

"Protect you from . . ."

"My goodness, you really are not from anywhere around here, are you? Haven't you heard? The Rebel army is around here somewhere! They'll be on to Washington next, if we don't stop them!"

"We?"

"They." She laughed brightly. "I meant 'they.'

Women have no part in war. Come on, we'll miss them!"

Soon Chambersburg Street opened into the town square, or The Diamond, as locals called it, and the girl ran off to join some friends. A young boy tugged on his stirrup and offered to sell him a plug of tobacco.

"No thanks, can't stand the stuff." Silas smiled at the puzzled expression on the boy's face before the child shrugged and tried for another customer.

Silas remained on the edge and watched smooth-faced boys in blue peacock about. *So you traded your textbooks and Bibles for rifles, did you?* His stomach soured for them, for their mothers and sweethearts. The beat of a drum hammered in Silas's chest as the high-pitched fife played "Yankee Doodle" to a backdrop of feminine cheers. Even the dripping, sullen sky seemed unable to dampen the throng now filling The Diamond.

How pitiful. How pathetic. They would not cheer if they knew what he knew. They would not believe him if he told them.

Their march ended, the uniformed students milled about the crowd, accepting pies and coffee from grateful townsfolk.

"You a seminary student?" Silas called down to a soldier near him. With cheeks bulging with cherries, the boy nodded in the affirmative. "Is Rev. Schmucker still teaching? He was my professor once upon a time."

The student-soldier's eyes brightened. "You don't say! When did you graduate?"

Silas rubbed a hand over his stubbled jaw. "Let's see—I was there in '57 and '58."

"Why then, you must have known Silas Ford!"

"As a matter of fact—" He stopped himself. "Why do you say that?"

"Oh every student from '57 on knows him. For pity's sake, the whole town knows about him. He's a legend! You know—'Silas Ford, man of the Lord'?"

Silas was stunned. "Man of the Lord?" He dared to believe it was true of him once, but—

"Of course! 'Silas Ford, man of the Lord, took slaves to bed and shot Pa dead'! Remember him now? Did you have any idea he was a bad egg?"

His blood turned to ice in his veins. "No, no, you must be mistaken."

The boy shook his head. "Hardly. Watch this. Hey Blevens!" he shouted to another soldier. "Finish this rhyme: Silas Ford, man of the Lord . . ."

"Took slaves to bed and shot Pa dead!" Blevens hadn't missed a beat.

Silas was going to be sick.

"You see?" The boy took another bite of cherry pie. "I can't understand how you don't know about him. Silas Ford is a cautionary tale. His mother wrote a letter to Rev. Schmucker explaining why he wasn't coming back, and word got out quick. Just goes to show no matter how close we feel to

God, we can all fall away as he did . . ." Another bite of pie.

Silas had heard enough. Clucking his tongue to Bullet, he began threading his way out of The Diamond.

Then he saw Liberty on the other side of the square, a simple blue dress gracing her frame as she climbed down from her buggy and joined the crowd. So she decided to put off mourning after all. *Does she know the rhyme too? Does she believe it?* Silas was glad she didn't see him. He wanted to watch her, unnoticed. She hadn't recognized him this morning, but what if she had a sudden recollection? Still, he couldn't help but watch Liberty one more moment as the old protective instinct for the orphan girl swelled in his chest.

Then he remembered why he was here in the first place, and the smile faded. Protecting the innocent was not part of his line of work. And it was certainly not what he was known for in Gettysburg.

Chapter Two

Bella could still smell that rye bread and rhubarb pie she'd made at the Holloway Farm as she let herself into her modest two-story house on South Washington Street. She was tempted to bake a pie for herself just to have that heavenly smell of buttery crust and tangy-sweet rhubarb permeate every corner of her comfortable home.

Large pink flowers bloomed on the creamy papered walls of her kitchen above wainscoting painted a mellow green. Open shelving revealed crocks of coffee beans, flour, lard, and sugar, while jelly pots sparkled with cherry and peach preserves. It was not furnished as finely as the homes of the white women she worked for, but it was her home—together with Abraham—and that was what was important. No mistress above her here. No master, no overseer, no driver. Here, she was her own mistress. As long as Bella had a choice, she would never consent to live in someone else's home again.

But there was no denying she still needed white folks as employers. Her eyes drifted to the baskets of laundry waiting to be ironed, and a sigh escaped her. At least it was already washed. Just the thought of toiling over a washboard in a bucket of water made her back muscles tie themselves up in knots. She much preferred tasks that allowed her to stand straight. Some days, judging by the way she felt, even she didn't believe she was only thirty-six years old. Maybe her body still suffered from years of bending over harvesting rice down on Georgia's St. Simons Island. Maybe the memory alone was enough to cause the ache.

Balderdash. She scolded herself as she dropped some kindling into the stove and lit the fire that would heat the iron on top. *That was a lifetime ago.* But a nest of hornets had buzzed in her belly this morning when she was hiding with the horses. Her past was not so distant that the idea of repeating it couldn't shake her to the core of her being. She had been lucky today.

Foolish is more like it, she could almost hear her friend Missy Pratt say. Not that Missy was anywhere near here anymore. She and most of her neighbors had packed up their belongings as best as they could and skedaddled as soon as Governor Curtin announced the Confederate army was now in Pennsylvania. Balancing bundles on their heads, pushing wheelbarrows or driving wagons of their earthly possessions, some fled to Yellow Hill, seven miles north of Gettysburg, some to the capital, Harrisburg, and some to Philadelphia. Others took the path of the Underground Railroad farther north, as if they were runaway slaves and not free blacks minding their own business in a free state. The western section of town was now all but vacant of its nearly two hundred colored folks.

The rain drummed harder outside, and Bella shivered as she tossed a glance at the Log Cabin quilt draped over the couch in the next room. How many times had she thrown that quilt over the clothesline outside as if she were airing it out? To the people who needed to hear it, the message was clear: *Welcome, night travelers. This is a safe house on your journey.* Only seven miles north of the Mason Dixon line, Gettysburg was among the first stops for many of them. The passing of the Fugitive Slave Law thirteen years ago gave slave catchers every "right" to come hunting for humans with their bloodhounds, and hunt they did.

Even Lincoln's Emancipation Proclamation of six months ago did not entirely stem the tide of runaway slaves. Freedom did not apply to slaves within the border states of Maryland, Delaware, Kentucky, and Missouri. Bella and Abraham would harbor the souls seeking freedom until it was time to secret them away to the McAllister Grist Mill where they would hide under the mill wheel until it was time to move again. Everyone hoped that Rock Creek and the pond by the mill would throw the dogs off the scent.

Humming "Wade in the Water," Bella gripped the iron with a potholder, turned it over and spit on the surface to test the heat. It was ready. As she ironed Mrs. Shriver's blouse, Bella wished it were as easy to smooth out the wrinkles in her life.

A sharp rapping on the door snapped Bella out of her reverie. As soon as she opened the door, the shining black face of old Hester King, or Aunt Hester, as everyone called her, beamed up at her.

"I saw a light in your window, baby, and just

thought I'd step in to check on you." She entered, and a whoosh of humid air came with her, like a puff of hot breath, sticking to Bella's skin.

She latched the door behind her and bent down to kiss Aunt Hester's cheeks in greeting. "I thought you'd be working at the Fosters' today."

"I have today off. I was fixin' to work in the garden, but not in this wet mess." She hung her shawl on a wooden peg inside the door and sat at the kitchen table, her usual sign she was planning to stay for tea. Bella moved the copper teakettle to the spot on the stove that was still hot from heating the iron, then sat across from her old friend.

"It's mighty quiet around here now, isn't it?" Bella folded her arms across the red and white checked tablecloth.

"Should be, after all that racket they all made skedaddling the place. Did you hear the way they were carrying on? The mamas and daddies scaring their children to death to keep up the pace."

"But you're not scared."

"No. If things turn ugly, the Foster family said they'd protect me." It was only right. She'd been their washerwoman for more than a decade. "And you? You're not afraid?"

Bella shrugged. "My feelings have little to do with my options."

Aunt Hester nodded slowly. "Don't I know that's right."

"If I leave, who will protect our home?" Bella raised her eyes. "Besides, three of the women I work for have all told me if I leave I won't be getting my job back."

"Ain't there no money coming in from Abraham?"

Bella clenched her teeth before responding. It was a question she'd asked herself every time the mail failed to bring her the answer she so desperately desired. "No. I don't understand it. He's off fighting only God knows where—and still no sign of a paycheck."

She clamped down on the rest of her thoughts on the subject before they spilled out of her. She wasn't proud of her sentiments. But how she wished she would have hidden the copy of *The Christian Recorder* advertising the fact that Frederick Douglass was speaking in Philadelphia in March! If he hadn't gone, if he hadn't heard the call for colored men to serve in the 54th Massachusetts, he'd still be here. She wouldn't be alone.

No, those were thoughts best kept hidden in the dark corners of her mind—the ones that needed to be swept out the most, but were most often neglected out of pure denial. Instead, all she said was, "My work is all I've got to keep us afloat right now. If I leave, we'll have nothing left."

Aunt Hester reached across the table and squeezed Bella's hand.

"It's not right that he should be fighting for freedom somewhere else when ours is in jeopardy right here."

"Don't you be listening to no nasty stories now, baby. You free, and I is too. Our days in bondage are over. We in charge of our own lives, and ain't nothing going to change that."

Steam billowed out of the teakettle's spout, and Bella jumped up to pour two cups, glad Aunt Hester couldn't see the tears welling up in her eyes. The truth was, she felt less like the mistress of her own life than she had in a long time, and the feeling chafed her raw. There had been a time when she had been able to shrug off stories of kidnapped colored folks. But that time was over. Now the stories weren't just rumors—they were headlines.

In spite of herself, her hands were unsteady as she placed the mismatched porcelain cups and saucers on the table. "Didn't you hear what Jenkins' Confederate cavalry did, just eleven days ago?"

"I heard." Aunt Hester grinned.

"Why are you smiling?" Bella was incredulous. "In Chambersburg, they captured between thirty and forty black women and children—*women and children*—and started driving them in wagons back down South."

"I smiling because the good white folks rescued them. The captives were freed."

Bella sipped her tea before saying that not all white folks would be so bold. Before reminding Aunt Hester that the entire town nearly paid the price. Jenkins demanded $50,000 in compensation for the blacks, who he claimed were his property. When the town leaders refused, Jenkins threatened to return in two hours to burn the town. Fourteen of the black women who had just been freed met with the town leaders and offered to give themselves up to Jenkins to spare the town. The town leaders refused, but Jenkins never returned. But not all such stories had happy endings.

Bella tightened her grip on her cup. "Did you see Tuesday's paper? The *Adams Sentinel*?"

"You know I can't read. Only news I get is what other folks tell me."

"Well, let me tell you. Rebels took possession of Hagerstown last Monday, and when they left two days later, they carried off with them horses and 'quite a number of colored persons.' But, the paper says, other than that, they did 'very little damage.' Isn't that a relief?" Sarcasm edged Bella's voice. "Very little damage! I'm sure the people on their way to the auction blocks would say otherwise!"

Slowly, Aunt Hester sipped her tea and replaced the cup on its saucer before folding her hands on the table. "And yet you still here. Ain't you? You gotta know that you will be protected from such a fate, otherwise wouldn't you be gone, too?"

Bella stared at the steam curling up from her tea for a moment before answering. "Chambersburg is twenty-three miles to the west. Hagerstown is in Maryland, thirty-two miles to the southwest. Gettysburg may be spared."

"Just so." Aunt Hester nodded, eyes twinkling. "The good Lord didn't bring you up from slavery to send you back down to it. You gotta grab on to hope, child, and make sure that hope is tied to God above. He is our hiding place."

Bella had too much respect for Aunt Hester to point out that God had not hidden the colored folks of Hagerstown very well. Most likely, it was sacrilegious even to think it, but she could not help herself. They were probably in the deep South by now, their lives forever changed. The old woman sitting across from her was serene, confident. Content. Bella would not take that from her. Instead, she nodded and dredged up a smile.

Aunt Hester's gaze flicked to the window. "Rain stopped! Well, baby, I do believe it's time for me to check on my spring vegetables. Stop by if you get lonely." She brought her cup and saucer to the dry sink, plucked her shawl off the peg, and let herself out the door.

After watching Aunt Hester amble down the wooden sidewalk, Bella returned to her chore as their conversation rolled over in her mind. Biting her lip, she pushed the iron across the linen, back

42

and forth, over and over. Truth be told, protecting her home and keeping her jobs were not the only reason she remained in Gettysburg. She had another reason for staying.

But that truth would not be told. Not ever.

Suddenly, her windows rattled. *Thunder? I thought the rain had stopped.* Bella stepped outside. Just a few blocks north, a dozen horsemen crashed pell-mell past South Washington Street on Chambersburg Pike. They were yelling. What were they yelling? Bella trotted toward the intersection, her heart rate quickly matching the horses' speed. People came out of their houses and lined the streets as the men raced up and down, their horses kicking up chunks of mud from the road. It was Robert Bell's Independent Cavalry. They were shouting the news, all of them, at the same time. Bella strained to make sense of their wild cries.

"The 26th has been routed!" *The 26th? The town's defenders? Already?*

"Most of them have been captured! The survivors are retreating to Gettysburg now!"

"Rebels in pursuit! They'll be in Gettysburg within the hour!"

And they left.

The 26th was in tatters. The Philadelphia City Troops, sent to reinforce the 26th, were nowhere to be found. Gettysburg's Independent Cavalry had just delivered their news and run away for their lives. Bella turned back. Her legs propelled her down the wooden sidewalk while women all over Gettysburg stood in their doorways and called for their children to come home. Windows shuttered. Doors slammed and latched. Quiet pulsed in her ears as Bella reached her house.

The rain had stopped, but another storm was rolling in. And the women and children were completely unprotected.

Liberty had gone to the Ladies Union Relief Society meeting expecting—no, hoping for—a sense of belonging. Support, even, for her decision to put mourning behind her. What she got instead, before she even opened her sewing basket, felt more like a slap in the face.

"You were a symbol," Geraldine Bennett said matter-of-factly. "A reminder to all of us here of the sacrifices our boys in blue are making. You were an inspiration to the town, a living remembrance of the ultimate price for freedom. You were the Widowed Bride. The Widow of Gettysburg."

The words were shards of glass, carving away her own delusion. *How could I not have seen it? They accepted me only because my husband died in the war.* If he hadn't, she would have still been on the outside looking in.

"I'd rather be known for who I am than for what—for who—I've lost." Liberty's voice sounded small. She did not want to anger Geraldine.

"My dear, any one of us can stitch and sew, scrape lint, and rip bandages. You were special."

Were. Tears pricked Liberty's eyes as the message washed over her, seeped into her pores. *You were valuable as a symbol. Taking away the symbol takes away the value. You are no longer special.*

"We were hoping you would be in the parade again this year, representing the Ladies Union Relief Society."

"I can still do that. I'm still a widow, aren't I? I still support our soldiers."

"But if you refuse to wear mourning clothes, why would we put you in the parade? Would any-one recognize you without your Widow's Weeds?" She trailed off. "You must understand, Liberty. You were a symbol." The hateful word, again.

And here I thought I was a person. Knowing full well she was breaching proper etiquette once again, Libbie swept out of the church without so much as a goodbye, leaving a group of tittering women in her wake. Whispers of "selfish" and "impertinent" chased after her into the street, but not one of the women tried to stop her.

Climbing into her buggy, Liberty slapped the reins on Daisy's back and the mare lurched into motion, never slowing until she stopped at Evergreen Cemetery.

Kneeling in front of Levi's tombstone, her body rocked with the torrent of emotion. She appeared braver this morning when a strange man came to her farm than she did when faced with a group of women. *Because I care what they think of me.* Maybe she shouldn't. Life surely would be easier if she didn't. But heaven help her, she did.

"Oh Levi," she said to the plot of earth in front of her. In the last two years she had said more to him right here than she had while they were alive. "If you wanted me to be happy, that should be enough for me. Please give me peace so I can live my life . . ."

A shadow darkened the tombstone, and Libbie looked up.

"Excuse me, Liberty. Were you praying?" It was Elizabeth Thorn, acting as the cemetery groundskeeper in her soldier husband's absence.

"No—why?"

"I thought I heard you ask for peace." Her hands rested on the swell of her belly. She'd have her fourth child by fall.

"I did."

"*Ja*, I thought as much." For having moved with her parents to America from Germany only nine years ago, her English was very good. "Lots of people talk to their loved ones in the ground. If they would talk to the good Lord nearly half as much, they'd be so much better off." She paused. "Do you pray, Liberty?"

Such a personal question. But then, she and Elizabeth had a close relationship—one of the very few that was genuine. It was impossible to stick to small talk and pleasantries when you only met in a graveyard. Elizabeth had comforted her after the deaths of both Aunt Helen and Levi. Her three boys had melted her heart and made her laugh. Elizabeth had earned the right, in the last few years, to ask the questions that dug deep.

"I pray." She looked up, thankful the summer breeze had blown the clouds from the brilliant blue sky. "But I must admit, it's hard to pray to a God I can't see, who doesn't talk back to me."

Elizabeth eased herself down on the ground next to Libbie, paying no mind to the wet grass that would dampen her skirt. "But you talk to Levi. Does he talk back to you?"

Words webbed in Libbie's chest, and she looked away. Levi had been quiet, studious. Still, "If I can remember what he said when he was here," she tried, "I can imagine what he would say to me now."

Elizabeth wrapped her arm around Liberty's shoulders, as she had done so many times before. "*Ja*, this is good. That's exactly right. Prayer works the same way. Share your heart. Remember what Jesus said when He was here—read the Gospels—and try to imagine what He'd say to you now."

Liberty sighed. "I'll try."

47

"I am proud of you." Elizabeth pinched the sleeve of Libbie's blue calico dress and gave a little tug. "For moving on. It is the right thing to do."

With a crooked smile, Liberty pushed herself up from the ground. "Speaking of moving on, I best be on my way." She lent a hand to Elizabeth and helped her pregnant friend up. Without bothering to visit Aunt Helen's grave, they walked back to the brick-arched gatehouse where Elizabeth's family lived and looked down from Cemetery Hill.

Everything looked so peaceful from up here. Split-rail fences stitched together rolling fields of green grass and purple clover with golden fields of ripening wheat, as if the landscape were a quilt spread over the earth, with seams of dirt roads and rushing creeks holding it in place. A little less than a mile to the east, Seminary Ridge bristled with oak and hickory trees. Farmhouses sprinkled the countryside. Just north of Cemetery Hill, white steeples gleamed in the sun while red brick houses clustered together. The village of Gettysburg was a hub, with spokes leading out in all directions, each one named for the town to which it led: clockwise from the north, it was Carlisle, Harrisburg, York, Hanover, Baltimore, Taneytown, Emmitsburg, Hagerstown, Chambersburg, Mummasburg.

"Elizabeth, look." Liberty pointed to Chambersburg Road. As far as the eye could see, it teemed with galloping cavalry. Dozens of them—hundreds—streamed into Gettysburg and collected in The Diamond like trout rushing down Willoughby Run.

"Do you recognize any of them?"

Libbie squinted. "No." Some of the townspeople appeared in their doorways, but no one rushed out with pie and coffee to greet them.

"Wait." Elizabeth disappeared inside the gatehouse for a moment before returning with her father and his field glasses. Muffled shouts carried on the breeze while Mr. Thorn took the first look. He cursed in a thick German accent and handed the glasses to the women, Elizabeth first, then Liberty.

Her hand trembled, blurring the view. The soldiers were not wearing blue. Some wore grey, but not the same shade—iron grey, sheep grey, old wood grey, and butternut, the telltale color of a faded Confederacy uniform. But many wore simply rags. It was surreal watching them like this, from a distance, and yet able to see the sweat running down their weather-hardened faces, the greasy strands of hair falling loose about their shoulders. Collarbones protruding against their skin. One man's spurs were strapped onto his bare feet.

A shudder passed through her as she passed the glasses back to Elizabeth. She did not need them to hear the hint of a crazed Rebel yell:

"Aaaaaiiiiiieeeeeeeeeee!" Sunlight glinted off gun barrels raised in the sky. Shots that must have terrified the people below sounded like sporadically popping corn.

Breath hitched in her chest as her gaze followed the current of men still streaming down Chambersburg Pike, through the town and into The Diamond, until it overflowed with Rebels and spilled over, flooding the surrounding neighborhoods. More than a thousand, more than two thousand, swarmed. Not long after someone raised the Confederate flag in the town square, a regimental band set up very near to where a band had been playing with the 26th earlier that morning.

They did not play "Yankee Doodle."

"Nicht gut, nicht gut," Mr. Thorn was saying, his face carved with wrinkles.

Elizabeth grabbed Libbie's arm, and she jumped. "Get you home, girl. Take not the main roads. Make haste!" Her eyes flashed, held Libbie's stunned face in their reflection. "They're here."

Baltimore, Maryland
Friday, June 26, 1863

The train to Frederick was already hissing in its impatience to depart by the time Harrison Caldwell arrived on the platform at the Baltimore

& Ohio Railroad station. White puffs of steam and black clouds of coal-flavored smoke belched from the engine as he bounded up the steps to board.

Threading his way down the narrow aisle, he pressed a handkerchief to his perspiring forehead and willed his heart to return to a normal pace. Missing this train could have cost him his job as war correspondent with the *Philadelphia Inquirer.* Not only did he have to get to the front, he had to get there before any major story unfolded without him. Being witness to a battlefield was never pleasant and always dangerous. But it was the price Harrison paid for a chance at earning distinction that could propel his career for the rest of his life.

"Caldwell?" A vaguely familiar voice called. "Harrison Caldwell! I'd recognize that carrot-top anywhere! Join us!"

Harrison instinctively put a hand to his orange-red hair as he turned and smiled at the sight of the best battlefield correspondents in the country sharing a compartment: Whitelaw Reid for the *Cincinnati Gazette,* Samuel Wilkeson of the *New York Times,* and Charles Carleton Coffin from the *Boston Morning Journal.* He had covered battles with them before. He should have known they would be following this lead, too. *Better to join them than to trail them.*

"White, shouldn't you be in Ohio covering that copperhead political meeting?" Harrison jibed as he pumped the hands of his fellow journalists. Like him, and unlike most gentlemen travelers, they carried cotton haversacks and canteens rather than suitcases and umbrellas. Though not in military uniform, slouch hats, not bowlers, topped their heads.

"Not when Lee's whole army is moving through Pennsylvania!" His lips quirked up beneath his bushy brown mustache in the grin of a newsman on the hunt. Whitelaw's smooth fair skin and full head of curly brown hair testified that he was the youngest of the group at age twenty-six. He had already earned the reputation of a distinguished reporter during the war. When he had first taken his job at the *Gazette* in June 1861, he had prepared himself by reading the standard manuals of war and studying the campaigns of Napoleon and Frederick the Great. When reporting from the front, he refused to gloss over Union mistakes or paint a cowardly picture of the Confederacy for spite, and Harrison respected him for it.

It took courage to be an objective war correspondent—and to be that correspondent's employer. When the *Philadelphia Inquirer* had run a story proclaiming the Confederate victory at the first Battle of Bull Run, an angry mob, fevered with Union patriotism, tried to burn down the paper's building. The next month, reporter Ambrose Kimball was stripped, tarred, and feathered in Haverhill, Massachusetts, for his perceived Southern-leanings in his editorials. They paraded him on a rail through town before releasing him. Harrison shuddered in sympathy at the recollection.

The train screeched and chugged into motion, and Harrison dropped onto the seat next to Whitelaw, facing the two older correspondents. With twelve years of experience as a news correspondent under his belt, forty-six-year-old Sam was the veteran of the group. Deep lines divided his mouth from his smooth-shaven cheeks, and an upside-down smile gave him a look of perpetual displeasure. Charles, or Carleton, as he preferred to be known, was forty, but would have appeared younger if not for the shadows beneath his sparkling blue eyes and the slight tremor in his hands, due to an overreliance on coffee to keep him going. Sitting across from Harrison now, his eyes looked tired already, and Harrison could relate. Being a war correspondent meant assuming the soldier's lifestyle to get the eyewitness accounts. Even Harrison's thirty-year-old body ached in anticipation of what lay ahead.

"Well, gentlemen, are you ready for this?"

But the question had no real answer. No matter how many battles they had covered, they would never get used to the sights and sounds. Or the smells.

"Could be like finding a needle in a haystack, but I'm hoping to catch a glimpse of my oldest son." Sam's piercing black eyes bore into Harrison's with that peculiar intensity he and his family were known for. His wife, Catherine, was the sister of Elizabeth Cady Stanton, outspoken abolitionist and women's rights leader. Elizabeth's Declaration of Sentiments, presented at Seneca Falls fifteen years ago, was still causing a stir. But now, at least for Sam, the focus had shifted to another family member. "Bayard is in the Army of the Potomac. Battery G, Fourth U.S. Artillery. If there's to be a fight—and we've no doubt about that—he's sure to be in it."

"I pray he'll be safe," said Carleton.

"Better to pray the boys do their duty, come what may." Sam's reply was quick and sharp. "You can trust that Bayard will."

"I've no doubt of that, my good fellow, no doubt whatever," Carleton offered before lapsing into silence. Outside the rain-splattered window, the brown and grey blur of Washington gave way to fertile green fields under a wool grey sky.

"Well," White broke in. "And what does Philadelphia have to say about all of this?" He motioned to the copy of the *Inquirer* on the seat beside him. "Come, Harrison, let's compare notes. Let's see if our stories match up." His eyes twinkled with good humor. "That is today's news, is it not?"

A wry smile spread across Harrison's face as he nodded and gamely unfolded the paper. It was only too true that the news, reported from so many different angles, and in such haste, was often contradictory. At worst, it was wildly inaccurate, reporting generals dead who were still alive, or giving victory to one side when the other had won the day.

"Our letter from Harrisburg," he began, then read directly from the paper. " 'At the present writing a comparatively large force of the army of the so-called Confederate States is in close proximity to the capital of the commonwealth of Pennsylvania. Jenkins holds Carlisle.' " He paused to glance up, and saw three nodding heads. So far, agreement. " 'The enemy is now within eighteen miles of Harrisburg . . .' " Harrison skimmed down further. " 'Many are the speculations as to the numbers and true character of the forces advancing toward us, but no definite and reliable conclusion has yet been arrived at. Refugees represent the force to be in the neighborhood of eight thousand, with reinforcements coming after, which is, in all probability, an exaggeration—' "

Grimacing, Harrison stopped reading. In another column in the same paper, a different correspondent quoted a nameless source as estimating Lee's army to be one hundred thousand strong. Not eight. *Humiliating.*

Harrison cleared his throat. " 'For the past few days the scene at the bridge which spans the Susquehanna, at this point, has been pitiful in the extreme,' " he continued. " 'The main road leading out of the Cumberland Valley has been literally jammed with carriages, wagons, and vehicles of all descriptions, bearing whole families of refugees, men, women and children, who have been driven from their once peaceful and happy homes, with the little of all their world's goods they have been able to save from the hand of the ruthless invader. Two or three thousand of these refugees have already passed through here. Many are still on the road, some of whom have not yet arrived, and others of whom are journeying on.' "

" 'Ruthless invader.' " Carleton's voice was low, thoughtful, as he absentmindedly stroked the neatly trimmed beard on his square jaw. "Ironic, isn't it? Has the North not invaded at Vicksburg, even as we speak? Have we not laid siege to a town of innocent civilians, shelling their homes and cutting them off from any source of food or news for the past thirty-nine days? And do we call ourselves ruthless?"

"Careful, Carleton, you'll be accused of treason, soon." Harrison winked at the serious gentleman across from him, but there was little mirth in it. He didn't have to be the Vicksburg, Mississippi, correspondent to imagine the havoc wreaked in that town. It was enough that he had seen the destruction in Virginia and Tennessee.

Sam glowered at Harrison.

"Listen, Wilkeson, I'm not unsympathetic to

the plight of the Cumberland Valley refugees." Harrison pulled a package of Necco-brand licorice-flavored wafers from his haversack and offered it to the others before popping a piece into his own mouth. "But you do realize that far more than three thousand refugees have been created in the South. And you can bet they are all rejoicing right now that it's the North's turn, once more, to be the host of war." The last time the South invaded the North was at Sharpsburg, Maryland—Antietam Creek—last September.

The candy soured in his mouth as unwelcome images, washed in red, flickered in Harrison's mind, as they always did at the faintest memory of the event.

"They are the ones who seceded from the Union, Caldwell." Sam's eyes darkened. "It's only right we should fight on their land."

"I don't want war in Pennsylvania any more than anyone else. This is my home state, for pity's sake! But if we're going to call the Confederates 'ruthless invaders,' we must be willing to admit we've done the same thing to them, but more often."

"Just which flag are you flying, sir—"

Harrison held up his hands in mock surrender. "Right or wrong, the facts are plain. We invaded them. Now they are invading us."

"Spitting mad, too," White jumped in. "Lincoln didn't just free their slaves. He armed them too.

What's the absolute worst nightmare of a slaveholding family? That their slaves will rise up against them. And then—the way they see it—a foreign government tells the slaves they are not only free, but they're morally obligated to take up arms against their homeland, including the people who once clothed and fed them."

"And enslaved them, abused them, kept them illiterate, treated them worse than dogs! If I didn't know better, Mr. Reid, I would say you are defending them."

White cocked an eyebrow. "Not defending anyone. I'm saying that under the circumstances, I predict that Lee's army is going to pour out its vengeance upon this land and its people the likes of which we have not seen before. Not at Sharpsburg. Not anywhere."

The chugging of the train through Maryland's fields filled the compartment as White's words hung in the air between them.

"The question, then, is where will this great battle be?" Harrison ventured as he tucked the rest of his candy away. "Harrisburg? Carlisle? Philadelphia?"

"No." Carleton's voice was steady, confident. "Not likely. I pick Gettysburg for the fight, or near it."

"Gettysburg, you say?" Sam wrinkled his brow. "Never heard of it."

"From what I've been able to learn, it's a small

village, about twenty-four hundred residents. The main trade is carriage and wagon-making, but they also have several fine educational institutions as well, Pennsylvania College and the Lutheran Theological Seminary being the foremost among them. On the map, it appears to be surrounded by farmland and topography ripe for a battle: ridges, hills, fields and valleys. Creeks and runs provide water sources throughout the area."

"If you're right about this, we'll see for ourselves, won't we?" said White. "What else do you see in your crystal ball?"

"Buy a paper and find out, whippersnapper." A rare chuckle escaped Carleton as he rapped White on the knee with a rolled-up copy of the *Boston Morning Journal.*

Harrison snatched it up and unrolled it to the front page story, written by Carleton himself. He read aloud:

> If Lee advances with nearly all his forces into Pennsylvania, there must be a collision of the two armies not many miles west of Gettysburg, probably among the rolling hills near the State line, on the head waters of the Monocacy . . . . I believe that Washington and Baltimore will not be harmed. I expect to see Adams, Franklin, Cumberland, and York counties run over somewhat by the rebels, and I also expect

to see Lee utterly defeated in his plans. His army may not be annihilated. Hooker may not achieve a great, decisive victory. But I fully believe that Lee will gain nothing by this move.

Harrison paused and rubbed his chin. "I hope you're right, Carleton—although your fortune-telling could be improved upon with a Union victory decisive enough to end to this war soon afterward."

Just not before I launch my career from it first.

Chapter Three

The Holloway Farm
Saturday, June 27, 1863

A scream sliced through the air, jolting Liberty straight up in bed. The nightmares were back.

Panting for breath and filmy with sweat, she waited, straining to hear padding footsteps in the hall. But no one came. She was alone.

And just who did I expect? She chided herself for her foolishness even as her heart continued racing. Tossing her thick braid over her shoulder, she reached over to her nightstand and turned the brass knob of her kerosene lamp until an amber pool of light fell in a circle around it. What she wouldn't give for a mother right now, to talk to and comfort her. But she didn't know her mother. *It was a mercy she didn't want to keep you,* Aunt Helen had told her. *And a mercy she died a short time after your birth. It's a blessing you'll never know her.* The shroud of shame was wrapped so tightly around her mother that Libbie dared not unwrap it. But she did have one link to her mother—a baby-sized crazy quilt her mother had made for her during her confinement. *Before she met and rejected you.* The poisonous thought washed over her, threatening to seep inside.

She closed her eyes—and the nightmare burst into her mind again. It was the same one that haunted her so much in the first year after Levi's death. In the dream, she stood in her wedding gown when a nameless messenger handed her the telegram. At once, the petals fell off every flower in her bouquet. The message told her only that he had been severely wounded, but her memory told her the extent of it: both legs blown off by a twelve-pounder. Half of the lower jaw removed from his face by a minié ball. Gangrene invading what was left. These wounds were both nightmare and memory, an awful reality she could not grasp as a seventeen-year-old bride.

Later, a letter from a nurse arrived. *Please come,* she had said. *Come quickly, he is slipping. It would be such a comfort to him to see you. But be warned, he is much altered from the man you*

61

last saw . . . Horrified by the magnitude of his injuries, in her own selfish immaturity, she had hesitated. By the time she had shored up her courage and travelled to the Columbia College Hospital in Washington City, the nurse told her it was too late. She had said he had not died alone, that she had been with him in his final moments. So had Major, the regimental canine who lost his hearing and an eye in the fight.

A nurse and a dog. *But not his own wife.* No, the only good she did was to escort his broken body back to Gettysburg. Major came too—somehow Levi had formed a bond with the dog that Major refused to believe had been severed. The dog smashed his body against the coffin, whimpering, until it was laid to rest at Evergreen Cemetery.

Did her past revisit her tonight to punish her for putting off her mourning clothes?

"It's been two years!" she yelled into the darkness. "I'm sorry! God, I am sorry! Am I to pay for my sins forever?"

A silent voice slithered into her ears: *Yes.*

"No!" Throwing back the covers, she snatched up her lamp and left the warmth of her bed. The cool of the hardwood seeped into her feet until she reached the braided rug in front of her bureau. She set the lamp down and opened the back of the frame holding Levi's image. With a ragged breath, she pulled out a folded sheet of paper and gently opened it to read the grey scrawl inside. It was a letter, pressed into her palm by the nurse who attended Levi, with the words, "Read it when you're home."

Dear Liberty,
    I know what it is to lose someone you love. You feel as if there is nothing left. Food has no taste, the sun has no warmth. Time seems to stretch out aimlessly and cruelly before you, while time on earth has ended for your loved one.
    But you are young. A very wise man once told me, in my own moment of desperate sorrow, something I want to share with you now. . . . A part of you will be buried with your husband. But not all of you has died. You live. You are young, and you still live. Live.

Liberty scanned a few more lines before her gaze landed on the nurse's parting words, which came from the Bible, the book of Philippians chapter 3, verses 13 and 14. Liberty read the verses aloud. ". . . forgetting those things which are behind, and reaching forth unto those things which are before, I press toward the mark for the prize of the high calling of God in Christ Jesus."
    Beneath the verses, the nurse had signed her name: Nurse Charlotte Waverly, United States Sanitary Commission.

Finally, Charlotte's letter hit its mark. Liberty looked in the mirror, repeated the verses. *Forgetting what is behind, reaching forth to what is before, I press toward the mark. Forgetting what is behind, reaching forth to what is before, I press. Forget. Reach forth. Forget. Reach forth.*

Her heart's frantic groping for hope slowly eased as God's Word became both her shield and her sword to keep the demon guilt away. *Lord,* she prayed, *if You're listening—I have confessed my sin to You. Help me believe I am forgiven. Please, let my soul rest. Help me leave my past in the past and reach forth unto what is before, whatever that may be. Help me reach forth.*

The grandfather clock in the hall downstairs chimed once. She needed to get back to sleep. *Maybe a glass of milk would help.*

Pulling a wrapper around her, Liberty brought her lamp to the kitchen, poured a glass from the icebox and stepped over Major, who kept his nightly vigil for Levi inside the front door.

Out on the porch, the half-moon was so bright she turned off the lamp and enjoyed the view in shades of blue and grey. Cool air feathered her face as she rocked. Inhaling the sweet scent of her wild roses, she relaxed to a chorus of bullfrogs and chirping crickets.

And Daisy.

Daisy? The horse never made a sound, unless she were angry. Or afraid.

Senses suddenly sharpened, Libbie picked up the lamp once more and circled the house, the ground like a sponge chilling the bottoms of her bare feet. She edged along the outside of the summer kitchen, crept around its corner until she could see the barn. A light shone fitfully between the wooden slats of the building.

In a flash, her neighbor's story from earlier today came back to her. A ragged set of Confederate cavalry had taken the town and were looking to take with them whatever they could get.

One impulse told her to run toward the barn for Daisy, another told her to dash back to the house and lock herself inside. While her mind played tug of war over the decision, her chest heaved with uncertain breath, her body stayed rooted to the ground.

Until she was lifted off her feet, with a dirty hand clamped over her mouth from behind. A scream trapped in her throat, her stomach roiled with the smell and taste of tobacco.

"Wade! Jud! See what I found sneaking around!" His fingers dug into her cheeks, the other hand pressed hard against her corsetless middle. Disgust curdled the milk in her stomach.

Two figures emerged from the barn, the taller of them leading Daisy, who was tossing her mane and twitching her tail. "Well, I'll be. Looks like we both got ourselves a feisty little filly, Amos!"

He came closer and raked over Libbie's body with his gaze. "Only problem I can tell is which one to ride first."

Liberty's stomach threatened to reject its contents. She squeezed her eyes shut, willing herself to retain control.

A drunken laugh gurgled out of Amos's belly, bringing with it a belch of whiskey. "I got use for her yet. Now listen here, girlie girl. I ain't never seen a summer kitchen so bare as this one here. Do you mean to tell me you got nothing else to give?" He removed his hand from her face. "Answer sweet."

Libbie rubbed her aching cheeks. "I have nothing else to give." Her voice shook. The taste of bile was thick in her mouth.

"The devil you don't. Get in there." Eyes suddenly flashing fire, Amos shoved her through the door and followed her in. "Jud, stay outside with the horse." He called over his shoulder to a boy who looked to be no more than fifteen years old, while Wade stumbled into the summer kitchen, too. The walls seemed to close in around Libbie as the lamp threw light and shadows in sharp angles all over the room. Broken shards of her ceramic mixing bowls were strewn about the floor, along with pots and pans. A drawer full of cooking utensils had been overturned. "You've already been here," Liberty began again, louder this time, "I have noth—"

A hard slap across her face and the metallic taste of blood from her lip silenced her.

Wade yanked and twisted her arms behind her back before she knew what was happening.

"Now you listen to me." Amos's voice was low, his breath rotten. The blade of a penknife glinted in the lamplight inches next to her face. "We here are hungry. And you know what's worse? Our women are too. Maybe you heard about the bread riots down South? How do you think it makes a man feel to know his womenfolk are in tatters, breaking into a bakery and fighting over a loaf of bread like common beggars?" His cracked lips quivered. "FEED US!" He pulled a revolver from his waistband, and Libbie jerked, squeezed her eyes shut.

A gunshot split the air and shattered the glass from the window behind her. Smoke floated from the barrel of Amos's gun, swirling in the air and choking Libbie.

"All right!" she said between sobs. "Just let—me—go." Preserving her supply of provisions wasn't worth whatever harm these desperate men were willing to inflict upon her. She had no idea how she'd recoup her losses. Right now, she didn't care.

Wade released her slowly. Pulling the worktable away from the fireplace, Liberty knelt to remove the loose bricks, fear and anger throbbing in her veins. A box of baking soda was the first to come out. The men tore it open and poured the white powder into their mouths while Libbie watched in wonder. The soldiers' appetites flared into a raging desire, and they shoved her out of the way to dig out the rest of her stores themselves. In seconds, the dirt floor was littered with flour, oats, preserves, tomatoes. As they stuffed their faces and their haversacks, Liberty sat on her heels and felt her face grow wet with tears. *I hate the Rebels! I hate them!*

"Put it back."

All heads turned to the doorway. No one had heard him enter, but there he stood in the edge of the lamp's amber glow.

"Where'd you come from?" With two grimy fingers, Wade scooped blueberry preserves into his mouth.

"I followed you when you snuck off from the railroad bridge at Rock Creek. You made it easy, too, leaving a scent trail of whiskey so thick it could make a man drunk just to smell it." He stepped around the food and knelt down in front of Liberty.

"I'm sorry," he said, green eyes penetrating hers. "Some folks just don't know how to treat a lady."

Libbie sucked in her breath. *The stranger who came for bread this morning!* "What? Who—? Do you know these men? But—but—" Her gaze darted between the soldiers eating flour off the floor and the man kneeling in front of her. "You don't look like a Rebel!"

And you don't look like a widow. Silas's heart lurched at the sight of her tear-stained face. The girl—*no, woman*—didn't deserve such hard knocks in her young life. Smelling of apples and cinnamon, her dark hair hung in a loose, glossy braid over her shoulder. Memory surged in Silas, and he saw her as the orphan he'd found crying here before. *I burned the bread,* she'd explained without looking up. *Aunt Helen says I'm worthless, and I should stop trying to help before I ruin anything else.* All he could do at the time was eat the loaf's blackened heel and assure her it was still good. This time, he could do more.

Resisting the urge to push a strand of hair off Liberty's forehead, he scanned her face. Was it anger he read in her expression? Or just confusion? Or— "They hurt you?"

Blue eyes glittering, she touched a finger to her split, swollen lip. A red handprint on her cheek sent a blade of heat slicing through his chest. He stood and rounded on the men crouched on their haunches, surrounded by their own mess.

"Stand up." Anger steeled his voice.

They frowned but stumbled to their feet, still chewing.

Undisciplined, drunken fools. Sorry excuses for soldiers if I ever saw any. "How dare you touch this unarmed woman!" Silas's hands

69

clenched into rock-hard weapons. But he would not fight, no matter how tempting. *Words, not fists,* he said to himself, and uncurled his fingers. He had to be careful. He had to control himself.

"She's a Yank!"

"She is a private citizen, and a lady!" Silas took a deep breath and grit his teeth, alarmed at the fire burning in his belly. He hadn't felt like this since—but that was in the past. *One, two, three, four, five. Breathe . . . Words, not fists.* He lowered his tone. "You do realize, gentlemen, that you are defying two orders right now? No drinking. And no harassing civilians. General Early is acquiring what we need by purchasing—not looting—supplies from the town merchants. You need not, and must not, raid private property."

"Didn't you hear?" Tomato juice dribbled into Wade's patchy beard as he spoke. "The town don't have enough goods to share! So you see, it's up to us to get the food we need, hats and shoes, too."

"It is not up to you." Silas stepped closer, straightened to his full height, and looked down at them. "We'll get more supplies from York tomorrow. You are to leave the civilians alone."

"Says who?"

"General Robert E. Lee, Order Number 73. Flyers were printed up and passed out to everyone—didn't you get it?"

Wade shrugged. "Gettin' it and readin' it is two different things, now ain't they?"

Silas pulled a paper from his pants pocket and held it out to them. "Read it."

Neither one took it.

"Chicken scratches," Amos finally said, and Silas understood. *They can't read.* He should have guessed as much. One out of every three soldiers he met in Lee's army was illiterate.

"Then allow me," said Silas, and Liberty rose to stand next to him, her lamplight falling upon the paper. " 'The commanding general considers that no greater disgrace could befall the army, and through it our whole people, than the perpetration of the barbarous outrages upon the unarmed, and defenceless, and the wanton destruction of private property that have marked the course of the enemy in our own county.' "

Silas glanced at the two soldiers' faces. They looked down at their splayed open shoes.

" 'It must be remembered that we make war only upon armed men,' " Silas continued, " 'and that we cannot take vengeance for the wrongs our people have suffered without lowering ourselves in the eyes of all whose abhorrence has been excited by the atrocities of our enemies, and offending against Him to whom vengeance belongeth, without whose favor and support our efforts must all prove in vain. The commanding general enjoins upon all officers to arrest and bring to summary punishment all who shall in any way offend against the orders on this subject.'" Silas tucked the paper back into his pocket.

"Bunch of big word balderdash, if you ask me." Wade licked his fingers as he flicked his gaze to Amos, who nodded. "Made no sense at all."

Silas sighed. "I'll make it simple for you. First, you are not to repay evil for evil. Let God do that. Second—" He pulled from his coat two pairs of handcuffs the provost guard let him borrow. "You are under arrest."

"You can't do that, you ain't got no rank!"

"Order Number 73 says I can." Actually, it said officers could do the arresting. But Silas could restrain and bring them to their superiors, who had their hands full burning the railroad bridge at the moment. And the two were drunk enough they didn't have enough wits about them to put up much of a fight, either mental or physical.

Handcuffs securely in place on both men, Silas surveyed the wreckage of the room before turning to Liberty. "I can fix this."

"Please just go. I'll clean it up myself." But her shaking voice betrayed her.

"I'm sorry—"

She shook her head, cheapening his apology, and a ringlet of hair slipped from her braid and bobbed next her face. "What about my horse?"

"Can't have her." Amos spat on the ground. "Contraband of war, and you know it."

"Horses of the Union army are contraband.

You take the horse of a private citizen, that's just plain stealing." He turned back to her. "The horse is yours."

She flattened her full lips into a thin line. "I don't know if I should thank you or tell you to get off my property, Mr. . . ." She looked at him expectantly.

Silas Ford, man of the Lord . . .

Wade grunted. "Hey Johnny, I'm about to need a privy, so . . ."

Billy Yank on the inside, Johnny Reb on the outside. It was as good a name as any, and a whole lot better than Silas Ford. "Just call me Johnny." Somehow, he managed a smile. "For your sake, I hope we never meet again. Now let's get your horse from Jud and leave you in peace."

But when they stepped back into the night, Jud and the horse were gone. He'd been proven a liar. Again.

Libbie awoke with a start and a crick in her neck. Peeling herself off her windowsill, she struggled to remember why she would have been sleeping, fully clothed, on a chair beside the window in her bedroom. Her mind still felt murky from exhaus-tion. Then she remembered. The Rebel raiders. The man named Johnny.

He knew the movements of Lee's army. He had a copy of Lee's order in his pocket! He had to be one of them. Didn't he? She should hate him, the

73

way she hated the others. She should not warm at the memory of how he looked at her. Defended her. She shuddered to imagine what could have happened if he hadn't come when he did.

Stiffly, she rose from her chair. After splashing some water on her face at the washstand, she sat at the vanity, unplaited her braid and gave it one hundred strokes with the horsehair brush, trying to wipe the stranger's face from her mind with every pull before taming her curls into a thick knot at the nape of her neck. *He did say he hopes we never meet again.*

With that thought firmly in her mind, she went downstairs and let the screen door bang behind her as she and Major crossed the dew-kissed ground to the barn.

Just as she suspected, it was empty. Daisy was still gone. In all probability, she was now the mount of a Confederate cavalryman, thanks to Jud sneaking off with her. The few chickens and the rooster Libbie kept for eggs lay silently on the sweet-smelling hay, their necks wrung. *Jud must have forgotten to take them when he left with Daisy.* No horse, no chickens, no eggs. The barn was a mere shell, with nothing left to shelter.

Numb, Liberty sank to the ground and stared absently at the dust motes dancing in the sunbeams streaming down through the hayloft. Major sat down next to her, sniffing the air. She wrapped her arm around the big dog's neck, and he leaned into her, the motion of his wagging tail gently rippling through his body and into hers.

She should get up. She should check the garden and the springhouse, with its crocks of butter and bottles of milk staying cool in the waters of Willoughby Run.

Sitting in a heap won't bring anything back, that's sure. Time to get busy. Libbie rose, brushed the dirt and hay from her skirt, and checked the rest of her outbuildings, Major ever at her heels. The summer kitchen was even more of a mess in the glaring light of day than it had been under the cover of semidarkness.

Major stayed in the summer kitchen lapping up the food on the ground while Liberty stalked back to the farmhouse to put on her apron, frustration churning in her gut. It was time to clean up.

Suddenly, footsteps whispered from somewhere inside the house. Alarm rang in her ears. *Not again!* She bounded up the stairs to the back door. Locked!

Heart pounding, she hiked up a fistful of skirts and dashed back to the summer kitchen, snatched up the first thing she could reach—a washboard— and rushed around to the front of the house.

Noiselessly, she slipped through the door, sidled along the front hall and peeked around the corner, palms sweating into the weathered wood frame of the metal washboard. *I should have grabbed the iron skillet. How much damage can a washboard do?*

"Liberty?"

The washboard fell from her hand and clattered to the floor as she wheeled around. There stood a woman draped in black, complete with a weeping veil covering her face. Liberty's body froze, her mind reeled. But not a single idea gained traction.

"It's me. Amelia Sanger. Your mother-in-law? I'm so sorry I startled you."

Liberty's breath seized as Amelia removed her veil. "But what—what are you doing here?"

"Please, call me Mama. We are family, aren't we?" In an embrace that smelled too thickly of lavender, Amelia pressed Liberty to herself before holding her at arm's length.

"I don't understand." Libbie's voice sounded more like a child's than a woman's, and she hated herself for it.

"I must say, Liberty, I don't either." Her eyes took her in from the top of her head to the red petticoat peeping out from beneath her blue floral calico. Just last week, she and the rest of the Ladies Union Relief Society had stripped all their white petticoats into bandages and sent them away, where they could be useful. "Have you forgotten my son so soon?"

She gaped, embarrassed at first. But hadn't she fought this battle already, over and over, to be free from Levi's death? Tasting anger, she found her voice: "The fact that I no longer wear the color black does not mean I have forgotten Levi, Mrs. Sanger." She would not call her Mama. She was not her mother. They were not family—not anymore.

The woman sighed. "You must forgive me. And if you won't call me Mama, at least call me Amelia." Her face looked pinched and pale. Snood-covered pecan brown hair was dusted with grey at the temples, reminding Libbie that Levi had been her miracle child, come later in life. "You can have no idea what I've been through to get here."

"Please, tell me why you've come, but sit first." She followed her to the front parlor where they sat at a marble-topped table. "You've chosen a fine time to travel. Don't you know Lee's army is here? Rebels raided the place last night. I thought you were one of them."

"You're not hurt, are you?" Amelia's eyes went round. "When I arrived and didn't find you at home, I began to fear all was not well."

All is not well. But, "I'm fine. They took my mare, killed the chickens, wreaked havoc in the summer kitchen, and helped themselves to the springhouse. But I am unhurt." She hoped her face bore no trace of Amos's slap.

Amelia nodded, and her eyes glazed. "I did not choose the time for our journey. Hiram—my husband—has just died, you see—"

"I'm so sorry," Liberty whispered, but Amelia waved the condolence away.

"We knew his time was near, and so did he. He made it very clear that he wanted our family to be buried together. 'Parted in life, but not parted in death,' he told us. Family was always the most important thing to him. To all of us." She dabbed her eyes with a black-edged handkerchief. "We never dreamed that Levi would be the first to be buried, but—well, the Lord giveth and the Lord taketh away. So here we are."

Confusion creased Libbie's brow. "You've come to take his body back to Ohio?"

"No, my dear girl." Amelia's voice warbled. "We considered that, but decided against it. Poor Levi has been moved enough, has he not?"

Liberty closed her eyes. She would not let her mind travel back to the awful trip she made by rail with his coffin.

Amelia nodded. "We have brought Hiram here, to be buried with his son at Evergreen Cemetery."

"But won't it be hard for you, to cover the miles when you want to visit their graves?"

"I'm not leaving." Her tone was laced with triumph. "There is nothing left for me in Ohio, not without Father. Now he and Levi are here. This is where our family is now. Including you." Amelia reached across the table and held Libbie's hand. "You are all I have left in this world. We belong together in these uncertain times. You don't deserve to be alone, my girl. I am your family, and I've done you wrong by not showing it more. But from now on, I'll stand shoulder to shoulder with you."

Libbie's mouth went dry. *Family?* She didn't know Amelia. She barely knew Levi when they married! "Where will you stay?"

"Here, of course. I can help you: cooking, preserving, sewing, needlework. We'll make a fresh start of it, together. The two of us. Hiram and Levi would have wanted it this way."

"But I—" Liberty's spirit flinched, but she could not say exactly why. Wasn't this what she had wanted? To not be alone? Yet this solution did not seem right. Like an ill-fitting store-bought dress, it pinched where there should be freedom; it hung loosely where it should have been snug. She licked her lips and tried again. "I mean no disrespect to you, nor to the memory of Levi or Mr. Sanger, God rest their souls. But death has severed the marriage bond that tied me to Levi. I could not ask you to stay and tie yourself to me, then."

"But I can help you! And Lord knows, my dear girl, I can't possibly go back to Cincinnati now. I had to sell Hiram's shop, and with the money I have from that, we can start over. Together. It would give me such pleasure to be close to you, dear. I want to know you and love you, because Levi did. I want to be close to him. You'll not deny me that privilege, will you? Levi would have taken good care of you had he been here. Hiram wanted the money he left me to benefit you, as well. You can't deny you could use a little help around this acreage—"

"I don't—I don't want to farm anymore. Very soon, I'm afraid there will be very little for you to do here."

"And just how will you make a living? Without a husband? Without a harvest?"

"I'm turning the farmhouse into an inn. This is a large house, with seven bedrooms not in use. The great hall upstairs can be turned into a recreational room of sorts, with a billiard table at one end and tables for checkers on the other. Perhaps a piano, too. If I can fill even some of the rooms more often than not each month, it will be enough money to live on and enough to put away for the future. I can even sell some of my quilts, and jars of applesauce and preserves. Adams County is famous for its apples. Travelers would be happy to bring some token home with them." Liberty took a deep breath.

"I see." Amelia's tone was thick with condescension. "And how many customers have you right now?"

"None."

"Well then, how many have you had up to this point?"

"I am still in the process of converting the

farm's purpose. I haven't had any customers yet."

"Yet you need money in order to make the place a pleasant accommodation, do you not? Let's see, you want to buy a piano, a billiard table, more beds, linens, washstands, basins and pitchers. Bureaus and writing desks would be ideal for each room, too. You can use my horses and wagon for the time being, but at some point you'll want to buy a horse of your own, too. Not to mention the expense of repairing the damages caused last night. Am I right?"

Out of nervous habit, Liberty reached for the ring that spun on her finger before crossing her arms instead. *My, how the list did go on.* At length, she nodded.

"Done!" Amelia beamed and grasped Libbie's hand. "Congratulations on your first customer!"

"You mean—"

"That's right, my girl! If you won't accept me as family, I'll rest content as a paying customer. Would you accept one dollar per night?"

Liberty gasped as she did the math in her head. Seven dollars a week! Of course, she'd need to use some of that money for more provisions if she would be feeding another mouth. And much of the funds should go toward obtaining a horse and purchasing furnishings for the rest of the rooms . . . Every room could have a theme, with the quilt as its centerpiece. She knew just what to do . . .

"I can work, too," Amelia added. "I'm still

strong. Give me some chores, and I'll see to them."

"I don't suppose you would be willing to pluck some chickens, would you? I just so happen to have three dead hens and a rooster we need to make use of before they spoil." She'd never admit it to Amelia, but she still couldn't clean a bird without feeling sick to her stomach.

Amelia nodded. "I make a delicious chicken pot pie, if you've got the vegetables."

"There are some onions, carrots, and beans in the garden that are ready for picking. You make dinner. I'll work on cleaning some of yesterday's mess. Would that arrangement be agreeable for you?"

"Absolutely."

"Well then, let me show you to your room so you can freshen up first." For the first time in a very long time, Liberty felt as young as she really was. "Welcome to Liberty Inn!"

Chapter Four

Gettysburg, Pennsylvania
Saturday, June 27, 1863

White hot pain reached up Bella's neck and wrapped its fingers around her skull. After hours of listening for the blood-curdling Rebel yell, she had fallen asleep tightly curled inside an empty barrel in her cellar. The musty smell crawled inside her nose and pulled her out of her sleep well after sun up. Only when she timidly moved her muscles did numbness give way to cramping. She would have to take her time getting out of this barrel.

THUD THUD THUD. Bella froze. Someone was knocking on her door. Had the Rebels come to search her place at last? The ability to pray escaped her. Terror seized her. She bowed her head low and hugged her knees to her chest, darts of pain spiking across her shoulder blades. Even her toes curled under as her body tried to disappear.

THUD THUD THUD. Perspiration beaded at her hair line, rolled down her forehead and clung to the end of her nose before dripping onto her crumpled apron. In seconds, dampness spread beneath her armpits and across the small of her back.

THUD THUD. "Bella! Are you in there?" Shock replaced fear at hearing her own name being called. Her eyes popped open, though it was still pitch black in the barrel.

"Bella! You in there, baby? It's safe, you hear? Them Rebels ran off! You safe, baby!"

Bella gasped at the sound of Aunt Hester, then found her voice after being silent for more than eighteen hours. "I'm here!" she shouted. "In the cellar! Wait!" *Oh, why in heaven's name hadn't*

Hester said who she was earlier? Too relieved to be irritated for more than a moment, Bella unfolded her body and stumbled awkwardly out of the barrel. "Wait!" she called again as she tripped toward the stairs.

By the time she opened the door, Aunt Hester was laughing. Bella kissed her and pulled her inside, and laughed with her, releasing a dozen emotions locked inside for too long.

"You fine, baby, you fine." Aunt Hester was saying. "See? Them Rebs done come to town, but the Lord watched out for you and me. Just like the Good Book says. We fine, ain't we now?"

Bella rolled her neck and rubbed her aching shoulders. "Are you sure they're gone?"

"Sure as sugar, baby. Wouldn't be here if I didn't know for sure. The little McCreary boy, Albertus, done told me so hisself, and he been tracking those soldiers for days." She let out a throaty laugh, her hands holding her jiggling belly. "Now I best get on back to my work now. Just wanted to check on you, make sure you was fine. And you is. Just like I said you would be." Aunt Hester winked at Bella and let herself out the door. *Thank goodness for Aunt Hester.*

With her stomach growling, Bella pulled out yesterday's bread, sat at the kitchen table, and ate. So much, in fact, she wondered if she rivaled Liberty's visitor from yesterday morning—the traveler.

Another knock at the door sounded. Though Aunt Hester had just reassured her that all was well in town, Bella couldn't help but stiffen.

"Mrs. Jamison?" Another knock. "It's Henry Stahle of the *Gettysburg Compiler*," he called through the wooden door. "I need to speak with you."

Caution slowing her movements, Bella opened the door.

"I have news of your husband." His puffy white face was grim.

Bella's hands flew to her cheeks. "He isn't— he's not—" Her knees began to weaken. This was too much, this couldn't be happening, not—

"Dead?" He huffed. "I think not."

A second wave of relief flooded her before she regained her manners. "Please." She held the door open and stepped aside. "Do come in."

He cleared his throat. "I think not. I just wanted to give you something that came across my desk at the paper." He thrust a dispatch toward her, holding the very end of it to be sure their hands wouldn't touch in the transfer. "You can read, can't you?"

He appeared relieved when she assured him she could. The top of the paper read: "The War in Georgia: The Destruction of Darien." From the *Savannah News*.

Her blood ran cold.

"Your husband is with the 54th Massachusetts, correct? Under Col. Robert Gould Shaw?"

Her power of speech now gone, she nodded.

Stahle huffed again, swelling his throat up like a bullfrog. "Apparently he's been involved in destroying a civilian town in Georgia. Now that's pretty big news, wouldn't you say? Black troops ravaging a white town in the South? I would ask you for a comment and run a story about it in the *Compiler*, but as you know, we have even bigger news in the making right here in Gettysburg. I'm giving this to you as a courtesy, Mrs. Jamison. If we see any more of Lee's army around these parts—or should I say, if they see you—how do you think they'll behave if they find out your husband just torched one of their innocent Southern towns? Does the word 'reprisal' mean anything to you?"

She could not have responded even if she'd wanted to. Her mouth was as dry as if it had been filled with sand.

Mr. Stahle pressed a handkerchief to his damp forehead. "Confederate troops just burned down Congressman Thaddeus Stevens's iron mill in Caledonia for his views on emancipation. Don't think for a moment they will hesitate to set your neighborhood ablaze if they learn what Abraham has done. Frankly, I love a good story, but I'd rather not see my town set on fire."

He turned and walked away.

Stunned, Bella latched the door and leaned against it, while the headline shouted at her: "The

Destruction of Darien." She took a deep breath and slowly exhaled.

Darien, Georgia. Just the name of the town was enough to unlock memories she had crammed into the farthest corners of her mind. How long had it been since she had been there? *Twenty-one years.*

She had been born just across the Altahama River from it, on St. Simon's Island, in a hut made of oyster shells and mud on Master Pierce Butler's rice plantation. As a child, she and her twin sister crossed the river to Darien by hollowed-out log most Saturdays to sell moss they had picked and dried from the live oak trees, which was used to stuff mattresses and furniture.

Once a month Bella's family and the rest of the slaves were allowed to attend a Baptist church for slaves in Darien, where they taught her from the Catechism for Colored Persons. She could answer those questions today, word for word, if asked.

How are Servants to try to please their Masters?

Please them well in all things, not answering again.

Is it right for a Servant commanded to do anything to be sullen and slow, and answering his Master again?

No.

But suppose the Master is hard to please, and threatens and punishes more than he ought, what is the Servant to do?

Do his best to please him.

The rote lines rolled through Bella's mind like a cannonball through barricades she had so carefully erected around those memories. She clenched her teeth. Religious instruction in that ramshackle, sand-sunk town of Darien had been just one more way their master reinforced the principle of blind obedience upon his slaves.

Now just what did my Abraham have to do with that place? Seating herself at the kitchen table, she studied the paper. The article consisted mostly of a letter written by a citizen of Darien, which began:

> What has been long threatened has at length come to pass. Darien is now one plain of ashes and blackened chimneys. The accursed Yankee-Negro vandals came up yesterday with three gunboats and two transports, and laid the city in ruins. There are but three small houses left in the place.

The next few paragraphs detailed the churches that were burned, the milk cows that were shot in the street, and the anger of the writer. From another letter, the *Savannah News* excerpted this:

> They took every Negro that was in the place, forcing some to go with their guns pointed at them all the time. One Negro woman ran from them and they shot her in

the head, and then carried her on board their boat. . . . The destruction of Darien was a cowardly, wanton outrage, for which the Yankee vandals have not even the excuse of plunder. The town had for a long time been nearly deserted, and there was nothing left in the place to excite even Yankee cupidity. It afforded a safe opportunity to inflict injury upon unarmed and defenceless private citizens, and it is in such enterprises that Yankee-Negro valor displays itself.

Bella bit her lip and reread the words, pressing her hand against her furrowed brow. The idea of Darien burning to the ground lit a smoldering satisfaction in the part of her spirit still dark with bitterness. But shooting a Negro woman? Abraham wouldn't do that. And from what he had told her of the 54th, not one of those men would have done that either. Some were former slaves, some were born free, but all of them, he told her, were anxious to prove they were just as brave as white soldiers, and deserved equal citizenship.

Shooting a woman in the head did not prove bravery. Burning a small deserted town—even one that Bella harbored no warm feelings toward—did not prove bravery either. Just the opposite.

This can't be Abraham's regiment. There must be some mistake.

But the article declared otherwise. Darien was "destroyed by a Negro regiment, officered by white men." If there was another regiment fitting this description, Bella did not know of it. According to the letter in the dispatch, "They left a book, which I found, and in which the following entry was made, and which, I presume, is a list of the regimental officers." Bella's heart dropped into her stomach as she read the names.

STEWART W. WOODS, June 11, 1863.
Company I, 54th Mass. Vols.
Penn Township, Cumberland County,
   Pennsylvania.
STEWART W. WOODS was born
   September 21, 1834.
Hidlersburg, Adams County,
   Pennsylvania.
ROBERT GOULD SHAW, Colonel of
   the 54th regiment, Massachusetts
   Volunteers.
Capt. G. POPE, First Lieut. HIGINSON,
   2nd Lieut.

Should these Yankee-Negro brigands ever fall into our hands, the above record may be useful.

And just what would happen if the wife of a "Yankee-Negro brigand" would fall into their hands? For pity's sake, even Adams County, of which Gettysburg was the county seat, was named in the book's incriminating inscription! One of the three local papers Gettysburg produced was named the *Adams County Sentinel.*

The Confederates may have left Gettysburg—at least, for now—but Bella felt as though she were still stuck in that barrel in the cellar. Trapped, and in the dark.

Frederick, Maryland
Saturday, June 27, 1863

Harrison Caldwell had a special talent for finding trouble—and then diving headfirst into it. His mother was the first one to notice, and pointed it out as a reprimand. As a freckle-faced, red-haired schoolboy, he took it as a compliment. Still did.

Now, in the lobby of the United States Hotel in Frederick, Maryland, he was right where he wanted to be. Surrounded by trouble, and on the brink of getting into more. He could feel it.

Literally. The hoofbeats of ten thousand Federal cavalry—Alfred Pleasonton's, Harrison was told—pounded the street between the hotel and the train station, and beyond. The great column did not halt at any point, but moved on through the streets and out on the roads leading north, toward Pennsylvania, like a winding, dark blue ribbon. Next came the Reserve Artillery, jarring the ground with the carriages and cannons rolling over the pavements. The rumbling outside rattled the hotel windows and reverberated in Harrison's stomach. The infantry was moving too, but not through Frederick. General Hooker had ordered them to move either east or west of it, but ultimately, north. To Pennsylvania.

"Well, what do you make of it?" Sam Wilkeson puffed on a cigar and eased into a red velvet armchair soaked in the late afternoon sun. The sweet-smelling, blue-grey smoke curled in the air.

"I'd say we're in the right place, wouldn't you? General Hooker is already here, and more infantry will be passing through tomorrow and Monday."

Sam grunted. "Dr. Brinton is here too, with twenty-five army wagon loads of battlefield medical supplies the medical director had him bring straight from Washington."

"Sounds like a generous supply."

"Quite so." Sam tapped his cigar on the nearby ashtray. "I'd say they overestimated the need, but better that than to err on the opposite end." He sighed and looked out the window, where the setting sun tinted the fleecy clouds rosy. "Soon enough we'll be off living army-style with the rest of them." The older man winced at the thought, but Harrison was thrilled. If this was to be the battle to end the war, it was going to be profound. Just the stuff on which he could build a name for himself.

"So they've got you on the review, too, I see." Sam pointed to a small book on the walnut table next to Harrison: *Journal of a Residence on a Georgian Plantation, 1838–1839*, by Frances Anne Kemble.

Harrison picked up the book and flipped through it. He had only just begun to read it on the train. "Her husband is a native of Philadelphia, you know." Frances Kemble, more commonly known as Fanny, was a famous British actress who, though staunchly opposed to slavery, had once been married to Pierce Butler, owner of rice and cotton plantations in Georgia. Every major paper in the country—at least in the North—would be covering the release of Fanny's new book.

"I do know. It was a New York paper that first carried the story of the Weeping Time."

But not yours. Harrison's lips tilted at the smug look on Sam's face. It was Harrison who had penned that story four years ago for the *New York Tribune*, but under a pseudonym for his own protection. The article covered the sale of more than four hundred of Butler's slaves in Savannah, Georgia, to pay off his gambling debts. It rained for days, until the last slave was sold, earning it the name the Weeping Time. Some said the story, which was reprinted as its own pamphlet, fueled the fires of abolitionism and convinced many that slavery was an issue worth going to war over— perhaps even more so than *Uncle Tom's Cabin*, for Mrs. Stowe's book was fictional, while the Weeping Time was fact. Harrison's pseudonym became a household name among those opposed to slavery. *Now if I can just earn as much fame for my real name.*

"I'm well aware of that, Sam," was all he said. He brought his coffee to his lips and took a long sip before he said anything else. The *New York Tribune* left an aftertaste far more bitter than his sugarless coffee. The editor there, Horace Greeley, was as inclined to shape the news as he was to report it. Some said it was the *New York Tribune*'s relentless pressure on the Union army that prompted the ill-conceived rush into the disastrous Battle of Bull Run in 1861. *Papers should report the news, not try to create it.* Harrison joined the news staff of the *Philadelphia Inquirer*, famous for its objective coverage of the war, and never regretted the decision.

"And," Sam began again, leaning forward, "Pierce Butler was arrested for treason and spent a few weeks in New York harbor's Fort Hamilton."

"True." Harrison set his mug back on the table and folded his hands. "But he's back in Philadelphia, sitting out the rest of the war. If anyone will get an interview with him about his ex-wife's journal, it's going to be me."

Sam glared as sunlight bounced into his eyes off bronze artillery rumbling by outside the window. "I seriously doubt he'll give it to any reporter at all. He's keeping his mouth shut tighter than a drum these days. No, young man, your story of this book will be the same as everyone else's: a simple book review. Interesting enough, judging by her inflammatory previously published journal. But in times like these, I wager it will be altogether forgettable. War news is what the people want. They are practically mad for it." He leaned back in his chair once more and smoked his cigar.

"Then that is what we shall give them." Tucking the book and his notebook under his arm, Harrison nodded at Sam, cut through the haze of his cigar smoke, and retired to his room for the night.

Finally enjoying a rare moment alone, Harrison hung his linen duster in the wardrobe of his hotel room and unfastened the top button of his shirt. The air was thick and heavy, despite the window being open. And thanks to the cavalry pounding the dirt street below, a fine layer of dust coated everything in the room. *No matter. I'll be sleeping on the ground before too long anyway.* With a satisfied sigh, he settled onto the bed with Fanny Kemble's journal and began reading by the light of the dipping sun.

The following diary was kept in the winter and spring of 1838–9, on an estate consisting of rice and cotton plantations, in the islands at the entrance of the Altahama, on the coast of Georgia.

The slaves in whom I then had an unfortunate interest were sold some years ago.

Harrison paused as images of slaves held in pens at Savannah's Ten Broeck Race Track surged before him. Poked and prodded for four days before the sale began, made to bend, twist, jump, crouch, and to show their teeth, as if they were livestock. To keep his identity as a Northern reporter hidden, he had pretended to inspect some slaves, too. Their faces still haunted him. Some were resigned and stoic. Some rocked back and forth, moaning with grief.

Gut twisting, as it always did when he saw their faces in his mind, he focused once again on the journal that would tell the stories of their lives before the sale.

The islands themselves are at present in the power of the Northern troops. The record contained in the following pages is a picture of conditions of human existence which I hope and believe have passed away.

A bell rang in Harrison's mind. He pinched the bridge of his freckled nose and turned the page. It was a letter to her friend, more like an essay, refuting all the arguments given by proponents of slavery. *I could write that myself,* he thought and flipped past several pages until he came to the first entry written from Georgia.

Darien, Georgia.

That was it. Darien, the small town that had just been destroyed by Yankee-Negro troops. Col. Robert G. Shaw and his men had been implicated, but Harrison would be more willing to believe that Col. James Montgomery and his South Carolina contraband troops had been behind it. Montgomery may wear blue, but he had very little use for Negroes and made no secret of it. It would be more his style than Shaw's to shoot that Negro woman in the head and torch the town. In any case, Fanny had been friends with Col. Shaw's abolitionist family in Boston.

Harrison closed the book and grazed his thumb over the spine. *There may be more to this story than a simple book review after all, even if I don't get an interview with that rat Pierce Butler.* With the link to Darien, and with a little extra digging, Harrison could turn this book into war news—the kind of news that would stir both hearts and conversations, just as the Weeping Time story had. Maybe he would recognize one of the slaves he'd met on the auction block in this little book he now held. If he could find a connection . . . but it would have to be good. Really good.

He opened it again and skimmed more entries. Fanny and Pierce's daughters had been children when they were in Georgia. Now they were grown women and both living in the Philadelphia area. Perhaps they remember plantation life, and would talk to him of their experiences. *Didn't I hear that Sarah was loyal to the Union, but Frances took up her father's affections for the Confederacy?* That may be a story. Not quite the emotional impact of the Weeping Time, but a start, anyway.

Outside the hotel window, night began unfurling upon the town. But in Harrison's mind, a new day was dawning. He was fully aware that the big news story to follow right now was the impending battle between Lee and Hooker. But it wouldn't hurt to follow one more lead until it was time to move out with the army. Turning the knob of the kerosene lamp, he determined to read as much as he could of Fanny Kemble's journal before slumber overcame him.

Frederick, Maryland
Sunday, June 28, 1863

Dreams of rice swamps, slave huts, and the driver's whip had held Harrison captive far too long. One glance out his window told him that something was up just one floor beneath him. He hurried through his morning routine, nicked his jaw with the straight-edge blade, and cursed himself for rushing through a shave yet again.

Pad and pencil in hand, he burst into the lobby of the United States Hotel to find it more packed than a church on Easter Sunday. Bewildered, he watched the crowd part to allow General Hooker to exit, alone.

Gen. George Meade, another Philadelphia native, was now the center of attention. With wispy grey hair framing his balding dome, he stood unmoving, staring at a paper in his hand. Soldiers in blue crammed in closer to hear what he might say.

Spying Whitelaw Reid among the crowd, with his own pencil and notebook at the ready, Harrison edged over to him. "What's this?" he whispered.

"Unthinkable. You nearly missed it, Harris."

"Missed what?" he hissed.

"Didn't you hear the train at the station last night?" He hadn't. "It came from Washington with two urgent messages from President Lincoln: one for Hooker and one for Meade."

"And?"

"Hooker's gone."

"Yes, I just saw him leave. He didn't look happy." He pressed a corner of his handkerchief to the cut on his chin.

"No." White shook his head impatiently. "Lincoln gave command of the Army of the Potomac to Meade."

Harrison blinked. "Now?"

"Just now."

"On the eve of battle?"

White cocked an eyebrow at him, then looked back at Meade expectantly.

What could the man possibly say? Harrison's pencil was poised to capture every word with shorthand. The sounds of pealing church bells and the trundling cannons floated in through the window as all men waited for Meade to speak.

Eyebrows knitted together, Meade cleared his

throat. "The country looks to this army to relieve it from devastation and the disgrace of hostile invasion. Whatever fatigues and sacrifices we may be called upon to undergo, let us have in view constantly the magnitude of the interests involved, and let each man determine to do his duty, leaving to an all-controlling Providence the decision of this great contest."

Harrison studied the general. He held his head high and his shoulders back in the perfect posture of a soldier. But apprehension collected in heavy, shadowy bags beneath his eyes. No one knew what Hooker's plan was but Hooker himself. The whereabouts of Lee's army was still a mystery. All they knew for sure was that a battle was imminent, and that it could determine the outcome of the war. And the Army of the Potomac had just been placed under new command. Unspoken questions tumbled in Harrison's mind. *How will Meade lead? Will the men resist or respond to his command? Can he formulate a plan in time?*

The rest of the speech took no more than a moment, and then Meade was gone.

"Harrison." White elbowed him in the ribs. "If we print this, you know it will give the enemy the advantage."

Harrison knew. The Confederates could read Yankee newspapers as well as anyone else, and they did. "Lee will attack—only God knows where—while the new leadership settles in."

"He has no time to settle in. There is only time to lead." White's voice was hushed, but his eyes blazed with conviction.

"All the more reason for Lee to strike now, during the transition." *Can the Union army possibly be ready in time?* Harrison rubbed the back of his neck and laced his way to the window. More artillery rumbled by, through air thickly scented from budding trees. "But what we imagine the Rebels will do with the information is of no account." He swiveled around to face White again. "We can't sit on the story in an attempt to influence the battle."

"No, by Jove, we can't. The rest of the press sure won't." White paused. "Coffee, Harris? You look as though you hadn't quite time for a cup yet today."

"Yes, thank you." Harrison smiled. It was a simple question with a simple answer, a relief to his muddled brain.

"No war correspondent should be without it. I'll go find some."

"I'll wait outside." The warm breath of a summer day filmed Harrison's skin as soon as he escaped the stuffy hotel lobby. In the distance, white steeples glinted in the sun and poked the cloud-flecked sky. Beneath them, no doubt, citizens sat in hardwood pews and listened to preachers tell them God was their protection. If he listened only to the birdsongs while a sticky breeze ruffled his hair, Harrison could imagine what a peaceful Sunday ought to be.

Until the earth shook once more. While churches swelled with hymn singing, here on the streets, men perspired under scratchy wool collars pushing 20-pounder cast and wrought iron Parrott Rifles, each one weighing more than 1750 pounds. Behind those, bronze 12-pounder guns, cast and wrought iron 10-pounder Parrott Rifles, 12-pounder Napoleon guns, and 3-inch ordnance rifles followed.

Today may be Sabbath, but it won't be peaceful for long.

Chapter Five

Holloway Farm,
Gettysburg, Pennsylvania
Tuesday, June 30, 1863

"It's right that I should be here with you, Liberty." Amelia's knitting needles clicked as she squinted at Seminary Ridge in the east. Rumor had it that Confederate soldiers had been spotted there not long ago. No one knew where they would turn up next. "Levi would not have wanted you to be alone at a time like this."

Libbie forced a smile as she sat in her rocker on the front porch and pieced together some blocks of fabric for a Union stars quilt. Near constant references to Levi in the past three days were not helping her "forget what is past" and "reach forth unto what is before." Hiram's burial at Evergreen Cemetery yesterday had been another emotional drain. But Liberty had to admit she would not have relished solitude right now, either.

The town's telegraph lines were cut. The railroad bridge over Rock Creek had been burned, and seventeen cars pushed over the edge, smashing into the creek bed below. There had been no mail since Friday. No news, except for the rumors slinging back and forth between farmers and townspeople. No trains bringing visitors or supplies. When Liberty had ridden into town with Amelia on Sunday for church, they had found the pulpit empty. Even the reverend had fled town.

Most folks called it annoying isolation. Only a few called it the calm before the storm.

For Liberty Holloway, however, it felt more like the fate of Gettysburg was a pendulum, swinging from one dramatic possibility to the opposite extreme. It was exhausting.

"What do we have for weapons here?"

Liberty pricked her finger and winced as a tiny dot of scarlet beaded on her fingertip. "Weapons?"

"Seminary Ridge is not that far away. If they come much closer, we'll need to defend ourselves, won't we? Do you at least have Levi's rifle?"

"What? Of course not, that was army-issued. All of his equipment belonged to the government and went straight back to the quartermaster when he died. But I do have a couple of washboards." She chuckled as she ripped out a seam and started over, stitching her own dreams back into place with every plunge and pull of the needle.

Amelia's laugh was thin. "I suppose humor is your way of dealing with grief. Although I must say, you do seem to have recovered quite fully."

Liberty's cheeks grew warm, and she fixed her gaze on the flash of her needle as it seamed together the patchwork. If only she could afford one of those Isaac Singer sewing machines like Hettie Shriver had . . .

"It's really quite remarkable. And his murderers just up on that ridge over there. I only wish I had the same talent for resilience that you display."

Amelia's words bit Liberty's ears like a sudden frost nipping the buds off her apple trees. Her hands stilled in her lap. "Murderers?"

"It was Rebels who killed him. Didn't they?"

Libbie tucked her head down again. She had heard that a mother's love was so strong, so fierce, that it could compel heroic acts in the face of danger—or be twisted beyond all logic in the face of grief. She should tread lightly.

"Well?" Amelia pressed. "I can read your face plain as day, my girl, you might as well say it outright."

"It's just that, well—'murderer' seems a bit strong."

Amelia's paper-pale face darkened into parchment, her eyes narrowed into slits. "What do *you* call it when someone deliberately kills someone else? Tell me, because if there's another name for it, I really need an education. Enlighten me, please."

The needle Libbie pinched grew slippery. *War?* But she said nothing.

The older woman threw back her head and laughed. "You look as though I might bite your head off! My mama bear growl was coming back just then, wasn't it? You mustn't be afraid of me. I'm sure your mother felt the same about you."

Liberty's skin prickled. "I'm sure she didn't." She stabbed the needle through a patch of dark blue.

"Liberty, look at me." Amelia set her knitting in her basket and reached between the rockers to lay a hand on Liberty's. "You are beautiful. You are smart. You are kind. Levi told me. He also told me your mother died when you were very young, correct? If she didn't love you the way every child deserves to be loved, it's only because she didn't have a chance to know you."

She had a chance.

Amelia settled back into her rocker and picked up her knitting needles once again. With a gentle push of her foot, she set her chair in motion, and her needles tapped to the swaying rhythm, a half-finished sock dangling beneath them. All traces of mama bear were gone, replaced instead with the countenance of a mother hen. "I would love to hear about your parents, Liberty, if you would care to share. It would do me good to get my mind off my own troubles—and those Rebels who may be on the ridge."

Liberty pulled brown thread through the square until it caught from the other side. "There isn't much to share." She poked the needle through the fabric for another even stitch.

"Then it won't take long. I'm ready when you are."

"All I know is what my aunt Helen told me."

"The woman who raised you?"

"That's right. Helen Holloway—this is her farm. *Was* her farm. My father, Gideon Holloway, was her brother." *But his wife was not my mother.* She knew better than to say that aloud. "He lived in Virginia, not thirty miles from here, but more than distance separated them. My father held slaves, and my aunt never forgave him for it."

Amelia's eyebrows bounced, but her knitting did not falter. "Was he kind to them?"

"I don't know. Aunt Helen never told me very much about him." *But she did tell me my mother was a woman of the night.* Liberty focused on her stitching. Up, pull, down, pull. Up, down. Up, down. The steady bobbing of the silver needle, glinting in the morning sun, soothed her. Piecing scraps of mismatched cloth together until they looked like they belonged that way soothed her.

And she needed soothing right now, as Aunt Helen's words came back to her—words she could never tell another. After an indiscretion with her father, Libbie's mother tried to use her pregnancy as leverage to get him to marry her. When he refused to leave his wife, she wanted nothing to do with Libbie once she was born. *To my mother, I was a bargaining chip in a gamble that failed. To my father, I was a liability, but he kept me out of guilt. My father's wife hated me.* She tied the thread in a knot and snipped the end off.

"So what became of your parents?"

Libbie threaded the needle once more and dove into the block again. "They were killed in a buggy accident when I was eleven months old. The will said I was to be sent here, to my aunt. So here I am."

"Your aunt Helen was like a mother to you, then."

"She tolerated me." Barely. *You don't deserve a real family,* were Aunt Helen's exact words.

"Well." Amelia started another row on the sock she was working on. "Someone certainly gave you a lovely name, dear."

Another symbol. But one Liberty was happy to represent. "I was born on the Fourth of July."

The sock dropped to Amelia's lap. "July fourth! Why, that's only four days away! Let me think now—you'll be twenty! Is that right?"

A smile spread on Libbie's face. "Yes. Hopefully there will still be a parade on Independence Day. I look forward to it every year. It's better than a party."

"But that's not for you, silly goose, that's for the country. No no no, we need to celebrate. Something special, just for you. What do you like? Cake? Pie?"

Libbie looked up. "I—I've never thought about it before."

"Do you mean to tell me, young lady, that no one has ever baked you a birthday cake?"

A lump lodged in Liberty's throat that no words could squeeze around. If Amelia only knew the full story, she would not think her birth was worth celebrating.

Amelia gathered her black skirts around her and swept over to Liberty's rocker. She bent down and placed two cool palms on Libbie's cheeks, looking straight into her eyes. "You are worth celebrating. You always have been. I'm just the first person—who knows how to bake a cake—who can see that."

"Please Amelia, you don't have to—"

"I know you don't want to call me Mama, Liberty. I hope one day you'll change your mind about that. Because I've never had a daughter.

And if it's all right with you, it sure would be my pleasure if I could love on you, no matter what you call me. I can already see you are special."

Special. That's what Geraldine had called her before she had clarified the word: symbol. Was she a symbol to Amelia, too?

Amelia pulled Liberty out of her rocker and into a tight embrace, whispering, "You are worth celebrating. Not just because you were my darling son's wife once upon a time, but because you are you. The sooner you realize that, the better."

But as she was enveloped by the soft, lavender-scented hug, suspicion grabbed her harder.

Liberty bit her lip as she stared at the third place setting on the dining room table.

"We only need two plates for lunch, Amelia." She gathered up the plate, napkin, and silverware and brought it back to the kitchen. "Unless there's a ghost living with us I wasn't aware of." She smiled, but her attempt at levity fell flat, again.

Amelia took the plate from Libbie's hands and plunked it back down on the table. "Perhaps, in a matter of speaking."

Libbie frowned.

"Call it what you will! But we are not cutting him out of our lives."

"Who?"

"Levi."

What about your husband, Hiram? But Liberty

didn't say it aloud. She certainly didn't want two vacant place settings at every meal. One was more than enough. Still, she wondered. Why would Amelia be so bent on preserving her son's memory when it was her own husband who most recently died? She wore bombazine now for Hiram, not Levi. Didn't she?

Amelia gripped the back of the chair she had placed for Levi's memory—*or his ghost*—and closed her eyes. " 'We shall meet, but we shall miss him.' "

Libbie blanched as Amelia recited the lines from "The Vacant Chair." The poem had been written for a Massachusetts soldier after his death in the Battle of Ball's Bluff in the fall of 1861 and had become popular all over the North and South. Now Amelia claimed it for Levi.

" 'There will be one vacant chair. We shall linger to caress him while we breathe our ev'ning prayer. When one year ago we gathered, Joy was in his mild blue eye. Now the golden cord is severed, And our hopes in ruin lie.' "

Liberty scraped her chair, loudly, across the floor as she sat down. "Yes, that's quite enough, thank you. Let me ask the blessing for the food." Libbie said grace for the chicken dumplings before the next stanza could begin, though she was losing her appetite fast. *Our hopes in ruin lie?* There had been a time when the words would have resonated with Liberty, but not now. After all, it had been *two* years, not one, as the poem said. She was still young. Her hopes did not lie in ruins.

Liberty was beginning to wonder if it had been a mistake to allow Amelia into her life like this. Still, she was a paying customer, and she sorely needed the funds. Later, when things settled down, her path would not be chosen by her need. Visions of customers coming to Liberty Inn danced through her mind.

A knock sounded at the door, and Liberty jumped up to get it. She reached down to scratch Major behind the ears as she stepped around him.

Surprise snatched the words from her mouth when she opened the front door.

"I wanted to check on you. After what happened, and not being able to help clean up the mess . . . I felt terrible."

She swallowed. She did not remember him being so tall. "Johnny, is it? I thought you never wanted to see me again." Why was her face growing warm?

Major ambled over and bumped into him for attention. He smiled as he rubbed the dog's fur. "Unfinished business always did bother me. I felt like I ran off too quickly with those two scalawags, and I should have checked the rest of your property to make sure no one else was lurking around."

She raised an eyebrow. He smelled clean, and his face was freshly shaven. His oak blond hair

111

was combed into place, except for a stubborn swirl of hair splaying up in the back.

"So, are you well?" His eyes skimmed over her as he passed a hand uselessly over his cowlick. "You look well."

Their argument over her mourning clothes came back to her, and a smile bloomed on Liberty's face. He would never guess how hard she had fought to stay out of mourning once she had decided he was right. Her smile wilted when she remembered black-draped Amelia and "the vacant chair" waiting for her in the dining room right now. Liberty had not escaped the world of death yet.

An idea sparked. "Are you hungry?"

He smiled, and laugh lines framed his eyes. For the first time, she noticed a sprinkling of grey above his ears. She wondered how old he was. *Maybe not so old.* War had a way of aging a person.

"I thought you'd never ask."

"So you are here for the food again?"

"No! Not—no." He sighed. "I told you why I came here. To check on you. But if you're going to offer me some food, I won't offend you by turning it down. It does smell divine." Eyes closed, he inhaled.

Perfect. "We just so happen to have a vacant chair that I would love for you to fill. Please come in."

Laughter bubbled in her chest as she led him back to the dining room and watched Amelia's face knot. "Please, sit down." Liberty motioned to the empty chair with the place setting all ready in front of it. "Amelia, we have company."

"Pleased to meet you, ma'am. How do you know Miss Holloway?"

"I'm her mother."

Liberty balked.

"Well, I'm the closest thing she has to it, even though she won't call me Mama yet."

Libbie's blood ran hot. "This is Amelia Sanger," she said firmly. *A woman whose grief makes her crazy.*

Amelia nodded. "Her husband's mother."

"No—" Liberty said a little too loudly. She lowered her voice. "My *late* husband's mother." She shot her a look that bordered on a glare. "She's visiting."

"I live here." Amelia smiled sweetly.

"As a guest of Liberty Inn. Here pass me your plate you must be starving." She strung the words together leaving Amelia no chance to jump in and twist the truth one more time.

Johnny handed her his plate and watched as she heaped steaming chicken dumplings high upon it.

"Whoa, that's enough." He laughed, and she realized she'd given him a triple portion.

"We do have plenty, you know. We just happened to have some extra dead chickens lying around." Liberty gave him a pointed look. "We've been eating chicken ever since."

He colored, but recovered himself. "It does seem like you have a lot to chew on." He took a sip of water and raised his eyebrows at Amelia, who she guessed he was referring to.

Amelia dabbed the corners of her mouth with a napkin and smoothed it over her lap. "Well. Pleased to meet you, Mr. . . . ?"

"Just call me Johnny."

Johnny. Liberty narrowed her eyes at him. *Johnny?* Her eyes popped wide open as she realized he'd just called her Miss Holloway. She had not offered her last name to this man. How would he have known that unless—Could he be? If he was, why did he not tell her right away? Racking her brain, she stabbed a piece of chicken with her fork and swirled it in the creamy sauce on her plate. After Levi had died, a soldier named Jonathan Welch had written to her, telling her that he had been friends with Levi, had been with him that day he died at Bull Run. Jonathan wrote to her that Levi had fought bravely, she should be proud, and that Levi had loved her. She had written back to thank him, and ask for more details. They had continued the correspondence sporadically, though they had never met face to face. Had never had a reason to.

Liberty looked at the man across from her now.

114

If this was Jonathan Welch, how had he gotten mixed up with the Rebels? *Is he a spy? Is that why he never offers a last name?*

He caught her gaze and held it from across the table. *He seems to know me. Is that why he wanted to make sure I was moving on after Levi?*

After the chicken dumplings, Liberty served them Bella's rhubarb pie and lemonade. When he took his leave, she walked him to the porch, where the scent of her wild roses permeated the sticky air. Curiosity overcame her.

"Johnny."

Silas looked down into her eyes and saw something that hadn't been there before.

"Do we know each other?" she whispered.

Silas groped for a response as the June breeze sighed through the hickory trees, smelling of hay and clover just as it had six years ago. He slacked a hip and leaned against the porch railing he built for Helen Holloway. The woman had not endeared herself to Silas one bit, but he had needed the odd jobs. He was going to buy freedom for his father's slaves.

Snatches of his conversations with Helen floated back to him now. *I think I heard your daughter crying in the hayloft. I thought you'd like to know. Is there anything I can do?* Her sharp retort: *She's not my daughter, thank heaven. But she is my cross to bear. Pay her no mind. I am paying you to fix the fences, replace the rotten boards on the barn. I am not paying you to be nursemaid to the child. Leave her be. She has to learn to make her own way.*

Silas had wished he could make things better for Liberty. He still did.

"Well?" she asked again, bringing him back to the present. "I feel like you know me . . ."

"Not nearly as much as I'd like to."

She smiled, dimples starring her cheeks, and he cursed himself for his uncalculated reply. It sounded like he wanted to court her. All he wanted was to protect her, like he would a sister.

"Will I see you again?" Her face reddened as soon as the words left her mouth.

His neck stuck to his collar. *Do you want to?* The question cleaved to the roof of his mouth. This was wrong, this was all wrong. He had come here under the illusion of blissful anonymity, only in order to make sure she was all right. If he had any notion she would expect more from him, he would not have come. Would he?

Silas tightened his grip on the railing as Liberty studied him with the same innocent blue eyes that had stirred his sympathies years ago. Before he could stop himself, he scanned the rest of her. She was petite—only coming to his shoulder—but the soft curves of her body reminded him she was no longer a child. She was a woman—capable, resilient—*and beautiful.* His pulse quickened. He could not, would not trust himself with her. She was not safe with him.

It was time to leave. For her sake.

"I best be on my way. Much obliged for the vittles. Be well." His bow was as awkward as his parting speech. As Silas mounted Bullet and rode away, he looked back and saw her standing on the porch watching his cowardly retreat. He tipped his hat at her, then spurred Bullet into a gallop, away from Holloway Farm.

No women, he told himself. *Not one. Especially not Liberty.*

Gettysburg, Pennsylvania
Tuesday, June 30, 1863

It began as a rumble. It grew to a thunder. By the time Bella Jamison had opened her window and peered down South Washington Street, the sound roared from an unseen source, like the crashing tide of Georgia's coastal waters hidden in the cloak of night. Clouds of dust lifted off the dirt road, announcing the power that rushed at her.

Then she saw them, and exhaled a breath she didn't realize she was holding. Union cavalry on well-fed horses, in smart blue uniforms, faces glistening with resolve.

Bella grabbed a tray, piled it high with rolls she had just pulled from the oven, and hastened outside, the June sun shining full in her face.

Soon, both sides of South Washington Street were lined with people—on sidewalks, in doorways, in windows, on balconies. The cavalry slowed their pace to grab slices of soft bread and tin cups of coffee from outstretched arms. White handkerchiefs fluttered like moths in the sky, and jaws flapped just as fast.

We're saved!

You're here!

The Rebs won't come around again now!

Won't you come to our house for dinner?

It was an absolute riot of relief. Young women stood in clusters at the intersections of Breckenridge, West High, and Middle Streets, greeting the troopers with smiles and songs: "Yankee Doodle" and the "Battle Hymn of the Republic." Small boys saluted the men and brought carrots and apples to the horses. Questions and answers sailed back and forth between citizens and saviors.

Straining her ears, Bella sifted all she could from the clamor. These were Brig. Gen. John Buford's cavalry, a force of thirty-five hundred.

Three cheers for Billy Yank! Down with Johnny Reb!

Buford surely suspected Lee's entire army was in the immediate vicinity.

Hurrah! Hurrah! Hurrah!

The people of Gettysburg must use caution.

The battle is as good as won!

For more than an hour, the cheers and songs and

offers of food filled the air, until the last of the column rode out of sight, past the Pennsylvania College campus, to set up camp.

A tug at Bella's sleeve pulled her attention to Aunt Hester. "We safe now, baby." She grinned. "See that? All is well. With them between us and the Rebs, nothing can hurt us now."

When Bella went to bed that night, she rested well for the first time in two weeks. As she folded down the quilt to rest at the foot of her half-empty bed, she did not wonder if she ought to hide in the cellar instead. As she pulled the crisp, soap-scented sheet up over her bone-weary body, she heard only crickets—not the Rebel yell or a shot of warning or hoofbeats thundering down the street. Her thoughts hovered comfortably around Abraham and the tasks that lay ahead of her. She would need to wake up early if she hoped to finish pressing and return Hettie Shriver's laundry before nine o'clock. After that, she would check on Liberty Holloway at the farm, and then . . . a yawn derailed her train of thought, and she happily surrendered to slumber.

Tomorrow would be a big day.

Act Two

THE
HEAVENS
COLLIDE

"IT SEEMED AS IF the heavens and earth were crashing together. The time that we sat in the cellar seemed long, listening to the terrific sound of the strife; more terrible never greeted human ears. We knew that with every explosion, and the scream of each shell, human beings were hurried, through excruciating pain, into another world, and that many more were torn, and mangled, and lying in torment worse than death, and no one able to extend relief. . . .Who is victorious, or with whom the advantage rests, no one here can tell."

—SARAH BROADHEAD,
Gettysburg housewife, age 34

Chapter Six

Gettysburg, Pennsylvania
Wednesday, July 1, 1863

"Did you hear that?" Hettie Shriver flung open the door of her Baltimore Street home to Bella. The large two-story brick house was flanked by a garden and had a ten-pin alley and saloon built on the back of the house, ready for business but waiting until Hettie's husband, George, returned. "Home by Christmas my foot," Bella often heard Hettie mutter. She hadn't seen George once since he had joined Cole's Cavalry in Frederick, Maryland, in August 1861.

"Hear what, ma'am?" Bella swiveled, a basket of freshly pressed laundry hugging her hip. During breakfast, a long line of Union cavalry and more wagons had passed by her home, going north on South Washington Street. But the brick sidewalks here on Baltimore Street were fairly empty now, and washed clean from the recent rain. Birds twittered from their perches in young trees lining the dirt road, the blue sky glimmered with gold-rimmed clouds. Romeo swished his tail contentedly as he stood at the hitching post, harnessed to Bella's wagon.

"There." Hettie raised her hand to silence her

daughters, though neither had made a sound yet. Mollie, a girl of just eight summers, and Sadie, two years younger, both clung to Hettie's work apron, their solemn blue eyes peering around at Bella vacantly.

Then she heard it. A bugle from the northeast, sounding the call for battle. Nodding but once, Bella locked eyes with Hettie for a heartbeat until the *pop pop* of small-arms fire carried faintly on the summer breeze.

Quickly, Bella stepped inside the butter-cream parlor and Hettie locked the door behind her.

"Mama?" Sadie tugged Hettie's skirt. "Is it Daddy?"

Color drained from Hettie's face. "No, darling."

"Then who is it? Are they good men or bad men?"

Both, thought Bella, as Hettie ushered the girls up to their playroom and told them everything would be fine.

The shots were so faint in the distance, maybe Hettie was right. Maybe, if a battle was to be had indeed, it would move farther away, not closer. Bella smoothed her apron over her green checked skirt and went into the kitchen to start baking for Hettie and her girls. She hitched her thoughts to the task as she would a horse to its post, concentrating on the dusting of flour on her fingertips, the scraping of the wooden spoon against the sides of the bowl, the spicy scent of the cinnamon and raisins waiting to be mixed in. It was something her mother had taught her long ago. When your thoughts run away, focus on what your hands are doing instead, shut out everything else. It was good advice—slaves' hands were rarely idle. Bella's mouth tilted up. *My hands are rarely idle now.* At least the driver's whip would not reach her here.

If only her memories would stay as far away.

Footsteps flew down the staircase over the kitchen, jerking Bella's attention to the doorway until Hettie filled its frame. Truly, the lines around her eyes and mouth spoke of a woman much older than the woman's twenty-six years.

"Bella, come quickly." It was a breath, spoken all at once, the kind that leaves no room for questioning. In one fluid movement, Bella dropped her spoon on the work table, wiped her hands on her apron, flicked her gaze to the window.

"No don't! Come away from the window at once." It was a whisper now, and frantic.

Hettie grabbed her arm then—something she had never done before—and pulled Bella forcefully out of the kitchen, down the servant's stairs and into the cellar.

"Stay here, at all costs, and don't make a sound." Hettie stood silhouetted in the doorway to the stairs, the light spilling over her shoulders from behind, the shadows hiding her face. "I will keep them away from you, I promise." She left. A latch clicked from the other side.

Bella was trapped. Again.

Fear shuddered through her, oozed out of her pores, until her collar plastered her neck, and her petticoats stuck to her thighs. Pulse pounding in her ears, she slid closer to the single shaft of light slanting into the cellar. The window was small, but not too small for her to spot the source of Hettie's alarm.

A dozen colored folks, men, women, and children, shuffled in a line down the street, Confederates with bayonets hemming them in behind and before.

"Goodbye!" one of the women shouted. "Goodbye! I'm going back to slavery!" No one corrected her. No one could deny she was right.

Bella squinted through the dirty glass. These were her friends, her neighbors, the only other colored people who had stayed in town. Aunt Hester was among them.

Bella wheeled away from the window and pressed her back against the cold bricks and chipping mortar. The tea and bread she'd had for breakfast threatened to reappear, uninvited. Were they searching the houses? Had they just missed her? Would they search a white woman's home looking for colored people—or Yankees? She wasn't safe. She wasn't safe here, and she wouldn't be safe at home. No matter where she turned, there was no way out. She had felt this way before.

The bricks of the Shrivers' foundation chafed the scars on her back through her dress. Crumbling to her knees, Bella pressed the heels of her hands to her eyes, tried desperately to fasten her thoughts once more to anything else—the musty smell filling her nostrils, the dampness clinging to her skin—to rein in the memories. But they ran away with her, unbridled, to the rice swamp of St. Simons Island.

Bella had tried to run away, then, and the other slaves had called her crazy. "What for you run?" her gnarled grandmother had said to her. "T'ain't no use. What use you run away? De swamp all round, you get in dar an starve to def, or de snakes eat you up. No, massa's Negroes don't neber run away." She had been right. It was an island, after all.

But Bella had run anyway, to the swamps where snakes slithered, hissing in the shadows, and her stomach fairly roared for food. Until she came back half-dead from starvation and was tied up by her wrists to a tree branch, her feet dangling above the floor so as to not afford a purchase for resistance. Driver Bran turned her shirt up over her head, exposing the flesh of her back.

Sweat itched across Bella's scalp and trickled down her face. She licked the salt from her lips as she remembered the leather thong scoring her body, filleting it open. In an attempt to heal itself, her flesh pulled tight as it breached the gullies carved out by the whip. The scars on her back burned with the memory of their birth.

She had run more than once, though she knew there was no way off the island. So many times, and with the same result, that she had been deemed insane.

Maybe she was.

She would run again.

Bella Jamison would not go back.

The line of captives had been snaking east. She would go southwest, to the Holloway Farm. She waited in the shadows of the cellar, ready to pounce as soon as Hettie opened the door. Bella was taken aback by the force coursing through her veins: the primal instinct to be free.

BOOM!

Cannon fire shook the earth, and the world shifted. This was not distant popping of musketry or a faint strain of bugle on the breeze. It was close enough to rattle the house. The children screamed from somewhere upstairs. A door slammed, and Bella watched as three pairs of feet ran past the cellar window. The Shrivers were running away? They would leave her here? Alone?

BOOM!

Before Bella had time to gather a plan about her, four pairs of feet came running back from the other direction. The door slammed again. Footsteps on the stairs. The latch clicked, the door opened and morning light streamed in again.

"We're leaving," Hettie said.

Bella, at her side, "So am I."

"Where?"

"To the Holloway Farm. I can hide there."

"On the other side of Seminary Ridge? You can't go there, that's where the fighting is. It's covered in smoke. Come with us."

"Where will you go?"

"My father's farm—Jacob Weikert. We'll be safe. He'll take us all in, I know he will. We're taking our neighbor's youngest girl, Tillie Pierce, to keep her out of harm's way, too. She is fifteen, and can help us with the girls . . ." She trailed off.

They reached the top of the stairs and found Sadie and Mollie clinging to Tillie, whose face was just as ashen.

"Ready to go see Grandpa?" Hettie's voice lilted in an effort, Bella guessed, to convince her girls this would be a pleasant outing.

BOOM!

The girls were not convinced.

"Where does your father live?" Bella prodded as Hettie locked the house behind her, and immediately covered her mouth. The air tasted of saltpeter from the gunpowder.

"Three miles south, away from the fighting. Safest place we could be. On Taneytown Road, on the eastern slope of Sugarloaf Hill, next to the Round Top. We go by foot—it's faster."

Holloway Farm,
outside Gettysburg, Pennsylvania
Wednesday, July 1, 1863

If her hands would only stop shaking, Liberty would busy them with quilting, or mending, or sewing new curtains for the guest rooms. Anything that would require the concentration of small, even stitching that had always calmed her nerves.

But how could she be still when the whole earth shuddered, when cannons roared, when the drummer boys beat out their call to battle on her very chest? The day had begun like any other. Liberty had taken Major out for a walk along the west bank of Willoughby Run. But she had let her mind wander, and her feet followed. The smell of freshly mown grass and purple clover clung to the breeze teasing tendrils of hair from her bun. Before she knew it, she and Major had crossed Hagerstown Road, about a mile north of her home.

Then everything changed.

Half a mile to her left, the crest of Herr Ridge squirmed with men just rising from the other side. *What are they doing?* Liberty whipped her head to the right and found her answer, which nearly knocked her off her feet. For there on McPherson's Heights was the Union cavalry, facing their enemy, their backs to the Lutheran Seminary.

Before the first shot fired, Liberty grabbed the scruff of Major's neck and turned him around to run home.

He knew. He could not hear, but he could feel the ground shake, the atmosphere change, smell the sulfuric belch of the field guns. It was enough. He kept pace with Liberty—though he could easily have outrun her—as she flew back home, and he would not leave Liberty's side as she now sat in the great hall, blood rushing in her ears.

You're crying wolf along with the rest of them. Her own words came back to her.

Don't you remember? In the end, the wolf actually came.

He was right, after all. In the end, the wolf had come.

Was this the end?

Amelia wrung her hands and paced the length of the room, her bombazine rustling in the gaps between the cannon fire. Liberty sat in a red velvet armchair and wished she could put words together to pray, but her brain was so rattled even that was difficult. *Then pray the psalms.* It was something Bella had taught her to do when her grief was raw. So she picked up a Bible with shaking hands and read Psalm 27, punctuated by shot and shell screaming through the air. It sounded closer than the mere mile that separated them from battle.

"The LORD is my light and my salvation; whom

shall I fear? the Lord is the strength of my life; of whom shall I be afraid?"

A small porcelain figurine toppled off the whatnot and shattered on the floor.

"Though an host should encamp against me, my heart shall not fear: though war should rise against me, in this will I be confident."

Major whined and brushed his head against Libbie's ankle.

"One thing have I desired of the LORD, that will I seek after; that I may dwell in the house of the LORD all the days of my life, to behold the beauty of the LORD, and to enquire in his temple. For in the time of trouble he shall hide me in his pavilion: in the secret of his tabernacle shall he hide me; he shall set me up upon a rock."

Blue-grey smoke blew in through the open windows, and Libbie rushed to slam them closed, to shut out the war outside her door. The war was not supposed to be fought here. It was supposed to take place somewhere else—somewhere far away. Not in fields of wheat, apple orchards, villages, and farms. Not where widows and orphans were defenseless. Not here.

She returned to her chair and continued reading. "Hear, O LORD, when I cry with my voice: have mercy also upon me, and answer me. Hide not thy face far from me; put not thy servant away in anger: thou hast been my help; leave me not, neither forsake me, O God of my salva—"

The front door burst open and Major, mis-judging the distance again, sailed into the intruder, wagging his tail, before stumbling back a little. The man staggered back a few steps, recovering his balance, but did not stoop to return Major's greeting. "You must not be afraid, but a very great many men are going to be brought here to this house. I'm Dr. Philip Stephens and I'll be staying here for quite some time." His Southern drawl and green-sashed, grey uniform triggered alarm in Libbie's mind. Yet she could make no sound.

"Here?" Amelia, at her side, unfurled. "This is a private house, not for military use!"

"My apologies, ma'am, but I'm not asking. I'm telling. If you care to leave, do so, but at your own risk. Those bullets out there won't dodge you just because you're civilians." His face was thin and pale, except for a drooping brown mustache and a tuft of beard below his lower lip. For a slight man, his voice was commanding.

"Now you listen to me—"

"Bring him in! Bring them all in!" The man was no longer talking to Amelia. A blustering widow and her mute companion were not his concern.

Bile replaced the words stuck in Liberty's throat as she watched horse-drawn ambulance drivers unload a wounded soldier outside her home. *Stay out, stay out,* her heart cried with every thud. *Not here, stay out, not here!*

But they came anyway. Past her roses, knocking

over the rockers on her porch, into her home, they came. The man being carried met Libbie's horrified eyes and threw her a single word: "Water." His eyes pleaded, then closed in a grimace that twisted his face.

"And just where do you think you're going to put him?" Amelia squawked.

The men shoved past her, around the corner and carried the patient into the first bedroom they came to—Amelia's room. Before depositing him on the featherbed, one of the men pulled the sheets from beneath the quilt and began tearing them into bandages. Hurriedly, the patient was lowered onto Libbie's best quilt, the lifeblood spilling from his shredded leg. One man drove a staple into the ceiling above the bed while another threaded a rope and pulley through it to create a swing to elevate the leg.

"You don't have to stay here," Dr. Stephens said to Liberty. "And I frankly recommend you don't. But if you're not going to leave, I would be much obliged if you would bring this man some water."

Liberty backed out of the room, her wobbly knees threatening to betray her.

Amelia grabbed her by the elbow in the hallway. "You can't."

She licked her lips. "I can't what?"

"You were about to bring them water, weren't you? Don't you care this is the enemy? It was a Yankee gun that shot this Rebel. You want to waste our ammunition? If you help this man live, he will go right back and try to kill our own men. You can't help, Liberty. You will only make things worse."

Memory ripped open inside her. You can't help, Liberty. It was Aunt Helen's voice. *You can't do anything right. Don't try to help, you will just make things worse.* Every time Libbie tried to learn something new, this was the mantra driven into her head. This was why Bella had to teach her the most basic things about keeping house. Liberty's lips thinned as her mind spun back to the day she heard that Levi was injured. Weren't these the same words that had held her back from going to him? *You can't help. Don't even try. You will only make things worse.* The forked tongue of deception had flickered in her ear, and she had believed the lie long enough to cause unending regret.

Liberty found her voice. "I can help. I'm going to help. This man is no longer a threat to the Union army, but he is still someone's son, brother, or husband."

Amelia's eyes shimmered. "And what about *your* husband, Liberty? Putting away your mourning clothes is one thing, but deliberately helping the army that put him in the ground? Have you lost your mind, child?"

Libbie swayed with the force of Amelia's anger. Then she tasted her own. She was not a child.

Even when she was young, she had had no childhood, and her prime courting years were spent in mourning.

"Aren't you known around here for your patriotism, your sacrifice? You told me they call you the Widow of Gettysburg. How would it look for you to turn your back on everything the Union stands for?"

"I take a different view of it." She moved to sidestep her, but Amelia blocked her path.

"Your name is Liberty. *Liberty.* Will you make a mockery of your very name by aiding the enemy of freedom itself? Whether you like it or not, young lady, you are at a crossroads. You must decide, today—this moment—who you are. And then act like it."

The words buffeted Libbie's ears. *Decide who I am?* It seemed too large a question to ask over the simple request for some water. But she did know who she did not want to be. A woman of guilt and regret. A woman who hid behind the lie she could not possibly do any good. Those were skins that itched and chafed, the scales she wanted to shed, as she had shed her Widow's Weeds.

"I am going to help. There is little I can do, but I will do it."

"They will ruin your house."

"I am going to help."

"They will take everything from you, Liberty. Your past, your present, your future."

The sound of tearing fabric split the air between them as men tore her linens to shreds. *They are only sheets.*

"Where is the water?" the doctor growled from inside the room.

Amelia remained planted in the hallway, but Libbie pushed past her, grabbed two pails from the kitchen and ran out to the well. The breath of the battle blew in her face, choked her, as she pumped. With each splash of water into the pail, she told herself she was doing the right thing.

The pails full, she carefully carried them in through the back door, grabbed a couple of old tin dippers from the kitchen, and walked to the great hall.

She gasped. While she had been pumping the water, men had brought in hay from the barn and spread it all over the floors, every inch, until it looked like her furniture had been brought out to the barn. Several more men had been carried in from the ambulances lining up outside the house, and their groaning mingled with the distant roar of battle. Blood darkened the straw beneath broken and shattered—and missing—limbs.

"God! God! Oh God!" one cried as he clawed for a leg that was not there.

Liberty could avert her gaze but with sloshing pails in her hands, she could not stop up her ears as she navigated a path through the men back to Amelia's room. One man called out for his mother. Another cursed her up and down when she nearly stepped on him, dribbling some precious water down the side of her bucket. One of them—*whistled?*

Slowly, she turned, and found Major, completely unbothered by the grotesque chorus, licking a soldier's face and nuzzling against his chest for affection—though whether it was to receive or bestow it, Liberty could not tell. She watched in awe as the former regimental canine did his work, blind to the color of the uniforms. He gently nudged their faces, offered a paw in handshake, and even laid his huge, black, one-eyed head on a drummer boy's chest while the boy clutched his fur and wept into his neck.

A tug on her skirt. She looked down. "Water?" he said.

She set down her pails, fished a dipper out of her apron pocket and poured some water into his mouth. He choked and sputtered. "Here," she said, and lifted his head onto her lap. "Let's try again." This time, a few tablespoonfuls made it into his parched throat. He looked up at her and smiled, a beautiful smile. "Be my girl?"

"What?" Nervous laughter escaped her.

"Oh come on." He lifted a blood-gloved hand from his arm. "Old saw-bones will take it off soon, and I've seen too many fellers give up their limbs only to lose their lives soon after. Always wanted a sweetheart to know I would be missed once I left this earth. Just never got around to it. Won't you say you'll be mine?"

"I—I'm a Yankee, you understand."

"Don't you worry about that. I won't hold it against you, if you won't hold it against me that I'm messing up your house like this. Just be my girl."

Ridiculous request. A dying wish.

"Just pretend, just let me pretend, somebody's going to care when I die. Such a pretty lie. I don't believe it would be a sin if you and I both know it ain't true, would it? If we just agree upon it?"

Liberty's heart buckled. "I'll be your girl." She forced a smile through her tears.

"Nice to meet you. My name is Isaac. I never dreamed I'd have such a pretty girl as you, Miss . . ."

"Liberty." She smiled again. "My name is Liberty."

"Well if that don't just beat all." His eyes closed. "The very thing we're fighting for. 'Give me Liberty or give me death' . . ." He faded, and Liberty stood.

"Nurse!" someone called. She spun on her heel to find the owner of the voice. "Water! Nurse!" *Is that what I am now?* Her rebellious stomach rejected the idea as she crushed the straw beneath her feet. But it did not matter what they called her. She would give them water.

When she finally arrived in Amelia's room, Dr.

Stephens instructed her to put the pails down and go fetch more. "You see only dozens of men now. There will be hundreds. Maybe more. Each will have a wound needing to be washed and dressed. And each will need to drink. Every bowl, every pail, every pan you have—fill it. It will not be too much. Go, nurse!"

"I'm not a nurse. My name is—"

"Not important. What matters is what you do. Now go! Nurse!" It was a verb, not a noun. Right now, who she was did not matter. Her actions did. This time, she would make them count.

Chapter Seven

Gettysburg, Pennsylvania
Wednesday, July 1, 1863

"I know a shortcut."

Hettie Shriver led her daughters, Tillie, and Bella down Baltimore Street, while cannons boomed incessantly, until veering off the road to cut into Evergreen Cemetery. A placard at the entrance read, "All persons are prohibited from destroying any flower or shrubs within these grounds." Inside, Union soldiers planted their cannon, and removed marble headstones from the graves, laying them flat on the lush green grass.

"Hurry along." An officer wiped the sweat from

his brow. "You are in great danger of being shot. The Rebels will fire their shells at us here any moment."

The women needed no other persuasion. Hettie lifted Sadie, Bella carried Mollie, and along with Tillie they fairly ran off the hill. A glance back toward the seminary showed the confusion of the battle. Troops double-timed into their positions, shells bursting in the air above them to form a great battle cloud over the ridge. Invisible waves of undulating air swept over Bella before each artillery blast could be heard.

This was no place for little girls. It was no place for women at all.

Once on Taneytown Road, they slacked their pace, put the girls down to walk on their own again, and caught their breath. Bella read in Hettie's face the fierce mother love that would stop at nothing to protect her daughters, and knew it was the same love that had sent Tillie Pierce away from her mother, to safety. It was love that drove Moses's mother to put him in a basket and send him down the Nile River.

Love like that was easy for Bella to understand. *Away from danger, whatever the cost.* Even if it meant not being his mother anymore. Yes, Bella knew. She knew the pain of separation, like a chamber of her heart being ripped away. Bella clutched at her chest, felt the erratic beating against her hand. She could live with a heart that was less than whole. She could not live with herself if she hadn't done everything in her power to ensure her daughter would be safe from the kind of life Bella had known. *Where is she now? Is she safe?*

An ambulance wagon overtook them then. Hettie called out, "What news?"

"Hard fighting," said the soldier. "General Reynolds shot through the head already this forenoon. He lies in back, we must see his body to safety. I would offer you a ride, but with a corpse in the back . . . it would not be pleasant for you or the children." The wagon continued to roll by.

"Where was the general killed?" Bella called out after them.

"In a field west of Seminary Ridge. We must go."

Liberty. The Holloway Farm was west of Seminary Ridge. The fighting could have been a mile or two distant from her, or it could have been within sight of her front porch. And she was alone. Bella's heart flipped.

"Bella." Hettie, several paces ahead of her on the road by now, looked over her shoulder at her. "Why ever are you just standing there? This is no time for dawdling."

Mud sucked at Bella's shoes, holding her there on the road as she turned her head toward the boom of cannons and rattle of musketry. The smoke over Seminary Ridge glowed orange with fire. Finally, "I must go."

"Yes! So make haste!"

"Not with you."

"What?" Hettie retraced her steps in the mud until she stood, chest heaving, right in front of Bella. "Where will you go?"

"Miss Holloway is alone. Over there, in that mess." She pointed west.

Hettie huffed. "I admire your loyalty to your employer, but may I remind you, I am your employer too, and today, Wednesday, is your day to serve *me*. And I am ordering you to come with us. I need your help—and besides, getting yourself killed will not help Liberty Holloway."

The words hung in the air between them. Bella looked once more at the ridge. How was she planning on getting through the lines of battle?

"Bella, didn't you see what happened to those colored people this morning? Even if you aren't killed outright, you could be captured by the Confederates."

Bella closed her eyes as dread settled on her like dust on a film of sweat. Hettie was right. And with what her husband had done, or was accused of doing, down South . . . she shuddered. The cannons now sounded like a continuous roll of thunder. She could not go there.

Once again, choice proved to be an illusion. She had no choices. Only escape routes.

"Mommy?" Sadie called out. "Are you coming?"

"Yes."

No. Tears pricked Bella's eyes. *Lord,* she prayed, *please keep my daughter safe.*

Back and arms aching, Libbie placed her hand on the iron pump handle, numb by now to the pressure on her blisters. Even if she had felt pain, she would have bit her tongue before complaining. There were men dying inside her house, making straw beneath them sticky with blood, and they did not make any sound.

And there were men who did. She could hear their screams and shrieks from outside the house, a mix of horror and pain. These were the screams that slowed Libbie down, the ones that made her stop and cover her ears.

They were getting louder.

THUD. She barely heard it. Twisting around, she scanned the house and ground, saw nothing. At least nothing that would have thumped. The ground was becoming littered with injured soldiers.

Ambulances continued to deliver their patients until they overflowed the first floor, and spilled onto the second floor, as well. Miraculously, they allowed Liberty's room to remain untouched. Amelia had retreated behind that door shortly after their argument, and there she had stayed ever since. Now, men covered the muddy dooryard, with nothing between them and the earth. Some were shielded from the glaring sun by the shade of hickory trees. Others were not so fortunate, and lay sweltering in the heat.

Squinting against the sunshine, Liberty began ferrying water to them until she heard a *thud* once more. This time, she saw it, too.

Her buckets fell from her hands and tipped over in the grass, soaking her feet with cool water.

Against the side of the house, where her purple phlox had stood tall just this morning, was a leg, severed from its owner. And an arm. *THUD.* Another leg. *THUD.* A foot. A hand. Her stomach revolting, Libbie looked up in time to see crimson-streaked arms dropping another load of limbs out the window.

She doubled over and wretched.

Her heart hammered on her ribs as she sank to the ground. "I can't do this! I cannot!" Her gasped confession was drowned out by the men inside who were coming apart at their seams. She buried her face in her hands and repeated a single word in her mind: *God!* It was prayer, plea, accusation.

"You done cryin' yet?" A soldier with a flattened arm propped against the side of the house grunted. "I reckon we feel the same way as you, to be honest. I keep praying I'll just pass out from the pain, but I reckon I'm a mite stronger than I'd like to be." His attempt at a smile pierced her heart, and shame almost swallowed her whole. These men were in excruciating pain, and fully aware of the fate about to unfold for them. The screams, the sound of saw on bone, the limbs thrown out the window, all of this was simply a preview of what came next for them.

She had no reason to complain, unless it was on behalf of these men.

But they are the enemy. The fact needled her, even though she had been so sure when she was arguing with Amelia rather than with her own heart. She scooped the remaining water from the bucket and drank it from her hand. *Levi, what would you say if you were here?* Should it matter what he would say? She was no longer his wife. Did she need permission from her past to do something in the present?

Elizabeth Thorn's words came back to her then, the suggestion to talk to God every time she talked to a dead man. *All right, Lord. What would You say?* He answered with Scriptures she had learned as a child.

Love your enemies, bless them that curse you, do good to them that hate you, and pray for them which despitefully use you, and persecute you; that ye may be the children of your Father which is in heaven.

Amelia wouldn't like it. But her heavenly Father would.

Rising, she shook her soiled skirts, apologized to the soldier for her outburst, and ventured back into her house.

Scraping together all the courage she had, she

stopped another blood-smeared doctor in the hall. "I need to talk to you."

"There are one thousand patients here, and counting, and only two surgeons to wait upon them. Do you suppose I have time to chat?"

"It's about your patients. The ones waiting to be—" She looked at his apron, his arms, his hands, all freckled with blood. *Butchered.* "Operated upon. The pile of limbs outside the window—it's in plain sight of all these poor men. Isn't there anything we can do about that?"

"Move them."

"Yes, that would be fine, move the limbs somewhere else."

"No, I meant *you* move them. If it concerns you so much."

Libbie sputtered. She could never do that, not after what happened to Levi. Acid juices from her stomach climbed into her mouth again.

"Or would you rather perform the amputations? One of us has to, you know. I find no pleasure in it either, but it must be done. The minié ball cannot be removed from the body like a round musket ball could. It shatters the bone, tears the tissue, utterly destroys whatever is in its path. If we don't remove the affected section, infection will certainly kill the patient over time —and painfully, too. So move the limbs, or don't, but do *something* useful, I beg of you."

"What else can I do?" Nothing could be as

offensive as touching that pile of deadened flesh.

"Feed them. Many of these men suffered through a forced march of more than twenty miles before they even arrived, sleepless, at the battle. Or bind the wounds. Have you ever bandaged before?"

She had torn yards of fabric into bandages. Rolled the strips into neat coils, two inches wide, one inch wide, and sent them on their way with the rest of the supplies from the Ladies Union Relief Society. But the unrolling and wrapping around an arm or leg to staunch the flow of blood—that was someone else's job. A nurse's job.

In her hesitation, men clamored for the doctor's attention, and she could tell he was growing impatient. "I'll show you, if you walk with me."

In the next thirty minutes, as he cared for the patients, she absorbed three ways to wrap a bandage and how to pack lint into a wound and keep it moist. Thirty minutes. Charlotte Waverly, the Sanitary Commission worker who had nursed Levi, had told her she'd trained for a full month at a hospital in New York City before nursing any of her own patients.

"Ready." His tone told her it was not a question. "Take these bandages with you, but start with food." She could read in his face that they needed far more than a single farm girl could give. "The most severe cases must have sustenance if they will survive the shock of the operations."

With bandages and lint bulging her apron pockets, she fetched peach preserves and applesauce from the summer kitchen. There wasn't much else left after Amos and Wade had been there, but there would have been nothing if not for Johnny's intervention. In the span of a single breath, she wondered where he was, blamed her boldness for his abrupt departure yesterday, and suspected she had scared him off for good, even if he survived this battle.

Back outside she hurried, and surveyed her dooryard. It was covered with men lying side by side. In that instant, her world shrunk down to the size of her own property, and still it was so big it threatened to overwhelm her. *How will I ever do this?* One patient at a time.

She would start here, at the porch, by her yellow roses, and move her way out toward the road. Liberty squatted in the mud next to her first patient, her skirts billowing around her. "Will you eat?"

A weathered face looked up at her. "Could you write a letter for me first?"

She blinked. "Yes, of course." She should have expected that in addition to water, food, and medical care, one of the most pressing needs was to notify family. It should not surprise her in the least, not after receiving such a letter from Charlotte. How very strange to now be the one writing the note.

Relief passed over his face and he sighed, clutching his chest. "I'm not long for this world, you see, and I just want to send a last message to my wife. I hate to think of her never hearing from me, never knowing what became of me. That would be worse, don't you think? At least if she knows, she can get on with her life. Wouldn't that be better?"

She nodded. It would be better. After she took down his message and the address of where to send it, he said, "Now I don't suppose y'all would let her come get my body until the war is over. But it would be a comfort for her to know where you bury it. And tell my wife where I am laid to rest. It would be a comfort for her to know. Promise."

Liberty promised, and her heart squeezed as she realized that no letter she would write for a Rebel would ever contain the words, "Come quickly." For Southerners would not be allowed to come bring their loved ones home, dead or alive. Unless, of course, the Confederates won the battle.

"But you might be fine," Libbie said, keeping her emotions in check. "You could pull through and be well in the end. Don't give up." But she could tell that he had. "Won't you please try some applesauce?"

He nodded, and she spooned the applesauce into his mouth, slowly, so as not to choke him. Her blood pumped faster as she looked around at all the mouths still waiting.

This was taking far too long. Spoon-feeding one man when there were hundreds waiting? What she needed, but did not have, was bread, to tear off pieces of it and hand them out. Let the men who can, eat at their own pace, on their own. *What I need is two of me!*

She looked up at the window of her bedroom just in time to see the curtain fall back into place.

Weikert Farm, near the Round Tops
Wednesday, July 1, 1863

Harrison Caldwell was on the right path, all right. He was just a little too late.

Taneytown Road was so cut up with wheel ruts and hoof prints, his horse sank more than a foot deep in the churned up mud before Harrison pulled him off to the side of the road for the rest of the journey. *The army has been here. And they were in a hurry.* Chest heaving from the gallop all the way from Taneytown, about fourteen miles south of Gettysburg, Harrison cursed himself for not being here first to see it all unfold.

Twilight dimmed the sky, and quiet pulsed in his ears. On his left was a large hill, covered with trees. Beyond that, a smaller hill, with steep, rocky slopes. *A perfect spot to defend, impossible to take from below,* Harrison mused as he approached it.

Finally he heard something. A mewling, perhaps. Like kittens hungry for their mother's milk. *Where was it coming from?*

Ahead, on the eastern slope of the smaller hill, a farmhouse and barn glowed, and women in aprons carried trays between them. *Of course.* The mewling came not from kittens, but from wounded men, most likely filling that barn. The same scene replayed in his mind from Antietam, Fredericksburg, Chancellorsville. The women the men had been fighting to protect were the ones picking up the pieces in the aftermath of battle.

Harrison pressed his heels into his tired horse and quickened his pace until he came to the farm.

"Hello there!" he called to the nearest woman.

She rushed over, a tin cup tied around her waist with string. "Have you news?"

A wry smile curled his lips, but the question burned his ears. He should have the news. But he had been too late. He dismounted to speak to her on eye level. His legs felt shaky after the hard ride. "Harrison Caldwell, *Philadelphia Inquirer.*" He extended his hand out of habit, then put it in his pocket. Her hands were full with a tray.

"Hettie Shriver. This is my father's farm."

"I've just arrived from Taneytown, but it appears I missed the battle."

"I wish I could say the same thing!" she said hotly. "Safest place to be, my foot. Would you believe I brought my daughters, my neighbor's daughter, and my hired help here to keep them *safe?*"

"What happened?" He pulled out his notebook and readied his pencil to take notes.

"Well! Shortly after we arrived, Union artillery hurried by, right before our very eyes, flying toward the sound of battle. Shouting and lashing their horses, they gave up on the rutted road and took to the fields. Then infantry came, and we all brought them water to speed them on to victory. And now this—" she pointed with her tray toward the barn. Moaning spilled from the doors and windows. Shrieks shot out like bullets. "They came back to us wounded, defeated. I thought I was bringing everyone to safety, but I brought them to the lion's den instead."

Looking toward the barn, Harrison rubbed a hand over his freckled face and sighed. He could imagine what was inside without entering.

"You'll be wanting to talk to them then, I suppose," said Mrs. Shriver. "Could you at least come to the kitchen and pick up some beef tea to bring with you on your way? I'd appreciate the help."

"Yes, of course." He tied his mount to a tree, hung a bag of oats around his head and let him feed while he entered the kitchen.

The smell of simmering beef tea washed over him, took him back to every makeshift hospital he had ever been in. Different battles, different women sweating over the steaming kettles, but the same smell. Fresh beef. Fresh horror. He had done this before, but these women hadn't. He could read in their eyes that they had witnessed pain they hadn't imagined possible, and he could see strength rising up in them that they did not know they possessed.

"This is Bella Jamison, my hired help." Mrs. Shriver nodded at a colored woman pouring beef tea into glass bottles, then set down her tray and checked on loaves of bread in the oven.

Bella looked up and greeted him, and recognition kindled in his mind. Those velvety brown eyes, skin the color of almond shells, wide cheekbones, full lips, straight nose. He had met her before. *Where? Where?*

"Pardon me, but have we met somewhere, Mrs. Jamison?"

She squinted those eyes at him. "I don't think so."

"Have you been to Philadelphia perhaps? I'm a reporter for the *Inquirer*." But he'd been all over the country. He could have met her anywhere.

"I'm from right here, Gettysburg." She handed him the bottles. They grew warm in his hands. He had never been to Gettysburg before.

"Travel much?"

"Only place I want to go is back across Seminary Ridge." The words were barely audible, perhaps not meant for him to hear. Her back was to him as she diced more beef to throw into a kettle of boiling water.

"Across Seminary Ridge? Is that where your home is?" He was unfamiliar with the land here, a fact he hoped to change at first light. He could fairly predict where fighting would take place if he could see the valleys, ridges, forests, and fields.

"No," Mrs. Shriver said as she sliced hot bread with a butcher knife. Harrison's stomach clamored for a piece, but his mind was made up. He would not take bread from wounded men. "That's where another employer of hers is. Where the fighting was today."

He looked at Bella for an explanation. "You want to go where the action was?"

"Just wanted to make sure Miss Holloway was all right, that's all." She slanted a glance at Mrs. Shriver's back as she exited with a tray of fresh bread. "I don't see why that's so unbelievable."

"You have special bonds with the women you work for, then?"

Bella looked up. "Do you always ask this many questions?"

"Afraid so. Goes with the territory for being a reporter. But—" he tucked his pencil and paper back into the pocket of his linen duster. "Do go on. I won't print it."

She turned back to her kettle and stirred the boiling water. "Miss Holloway is special." She spoke into curling wisps of steam. "An orphan, raised by a spinster aunt who made no secret of the fact she didn't love her. Helen called her the thorn in her side until she died, although I'd say it was the other way around. Then Liberty married when she was only seventeen, became a widow weeks later."

Harrison moved so he could watch Bella's face when she spoke. "The war?"

"First Bull Run." Her profile glistened in the cloud of steam.

He nodded. He had been there, too.

"And now, this battle—the fighting was so close to her farm today. I worry about her. I don't know how much more she can stand to lose without breaking."

"I can certainly understand that." He had seen some women rise above expectations during this war. He had seen others die from overwork, or a broken heart. Harrison sighed. "I hope you find her well. And now, I best get out to the barn and talk to some soldiers."

She nodded, then turned back to her kettle and rolled the kinks out of her neck.

His eyes widened as another scene overlaid his vision: one of a mulatto woman rolling the kinks out of her neck. Same skin color, eyes, nose, mouth, everything. But a very, very different setting.

"Georgia!" he blurted out, and she jumped, dropping her spoon.

"Pardon me," he said, picking it up for her. "But

I just remembered where I'd seen you before. Four years ago, Ten Broeck Race Course, near Savannah, Georgia. The Weeping Time."

He had frightened her, dredged up unwelcome memories, he could see it in her eyes. How selfish of him. "But you're free now!" *Oh no, does she still think I am pro-slavery?* "Mrs. Jamison, I was there as a reporter for the *New York Tribune.* I had to act like a slave owner so they wouldn't throw me out—and so they wouldn't kill me. But I've never held a slave."

She backed away from him. Why was she so afraid? "I'm sure it was you. I never forget a face." Hers had been twisted in agony at the time. That's why it had taken him so long to place her.

"I've never been near Savannah. You must be mistaken." Her eyes glimmered before she drew a veil over their spark. He had seen that vacant look before, mostly in slaves on the auction block, or runaway slaves who had just been recaptured. He supposed it was a sign of resignation to their situation. Or perhaps it was an instrument of self-defense, a shielding of their spirit whenever they sensed danger.

The beef tea bubbled over, sizzled on the cast iron stovetop. Bella went back to skim off the fat. She did not turn around this time when he took his leave.

She was hiding something. And he would find out what it was.

Chapter Eight

Holloway Farm,
outside Gettysburg, Pennsylvania
Wednesday, July 1, 1863

"I need help."

"Please, please I'll do anything else." Liberty hooked a curl of hair behind her ear and bit her trembling lip.

"This is the help I need." Dr. Stephens' eyes gleamed in the moonlight, unblinking. A kerosene lantern swung from his hand.

"You don't understand. My husband—late husband—had both legs amputated and I wasn't even brave enough to go visit him afterward . . ."

"What does that have to do with right now?"

She blanched. "Isn't it obvious? If I wasn't strong enough to visit a recovering amputee—my own husband—how could I be strong enough to assist in the carving of a man?"

"Selfish." He spat the word upon her. "What a selfish excuse. You want only to protect yourself from a sliver of emotional pain, when you have in your power the ability to prevent physical suffering you cannot imagine. Look around." He waved his arm in a wide-swinging arc. "There are now exactly fifteen hundred forty-two patients

158

here, and only three surgeons. The patients upon whom we do not amputate within twenty-fours get no anesthesia, for if they do, they will not wake up. Darkness is already upon us, which means we have roughly fourteen to sixteen hours to perform these operations in the most humane way possible. We three surgeons must all amputate through the night. I need you to hold the light."

In her moment of hesitation, he jumped in again. "You don't know what you can do until you are required to do it."

"I am only a young widow!"

"And I was only a father!" He dropped his eyelids. "Required to amputate the leg off my own son at Antietam. To save his life, you see. He begged me not to, but I had no choice. It had to come off, there was no other way." His voice wavered. "When he was a child, he fractured his leg, and I set it right again and it healed. To be required to then cut off that leg . . ."

How perfectly barbarous. Eyes filling with tears, Liberty held her tongue and waited.

"I killed him." He brought his gaze to hers, as if measuring her response.

She offered none.

A lump shifted in his throat. "I gave him too much chloroform. I didn't want him to feel any amount of pain at all." He sniffed. "He didn't. He was dead before I finished. Because I was afraid

159

of his pain, and of my own part in it. That is why he died."

Liberty's breath seized in her throat.

"So don't tell me you can't hold a lantern. Don't tell me it's too much." His words, edged with pain, stripped her. She felt exposed. Selfish.

No more.

When Dr. Stephens held out a kerosene lantern, she took it with shaky hand.

"Hold it close."

Her stomach threatened to rebel, and she was glad it was completely empty as she turned her attention to the improvised operating table. It was her barn door, ripped from its hinges and laid atop empty barrels. The other door was in use for the same purpose on the other side of the barn.

They are only doors, Liberty had told herself when they had first been torn out, when the smell of blood overpowered the smell of hay. *It is only a barn.*

"Closer." His tone was impatient. He had been amputating for more than fourteen hours in the wet flannel heat of summer, with no break at all.

Libbie held it over the body, moving it a little this way, a little that way, as instructed, for she did not trust herself to lay her own eyes on the mangled body without flinging down the light and running. *I can do all things through Christ which strengtheneth me. Lord, strengthen me.*

Dr. Stephens lifted the patient's head and tipped

some brandy into his mouth, then gently laid him back on the door. Next, he took an eight-ounce tin canister of chloroform and a small metal flattened cylinder, less than three inches long and one inch wide. Two small tubes protruded from one end. "We used to fold a cloth napkin into a cone and drip one or two ounces into it before holding it over the patient's nose and mouth. This is much more efficient."

Whether he thought she was truly interested or just trying to distract her from the wound, she was grateful for something to hold her interest. "You need only drop one-eighth of an ounce into this perforated disc, like this—and it goes onto a small sponge inside. Now we insert the tubes in his nose —there we are. Now breathe in, my good man."

The patient inhaled, and all three of them waited for the anesthesia to take hold. The patient began muttering something, then cried out, and tried to rise from the barn door. Dr. Stephens did not look alarmed, and Libbie guessed this excitement was the first stage of the drug's effect. Every amputation she had heard today had begun with the patient's wild flailing before succumbing to unconsciousness.

"It is all right, my good man," Dr. Stephens murmured a few times until the man relaxed fully. He touched his eyelids, and they did not contract. "Ready. Watch his coloring, Miss Holloway, and monitor his pulse."

Her eyes darted between doctor and patient.

"If his tongue slips back into the glottis, he will suffocate on the table and die. He will turn grey if there is danger. If that happens, seize his tongue immediately and pull it out."

"But—how often does that happen?" Libbie sputtered.

"Once is too often. Just watch."

Swallowing hard, she pinned her gaze to the patient's face, and held the lantern as steady as she could while the doctor turned the screw on the tourniquet, tightening the strap high on the arm. Light glimmered dimly on the knife's stained blade before it met the man's flesh.

Her heartbeat sounded in her ears. Dr. Stephens swore, and Liberty jerked, exposing her tattered nerves.

"Hold still, woman!" The doctor yelled at her, bent over the table with his knife, and cursed again.

"What is it?" Libbie wondered if the patient could hear anything while he slept, and when he might wake up.

"The blades are dull."

Dull blades didn't slice. They tore. She gritted her teeth and while Dr. Stephens labored to divide muscles, veins and nerves, she prayed in short bursts. *Strengthen me. Strengthen him. Help. Help them, help us. Please, please.*

"Now the retractor." The doctor's voice was

tired. Liberty flicked a glance at him and watched great beads of sweat roll down into his eyes. He wiped his face with the back of his hand, and she averted her gaze again.

"I would consider it a great personal favor," he said, "if you would just hold tight to these straps while I cut. You don't have to watch, just grab on to the retractor and pull it snug. Otherwise, the muscle tissue will get in the way of the bone when I—"

"Yes, yes, that's fine." She didn't need to hear any more. She held firmly to the linen strips with one hand, kept the lantern steady with the other, and focused her gaze on the patient's complexion.

The doctor hesitated. "Set the lantern down. Here."

"What?"

"I need you to steady the limb as I cut."

She froze.

"Don't you dare tell me you can't."

Stuffing down her fear, she held the retractor strips with one hand, and the patient's arm with the other. The saw rasped against bone until she held a severed arm in her grasp. She let it fall to the ground.

He took the retractor from her hand and she closed her eyes in relief. *It's over.*

"It's not over. Pick up the lantern again and hold it close. Keep watch of his face."

163

Liberty shifted her position, switching the lantern from her right arm to her left.

Dr. Stephens picked up a long metal file and grated it against the bone as one would draw a bow across a cello's strings, until he was satisfied the edge was smooth enough. "It will never heal properly if the edges are sharp."

Next he moistened the end of a silk thread in his mouth, bent low with some thin, long instruments, and was silent for several moments as he sewed. Then he sprinkled some powder on the open stump. "Opium is a miracle drug. Stops bleeding, relieves pain. It's the one battlefield drug I would never choose to go without."

Straightening somewhat, he turned the screw on the tourniquet and released the pressure, slowly. "Good." He exhaled. "The ligatures held. Now to separate the nerve endings and sew any smaller veins shut."

Moths beat chaotically against the lantern while Liberty waited for some signal that the operation was complete. Dr. Stephens tugged the muscle and skin back down over the stump, then smoothed adhesive strips of plaster over it to strap the skin back together.

"Won't you sew it shut?" Liberty asked.

"Not necessary. The skin will fuse itself back better without stitches. This is better, so long as we leave room for drainage and the ends of the ligature threads so we can pull those out later.

Now watch. This part isn't hard, you could do it next time." He bandaged a wad of lint onto the end of the plastered stump. "Now the drainage will stay inside the bandage. You see why the dressings must be changed regularly." He sought her eyes with his. "Why I can't care for these patients without your help." She could not deny it.

After wiping his blades on his apron, Dr. Stephens set them back on the end of the barn door, at the patient's feet. The doctor's hands were filthy, sticky with blood and pus, gummy with adhesive and plaster, sprinkled with lint. He wiped them on his apron, too.

"He will awake soon, and we'll help him down so we can do the next operation."

Libbie lowered the lantern and stepped away from the table, bumping into something with her foot. She looked down. *It is only an arm.* And for the first time all day, she did not quake.

She could do this.

"Thank God you have anesthesia," she whispered.

"We don't. Union blockades, you know."

She frowned. "You don't have medicine?"

"Very little, plus what we smuggle."

"Then how—"

"I have my own amputation kit, and the small chloroform device is mine. But the rest of these supplies—the tourniquets, silk thread, bandages, chloroform, opium—all of this was captured from the Union hospital at the Lutheran Theological Seminary."

Liberty flinched. "Then what do they have?"

He shrugged. "A hospital full of patients who can't be helped, or at least not with anesthesia."

"So helping these men means that Union soldiers must suffer?" Union boys housed in the very seminary where Levi studied!

"Oh, I'm certain they are quite miserable."

"I can't be a part of this!"

"You already are."

Indignation flared in Liberty's veins. Was this what loving one's enemies required of her? "I didn't know these supplies were stolen from the North!"

"And what do you call the Union blockade on the South? We would have gladly purchased all we need, but we have no way to get it! Do you deny these men deserve medical attention?"

Her frustration pulsed. Her mind could form no rebuttal.

"Look, the patient is waking. It's time for the next operation, and I need your help, you know that I do. Will you now refuse to give it?"

Part of her wanted to swish her filthy skirt and storm off in a tempest, taking the lantern with her. This was an impossible position for her to be in. The Widow of Gettysburg helping provide medical care to the Rebels, possibly preventing Southern women from becoming other widows of

Gettysburg? She could almost hear Amelia now. *Whose side are you on?*

Love your enemies.

She looked up at the moon then, and sighed. *Who I am doesn't matter as much as what I do. Lord, help me want to love my enemies.*

By the time the next patient was on the door, Liberty was there with the lantern.

General Lee's headquarters, Seminary Ridge, Gettysburg, Pennsylvania Thursday, July 2, 1863

Do we know each other?

Not nearly as much as I'd like to.

Will I see you again?

"Ford."

Silas jerked his head up and cracked it on the stone wall behind him, as his disoriented mind swam back to wakefulness. The vision of Liberty Holloway that appeared whenever he closed his eyes vanished, replaced by the stern, bearded face of a Confederate officer.

"Pardon me, sir." Silas fought the urge to rub the back of his head as he stood. He had come to the one and a half story stone house serving as Lee's headquarters more than an hour ago to report on the Union position. But Lee was away speaking with General Ewell, and Silas was asked to wait for Lee's return. He had tried to stay awake

167

reading a cross-stitched wall hanging of the Lord's Prayer, but he must have nodded off between "Forgive us our debts" and "deliver us from evil."

"He will see you now."

Strong tobacco flavored the officer's breath, the foul smell pinching Silas further awake. Hat in his hands, he approached the very tired-looking General Lee. The first day of battle had come and gone, and at twelve-thirty on Thursday morning, Lee sorely needed rest. Everyone did.

"Please, do tell me what you have learned this night." Weariness cloaked his voice.

Silas cleared the sleep from his throat. "Sir, the Union line regrouped south of town after their retreat. They are still on the high ground near the cemetery. General Ewell did not attack the hill, sir, and they are working to strengthen their position there." Silas paused.

"Go on." So far, clearly, this was nothing Lee did not know.

"Sir, it sounds like there is movement on the other hill, as if Union troops are deploying there as well. This would be their right flank. On their left, they have positions on the high ground crossing Taneytown Road and south along the ridge for about half a mile or so. Reinforcements are arriving from the south and southeast along Taneytown Road and the Baltimore pike, sir."

Lee nodded, slowly, his gaze fixed on the map curling up on the table before him. "Those two roads are blocked, and we have lost an opportunity to capture the high ground of Cemetery Hill and Culp's Hill. Have you any word of General Stuart?"

"Sir, I have found no one who knows anything of General Stuart's position."

Still looking at the map, Lee muttered, "I have no idea where he is, and his cavalry was to be my eyes and ears on the Federals." Stuart should have been here by now—no, days ago—providing both reinforcements and intelligence. But his whereabouts remained a mystery.

Candlelight gleamed in Lee's eyes as he faced Silas. "It most assuredly would be to our benefit to know where he is, and more than that, to know what he knows. Perhaps he has been cut off from us by Union lines. If so, will he not know the nature of those columns? Their direction, their number, their condition?" He paused. "We need more information. Ford, you will get it for us."

"Sir." Silas stood at attention.

"Go get Jeb Stuart, and bring him back."

Silas understood the urgency as well as the order. "Yes, sir." His heart fell into his stomach like a chunk of johnnycake. With every mission, it was becoming more difficult to reconcile his personal convictions with his role in the war.

"Lose not a moment's time," Lee added. "Spurs and gallop. He could be anywhere in Pennsylvania, but chances are he is east of here."

Silas took his leave, calculating distances against time as he mounted Bullet and dug his heels into his sides. Day would break just after four thirty. There was little time.

Moonlight and shadow danced on the road in front of him as he and Bullet passed under the spreading branches of an oak tree. If he believed God would answer his prayers, he may have asked for divine guidance. But what did David, the psalmist say? *If I regard iniquity in my heart, the Lord will not hear me.*

That's right. Iniquity. Silas was on his own.

He turned Bullet east on Chambersburg Pike and dug in, and the horse's lean but powerful hindquarters responded. In less than ten minutes, he had crossed the slope down from Seminary Ridge and into Gettysburg, where streetlights glowed along the main road. The sharp smell of ammonia pinched his nose, announcing the presence of soldiers and horses before he saw them. In the absence of an adequate number of privies, man and beast alike relieved themselves wherever they pleased.

Slowing Bullet's pace, he caught glimpses of Confederate soldiers sleeping on the street, some on church steps, some in the doorways of houses. Puffs of tobacco smoke floated toward Silas, choking him with the stink. Several women were at their wells outside, pumping water and hauling it back down into their cellars. He guessed they had remained hidden, below ground all day during the fighting.

From within Christ Lutheran Church, where he had once practiced preaching, the distinct drone of the wounded drifted out to him. Silas blanched. Like his own heart, what was once filled with worship now bore the stains of man's sin.

Across the street from the church, a woman carried two pails of water toward her door. "Pardon me, ma'am," Silas said to her. "Could you spare a cup of water for me?" He could not read the expression on her face, but her tone of voice was clear.

"Are you Union?"

He shook his head.

"Well then, are you wounded?"

No again.

"Then no, I can't spare it. I've got seventeen people—civilians, mind you—in my cellar below, and not a drop to drink or a crumb to eat all day. Six wounded are in my parlor, and you can tell from here there's more in the church. If you'll excuse me, I've got to bake some bread so we don't all faint from hunger. You'll find the same story in every other house around here that hasn't been abandoned by the owners."

He tipped his hat to her as she trudged off, and did not blame her in the least, though he was still thirsty and hungry himself. Silas wondered if Liberty would even give him food and water if she really knew who he was. He should not have high-tailed it away from her like he did. Hadn't she been left by enough people? He should have owned up to his past. *But no, I just had to light out of there.* Running had become a way of life for Silas.

Lose not a moment's time. Lee's directive rang like an alarm in his mind. Silas urged Bullet into a canter straight through The Diamond, through the last few blocks of town, then galloped out onto the road leading northeast, toward York. If he didn't fall asleep on his mount, the forty-mile ride would give him plenty of time to think.

Just what he didn't want.

Before the war, he used to love midnight rides on horseback. Even if there was no one else in sight, he couldn't possibly feel alone with the canopy of stars twinkling above him, as though God had pricked holes in a black velvet canvas and let the heavens shine through. Back then, he had felt close to God even while enveloped in darkness.

Those days are long gone. That was before the war. Before he started on a path that allowed no turning back.

Silas's legs tensed around Bullet's body as his father's face surged before him: creased with rage, twitching with fury, and as red as the glowing iron he had used to brand his slaves. *How could you have defied me in this way?* The tobacco smell of slave labor was heavy on his father's breath. *How can you live with yourself?* had been Silas's response. Enraged, his father ended the argument with the whip, filleting Silas's back with lash after lash, until the overseer finally wrestled it out of his grasp. When his back finally healed, the flesh rippled with scar tissue. *I would do it again,* Silas thought. *Some prices are worth paying.*

An owl hooted overhead as Bullet carried Silas toward York, and Silas wiped thoughts of his former life from his mind. Like it or not, he had a mission to complete.

He could not stop running yet.

Chapter Nine

Carlisle, Pennsylvania
Thursday, July 2, 1863

Bullet was all but spent, and so was Silas. Thirty-five miles from Gettysburg to York would have been no trifling journey in the daylight. But traversing the road before dawn revealed it, with no rest or food or water—Silas was not surprised that Bullet could not sustain a gallop, or even a canter for much of it. Fatigue and constant vigilance had weakened horse and rider alike.

And Stuart had not been at York. After three more hours of hard riding, Silas and Bullet arrived in Carlisle, thirty-two miles west of York. Smoke clogging his already parched throat, Silas dismounted his exhausted horse in front of the blunted remains of Carlisle Barracks. *Stuart was here.* And he may have just missed him.

"Pardon me, young man, but could you tell me when this happened?" Silas approached a young boy climbing around on the rubble.

The boy was only too eager to tell the tale. Stuart had been here all right. If the boy could be believed, he had lobbed some shells into the town last night, made some demands for supplies, and been refused, evidently because Confederate General Ewell had already cleaned them out. So he lit Carlisle Barracks and headed south toward Gettysburg.

"Can't miss 'em," said the boy. "He left with one hundred and forty brand-new, fully loaded wagons and mule teams, all of them Federal. Counted 'em myself. He shouldn'a done that." He scowled.

With that long of a wagon train, Stuart wouldn't be able to go any faster than a walk. Silas was feeling rather slow himself at the moment, and he knew Bullet needed a rest. His hide was filmy with sweat and he frothed around his bit. The poor beast needed a break.

"I don't suppose you know of a fresh horse I could borrow?" he asked the boy. "I'd leave this one here with you until I could come back for him."

"Stuart took all the good horses we have." *Of course he did.*

"All right, Bullet, we'll rest a short spell, and then it's back on the road."

But the short spell stretched out on the bank of the stream that curved around the smoldering barracks. When Bullet nudged the hat off Silas's face, the sun glared almost directly down on him.

Silas stumbled to his feet, scolding himself for sleeping that long. Swinging back in the saddle, he winced as his thighs hit his mount, and spurred Bullet toward Gettysburg. If Stuart had headed there himself, there was only one road he would have used. Silas might catch up to him yet, if he was lucky.

He was. Headed south on Carlisle Road, Stuart's wagon train, laden with weight that sunk the wheels into the ground, labored to move at a crawling pace. Silas steered Bullet off the road and trotted to the front of the line until he found Lee's absentee general.

"Sir." Silas saluted Stuart. "General Lee is anxious for your arrival in Gettysburg." He knew better than to say any more.

Stuart slanted a gaze at him. "I can go no faster, as you see with your own eyes." At this rate, he would not likely enter town until evening. Directing his gaze into the distance ahead, he did not look at Silas again. The conversation was over.

Saluting once more, Silas urged Bullet forward, past the wagon train, and veered back on the road. By midafternoon, he was back at the Confederate headquarters on Seminary Ridge. Completely sapped of his strength, Silas sighed as he dismounted and approached the two guards flanking the door.

"I need to report to General Lee. I have news of General Stuart."

"The General and Major Taylor went south along the ridge with Longstreet," one of the men responded. "You may find him there."

Silas nodded, slowly turning back to his horse.

"Ford. Need water?" He pointed him to the well. "You look about dead on your feet."

After slaking his thirst, Silas filled his canteen and let Bullet drink before stiffly climbing back in the saddle. Mustering the very last dregs of his energy, they traveled south along Seminary Ridge. Muscles quivering as he fought to maintain balance, he threaded a path through a buzzing swarm of Confederate soldiers, asking for General Lee along the way. There were hundreds of soldiers, with more collecting by the minute, but so far, none had seen Lee. "He may yet be coming," one of Hood's men told him. "Come back in an hour."

Gladly. Silas retraced his path north, just beyond the bevy of soldiers, and stopped to rest in the shade before he collapsed off his horse completely. Back aching from the constant jolting on his horse, he sagged against a tree trunk and closed his eyes.

And did not sleep. Without looking, he knew that not two miles from where he sat was the Holloway Farm, and Liberty. Groaning, he covered his face with his hat. His conscience would not let him rest until he checked on her welfare one last time, now that battle had come to her doorstep. He would assure himself that she was fine, and then he would leave. He would not turn tail and run away as he had last time, but he would make his exit like a gentleman who knew not to overstay his welcome.

With a sigh of resignation, Silas rehearsed in his mind what he would say to Liberty. Once he told her who he was, what he'd done, she would reject him outright, and all would be well. His heart would be safe, and so would she. All he had to do was tell her the truth. Most likely, she already knew one version of it. *Silas Ford, man of the Lord, took slaves to bed and shot Pa dead!*

It was easier if he wrote it. Yes, he would write her. Reaching into his haversack, he retrieved paper and pencil, and let the story unfold in a letter. He told her almost everything. Perhaps some things were better left unsaid.

After signing and folding the paper into his trousers pocket, he let his head fall back against the shaggy bark of the tree trunk and closed his eyes once more. Visions swirled in his mind. A flash of sunlight on the silver barrels of two lacquered walnut dueling pistols. Smoke pouring out of his gun. His father's face before he fell. A full jug of moonshine. An empty jug of moonshine. A stranger pointing to an enlistment paper. His name, but not his signature. A gun to his head.

Darkness.

Round Tops,
Gettysburg, Pennsylvania
Thursday, July 2, 1863

Congratulating himself on his perfect timing for the brewing fight, Harrison Caldwell ran up the eastern slope of the smaller Round Top hill, crunching last year's dead leaves beneath his feet, as Union regiments double-timed into place. From beyond the wooded hill, the Rebel yell vibrated the air before a single enemy soldier could be seen.

But they were coming.

Harrison crouched alongside the reserves of the 20th Maine regiment, twenty yards behind the front line, and found himself next to a private he'd already met. Theodore Hopkins, the last of his brothers to go to war, and the only one still alive.

"Well, Hopkins, what can you tell me?" Harrison asked as he pulled out his pad and pencil. The air filled with the sound of sharpening knives, and

Harrison looked up to see every man on the front line ramming his rod down the barrel of his Springfield rifle, each one glinting silver and bobbing like a giant needle.

"We're the left flank, and the 83rd Pennsylvania is to our right. Col. Chamberlain says we've got to stand our ground here or the Rebels will sweep over the rest of the line. So it's up to us." He tore open a cartridge with his teeth, poured the powder and bullet into the barrel, and rammed his metal rod down in after it. "When there is a hole on the front line, we are to fill it. I've got to be ready." He dropped his rammer in the dead leaves, and groped around for it for a few seconds before returning it to its slot and priming the gun. In training, the best men could fire three times in one minute. In the heat and confusion of an actual battle, Harrison had seen less experienced soldiers take far longer than that. He hoped Hopkins' fumbling hands would not be the death of him.

"Here they come!" shouted a soldier on the front line, and new energy coursed through Harrison's veins, heightening all his senses.

Every gun in the Union line seemed to fire at once, cracking the air as lead balls rushed at the enemy. Clouds of smoke hung in front of the barrels, saltpeter and sulfur replacing the scent of rotting leaves and warm, damp earth.

While the soldiers in front reloaded their rifles, Hopkins chanted with quavering voice. "For right is right, since God is God, and right the day must win; to doubt would be disloyalty, to falter would be sin. For right is right, since God is God, and right the day must—"

Rushing footsteps in the underbrush grew louder, like the tide coming in, as the Confederates charged up the rocky western slope.

The Union guns fired at will, sporadically this time, dropping Confederate soldiers mid-stride, their bodies blending in with the felled tree trunks scattered on the slope. Orange-red sparks spat out of the barrels like lizard tongues lapping at the smoke.

A Maine soldier slumped silently over the hastily built pile of rocks in front of him, dead. Another fell back as a bullet slammed into his shoulder. Rebels were beginning to perforate the Union line.

Harrison glanced at Hopkins. A film of sweat coated the boy's face under his kepi, his knuckles were white against his barrel. Expelling a breath, he pulled out another cartridge and put it to his teeth.

"You've already loaded it." Harrison laid his hand on Hopkins' shoulder. "You're ready."

"I'm going to be sick. My mother told me not to enlist. I can't die. She'll be all alone. I can't die."

Harrison groaned inwardly. It was the same story he'd heard countless times, yet no less tragic despite its repetition. Young man wants to prove bravery. Mother says no. Man enlists. Man dies. Another mother mourns.

"Private!" An officer stood over him. "Fill that hole. Now."

Crouching low, Hopkins crept up to fill the breach in the line, pulling another cartridge packet from his box as he went.

Time stretched as men in blue traded shots with men in grey. Harrison stood to get a better look, but dropped down again when a bullet whizzed past his head, taking a notch out of his straw hat.

Minutes crawled by, punctuated by showers of musket fire and the thunder of artillery from elsewhere on the hill. Until an explosion in the line twenty yards in front of him made everything else sound like rain.

Dread trickled over Harrison, seeped into his skin. He looked down and saw the torn papers from eight cartridges that had not been there when he had first arrived. *Eight!* His stomach roiled. Hopkins must have gone mad with fright, and reloaded his gun out of nervous habit, jamming the barrel with gunpowder and lead before ever taking his first fatal shot.

"They're falling back!" someone called. The shots tapered off to an eerie calm. Smoke swirled in long shafts of sunlight falling through the trees. "Remove the wounded, gather their ammunition."

Harrison watched as soldiers dragged their comrades from the stone wall and moved them back to the reserves line, out of danger's reach.

Some men grimaced in pain, while other faces were already frozen in death. One face had been blown off completely. So had his hands. It had to be Hopkins.

Such a waste.

A sheen of moisture stung Harrison's eyes, and he wiped them angrily. *A war correspondent has no business getting weepy over a single casualty when thousands fall.*

He had seen too many boys and men—sons, fathers, husbands, brothers, sweethearts—pass ingloriously into the next world. The hardened reporter's shell he had built around his heart was beginning to crack, and it frightened him. If he was going to make a name for himself with a profound story as a war reporter, he needed to toughen up.

I'm too close. What Harrison needed was a big picture view, not a character study.

"Here they come again!" A new wave of Confederates came charging up the hill.

With bullets zipping through the air above him, Harrison scurried down the eastern slope to retrieve his horse from the Weikert farm. He needed a different observation point, that was all.

Then he saw her, Bella Jamison, running frantically back to the farmhouse with the rest of the women and children.

"Mrs. Jamison!" He called out, but she did not

hear him. When he got close enough, he grabbed her elbow, and she whirled around and punched him in the gut. He doubled over for a moment, and vaguely registered that she had laid a hand on his back in apology, he guessed. He stood again.

BOOM!

"I need to get over to Seminary Ridge!" he shouted over the roar of Union artillery. "Do you still want to go?"

BOOM!

Her eyes went wide, she nodded, and together they ran to his horse, the earth rumbling beneath their feet. He helped her up into the saddle, swung himself up to sit behind her, and kicked his heels sharply into the horse's sides.

"I need to watch the rest of the battle from the Ridge," Harrison shouted, "and then I'll take you wherever you wish."

Blue-grey powdery smoke rolled down the hill, chasing them as they left.

Holloway Farm,
outside Gettysburg, Pennsylvania
Thursday, July 2, 1863

Shock rippled through Bella as Harrison's horse carried her onto Liberty's property. Three horses wandered about in the nearby field, grazing on and trampling the wheat. The fences that had once neatly enclosed the garden were gone, used for kindling, Bella surmised, for the fire that crackled loudly in the sweltering summer afternoon. Black smoke billowed up from behind the house, sending noxious fumes of burning horseflesh into the air.

"I take it this is not what you expected to find."

Coughing, she drew a hand over her mouth and nose, but the smoke had already snaked down her throat.

"Nasty business, burning dead horses," Harrison muttered as he helped her dismount. "But it's the only way to be rid of them, and the sooner the better. Are you going to find her?" He tied his horse to an apple tree bearing small green promises.

Bella's feet remained rooted in the ground. Another smell, the strong odor of ammonia, pinched her nose. If the men had bothered to dig a ditch for their own waste, they had not bothered to turn soil onto it, or throw in chloride of lime. The dooryard and much of the land was covered with men in bloody bandages, and men who had come apart. A buzzing layer of flies covered a pile of festering limbs outside the summer kitchen. The loping Southern accents that drifted to her told her they were not Union men even without looking at their uniforms.

Confederates!? Here? Her heart pumped faster to keep up with her whirling thoughts. If any one of these men had laid a hand on Liberty—

"Come, I'll go with you." Harrison offered Bella his elbow, and she hooked her hand through it, keenly aware she was doing two things she'd never dreamed of in this life: she was being escorted by a white man, and she was willingly walking into a sea of Rebel soldiers. *At least they are all wounded.* "They won't harm you now." For once, she was glad to have this nosy reporter around.

"Bella?"

Bella jerked her head around until she saw Liberty. Her brown gingham dress and broad apron were speckled with dark red spots, the hem lined with mud. Black curls fell loose from their bun and clung to her neck. But it was her eyes that told on her. That she had seen too much, had seen things that would haunt her for the rest of her life.

Liberty hitched up her skirts and wove her way through the men on the ground until she was right in front of Bella. She grasped Bella's hands, and squeezed. "You're here! Oh thank God, thank God you're here." She threw her arms around Bella's neck. Bella hugged her tightly, and noticed she no longer smelled of apples and cinnamon, but of sweat and fear and pain. But she was safe. Her daughter was safe.

Libbie stood back.

"You're all right," they both said at once. Harrison chuckled at Bella's side.

"Oh, Liberty Holloway, this is Mr. Harrison

Caldwell. He's a reporter for the *Philadelphia Inquirer*, and he brought me here from Cemetery Ridge."

Liberty shook his hand. "Pleased to meet you. Thank you for bringing her to me. And these—" she spread her arms wide and glanced over her shoulder. "These are my patients."

"Excuse me? *Your* patients?" Alarm rang throughout Bella's spirit.

Liberty raised her eyebrows. "Well, yes! I know they aren't Union soldiers, Bella. I would have preferred to care for our own—actually, if you had asked me two days ago, I would have said I preferred to be left alone completely. But these men need help, and I have been doing that ever since they arrived."

"Doing what, exactly?"

"Bringing them water, brandy, food. Writing letters for them. Assisting the doctors."

Visions of the mangled bodies at the Weikert farm swam before Bella's eyes. The sights had been so gruesome, she was grateful to be able to spend all her time laboring over a hot kettle of beef tea in the kitchen instead. How on earth had Liberty been able to stand it? "Assisting the doctors? Really?"

"Don't look at me that way. I know what you're thinking. But I did it. Just ask the doctor."

"Or me."

All three heads turned to see a patient grinning

up at them. "She was right there when saw-bones nearly took my arm. A braver, more beautiful gal I never did see." That Southern twang, combined with the hungry look he gave Liberty, was enough to make Bella's stomach sour.

But Libbie smiled at him. *Smiled at him!* "Thank you, Isaac. Is your arm feeling all right now?" She turned to Bella and Harrison. "It was only a round musket ball, not a minié ball that entered his arm, so the doctor was able to pull it out fully intact."

"I feel right as rain whenever you're around, Sugar. Liberty's my girl, now. Aren't you, Liberty?"

Bella stared at Liberty. This could not be happening. This was not right. Liberty was in mourning for a man who died for the Union. She would never put up with this—

"Right, Isaac. Remember, you and six others."

Bella gasped, and Liberty offered her a wobbly, guilty-looking smile. Harrison seemed amused by this exchange. She wasn't amused. She was horrified. Liberty Holloway was *flirting* with a Rebel? She had no idea what she was doing.

With a hand on Liberty's shoulder, Bella spun her aside and hissed. "Just what is going on here? Have you changed so much in six days' time that I barely recognize you myself?" Her forehead ached, and she pressed a hand to the pain. She sounded more like a mother than the hired help.

She needs a mother right about now. "Have you forgotten who you are?" The words slipped out before she could catch them. Before Bella remembered. *She doesn't know who she is.* Bella had always thought it was better that way. Now, doubt shook her.

Astonishment bloomed on Liberty's face. "You sound just like Amelia."

"Who's Amelia?" Exasperation laced her tone.

"No, who are you?" That Rebel, Isaac, rose and jabbed a finger at her. "I don't appreciate you talking to my girl thatta way."

Your *girl?* Your *girl?* Bella glared at the little Rebel.

"He's not serious, Bella, it's only in jest." Liberty whispered, tugging on her sleeve. "The doctor told me to play along, to raise their spirits. It's only a game."

"Oh, I am too serious. Lookit you. You think you're as good as white just because your skin ain't black as pitch."

Bella's blood ran cold. He was thin, his chin was weak, and he was no taller than she was—but that didn't mean he wouldn't crack a whip over her back. Or worse. She had seen his kind before.

"Why, Isaac Tucker—"

He held up a hand to silence Liberty. "No, Sugar. She oughta be servin' you, not scolding you. Or serving me." He raked his gaze over Bella.

She closed her eyes, shutting out his face, while the old memory dredged back up again. The weight of a man's body crushing the breath out of her, the tobacco on his breath. Her own tears rolling down the sides of her face and filling her ears before spilling onto the pillow.

"You get on outta here now. Go on. Make yourself useful and fry us up some chicken and biscuits." Isaac snickered. Other patients did not. Most just stared, but one of them told him to hush his mouth and sit down.

"Now see here—Isaac, is it?" Harrison stepped in and blocked the Rebel from her view while Liberty whisked her away, toward the shade of the oak trees next to her house.

"I'm so sorry, Bella," Liberty whispered.

"Me, too." Her throat tightened with unshed tears. "How could you care for a man like that?"

"I don't care for him as a man, understand. I'm simply caring *for* him as a patient. See the difference?"

Bella studied Liberty's face and nodded. "I do. I see a big difference." She raised an eyebrow.

"If you're referring to the changes in me, then yes, I freely admit I'm different from the girl I was last week. I still love the Union. I still hate slavery and hope the Confederacy is defeated soon. The sooner the better. But aren't we supposed to love our enemies?"

Bella grit her teeth.

"We can talk about all that later. First, I want to hear how you are. Where were you these last couple of days? Walk with me."

Bella told an abbreviated version of her tale as they walked to the spring house to fill Liberty's basin.

"And your horse?" Libbie asked as she bent to scoop up the water.

"Left him tied up on Baltimore Street and never went back for him. Mr. Caldwell says that when the Confederates took the town yesterday, they surely took him."

Liberty pressed her lips together and led the way back into the sunshine. "It will be harder to serve your clients without a horse."

Only one client interested Bella right now. The cries of broken men grew louder as they neared the house. "They're inside, too?"

Liberty nodded. "No vacancy."

Bella shuddered to imagine the mess that had overwhelmed the place where Liberty had pinned her dreams of a brighter future. "It will be harder to have an inn without—an inn."

Liberty looked as if she might cry, but she laughed instead. "I didn't even get a chance to tell you, I got my first guest for Liberty Inn last weekend."

"And now you have hundreds!" Bella hoped to tease a smile from Liberty. It worked. "But tell me, who was the guest?"

"Is. She's still here, locked in my room. I think."
Liberty looked up toward her own window
before sighing and telling Bella about Amelia
Sanger, Levi's mother. Bella's heart sank when
Libbie told her Amelia wanted her to call her
"Mama," and soared when Libbie said she
refused. Then, "Yesterday we had an argument."

"Oh?"

Liberty sighed. "She didn't want me to bring
water to the patients. Didn't want me to do anything to help at all. She said they would take
everything from me."

Bella let the words hang in the air for a moment.
"Was she wrong?"

"I've been trying not to think about that,
actually." Absently, she wrapped her apron strings
around her fingers before dropping them. "I have
work to do. Coming?"

"I beg your pardon?"

"We can keep talking, but I need to get back to the
patients. I could surely use your help, too, Bella."

"Are you in earnest? Did you not hear the way
Isaac spoke to me back there?" Indignation had
crept into her tone, but she didn't care.

"That was wrong of him, I know it was. But he
is just one patient. There are many, many others
who just need us to drip water on their lint or
bandages, to keep them moist. Most of them won't
even know we're there at all. Won't you please
help me? I need you."

"And I need you, young lady, to *think* for just one moment, exactly what it is you are asking me to do." Her fists were on her hips. "These men held my family in slavery for generations and would love to see me taken back to the auction block today."

"*These* men did?" Liberty narrowed her eyes. "Really? Do you recognize any of them?"

"You know what I mean, Lib—Miss Liberty, don't be contrary."

"Please. You have opened my eyes, just a little, to the prejudices you have faced because of the color of your skin. People make judgments about you as a person without getting to know you. They reduce your personality, your skills, and gifts to a broad category."

More than one category, actually. Former slave. Mulatto woman. The help.

"Well?" Liberty's eyes were circled with exhaustion. "Aren't you doing the same thing now? You're assigning the sins of your slave masters to every one of these men just because they are from the South. I met lots of men here who have never had a slave in their life!"

"And I've met plenty of men in the North who have no use for colored folks once they're free."

The women faced off, truth clashing in the air between them. Tears filled Liberty's eyes, and the tip of her nose pinked. This was not the way Bella had wanted their reunion to go.

"You don't understand the risk you take," Bella tried again, softer this time. "Do these men respect you enough to leave you be? Or are you a symbol to them, the embodiment of everything they hate?" A chill swept over Bella. This wasn't supposed to happen to her daughter. Not to a woman who looked just as white as anyone else. *How can I make her understand the danger?* "You are a Yankee. They are Confederates. Worse, they are wounded Confederates, which means their pride is already sore. What is to stop them from hurting you to make them feel like men again?"

"Most of these men seem to be perfect gentlemen, if not perfectly educated."

"All it takes is one man who thinks he owns you. One man who believes degrading you will raise his own status."

"I will be fine."

"How do you know that? You don't know, you can never know. I didn't know when—" Bella bit her tongue on her frantic speech. She had almost said too much.

" 'Though an host should encamp against me, my heart shall not fear: though war should rise against me, in this will I be confident.' "

"Your heart may not fear, Liberty Holloway, but that doesn't mean that bad things might not still happen to you." This was a thin line to tread. Did she really want to deflate her faith that God would keep her safe?

Questions glimmered in Liberty's eyes. "Bella, such an outburst. Why are you trying to scare me like this? Remember your place."

Oh, I remember, child. If you only knew.

"I have to go." Liberty sniffed, and took her basin and sponge to the nearest Rebel.

"So do I," said Bella, stunned.

Liberty looked up. "Where will you go? You have no horse. The Confederates have taken the town. There's no telling when or where the next fight will break out."

"Anywhere but here." And she stalked away from Holloway Farm.

Seminary Ridge, Gettysburg, Pennsylvania
Thursday, July 2, 1863

"Oh, no you don't."

Silas Ford jerked awake to find himself being yanked to his feet from under the tree where he'd fallen asleep.

"You're not sitting this one out, soldier." A barrel-chested Confederate half-dragged Silas from the shade with one hand, while the other gripped his Enfield rifle.

"I'm not a soldier." Silas shook the fog from his brain as he stumbled along. Bullet was nowhere in sight.

"Don't matter what you call yourself, but your

haversack there says C.S.A. You're a Rebel, and you're coming. Or you're a deserter, in which case I'll shoot you myself."

Any further argument was useless as Silas was dragged into a regiment marked by the palmetto symbol of South Carolina, their rifles bouncing sunlight into his bleary eyes. The crowd of soldiers he had searched an hour ago had swollen to a large battle formation. As though in a dream, Silas watched a contest from the inside for the first time.

Twenty yards to his right, four regiments were already advancing, across Emmitsburg Road, over a stream, toward a wooded area. Then an order was shouted, and the regiment surrounding Silas began to move forward. The boy next to Silas wet himself with fear.

Shots cracked the air ahead and to the right as they crossed Emmitsburg Road toward the Union positions. Gun smoke knit together in the air in a surreal blanket of haze as rifle fire grew to a near constant rattle in Silas's ears.

Billy Yanks locked with Johnny Rebs, grinding and churning like a plough through rocky soil. Yards of ground gained were soon lost again. Grey pushed back Blue, Blue drove back Grey, thrusting and reeling in waves as the ground grew red beneath them.

"Take up a weapon!" A Rebel shouted at Silas while ramming his rod back into his musket barrel.

Silas had no weapon.

Time suspended, impotent to end the fight by its passing. The battle raged, sweeping the soldiers into a wheat field where ripening grain smoked with gunpowder. The strong unflinchingly fired their guns while men were hurled from life to death on every side. The weak clung without pride to the bellies of fallen horses, taking cover behind their girth. Some boys became men in an instant. Some men cried for their mothers. Bullets pierced courageous and cowardly alike, while riderless horses reared and plunged. Men came apart.

Union twelve-pounder Napoleon guns blasted canister shots at the Rebels, the balls spraying into the wheat like hail. A shell screamed overhead and Silas splayed his body against the ground, crushing stalks of wheat beneath him, while men slammed into the soil around him. Thin golden stems snapped while the field grew ripe with a harvest of bodies.

Minié balls whirred and moaned over Silas's head, somewhere in the battle cloud that hid the blue summer sky. His parched mouth filled with the tastes of nitrate and sulfur. "God! God!" The staccato prayers of the wounded passed through their bloody lips, and Silas matched them with his own silent plea.

"*Fight,* for Pete's sake! Take a rifle from the wounded!" The soldier's eyes were veined with red, his face sketched black with gunpowder from tearing tops off the cartridges. But Silas would not pick up a weapon ever again, had not touched one since—

BOOM! The ground shuddered as the Napoleons fired their canisters again, and Silas shielded his head with his arms. Mud coated his face as he pressed his head down. If he stayed, the Yankees would kill him. If he fled, the Confederates would kill him.

Confusion swelled and swirled in the smoke-filled field. The late afternoon sun permeated the haze, baking Silas's sweat-soaked back as soldiers in blue and grey fired through the wheat. There was no way of knowing how many Federals the Confederates now faced in this hazy maze, nor who held the field.

"Fool!" The soldier yelled at Silas again as he reached for another cartridge. "See that rifle there—" A bullet cut short his sentence, tearing through his throat, and a jagged crimson stream arced forth. His eyes bulged, he stumbled, fell, the thud muted by the surrounding cacophony.

"Bayonets!" The cry came from somewhere in the fog, bristling Silas's skin, as he stripped the shirt off his back. Quickly, he twisted the shirt into a bandage, but by the time he brought it to the soldier, life had already left his body.

The rattle of musketry ceased as soldiers on both sides fixed their bayonets to their muskets. Silas's heart banged against his ribs, pulsed in his ears. He swiveled on his knees, warm mud seeping into his trouser legs. All around him, men were cut down, as if by a giant scythe. He dropped to the ground and wormed between the dead, away from the fray.

"How bad is it?"

Silas startled, and turned toward the feeble voice. The soldier beside him was not dead yet. His left thigh bone had been shattered, bits of bone sprinkled and embedded in the exposed red muscle. Flies buzzed above his wound.

"You'll be fine, we just need to get you to a surgeon." Sweat spilled down Silas's bare back as he threaded his shirt beneath the soldier's leg and then tied it snugly against the flesh, above the wound.

"Charge!" The call sounded far away, but Silas didn't trust his ears. Everything sounded far away after being caught in the thunder of battle. If he didn't get this soldier to safety, he'd bleed to death or be killed by bayonet. *And so will I.*

"Take his uniform," the soldier pointed weakly to a fallen Union soldier yards away. "If they are close enough to charge us, they'll be close enough to see you're a Yankee."

Silas hurried over to the Union man and found him unconscious, if not yet dead, his hair matted with blood. He ripped off the dark blue jacket and stretched it on over his torso, not bothering to put on the shirtwaist beneath it. Silas's own trousers were already a grey-blue color, and would suffice for the hasty disguise.

Sweat beaded at Silas's hairline and rolled down his face, mixing with mud, as he hustled back to the soldier.

"Get down, down," the soldier said. "We'll not be killed by bayonet if they think we are already dead."

Silas dropped to the ground before the blanket of gun smoke unraveled above them. The clash and clamor of hand-to-hand combat reached a fever pitch before receding beneath the more insistent sounds of fresh pain, until the fight had gone out of the men completely. There was no way to tell who won.

Silas glanced at the wounded man beside him. Short gasps of pain were the only sign that he hadn't yet succumbed to unconsciousness. Silas was glad. If he fell asleep now, he might never wake up. He had to keep him talking.

"I never did catch your name, lieutenant." Silas tried to sound casual as his mind spun for a way to get him help, fast.

"Holmes. Pierce . . . Butler . . . Holmes."

"And where is home for you, Holmes?"

"Little town . . . Darien . . . Georgia."

Slowly, Silas stood and spun in a slow circle to view the wreckage of the trampled field. Until—
"There! An ambulance. We're in luck, Holmes." He turned back to the ambulance. "Stretcher!" But

none came. The driver stumbled away from the wagon and wretched before looking up at Silas.

"I quit!" he shouted, shaking. "I hope I never see so much as a scratch on a man again!" With that, he staggered away from the empty four-wheeled wagon, tripping over bodies as he went.

Silas grit his teeth, but said nothing. He would load this man into the ambulance himself, along with any others he thought may yet be saved, and take them to a surgeon. The Holloway Farm was three miles from here, perhaps a little further. Silas was sure it had been taken for a hospital by now. If it was held by Yankees, his uniform would be his protection. If it was held by Confederates, they would welcome this wounded soldier. Either way, he had to try.

Willoughby Run,
outside Gettysburg, Pennsylvania
Thursday, July 2, 1863

Bella Jamison tramped along the west bank of Willoughby Run, away from Holloway Farm. Where she was going, she did not know, and she did not care. The only thing she cared about right now was Liberty.

But to Liberty, Bella was the hired help. Nothing more. Hired help was paid to wash clothes, bake bread, curry the horses—not to direct the course of one's life. That was the role of a mother.

A role Bella had given up long ago, and willingly. As long as she could be part of Liberty's life, in some small way, even if it was as the help. This was the role she had chosen to play. She could not deviate from it now, without an explanation, any more than an actor on stage could suddenly switch characters. It would upset the entire performance.

Better that no one knew Liberty was one-quarter Negro. Even in the North, being mixed race meant more questions and fewer opportunities. This close to Mason and Dixon, it meant living with the possibility of being sold into slavery. Being subject to other people's wishes and control. Spit upon. Ridiculed. Rejected.

She had watched too many times as her mother had been hauled off to the overseer's house on St. Simons Island, then come home the next day, with his seed in her womb. Nine months later, a baby would come, and so would the overseer's wife, who beat her into a hospital bed. Between the overseer and his wife, Bella's mother had no escape. No choice. No relief.

And Bella had thought she could change all that. Bella sniffed at the memory. *Foolish girl.*

No, that kind of life would end with Bella. It would not be passed on to her daughter, or to her daughter's daughter. It ended here.

Bella knelt by the water and gazed into the glassy stream. *Still, I wonder . . .*

It doesn't matter. Bella dropped a hand into the cool water and let it flow between her fingers. *And if she doesn't know my story—her story—how can I expect her to be afraid that a version of that history will repeat itself?* Bella sighed. She couldn't.

But there was no denying that girl needed a mother. "When my father and my mother forsake me, then the Lord will take me up." *I have not forsaken her, Lord, but she doesn't know that. Please, take her up. Speak to her in a way that I can't.*

Bella stood and rubbed the knots from her shoulders as the night air settled upon her skin. She may not be able to play the role of mother to her own daughter, but she would not leave the stage completely. Liberty had hired her as the help. So, God help her, she would.

"Easy, easy," Silas murmured to the horses he drove, more from habit than from the belief that it would help matters one whit.

The ambulance allowed Silas to move six wounded men from the battlefield, including Holmes—but judging from the sounds coming from the rickety wagon behind him, the journey felt more like torture than salvation for those he intended to help. With no straw to cushion their bodies, every bounce of the wheels intensified their pain. By now, all but Holmes had passed out from it, if they had not been unconscious already.

As they approached Willoughby Run, Silas expelled a sigh in relief. "Almost there, Holmes," he called over his shoulder. "Only five hundred yards past this creek and you'll get—"

CRACK! The ambulance pitched left, the horses skittered sideways, and Holmes cried out in agony. The wobbly front left wheel had finally bounced clear off the axle, leaving one corner of the ambulance sloping to the earth. Silas wiped the back of his hand across his forehead and squinted toward Holloway Farm. Surely, they were close enough.

Climbing down from his seat behind the horses, he walked to the bank of Willoughby Run and waved his arms. "Hello!" he shouted. "Over here! Help!"

No one looked his way.

"Help!" He tried again, but his voice was still hoarse from the gunpowder he'd swallowed.

Silas leaned against the wagon. "Well Holmes, our wagon has just mustered out of service, but I can see the hospital from here."

"They see you?" Holmes whispered.

"Not yet. But don't worry—"

"Take my gun."

"What?"

"As a signal. Fire into the air."

No. Silas shouted and waved his arms again, but

still no one turned his direction while six men lay dying in the wagon.

"Please. Take it." Hand shaking, Holmes held up a pistol by the barrel.

It's just a flare, Silas told himself. *Not a weapon.*

As he grasped the handle in his sweaty palm, his father's contorting face flashed before him once more. He shut it out, pointed the pistol to the heavens, and squeezed the trigger. The shot tore through the sky, silencing the chatter outside the farm.

Finally, people saw. He handed the pistol back through the window to Holmes.

"Look! Over there! A Yankee!"

"He's shooting at us!"

"Shooting at a hospital!"

"Take him down!"

With sickening clarity, Silas remembered the Union uniform he now wore. "No!" he shouted. His sweat turned cold on his body, chilling him to his core. "I'm Confederate, and I have wounded Confederate soldiers here!"

They were ramming their rods down on their powder.

"I tell you I'm not the enemy!" His mouth turned dry, he could barely make his tongue obey. He walked closer to the creek, to be heard. "I escaped with this jacket—" But his voice would not carry.

Get down! His brain told him, but his body had become wooden.

A bullet sliced through the air.

Hit its target.

Dropped him to the ground.

Instinctively, he sat up, reached for the pain, and gasped when his hand came back to him bleeding from its palm, stabbed by the bone jutting out of his trousers.

Another bullet whistled by his ear and he dropped back to the ground, smacking his head on a rock.

Silas closed his eyes to stop the dizziness. Vaguely, he could hear the footsteps of two men running toward him. Their voices were muffled. He heard them grunt as they carried the wounded out of the ambulance. And then they were gone.

They will come back for the rest.

But they did not come back for him. Darkness fell between Silas and Holloway Farm. He was still alone in the field, bleeding into the grass. Rejected and forgotten by North and South alike.

Like a lamb walking into a pack of wolves, Bella returned to the Holloway Farm hospital and prayed God would help her. Relief washed over her when she saw Liberty smile at her in welcome.

"I'm so glad you've come back," Liberty said.

Before Bella could reply, two men in grey carried a new patient over to a barn door on barrels.

"Miss Holloway." A man with a stethoscope around his neck bellowed as he stormed by. "I need light, and I need it now."

Liberty scampered after him, pulled matches and a tallow candle from her apron pocket. She lit the candle, and held it over the mangled form. "We have no more kerosene."

"So we have a single flame?" The doctor growled. "That's not enough light to cut a steak, let alone a man."

Bella swallowed the acid in her mouth and stepped forward. "Is there another candle? I can hold it for you." *Lord, help me.* "If you'll allow it."

The doctor looked her up and down and grunted. He did not turn her away.

Harrison Caldwell approached and offered to hold one, as well.

"Still here?" Bella asked Harrison, her tone low.

He nodded. "Fighting's over for the day anyway. I've been interviewing these men about the battles in which they fought. Helps me get the overall view of things." His voice was steady, but his color paled in the candlelight.

Bella turned her attention back to the table, where the doctor was tipping some brandy into the patient's mouth.

"Soldier, can you tell me your name?"

He swallowed and licked his cracked lips. "Pierce Butler Holmes."

No.

No no no no no.

Pierce Butler Holmes?

Here?

The name seemed to slither around her throat like a snake, tightening, slowly.

"Oglethorpe's Light Infantry. Eighth Georgia."

Her throat squeezed. She knew him. Lord have mercy, he was the son of the plantation's physician, and the godson of Master Pierce Butler himself! He lives in Darien—or at least, he lived there before the Union troops burned the town. *My husband's troops.*

"Pierce Butler Holmes, you say?" Harrison leaned in closer to the patient. "Are you a relation of my fellow Philadelphian, Pierce Butler, the former slave owner? Ex-husband of Fanny Kemble?"

Holmes blinked. "He's my . . . godfather. Good as . . . family. My father . . . was the doctor . . . for his slaves."

Harrison raised his eyebrows, but mercifully prodded no further.

This can't be happening. Bella stepped back.

"Light, woman! Bring it close!" the doctor snarled, then looked back at the patient. "Can you tell me when you were wounded, man? Was it today?"

When Holmes nodded, the doctor dripped some clear liquid into a small metal device and held it in Holmes's nose. Harrison leaned over and whispered to Bella the reason for the doctor's question. "If it's been more than twenty-four hours since the wound, they can't use anesthesia. Might not come out of the sleep, you see."

Bella quelled the instinct to run. So he was going to sleep in a moment. *Fine. All right.* She could hold on a moment longer, and soon it would not matter who he was. He would just be one more patient, lying on the table, helpless under the knife and saw. He would not be able to harm her.

Suddenly, his eyes snapped open and flashed with fire. Bella's breath caught in her throat as he clamped a hand around Liberty's wrist and pulled her close to his face. Her candle dripped hot wax on his face, but he did not flinch. Or even blink. "Why, you're the very likeness of Roswell King Junior!"

Bella's candle shook, her knees buckled.

"It's the chloroform," Harrison said. "It makes them crazy before they drop to sleep."

He wasn't crazy.

"That's a good man, now let the young lady go." The doctor pried his white-knuckled fingers off Liberty's wrist, but Holmes twisted and writhed until he was up on elbows, staring at Bella.

She could not breathe. She could not move.

He pointed at her and laughed maniacally. "So are you! You're twins! That is, except for your skin color . . ."

"He is mad with the drug," said the doctor.

Holmes spoke again, his voice eerily high-pitched. "I would know a King anywhere, even away from Darien. But how did you escape? You all have the same—eyes, I think. No, lips. Nose and lips, that's it."

Liberty looked at Bella, unspoken questions written in the lines on her brow. Bella shook her head, as if to say, "He is only mad. Pay him no mind." But no words formed.

He knew her secret.

And Liberty's.

Only when he fell back, unconscious, upon the table, did Bella realize she was covering her face with one hand, and leaning against Harrison. The nosy reporter who had seen it all.

After the tenth amputation since Harrison had been at the table, Dr. Stephens dropped in a dead faint from exhaustion.

Finally, the morbid candlelight vigil came to a close. *At least for now.*

He let out a breath and noticed his stomach cramping. His supply of licorice Necco wafers depleted, Harrison reached into his knapsack and pulled out some hardtack and vegetables. *Desecrated vegetables,* as the soldiers called them. Army fare wasn't particularly appetizing, but it was portable, and it took the edge off his hunger. If it was good enough for the Union army, it was good enough for him. In small doses.

"Excuse me, Mr. Caldwell." Liberty's eyes looked hollow in the sputtering glow of her candle. It would surely be out soon. "Is that—food?"

"In a manner of speaking, yes. Tasteless hardtack, and a cake of dried vegetables." He held up the squares.

She stared at them, and her stomach growled.

"I don't suppose you'd care to try one?"

She grabbed the vegetables from his outstretched hand and ate it a little faster than was generally considered polite. Wiping her mouth, she turned toward a mass of men begging for water. "I need to go. Bella, there is enough for both of us to do—there is enough for a dozen of us." She sighed. "But I will not require it of you. Do as you please." She walked away, her steps heavier than they had been when he first met her hours ago.

Indecision etched on Bella's face, and Harrison seized upon her hesitation.

"Mrs. Jamison, I couldn't help but notice you seemed quite upset by Lieutenant Holmes's outburst. While the chloroform was taking hold."

She looked down at her fingers, twisting in the folds of her apron.

"Why were you so shaken?"

"I wasn't—I was—it was just—I've never stood so near an amputation before."

Harrison frowned. "No, no, this was before

Dr. Stephens brought a knife to the skin. It was something Holmes said that bothered you."

Her chest rose and fell in quick, shallow breaths.

"Mrs. Jamison, where is your husband now?"

Her eyes narrowed, she flattened her lips.

"He's a soldier."

"In training?" Just last week, colored troops had begun training at Camp William Penn, eight miles north of Philadelphia.

"Active."

The only active duty colored troops were the 54th Massachusetts and the 2nd South Carolina Volunteers. Being from Pennsylvania, he would be in the free black troops of Massachusetts. The South Carolina regiment was made up of contra-bands—former slaves. But they had recently joined together for a controversial action in—

"Darien, Georgia. Yes? The home of Pierce Butler Holmes?" Harrison casually broke off a piece of hardtack and popped it in his mouth, gauging her reaction.

The sparks in her eyes flared brighter.

"Yes. My husband is in the 54th, which recently burned down the lieutenant's hometown. If he knew, I don't know what he would do. Wouldn't he want to retaliate? Wouldn't I be the perfect target?"

Harrison swallowed. "Good news, Mrs. Jamison. You must have read only the earliest report of the Darien raid."

"Our telegraph has been out."

"Allow me to put your mind at ease. Further reports have shown that it was Captain Montgomery of the 2nd South Carolina who gave the orders to torch the town. Not Colonel Shaw. In fact, more than one of Shaw's letters to his superiors have since been published in the papers, expressing his disagreement with Montgomery's methods. It's widely known now, that if the 54th had any involvement in that raid at all, it was minor, and only because Montgomery forced it upon them. Your husband, Mrs. Jamison, has done nothing wrong, I am quite sure of it. You need not fear revenge on his behalf."

The night was deepening, and Harrison could barely see her face anymore, but a flash of white teeth told him she had understood.

"Thank you, Mr. Harrison. I am much relieved to hear it."

"My pleasure. It's not every day I get to bring glad tidings."

She nodded. "Now, if you'll excuse me, I will go help Liberty bring the men water."

"You have nothing to fear."

But as she walked away, her shoulders still sagged.

Harrison bit into a cake of dried vegetables and mulled over her curious behavior.

Aha! Roswell King Junior. Those were the words that sent Bella backward until she leaned on Harrison for support. He had grabbed Liberty, and said—she looked like him. That couldn't be right. He had also said Liberty and Bella were twins, and that obviously was wrong, too. Still, there was something there.

He chewed another piece of hardtack, and hoped he wouldn't break a tooth on it. Roswell King Jr. was Pierce Butler's overseer on the Georgia plantations. Butler prized him for his efficiency.

But according to Fanny Kemble in her *Journal of a Residence on a Georgian Plantation*, he did more than manage the property. He personally populated the estate with new slaves.

Harrison reached into the bottom of his haversack and drew out the neglected journal, cringing at the curled corners and water stain from where moisture had seeped into the bag from the muddy ground. Though the moon shone brightly, it was not enough light to read a book, so he lit another candle and buried the end of it in the ground beside him until it stood steady on its own.

Hungry for clues, he began flipping through the book. As was the style, Kemble did not always print full names in her accounts, using only initials instead. But from the context, it was clear enough that "Mr. K—" or "Mr. R—K—" referred to Mr. Roswell King, Jr. "Old Mr. K—" referred to his father.

References to the son were abundant. Betty, the wife of headman Frank, had at least one son by King, with "straight features and diluted color." Another young man who bore a striking resemblance to King was born of a Negress named Minda.

A little more than halfway through the journal, Harrison had bracketed a particularly chilling account:

> Sophy said she had never had any husband, that she had had two children by a white man of the name of Walker, who was employed at the mill on the rice island; she was in the hospital after the birth of the second child she bore this man, and at the same time two women, Judy and Scylla, of whose children Mr. K— was the father, were recovering from their confinements. It was not a month since any of them had been delivered, when Mrs. K— came to the hospital, had them all three severely flogged, a process which she personally superintended, and then sent them to Five Pound—the swamp Botany Bay of the plantation, of which I have told you—with further orders to the drivers to flog them every day for a week.

Harrison closed the book. He had never met Roswell King Jr., but he assumed that Lt. Holmes had. They shared a hometown, after all, and Holmes's father was the plantation physician.

Would not Holmes have accompanied his father on his calls?

Holmes had said Liberty bore King's resemblance. So did Bella. Was he saying they were *both* King's illegitimate daughters? Were they half-sisters? Bella had called Liberty her employer, but had not mentioned any family relationship between them.

But would she?

Bella's insistence on getting back to Liberty during the fighting replayed in his mind. Strange, that she had said nothing about her own home. Her only desire was to get here. To Liberty. And even after she had seen it was full of Rebel soldiers, she had come back. To help Liberty.

Harrison chewed the end of his pencil before jotting some notes in his pad. They had to be related, even if Bella wanted to keep that hidden. Besides, even if only one of them were related to King, it would be remarkable. This could be the story he had been looking for. A sequel to the Weeping Time story, but penned under his real name.

Imagine! A former slave, the daughter of the Butler plantation overseer, now helping Rebel wounded at the battle of Gettysburg. And her husband had watched the burning of Darien! He may have even helped torch it. How poetic!

But so far, all was conjecture. He needed proof—facts and testimony—or his story would be mere speculation, a gossip column. The last thing he wanted. He needed Bella and Liberty to be straightforward with him. He had to win their confidence.

"Exactly who is Bella Jamison?" he said aloud to no one but the crickets. "Who is Liberty Holloway?"

"Now that, young man, is a very good question!"

Harrison jumped to his feet. He had been so lost in thought he hadn't noticed the inky outline of another person standing beside him. He bent and picked up his candle so he could see her face.

"I'm sorry to startle you. I'm Amelia Sanger, Liberty's mother."

Harrison narrowed his eyes. "I was told she was an orphan."

"Oh, that. Technically, yes. I'm her mother-in-law. But I might as well be her mother. We're very close."

His face knotted in confusion. "I thought she was a widow."

"Fine! My son—her husband—was killed two years ago! But you probably already knew that too, Mr.—"

"Harrison Caldwell, *Philadelphia Inquirer*."

"Oh, a reporter! Well keep digging, newsman. There's a story here."

"Is that so?"

She nodded. "How does this strike you: 'Union Widow Shamelessly Supports Late Husband's

Killers.' " She jiggled her eyebrows at him. "Well? Have you seen her with these Rebel hooligans?"

"Some. Have you?"

"I've seen plenty. From right up there." She nodded toward a window on the second floor of the farmhouse.

"Ah. So you've locked yourself in your bedroom ever since they arrived?"

"Liberty's bedroom. They took mine as an operating room first thing. Imagine!"

"So let me make sure I've got the facts straight. You've been sleeping in Miss Holloway's bed while she has been out here, feeding and watering the men, wetting their bandages, assisting with amputations."

Amelia glowered. "And why shouldn't I shut myself away? If your own mother were here, wouldn't you rather she stayed out of it as well as she could?"

"Quite." He raked a hand through his hair. "So, what brings you out of your sanctuary this fine evening?"

"Mind your own beeswax."

His gaze dropped to the chamber pot she held in her hands. "I do beg your pardon."

"Now if you'll excuse me." She began to saunter away, but turned back. "You keep digging, newsman, and you'll find a story surrounding Liberty Holloway, that much is certain!"

He had a feeling she was right.

Chapter Ten

Holloway Farm,
outside Gettysburg, Pennsylvania
Friday, July 3, 1863

Liberty's stomach revolted at the smell of flesh spoiling in the broiling sun. The air was thick with it, and it was terrible for the morale of the patients.

"Dr. Stephens." Liberty approached the doctor as he was probing for a bullet in someone's shoulder. His movements were slow, lethargic. Surely he needed sleep. "I really must insist we do something about that pile of limbs outside the summer kitchen. Do you really plan to let them stay there forever? When the wind blows from that direction, the smell alone is enough to make the men sick."

He looked up at her, eyes red and glazed. "Do sssomethin' yerself."

Her brows knitted together. "Are you quite well?"

The doctor wagged his head, wincing as if the movement pained him. "I've gotta sssplittin' headache." He wiped his nose with a handker-chief. "Ssplittin'. And close to a thousand patienz to see. So go fix yer own problems. Oh see there, Collins is taking careofit. Now lemme be."

Astonishment filled Liberty as she watched a one-armed patient pulling a wheelbarrow backwards toward the pile. *Does he mean to move those limbs himself? Why, he will meet his own arm again!*

Liberty hurried over to him at once. "Mr. Collins, what on earth can you be doing?"

"You're right, Miss Holloway. This pile must be taken care of. And since my arm is in there somewhere, I figured I would help put it away. Didn't your mother teach you to put away your own things when you were done with them?"

He smiled, and Libbie's eyes widened. "Are you quite sure you want to do this?"

"Quite sure."

"At least let me tie a handkerchief around your face." But she had no more handkerchiefs. "Excuse me a moment." She went to the other side of the summer kitchen, lifted her skirt and tore a wide section of fabric from her red petticoat. Tearing that in half, she had two cloths that would serve the purpose. Her conscience needled her as she returned to Collins with the handkerchiefs.

"Bend down a little, please, and I'll tie this on you. There." She peered up at him. "Do you—do you want me to help?"

"No ma'am." His voice was muffled behind the red triangle covering his nose and mouth. "At least, not with handling the limbs. I can use a rake to get them into the wheelbarrow, but I don't believe I can manage to steer it with one arm once it's loaded. You know, to the burying place. I'll need your help then. I know it's an awful lot to ask of a lady."

She did not feel like a lady in the least. She hadn't bathed properly in days and had only changed her dress once. Her hair was unkempt, the curls falling out of her pins. And now her only petticoat had a large hole torn out of it.

"Would you call me Romeo if I offered to do that for you?" Isaac sidled up to Liberty and took her hand.

Liberty slipped out of his grip. "I don't promise you that, but I would be so grateful for any help you can give. We need to bury this pile as soon as possible."

Isaac wrinkled his nose, and Liberty held out the square of fabric she'd torn from her petticoat. "Put this on. It will keep the flies out of your mouth and nose while you work."

"This is what we have Negroes for, down south. Where is that colored woman I saw yesterday? She looked plenty strong enough for the task."

Liberty's face flooded with heat. "I'm not asking her to do this, Isaac. I'm asking you. Please."

The sulky look on his face reminded Liberty of a small child after being told he could not pass off his chores to someone else.

"My arm still hurts."

"My arm's still gone." Mr. Collins glared at Isaac.

"Yes." Impatience threaded Liberty's tone. "If Sergeant Collins is helping, you should be able to as well." Isaac's injury had not been so severe that he could not lend a hand. In fact, soon he should be able to rejoin his regiment.

"Fine, Sugar. If it makes you happy."

"If you don't help, I'll have to. So consider it a personal favor to me."

"Anything for you. After all, you are my girl, aren't you?"

Liberty cleared her throat. The charm of this little game was wearing quite thin. "Thank you. I do appreciate it. There are rakes and shovels in the barn. I can show you where to bury them."

Isaac followed her to a spot a distance from the house, in the apple orchard.

"This should be fine, wouldn't you say?" she asked him. Fine had become such a relevant term these days.

"I'll tell you what isn't fine, Sugar. Taking sides against your man isn't fine." His eyes glowed. "You shamed me back there. Don't do it again."

Liberty propped a fist on her hip. "I'm sorry if you felt embarrassed. But you must realize this little make-believe courtship you've drummed up isn't going anywhere. As soon as the battle is over, which has got to be soon, you'll be on your way, and I will stay here and do my best to pick up the pieces from this wreckage."

"Oh, I'm not leaving you, Sugar."

"Pardon me?"

"We were meant to be together, you and me. I'm staying, for good. I love you."

Libbie laughed, but she was the furthest thing from happy. "You don't even know me! You certainly don't love me."

"Then why in tarnation did I just agree to bury a bunch of dead arms and legs?"

"Because it's the right thing to do."

"Sorry, not a good enough reason for me." A grin slithered over his face. "You owe me. That's why I'm doing it. You owe me now."

"I owe you nothing." Anger sharpened her voice. "If anyone owes anyone here, it's you and your army who owe me. Did you know I was married once? Lost my husband in the Battle of Bull Run. The Confederates took my husband, and now my home."

He gripped her wrist and twisted. "You lost your husband, did you? How lonely for you. Let me pay you back." He pulled her close and clutched her squirming body against his. With one hand against her back and the other pressing against the back of her head, he kissed her, deeply, until she bit his lip and stomped on his foot as hard as she could. He released her with a yelp.

"You stay away from me, Isaac. The Union will win this battle, and then you'll leave in disgrace. The sooner the better! I'm not your girl!" Face burning, she ran back to the farmhouse.

"Oh yes you are! I like a little spice with my Sugar!" he called after her, laughing.

But Liberty did not turn around. She was done playing this little game. *I'm sorry I ever started!*

Meade's Headquarters, Taneytown Road, Gettysburg, Pennsylvania
Friday, July 3, 1863

Something was wrong with Harrison Caldwell.

Nightmares were not so unusual. But now, even in the light of day, he saw mangled forms on the landscape even where there were none. When he saw a perfectly whole soldier, Yankee or Rebel, he imagined—against his will—an arm being blown off by a shell, or a twelve-pounder taking his legs off.

When he had covered the battlefields this morning on his horse, he had vomited. Twice. At least no one had been around, aside from the unseeing corpses, bloating and blackening in the sweltering summer sun. There were bodies—both of men and horses—everywhere.

In shallow mounds of freshly turned earth, hands and arms thrust up through the scant covering, as if begging for more earth to hide them from the glare of day. Some bodies lay flattened against the rocks as if thrown there by a giant hand. Heads, arms, and legs nestled among the branches and twigs that had also been severed from their trunks by the leaden hail-storm.

Would it never end, this human waste? An overwhelming sense of sadness penetrated his spirit.

Harrison had seen enough of the dead. It was time to talk to the living.

When he arrived at Meade's headquarters on Taneytown Road behind Cemetery Ridge, he found Sam Wilkeson and Charles Carleton Coffin already there, on the shady side of the widow's home. Harrison tied his horse to the fence along with the rest.

"My boy's been wounded." The first words out of Sam's mouth.

"I'm so sorry." Harrison clapped a hand on his back. "Do you know, is it quite serious?"

"I know very little." His eyes were red. Harrison would not be the only correspondent having trouble reporting on this massive battle.

Before Harrison could reply, a mass of artillery roared to life all at once, the sound as if earth and sky were crashing together. The fiery thunder filled the air as suddenly and as completely as the notes of an organ would fill a church with Handel's "Hallelujah Chorus" on Christmas morning. Taking up his field glasses, Harrison counted close to one hundred fifty Confederate cannon blazing with spark and billowing smoke on Seminary Ridge. Seconds later, shells shrieked across the sky, whirling across the valley until landing on the center of the Union lines on Cemetery Ridge.

But not all of them hit their mark. Those that overshot their target exploded above, around, and through Meade's headquarters. As many as six shells per second burst in the sky above Harrison's head. The men scrambled to safety some distance behind the house, leaving the tethered horses to rear in terror.

For one hour that felt like ten, the inferno of the Confederate artillery raged against Cemetery Ridge, and the Union guns blazed back. Shrapnel rattled in the trees like hail. Clouds burst into view where before there had been blue, unsullied sky. Several Yankee soldiers on Taneytown Road were torn to pieces. Harrison would hear their screams again, in his dreams, he was sure.

Finally, a lull. Harrison watched in horrified awe as a mass of men, perhaps twelve thousand strong, marched forward in perfect order across the open field, a mile wide, right up to the very muzzles of the guns, until the Yankees opened fire and tore lanes through the Rebels as they came.

"They are committing suicide!" said Wilkeson.

"They are following orders." Carleton's voice was tempered by amazement. "No one can say they are not brave. And they will go down in a blaze of glory."

Glory? Harrison could barely keep himself from shouting that all was madness. Though his loyalties were firmly on the side of the North, he could not rejoice to watch this slaughter. *What was Lee thinking to issue such a command?* This was not a fair fight. It was a squandering of human life on a monumental scale. There was no glory on this field. Only carnage.

For fifteen minutes, the Union gunned down men who, by now, were running at them like wild men, as if minié balls and bayonets could be a match for cannon and high ground. Until the last gun fell silent, the last Rebel yell and Yankee huzzah faded away, and the Union still held Cemetery Ridge.

The field smoldered with charred and grotesquely mangled forms in every conceivable position, laid out in the track of the great charge. It was scattered with caissons, canteens, muskets, cartridges, horses. Men.

"How can Lee recover from such a blow?" Harrison muttered. The words sounded distant and muffled after the earsplitting battle.

"He won't. He must withdraw." Carleton's prediction. Harrison had never known him to be wrong.

Back at Meade's headquarters, they found the one-room widow's house perforated with shell. All sixteen horses lay dead on the ground, still tied to the fence.

Rehearsing potential opening lines to his story in his mind, Harrison walked the ridge back to Cemetery Hill. Cannons blackened with their own smoke and covered in mud rested, finally spent, among the graves. Harrison sat with the dead, then, some below the ground, some above it, and looked out over the battlefield. Just two days ago he had looked out from this vantage point and seen mostly fields of wheat, barley and rye, peach orchards and apple orchards. Now the land was war-trampled and destroyed. Green fields turned into dirt and dust, the grass ground into a layer of jelly. Mounds marked mass graves so shallow that the hair on the corpses' heads was ruffled by the wind. Some graves had been marked with chalk on the tops of cartridge boxes. The names would be washed away in the next rainfall, perhaps in the next heavy fog, and the bodies would be lost to their families forever.

Holding his head in his hands, Harrison tried to think. His editor would be clamoring for a story as soon as Harrison could write it. How could he tell this tale? How could he make the public, people who had never been on a battlefield, understand exactly the toll war exacted?

Unbidden, the faces of men wounded and killed at Antietam, Bull Run, and Fredericksburg passed before his eyes, a cadre of ghosts he'd learned to live with. Gettysburg would add another host to their number.

Eyes squeezed shut, Harrison clenched a thatch of hair and grasped for what was left of his decomposing sanity.

Act Three

IN
THE
FOG

"[I HAVE] DONE WHAT I never expected to do, or thought I could. I am becoming more used to sights of misery. We do not know until tried what we are capable of."

—SARAH BROADHEAD,
Gettysburg housewife and volunteer nurse,
from a diary entry dated July 7, 1863.

"I OFTEN LOOK BACK upon those days and wonder how we all were able to do what we did during those three terrible days of battle, and the weeks succeeding them. Surely we should have failed utterly, had the Lord not sustained us by His strength, and held us up by His power. To Him be all the praise."

—FANNIE BUEHLER,
Gettysburg housewife

Chapter Eleven

Holloway Farm
Saturday, July 4, 1863

Lightning cracked open the sky above Seminary Ridge, and sheets of rain spilled out while thunder rolled like distant artillery. Water sluiced over hills, ridges, fields, and bodies, washing away the blood that had collected. It almost felt like baptism to Liberty, an attempt at purifying the stained. Stepping off her porch, she lifted her face to the angry sky and let the heavy drops splash her skin.

The battle was over.

In addition to the officers who had already been taken prisoner, including Lt. Holmes, almost a thousand patients had vacated Holloway Farm this afternoon, joining in a wagon train of Confederate supplies and wounded that was at least seventeen miles long. The patients who could walk hunched their shoulders against the rain and shuffled between the wagons. Those who could not were laid on the bare planks of the wagons, without straw or springs to cushion the jolting over the washboard roads. Their agony echoed throughout the wagon train as it snaked by on its retreat to Virginia, a macabre Independence Day parade.

Her birthday.

The screen door banged closed as Dr. Stephens came out on the porch and leaned against a weathered post. The other two surgeons had left with the wagon train, leaving Dr. Stephens in charge of the remaining patients at Holloway Farm. Liberty was glad he had recovered from whatever ailment had slurred his speech and glazed his eyes. Most likely exhaustion. The man had risen at two in the morning and worked steadily until midnight the last few days. "The place feels almost empty, doesn't it?"

"Almost." Liberty climbed back under shelter and scanned her trampled dooryard.

"I suppose it is a great relief to you to see them go."

Liberty measured her response. "It is a relief to see an invasion come to an end. But in truth, I wanted to say goodbye to some of those men. Three days is such a short time, but three days of crisis wraps the bonds much tighter than usual, wouldn't you say?"

He nodded. "You say you wanted to say good-bye. Did you not?"

She looked down. "I was afraid it would sound like mockery. I'm so glad you stayed, though."

Hinges squeaked as the door swung open again, and Bella joined them. Her apron and dress bore the marks of almost three days and nights of service, but she held her head high as she stood silently near Liberty.

"Of course." Dr. Stephens sniffed, wiped his nose on his sleeve. "We still have five hundred who need care."

Liberty knew. Those who overflowed the house and barn lay sinking in the mud under the eaves of the house and outbuildings, their stomachs growling and wounds crying out for relief and fresh dressings. But their medical supply had dwindled to almost nothing. The only people here who were comfortable were the ones buried in the orchard.

"I don't know what I'd do without you."

"What about me, Thugar Plum?"

Liberty's spine tingled as Isaac Tucker bounded up the porch steps and smiled, revealing a gap where his two front teeth should have been.

"Come on, Thugar, don't tell me you're not glad to thee me." Soaking wet, he was narrow as a musket rod, and looked almost as strong.

"What on earth happened to you?" Liberty asked over the doctor's groan.

"You're the worst kind of coward, you know that?" Dr. Stephens growled.

"I'm injured!"

"Self-inflicted."

Warning flared in Bella's eyes. Liberty swiveled between the two men. "I don't understand."

"It'th a mythtery to me, too, but the important

thing ith that the army doethn't want me any-more. Can't tear open a cartridge, thee? Front teeth required. And I'm plum out." He smiled again. "Told you I wath thtaying."

"So, you've been discharged?" His lisp continued to distort his speech, but Libbie's ear quickly tuned out the hint of childishness.

He shrugged. "More or less."

"Mr. Tucker." Dr. Stephens towered over him. "Since you no longer require medical attention, you are ordered off this hospital grounds at once."

Isaac laughed, and a curl of black hair dripped on his forehead. "That's the great thing about being discharged. It means I don't have to take orders from you or anyone else in the army anymore. Ever. You've got no rank on me. You can't tell me what to do, see? The only person here I'll listen to is this little lady right here." He turned his gaze back to Liberty, and she fought the urge to smack that smile off his lisping mouth.

Her chest heaved. This boy was crazy. *Crazy!* The thought of his sloppy kiss made her want to run.

"Miss Liberty. A word, please." Bella cut her voice low, guided Libbie by the elbow to the corner of the porch. "Whose farm is this? Whose house? Whose property are we on right now?"

"Mine."

"Then start acting like it." Bella held Liberty's shoulders, her brown eyes penetrating. "That boy

234

over there is a coward and a fool, but he means to please you. Make him work for it. Lord knows there's work enough to go around." She flattened her lips for a moment, as if weighing her words. "Take charge. You are the mistress of this place. Step up, Miss Liberty. This is your land. Don't you dare let them think it isn't." She released Liberty's shoulders. "Do you understand me? Rise up."

Liberty nodded. Bella's words fanned into flame the fire that had been kindling in her spirit. Bella was right. This was her home. Her future. She would fight to get it back.

They walked back over to the men. "This is still my home, Isaac, and I'll not permit you to stay for free. This farm was an inn before your army overtook it, and I mean to turn it back into one. You're going to help me. You can start by raking and shoveling all the soiled hay out of the house and combing the countryside for fresh straw, milk, food. And you will assist Dr. Stephens. You don't need all your teeth for that. We have a lot of patients here and they all need help. So do whatever the doctor tells you to do, or I'll have no use for you either."

A scowl slashed across Isaac's face, but Liberty folded her arms and raised an eyebrow at him. A lashing was ready on the tip of her tongue if he but tested her resolve. The Rebels had torn down her fences. Now it was time to erect new boundaries. Dr. Stephens grunted. "Miss Holloway, I should mention—some of the walking wounded, when they were getting ready to move out today, discovered a body just over there." He pointed to the bank of Willoughby Run about five hundred yards away.

Liberty's brows knitted. *A body? Hardly unusual after the last three days.* "Yes?"

"Well, he was still alive, and they brought him to the barn, but I haven't treated him yet." He looked guilty as sin.

"Why ever not?"

"He's a Yankee."

"Dr. Stephens!" She yelled at him, giving full vent to her frustration, stopping just shy of stomping her foot. "I've given my house, my orchard, my food, my bedding, my *clothing* and all the strength and courage I could possibly muster to care for *Rebels* for three and a half days, and you won't treat a single Union soldier? Shame on you! Shame!" Her face burned with anger. She could feel Bella watching her in amazement.

"Now hear me." His eyes shimmered with his own defense. "I am a Confederate surgeon, and my obligation is to Confederate wounded. There are dozens of patients here whose wounds are not healing properly, upon whom I may need to amputate further. After I'm satisfied that I have cared for all my own patients to the best of my ability, then, and only then, will I look after the enemy."

"If he's wounded, if he's on the brink of death, he can't fight anymore, so he's no longer the enemy, is he? He's a patient. And you're a doctor." She looked at Dr. Stephens expectantly but he did not move.

"Fine." Liberty twisted her loose curls back up under her pins, then wiped her hands on her thread-bare apron. "I'll look after him myself."

"Be advised, you'll have very little to work with. Our supplies are all but gone."

"The captured Union supplies, you mean. The ones intended for the care and relief of Union wounded. The ones we used on fifteen hundred Rebels. Those supplies?"

"Careful, Miss Holloway." Dr. Stephens' eyes were red, his cheeks hollow. "We've been over this before."

Words netted in her chest, fluttered madly, as if to escape. Until, "What is left for my Northern boy?"

Dr. Stephens extended a hand into the down-pour just beyond the shelter of the porch, letting it stream through his fingers and slide down his arm, soaking his filthy, rolled-up sleeve. "Water."

"No brandy?"

"Water."

"What of opium?"

"It's not for him."

"Laudanum? Morphia?"

"No."

"Bandages and lint!"

"No!"

Liberty snapped her attention to Bella. "You will please go into my bedroom and strip the sheets into bandages, and I don't care what Amelia says. Then take a razor to my flannel wrapper and scrape all the lint you can. If it isn't much, which I fear may be the case, please cut small squares of cotton from my dresses, and we'll use them as pads. Please bring a supply to the barn as quickly as you can."

"Yes, Miss Liberty." Bella ducked back into the house.

Still brimming with frustration, Liberty plunged down the steps, mud sucking at her ankles, rain-wrapped wind licking her skin, determined to save the one Union soldier on her farm.

The barn creaked in the wind while rain sprayed through the open doorway like shrapnel. Pale grey light and streams of water trickled through weathered planks. Sodden skirts tangling around her legs, Liberty threaded her way through the greybacks until she found a soldier in blue.

There.

With both compassion and dread swelling in her chest, she hastened to his side, sloshing water over the sides of her pails as she did so. She had brought one for washing, and one for drinking. His face was layered in mud, shadowed by stubble. Kneeling, she slid her calloused palm into his. It radiated with fever. Libbie breathed a silent prayer of thanks that he was still alive.

"Hello, soldier." She kept her voice low, relieved that her gag reflex had worn out by now. From the smell and looks of his body, he had been injured and left in the field more than a day ago. His Union jacket was encrusted with blood on the midsection, but the fabric of the uniform remained whole. *Someone else's blood?*

She edged a little closer to his face. Turning up her skirt at the hem, Liberty ripped off another strip of her tattered petticoat. She wet it, then wiped his burning forehead with slow, gentle strokes. His eyes fluttered open for a moment, then closed again.

Green eyes. The color of moss.

She inhaled, sharply, as shock rippled through her. "Johnny? Jonathan?"

His eyes became green slits, and his lips twitched in a failed attempt to smile. "I know, I know." His voice was hoarse. "I don't look like a Rebel."

She swallowed the tears gathering thickly in her throat. "It doesn't matter what you look like."

"I was hoping I'd see you again." He paused for breath, taking shallow sips of air. "Just not like this."

"Please, say no more. Will you drink?" She cradled his head on her lap, then brought a dipper of water to his lips. Some escaped his mouth, trickled into his beard. She hazarded a glance at his leg once more. "We'll fix you up in no time."

He gave her a crooked smile, obviously reading the truth on her face. Fixing meant cutting. He was going to lose his leg. Without anesthesia. "I know."

Liberty tipped more water into his mouth before laying him back down to rest. What she wouldn't give for fresh straw to cushion his broken body right now.

The doorway darkened, and Liberty looked up to see Bella and Amelia blowing in, with Major between them. When the dog spotted Liberty, he picked his way to her and then wedged himself beside Johnny, putting his wet head on his chest. Johnny didn't respond.

"Here." Bella held a tray of freshly rolled bandages, wads of lint, and calico pads. But they both knew what was really needed was not on the tray. They needed Dr. Stephens to amputate.

"Oof! What is that *awful* smell, I *knew* I was right to hide away in my room all this time." Amelia pinched her nose as if the stench of the field hospital had not pervaded the entire property.

Liberty glared at the woman. "My room. You're still a guest, Amelia, and you are free to leave at any time." In fact, Liberty had half a mind to show her the door right now. "Just what is it that has brought you out in the rain?"

Amelia looked down her nose. "I've been waiting all day to give you your birthday present. But as you seem to have no intention whatever of coming in until after I retire, I have come to you."

"Surely not a cake." Liberty stood, her mouth nearly watering over the word. She would have been happy with more desiccated vegetables, in fact. Anything for the aching void in her middle, and for something to feed the men.

Amelia pressed something cool and smooth into Liberty's hand, while Bella watched silently. It was a brooch about half the size of her palm. The small design within the seed pearl-edged border was of a weeping willow over a tombstone.

"It's Levi's hair!" Amelia announced.

A few yards distant, a cheeky one-armed soldier named Fitz shouted, "Where? Where's his hair? Why don't Levi have his own hair?"

But Liberty was not laughing. "You didn't."

"No, I don't do hair work myself. Far too tedious and intricate for my fingers. I sent two locks of his hair out to be done through a mail order catalog. I had one made for you, and a matching one for me." Her bosom swelled with pride, and Libbie spotted the hair brooch pinned to her dress.

Liberty dropped the brooch into her apron pocket and forced a smile. "Thank you."

"Will you not wear it?"

"No." Liberty cocked her head. "But you've brought up quite an excellent point, Amelia."

"Oh?" She smiled, blinking rainwater out of her eyes.

"Indeed. Levi's things. There is a box of his clothing under the bed in my room, doing nothing useful at all. Bella, would you please bring down one of his shirts? This soldier desperately needs a change of clothing."

Southern voices piped up all over the barn—"I want one! I'm dirty too! Change me!"

Amelia's jaw dropped. "You would scatter your late husband's garments amongst the enemy?"

Liberty shook her head. "No, I'm not quite ready for that. But a neglected Union man about to undergo amputation? Yes. I will." To Bella, she added, "Please bring the quilt off my bed, as well."

"Absolutely indecent." The older woman huffed. "Do you dare believe that playing dress-up by putting Levi's clothes on this man makes him worthy of your attention?"

No. He already is. "You may as well get used to the fact that I won't be confined by my losses. It's time to rise above them, and go forth." Liberty caught Bella's smiling eyes and nodded.

"You heard the lady," Bella said to Amelia. "Go forth." She motioned toward the open door. Liberty stifled her laughter as Bella shooed

Amelia out of the barn like a clucking hen, and into the rain once more.

The swirling sky darkening, Liberty knelt once more by Johnny's side. With circular motions, she tenderly wiped the grime and sweat from his face and neck, and the furrows in his brow relaxed.

"I must tell you something . . ." He trailed away, and her pulse throbbed.

"It will keep. Save your breath, just rest for now." She dipped her rag in the washing pail, then took his hand in her lap and wiped the dirt and blood from between his fingers. She wondered if he had fallen asleep until, when his hand was clean, he closed it over hers, squeezed, and whispered, "Happy birthday."

She smiled, even as her heart cracked open.

When Bella returned with the quilt and blue denim pullover shirt, Liberty insisted Bella be the one to help Johnny into it, if need be. Liberty had grown accustomed to washing strange men during the past four days. But Johnny was no stranger, and washing his face and hands had felt intimate enough. She turned her back and let Bella take over.

"There's something in here." Bella joined her just inside the doorway to the barn and opened the dirty Union jacket. Pinned to the inside was a foolscap page, folded into thirds. "A letter." She unpinned it and gave it to Liberty, her face knotted in confusion.

It was addressed to Liberty, who froze as soon as she read her name.

"Miss Liberty, I know this is none of my never mind, but if you would you care to explain to me why your name is on that letter, I would be more than happy to hear it."

A nod, barely perceptible. Who else could she tell but Bella, anyway?

Bella tossed a glance back at Johnny and the rest of the patients. "Come, your work here is done for now."

Back through the rain, they returned to the porch. Amelia was holed up in the bedroom, and this was not a story Liberty wanted to share in her presence.

She needed no prompting. Bella's eyes bore into Liberty's as the story gushed out of her, beginning with the first letter Jonathan Welch had written her after Levi's death. They continued writing sporadically, but when he mentioned wanting to meet her, she had ignored the idea. Eventually, she stopped responding to his letters altogether, afraid of trespassing on Levi's memory and honor. "Then he came."

"Pardon me?"

"The stranger that came that morning when you and the horses hid—it was Jonathan. But he didn't tell me it was him."

She then told Bella the rest of the story—his prophetic words before the battle, his intervention during the raid, his filling the "vacant chair" Amelia had intended for Levi.

"And now he's filling Levi's clothes." Bella raised her eyebrows, and rain splattered the silence between them. "Well, aren't you going to read the letter?"

"I can't make it out in this light," Liberty hedged.

Bella pulled a match and candle from her apron pocket and lit it. Carefully, Liberty opened the letter and scanned the slanted grey script until she came to his signature: "Please say yes. Jonathan." The words blinked at her in the flicker of candlelight as if begging for response. She pressed it against the staccato beat of her heart and looked at Bella.

"He said . . . he—that is, if he lives beyond the battle, he—wants to marry me."

Bella sucked in her breath, reminding Liberty to take one. Johnny's face surged before her then, as he had appeared the first time she saw him. Handsome, insistent, and slightly mysterious— but she knew the secret now. *To think, I took him for the enemy at first!*

"Will you?" Bella faced her squarely. "Will you take a husband?"

Liberty cleared the shock from her voice. "He said if he survives the battle. We don't know what that verdict is quite yet. I'm sure you saw his leg."

"A man can live with one leg. Will you marry him if he survives? He will want to know."

"No. It's you who wants to know." Liberty laughed nervously.

"I'm serious. You must decide."

"How can I marry him? We've only met on a few occasions!"

"But you've known him for two years."

Liberty sighed, exasperated. "Well, I'd hardly call it a courtship. I can't possibly love him yet. Such a hasty proposal!" Her cheeks warmed at the thought of the letter. The thought of him.

"Love is only one reason to marry." Bella held Liberty's gaze. "Security is another. Marriage can be and should be a safe place, protection, provision. Life is hard for an unmarried woman."

"Life is going to be hard for Johnny. He'll lose his leg tomorrow, if nothing else."

"I'm not talking just about him, although if you were to marry him, I'm sure he'd find a way to provide for and protect you. I'm saying if you aim to marry, you ought not wait for cupid's arrow if a reasonable opportunity presents itself." She took a breath. "I don't know how you'll recover from this alone."

Liberty wiped her forehead with the ragged hem of her sleeve, hoping to hide the tears pooling in her eyes. Recovery would be a long road for everyone.

"Forgive me. I do run on." Bella twisted her fingers in her apron.

"Yes, you do." Liberty's lips curved up. "Then may I ask—don't you love Abraham?"

"I love him plenty. Now." A smile softened Bella's face. "Real life love isn't like the romance love in your novels. Love can grow out of companionship as well as it can from—well, anything else. Love is a commitment, and Abraham and I committed to each other when we married. The warm feelings followed. But at the time, I was more interested in the practicality of the arrangement."

Libbie tilted her head and studied the woman before her. There was so much about Bella she didn't know. But, "Dr. Stephens said amputees can often die of secondary hemorrhage. What if he dies right after I marry him, and I become a widow all over again?" She pressed her fingers to her throbbing temples. "Am I doomed to be the Widow of Gettysburg forever?"

"He isn't dead. We don't know the number of days appointed for any of us. You could marry any man in Pennsylvania, and the Lord might take him up the next day. Carriage accident. The fever. Could be anything, not just war. You can't refuse to marry again just because the man might die. Didn't I just hear you say to Amelia that you weren't confined by your losses anymore? That it's time to rise above them and go forth?"

"Yes."

"So go forth. I'm not saying you have to marry him, I'm just saying it would be folly to let your past dictate the rest of your life. Forgive me for speaking so freely. But *you* make the decision. No one else—living or dead—gets to do that for you."

Liberty's thoughts churned as laboriously as wagon wheels through the mud. Her muscles ached beneath her sodden dress as she folded the letter and tucked it into her pocket. She would make her decision.

But not tonight.

Chapter Twelve

Holloway Farm
Sunday, July 5, 1863

Though dawn had lifted night's curtain, a grey veil of rain still hid the risen sun. Liberty's hands quavered slightly with the buttons and ties on her tired-looking dress. After four days without food, she could not control the tremors.

A knock sounded on her bedroom door. "Liberty! Liberty!"

She opened it with a frown, her hair still in a braid down her back. "You may call me Miss Holloway, Isaac." It was high time he realized he had curried no favors with her.

"It's Dr. Stephens. Something's wrong with Dr. Stephens." His lisp contorted his message, but Liberty dashed out after him just the same.

"If this is a trick to get me alone with you, Isaac, I will knock out your other teeth."

"No. No trick. Just see." His charm vanished, raw fear gaped open in its place. Liberty's heart thundered as they approached the doctor, convulsing in the corner of the great hall. "What happened to him?"

"I don't know!"

"Tell me something, Isaac. Anything. When did you find him like this?"

"Just now. He was saying all kinds of crazy stuff all night long. I bet he didn't sleep more than an hour, which meant I didn't sleep more than an hour. About half an hour ago, he started hallucinating."

"How do you know?"

"He was hugging the air, talking out loud some nonsense like, 'Oh my boy, my boy, you've come back to me.' Then he started mumbling about a leg, and apologizing, and crying all over himself like some milksop."

Chills rippled over Liberty's skin. "Then what happened?"

"I couldn't stand to see him weeping like that, and he didn't answer me when I asked what the blazes was going on. So I left. Went outside to use the trench—which is full of water I'll have you know, about two feet, just right in there, with all manner of floating—"

"Enough! The doctor. Focus."

"I'm just saying if the trench floods we're going to have a whole lot of *mess* we didn't count on. But anyway. When I came back in, the doctor was curled up on the floor like this."

Liberty watched as the doctor's body finally relaxed, his eyes rolled back into his head.

"Dr. Stephens?" She knelt by his side. His lips and fingertips were blue. With her fingers against his neck, she barely detected his pulse.

"What happens if he dies?" Isaac asked.

"He won't die."

"Come on, Lib—Miss Holloway, he looks near gone already. What'll we do with all these patients? He's the only one—"

"Isaac! Honestly!" *What would they do without a doctor indeed?* Fear churned in her belly. *What would happen to Jonathan?*

She knew the answer. His body burned with poison-induced fever last night. Today he would only be worse. If the leg did not come off, and soon, he would die.

Liberty could not let that happen. She could not hesitate like she had before. This time, she could not fail.

"What do you do when someone is sick?" Liberty looked from Dr. Stephens to Isaac. "You go for a doctor. . . . Another doctor."

"I'll go at once." It was Bella. "You'd best see to the boys outside."

Liberty flew to the window. Water flooded the dooryard, overflowing wagon ruts and holes, rushing in tiny streams under and around the bodies of the men too weak to sit up. Willoughby Run had escaped its banks. The ground had been so churned up yesterday with men, horses, and wagons tearing up the earth, it was an absolute quagmire in the deluge. The men would drown.

She rounded on Isaac. "Quickly. Go to every man in the house and find the ones who have passed in the night, just stack their bodies in the hallway for now. Make note of how many spaces we now have inside, then fill them with men from outside. Fill the porch next. I'll go to the barn. Can you do it? Isaac! Can you do it?"

Isaac nodded and she flew down the stairs, slammed open the screen door and plunged into the mud in front of the porch.

"Help is coming," she called out, though she sank in the sludge past her ankles, and her skirts swirled and swam around her legs.

It had been hours since Bella had left, and though the sun now shined in a crisp blue sky, Liberty's mood did not match it. Muscles aching from this morning's emergency, she stooped over Dr. Stephen's cool, clammy body. He was awake, but weak and confused.

She sat on her heels in her ruined dress, on her ruined floor, in her ruined house, too tired to care about any of it.

Amelia remained sequestered, busy with needlework. Isaac was next to Liberty, mercifully silent. He had risen to meet the need, and she was grateful. Not a man had drowned. Johnny was still alive, but slipping out of wakefulness for longer intervals. His skin was bright and moist with the poison of his shattered leg.

At long last, the screen door downstairs slammed. Two sets of footsteps grew louder on the stairs until two breathless, shining faces appeared.

"Owen O'Leary, United States Christian Commission, at your service." A young man in his thirties with short brown hair that curled over the tops of his ears and a neatly trimmed mustache shook Libbie's hand. Her gaze travelled to the bag in his hand.

"Liberty Holloway. I hope that's a medical kit."

"Indeed it is, and here we have a patient. Perfect fit, wouldn't you say?" He bent to examine Dr. Stephens and Bella leaned in to Liberty.

"He's a physician from Philadelphia, and a delegate of the Christian Commission. It's similar to the Sanitary Commission, but they care for the spirit as well as the physical body. Came here on his own to offer his services free of charge for the wounded. He says wagonloads of supplies are on their way for the wounded, he just got here ahead of them."

"Thank God."

Dr. O'Leary pulled back Dr. Stephen's eyelids then let them fall closed again. "Tell me what you know."

As Isaac recited his story once more, Dr. O'Leary pushed down Dr. Stephens's chin, opening his mouth, and smelled his breath.

"Opium overdose."

"What?" Liberty fumed. "He told me we were out of opium!"

"No, he didn't." Isaac's gap-tooth grin grated on her. "He said it wasn't for the Union boy. Big difference."

"I don't understand. He said opium was the most essential drug in battlefield medicine. To stop bleeding, to relieve pain. We still have hundreds who need it! Why would he take it himself?"

Dr. O'Leary rummaged through his leather bag and extracted a bottle of watery white liquid labeled zinc sulfate solution. "A number of reasons. Doesn't surprise me at all. In fact, doctors are quite susceptible to overdose because of the access they have to the wonder drug. It not only relieves physical pain, but emotional pain as well. Reduces nerves, helps one sleep. But ironically, taking opium can cause a depressed spirit, prompting the user to take more of the drug—and so on, in an endless cycle."

He drew some solution into a glass dropper, then carefully squeezed it into Dr. Stephens's mouth. He swallowed. "I'll need four pints of water, please, and an empty bowl or chamber pot." Bella went to fetch them.

Five minutes later, Dr. O'Leary dosed Dr. Stephens again, and again at the same interval until ten doses had been given. The minutes between each seemed to drag on for Liberty as she thought of Johnny in the barn.

Fifteen minutes after the last dose had been given, Dr. Stephens vomited into the bowl.

"Just as I thought." Dr. O'Leary sniffed the air. "Opium. Funny thing about drugs. They can heal, and they can kill. You must only use them as they are intended." He snaked a tube down Dr. Stephens's throat and flushed his stomach with the water.

"That should do nicely. But he's in no condition to see patients for some time yet. The drug impairs mental capacity and interferes with physical coordination. No, he needs to rest. Fine way to spend a Sunday."

"Oh! Is it?" Liberty hadn't thought of church once today.

"It is. But there is no place I'd rather be than right here, at the seat of the emergency. If Jesus healed on the Sabbath—which He most certainly did—then so can I. Now. I imagine there are others you'd like me to attend?"

"Yes!" Liberty's answer burst out of her. "We have a soldier who desperately needs a doctor's attention. Wounded days ago, I believe, and suffering with fever from his injured leg."

"After you." He extended a hand.

Liberty paused. "Is it true that the Christian Commission is sending supplies into Gettysburg for the wounded?"

"It is. Medical equipment, tents, clothing, stimulating drinks, food—"

"When will they arrive?"

"This very evening, before dark."

"I'll go again," Bella volunteered. "I'll be there when the wagons arrive, Miss Liberty, and bring back whatever I can."

"Isaac, you'll go with her. She could use an extra pair of hands." Liberty crossed her arms. "If you give Mrs. Jamison one lick of trouble, I'll banish you from the property. Understood? These patients are counting on the two of you for supplies. Cooperate." She turned back to Dr. O'Leary and led him to the barn.

"He needs an amputation," Liberty heard herself say. "Please, Dr. O'Leary, as quickly as possible. I'll help."

Color drained from the doctor's face. "Where do the operations take place?"

"Outside on the barn door." She cringed, aware of how ridiculous it all seemed. But the rains, at least, had washed the improvised table fairly clean.

"Do you have your own kit? Or shall I fetch Dr. Stephens's supplies?"

Dr. O'Leary shook his head. It looked more like a twitch. "I have my own. Let's bring him to the table. Have you a stretcher?"

"All the stretchers retreated along with Lee's army."

"Now, before we do anything else, I hope you don't mind if we get rid of those maggots. They are distracting me." He reached into his large leather bag and pulled out a tin of turpentine.

Once Johnny was centered on the barn door, Dr. O'Leary pulled from his bag a rectangular mahogany box about fifteen inches long and only five inches wide. An oval brass plate clearly read *G. Tiemann & Co. Manufacturer of Surgical Instruments, 63 Chatham St., NY.* When he opened the case with the sliding brass latch, sunlight bounced off the perfectly polished silver saw blade.

"Please, tell me you've done this before."

"Fortunately for my patients . . . no." His lips slanted, but his eyes were serious. "But you have an immediate need, do you not? And I have—a book." He produced a book labeled *The Practice of Surgery* and slapped it upon the door.

"Did they not teach you this in medical school?" Liberty was stunned. Terrified.

"In my six months of lectures, not one person

volunteered for us to practice our amputation skills upon them. Can you imagine that?"

She closed her eyes and remembered the speed at which Dr. Stephens had cut through his patients with a dull blade. On a good day, he could amputate a limb in five minutes, have the man stitched and bandaged by the end of eight.

Liberty expelled a breath of air. "You don't know what you can do until it's required of you."

He nodded. "I can do all things through Christ which strengtheneth me."

"Yes, you can. Now let's get to work."

Since there was no brandy, Liberty did not tell him the stimulating drink should be poured into Johnny's mouth. Since she did not see a flask of chloroform, she did not mention it was too late to use anesthesia.

"Would you please turn to the section called 'Amputation of the Thigh'?" He picked up each tool from his kit, hefted the weight of it in his hand.

"Secure the tourniquet." She did not need to open the book to know the first step by now. "Place the pad directly on the femoral artery and tighten."

"Of course. I know that."

As he did, she flipped through the book until she landed on the page Dr. O'Leary requested.

"Read please."

She read down, turned the page, went to the

next. On and on, the author droned about the benefits and dangers of various methods and philosophies of incision. Aha. There in the last paragraph of this section. "It says do it as quickly as you can, with one sweep of the knife—yes, that's right the long knife, not the saw—with one sweep of the knife or two, but for heaven's sake get it done quickly for it is the most painful part of the operation."

His mouth twitched. "So that's what it says."

"Yes."

Perspiration glittered on Dr. O'Leary's forehead as he grasped the knife's handle and nodded at the injured leg. "I'd be much obliged if . . ."

She laid the book on the table and her hands on Johnny's leg. "Like this?"

"I believe so."

"Just say yes."

"Yes."

Liberty closed her eyes and turned her head, praying with all her might that God would help her forget whose leg she gripped, and that he would allow Johnny to remain unconscious to protect him from the pain. *It is only a leg under my hands. It is only another patient.*

Finally, a puff of air from the doctor's mouth. Then, "What next?"

Releasing the thigh, she picked up the book and once again scanned dense blocks of text. *Exposed bone . . . create a groove . . . backward sweep of the saw . . . They are mere letters on the page, a spelling list,* she told herself, and heard herself read with unshaking voice.

Dr. O'Leary nodded, and with steady hand, followed her every direction. Her recitation complete, Liberty kept an even pressure on Johnny's leg and lifted her gaze to the vanilla clouds drifting above Seminary Ridge like sails through the deep blue sea. *I will lift mine eyes unto the hills, from whence cometh my help. My help cometh from the Lord, which made heaven and earth.* Psalm 121 sprang to her mind, a blessed relief. *He will not suffer thy foot to be moved: he that keepeth thee will not slumber. The Lord is thy keeper: the Lord is thy shade upon thy right hand. The sun shall not smite thee by day, nor the moon by night.*

By the end of the sixth verse in the chapter, Dr. O'Leary had accomplished his task. "Thank God," he breathed, then delicately tied up the ligatures. Johnny stirred. He was waking up. Liberty's heart lurched as a faint moan rumbled up through his chest.

They were nearly through. There was no bone file in Dr. O'Leary's field amputation kit, but with such a clean slice, maybe all was well without it. The edges of Dr. Stephens's patients' bones were surely serrated and jagged from the dull blade.

"Cover the stump," she urged, and told him to

let the ends of the ligature threads hang out the seam. "Do you have adhesive bandages?"

"In my bag." He did not look up as he tugged the skin back in place.

Before he had to ask for them, Liberty placed the adhesive strips over the stump until Dr. O'Leary's hands were free to help as well. Once secured, he asked for lint and unguent.

Lint she had, but, "Unguent?" Dr. Stephens had never asked for this. Perhaps he did not have it.

"Yes of course, the ointment to place between the lint and the stump. Otherwise, when it comes time to change the dressing, the lint will stick to the skin between the adhesive strips. This much I *do* know. Very unpleasant for the patient, which in turn, is quite unpleasant for you."

Oh no. Hundreds of amputee patients had been dressed without any unguent. Many of them were still here, waiting for their dressings to be changed for the first time. The dressings should all be changed by the fourth or fifth day. That meant today or tomorrow. She kept reading.

The favorable healing of a stump will depend very much upon the skill and tenderness with which the dressings are changed, more especially the first dressings.

Her heart rate double-timed. The favorable healing of a stump depended on—her. Unless . . . "Dr. O'Leary, will you stay?"

"My dear," said he, upon finishing, "I would

260

like nothing better in this world. To be right where one is needed most, at precisely the time one is needed—" He flung a glance around her desolated property. "And to be able to relieve the suffering of mankind . . . What could possibly be better than that?"

Liberty looked at Johnny's body on the barn door and was filled not with sadness for his losing a limb, but with joy that he may yet still live. *What could be better than that, indeed?*

From somewhere on the other side of the barn, the distinct, twangy voice of Fitz drifted on the breeze to her, followed by a chorus of masculine laughter. All was not darkness and gloom here. There was healing, and life. And though she could not deny the presence of suffering, neither could she deny the presence of God as the last two verses of Psalm 121 rang out clearly in her heart. *The Lord shall preserve thee from all evil: he shall preserve thy soul. The Lord shall preserve thy going out and thy coming in from this time forth, and even for evermore.*

Chapter Thirteen

Philadelphia, Pennsylvania
Tuesday, July 7, 1863

Outside the office of the *Philadelphia Inquirer*, South Third Street teemed with life. Carriages trundled over cobblestones taking stockbrokers to the Merchant Exchange and ladies to do their shopping, while newsboys hawked papers between the gaslights that lined the street. The U.S. flag flying just outside the *Inquirer*'s sixth-story window snapped and shuddered in the wind, a blur of red, white, and blue.

Harrison Caldwell felt like a blur himself. Hands quivering from too much caffeine, he held his breath as his editor, Boris Trent, read the story he had just submitted on the battle of Gettysburg. No, on the people of Gettysburg and how they were affected. He was done writing about shot and shell.

Boris slammed the paper down on his mahogany desk, and Harrison jolted.

"OK, Caldwell." Boris folded his arms across his paper-strewn, coffee-stained desk, jutting his head forward like a bulldog, bottom lip protruding. "I'm waiting."

Harrison coughed as cloying scents of musk

and vanilla from the nearby perfumery floated in through the window. "Sir?"

"For your story. Because surely, this is just a joke." His small black eyes sparked over the top of his spectacles.

Shifting in his chair, Harrison braced himself for the coming tirade.

"Hang it all, Caldwell!" Boris slammed a beefy fist on his desk. "Gettysburg was the greatest battle in the history of the war! Wouldn't it be logical, then, for my war correspondent to produce the greatest story of his career from it? Why on earth would you be talking about the people of Gettysburg?"

"There's a story there, Mr. Trent. If you'll give me time to revise, I'll do it, but—"

"No Caldwell, there's a story in the wounded! The maimed! The dead!" Harrison knew. The twenty-five wagonloads of medical supplies he'd seen at Fredericksburg had been ordered to the rear, in favor of ammunition. They only reached the field on July 4—days after they were needed. Yes, there was a story here. But not the one Harrison had the stomach to write.

"This—" he rattled Harrison's paper in front of his face. "This is drivel. If you're going to tell me about the people of Gettysburg, then tell me something shocking! Make me mad!" He rifled through a stack and shoved a copy of the *New York Times* at him. "Read it!"

Harrison picked it up and cleared his throat. " 'Let me make it a matter of undeniable history that the actions of the people of Gettysburg are so sordidly mean and unpatriotic as to engender the belief that they were indifferent as to which party was whipped.' " He stopped. "Mr. Trent, this is shoddy reporting, absolute balderdash. Mean and unpatriotic? Indifferent as to which party was whipped? How dare he call this undeniable history. He does not get to rewrite what happened!" Heat prickled his skin.

"Careful, Caldwell. Your Irish is showing."

He did not care if his cheeks flamed red with anger. "The people there went hungry for days. They gave all their food, their farms were destroyed, and a twenty-year-old girl was killed by sniper fire while she baked bread for the soldiers."

"Killed you say?"

"Yes, Jennie Wade. It's in the story. And there is a Union widow, quite young, who was forced to let her farm be used for a Confederate field hospital. Completely ruined the place. Another woman with three children and currently with child is running the local cemetery in her husband's place while he guards Washington. The cemetery was virtually destroyed, and she is left to pick up the pieces."

Boris grunted. "Keep reading." He pointed his cigar at the *Times*, sprinkling ash on the newsprint.

264

Harrison raked a hand through his hair and tugged at the cravat at his neck. Then he read:

> On the streets the burden of their talk is their losses—and speculations as to whether the Government can be compelled to pay for this or that. Almost entirely they are uncourteous—but this is plainly from lack of intelligence and refinement. Their charges, too, were exorbitant—hotels, $2.50 per day; milk, 10 and 15 cents per quart; bread, $1 and even 1.50 per loaf; twenty cents for a bandage for a wounded soldier! And these are only a few specimens of the sordid meanness and unpatriotic spirit manifested by these people from whose doors our noble army had driven a hated enemy. . . . This is Adams County—a neighbor to Copperhead York, which is still nearer to the stupid and stingy Berks.

Harrison tossed the paper back on the desk. "I've read enough."

"Well? What have you to say to these charges?"

"I never saw any such profiteering from the citizens. It could be that this writer, Lorenzo J. Ellis, found a few people demanding compensation, but this is not the norm. On the whole, everyone I came in contact with sacrificed everything they could for the emergency. I suspect many of them will never recover from it."

Boris lit a cigar, inhaled, sent tangy blue smoke curling into the air. "That's not a story."

"Perhaps not a story that will sell, but it's a story, all right."

"Well, in this business, Mr. Caldwell, we print stories that make money. I sent you to a battle. I want a battle story. Samuel Wilkeson's report is the talk of the nation."

"He had a son in battle."

"And lucky for the *Times*, he died there. Apparently had to amputate his own leg with a penknife first!" Boris picked up the *Times* with a flourish and began reading: " 'How can I write the history of a battle when my eyes are immovably fastened upon a central figure of transcendently absorbing interest—the dead body of my oldest born son, caused by a shell in a position where the battery he commanded should never have been sent, and abandoned to die in a building where surgeons dared not to stay?' " Boris peered over the top of the paper. "Beat that."

"Beat it!" Harrison was out of his chair now, pacing in the cramped, smoky office. "He lost his son! I can't 'beat' that. I'm not writing about the dead. I've had enough dead to last me a lifetime."

"Then what in the Sam Hill will you write about? What you gave me tonight won't sell papers."

"But it's a story that needs to be told. Not all the glory should go to the dead. So much is required of the living, and so much of that from civilians, women and children!"

Boris leaned back in his chair and threw his feet up on the desktop with a clunk, cigar smoke swirling around his head. "I'll make you a deal. You write me a Gettysburg battle story that sells papers, and I'll print your little story about the sacrificing civilians."

"And then I'm off battles all together. Until I'm ready again. I need a change of pace."

And scenery. Harrison crossed to the window and looked past the classical façade of Girard's National Bank across the street, until his gaze rested on the spire of Independence Hall, just two blocks beyond it. Birthplace of the Declaration of Independence and home of the famous Liberty Bell.

"Funny, isn't it?" Harrison mused aloud. "Both North and South point to our revolutionary founding fathers to justify their points of view. But it was Northern abolitionists who made the State House bell their icon, renaming it the Liberty Bell for its inscription." Growing up in Philadelphia, Harrison knew it well: PROCLAIM LIBERTY THROUGHOUT ALL THE LAND UNTO ALL THE INHABITANTS THEREOF. LEVITICUS XXV X.

Boris heaved a sigh. "States' rights. Slavery.

Either way, it's all about liberty. But enough about that." He waved a hand, swirling the smoke above his head. "What kind of story did you have in mind next? After your Gettysburg articles, that is."

The Liberty Bell Harrison pictured in his mind dissolved as he thought of Liberty Holloway. And Bella.

He was on to something. If he could just connect the pieces of the puzzle . . . "Fanny Kemble's journal."

"A book review?" Boris scoffed. "Too late, already done."

"No, to follow up what happened next. What happened to the slaves she mentions in the journal? Where are they now?"

Boris chewed on the end of his cigar for a moment. "Do you have a lead?"

"I believe I do. Right here in Pennsylvania."

"If you can deliver a story like that, Caldwell, you'll make us both rich."

Not to mention famous.

Holloway Farm,
Gettysburg, Pennsylvania
Tuesday, July 7, 1863

In his dream, Silas Ford was whole again, riding a horse bareback through the wooded hills of Tennessee, his father on his own horse beside him.

Sunshine spilled through towering hemlocks, splashing his skin with warmth, infusing him with joy. Then his father's horse veered off the trail. Silas chased after him, but found only darkness. A jackal latched on to his right leg and—

"Johnny. Can you hear me? Johnny."

Silas awoke with a start and sat up on the barn floor, half-expecting to see a wild animal on his leg.

But there was no leg at all. Only pain. He reached past the stump of his right thigh and waved his hand through the air where his leg should have been. Silas grimaced, felt his face pull tight over his teeth as pain bit the leg that wasn't there, tore at it, chewed on it, stabbed it with a red hot poker. He squeezed his eyes shut, felt the warmth of a hand on his back.

"Do you need morphia?"

He could barely breathe, let alone answer Liberty. He felt her presence, hovering over him, watching his mute agony, his shoulders hunched over his butchered leg. He wanted no audience.

"Breathe, Johnny."

He had not realized he held his breath. He concentrated on breathing in, breathing out. In. Out.

The invisible jackal clamped down on his absent calf again, and Silas gripped the end of his stump, sending fiery darts shooting up the short distance to his hip. It was like having a nail driven

269

into his palm and only being able to hold his wrist instead. *Useless!* Panic bloomed in his veins, swelled in his chest.

"Where is the pain? At the bottom of the stump, or is it higher? Please, tell me if you can, Johnny, we must know if there is some infection further up."

"Don't touch me." He gasped out the words, tasting their bitterness as they left his mouth.

"I'm trying to help."

He didn't look at her. He wished she would not look at him. The muscles in his jaw bunched as he clenched his teeth against the pain.

The pain is in the air near my stump. If he told her the truth, she would think he was crazy. He almost believed it himself.

The pain seeped away now, until he could stand to open his eyes.

Liberty was still there, striped with sunlight that fell through the barn planks. "I came to see if you'd like soft bread and beef tea, compliments of the Christian Commission. But you seem like you need the doctor." A warm breeze played with the curls that had escaped her snood, and carried with it the smell of fresh bread and chloride of lime. Someone was disinfecting the property.

"I'm not hungry."

"You must eat." She sat on her heels next to him on the straw-covered floor.

"I have no appetite." *For anything.* Silas turned his head away and stared at a row of abbreviated men, asleep.

"Please, Johnny."

Why wouldn't she leave?

"Tell me what you want me to do. I'll help you however I can. May I see your—bandages?"

"I don't want your help. You've done enough." He glanced at her face and saw that the words he'd flung at her had hit their mark, embedded themselves like shrapnel in her heart.

Her face hardened as she looked down at the rejected offering in her hands. But still, she would not leave.

Pain sharpened his tongue and he thrust again. "You told me that you've always felt so guilty for not seeing your husband after you heard he'd been injured."

She raised glittering blue eyes to his. Nodded.

"But who asked you to come?"

"The nurse wrote to me and—"

"Exactly. It was the nurse. Not your husband. He didn't want to see you. He didn't want *you* to see *him*. Did you ever consider that you were doing him a favor by staying away?"

"How do you know that? Why would you say such a thing?" Lines deepened in her forehead. Her chin trembled.

His heart galloped in his chest as he twisted his weapon in her heart. "Because I don't want to

see you. Do me a favor, Liberty, and stay away."
Truly, it was for the best.

His words grew blades, dug into her, slicing away the illusion that he would be grateful for her help, for life itself, and that they could get past this nightmare together. The joy that had surged when she realized he would survive the operation drained away now, with the idea that perhaps he had not wanted to. Or perhaps, it was just her that he no longer wanted.

Tears threatening to spill down her cheeks, Liberty studied his face. His jaw was set, but his eyes glistened, and the end of his nose was pink with emotion. He could not mean what he said, truly, could he?

"I found your letter, Johnny. It was in your clothes."

He looked up at her, and she read a dozen questions in his eyes. "Then you know," he said. "You know everything."

"I do." Her lips flattened as she watched him, waiting for more of a reaction.

None came. Until, "Then why are you still calling me Johnny?"

That was all he had to say? She cleared her throat. "I know it isn't your given name, but it's what you asked me to call you. It seems to fit somehow."

He laughed through his nose, a single short

puff of air. "I thought you'd be upset, considering where your loyalties lie."

Liberty had been loyal to Levi for long enough. "Do you remember what you said to me when we first met? There's so much more to life than death."

"Yes. Like convalescence." He looked at his stump, and she winced.

"Please don't be angry." Her voice hitched. She had not considered, in her rush to save his life, that he might not forgive her for the loss of his leg.

Johnny sighed, rubbed a hand over his face. "Forgive me for not hopping around on one leg, full of joy at my current situation."

"Miss Liberty." Bella stood in the barn door.

"Coming!" She turned back to Johnny. "I need to go. Should I bring back some morphia?"

"Don't come back." Bitterness sizzled between them. "Send it with someone else. I want another nurse."

Anger knotted her face. "*Who,* Johnny? Who? Whether you like it or not, I'm all you've got right now, besides Bella cooking and two doctors tending more than five hundred patients. If you want a nurse at all, you're going to have to get used to the fact that it's got to be me."

"I don't want you."

"I thought you did."

He looked away.

Liberty left without another word, Johnny's silent response still pulsing in her ears.

Gettysburg, Pennsylvania
Wednesday, July 8, 1863

The ride into Gettysburg was perfectly desolate, like a scene out of Dante's *Inferno*. Liberty was grateful for Bella's presence beside her on the buckboard wagon. They made the journey in silence, save for the whinny of Dr. O'Leary's horse.

Fields once green were trampled brown and turned to marsh by the recent rains. On either side of the miry road, dead horses bloated to twice their size. Bodies began to rise from their shallow graves, uncovered by wind and rain. Fences gone, cows, pigs, sheep, goats, and chickens alike freely roamed the countryside, routing in the mounds of freshly turned earth.

The debris of battle mingled among the dead: broken gun carriages, muskets, bayonets, swords, canteens, cartridge boxes, like a strange and terrible crop. Not a single vulture circled overhead, but blankets of green flies had descended like a plague.

The odor in the countryside was nothing compared to the stink of the town. Without freely sweeping wind to clear it, the air in Gettysburg pulsed with stench. Liberty and Bella covered their noses as they rode toward the Sanitary Commission headquarters at the Fahnestock Brothers Store in The Diamond. People walked about with bottles of pennyroyal or peppermint oil beneath their noses, and kept their windows closed despite the sweltering July heat. White picket fences were perforated with balls, wooden shutters were riddled with bullet holes, brick homes spotted with the blue of lead.

Women on hands and knees scrubbed the pavement in front of their doors while others threw chloride of lime in the streets. Liberty lost track of how many yellow flags were thrust out of windows of private homes and public buildings, signaling they had been turned into hospitals. The white cornettes of visiting Sisters of Charity flapped like angels wings about their heads as they carried supplies through the streets. Regimental bands played lively tunes outside buildings crammed with wounded to drown out the cries from within.

It didn't work.

Embalming parlors, never before seen in Gettysburg, sprouted suddenly along the main roads. One sign advertised full-service rates: $15 for embalming, $5 for a coffin, $24 for express shipment to home state. A preserved corpse stood upright in a coffin outside one parlor as proof of what the embalmer could accomplish. *Ghastly.*

The Sanitary Commission headquarters was an oasis of supplies for a town in grave need. Liberty recognized many of the citizens waiting in line, and imagined they were just as hungry and desperate as she was. After waiting their turn, Liberty and Bella told a Commission agent their names and location of their hospital. A round-faced young woman, blonde hair misbehaving in its disheveled bun, sat on a barrel next to the brick wall of the store, and watched. A worn carpetbag slouched at her feet, half-hidden by her green and tan gingham work dress.

"And how many Union patients have you?" A bald man with kind eyes and a white goatee asked Liberty.

She looked at Bella. She should have known the Sanitary Commission, an organization composed of Northern women, would exist to relieve the suffering of Northern men.

"How many, my dear?" he asked again.

"One." Her heart sank at the look of surprise on his face.

"And five hundred fourteen Southern wounded," Bella added.

His eyebrows raised. "Who is caring for these men?"

"We are," said Liberty. "Plus a Confederate surgeon and a volunteer from the Christian Commission, a doctor from Philadelphia who has been perfectly wonderful."

"Hey!" A man three spaces back in line came up to the front. "You're caring for Rebels? Liberty Holloway is caring for *Rebels?* How *could* you?"

"Let's leave the battles to the armies, not the

civilians. The wounded on my farm are not my personal enemy."

"Says who?" the man snarled. "Don't you know what they've done around here? Seven families in the country have lost their barns or houses, or both. A few civilian men have been marched off as prisoners. A Rebel bullet put Jennie Wade in the ground. They looted houses, broke furniture, smashed dishes, used the parlors as privies, stole food and horses. In one house on my street, they mixed a half barrel of flour with water to make a thin paste, threw feathers into it, and threw the whole mess over everything in the house. Don't tell me they don't fight against civilians. Don't give her anything! Liberty Holloway, you traitor! You copperhead! For shame!"

Liberty's eyes narrowed in self-defense while Bella gave the man a tongue lashing. She was hungry. She was tired. And for the love of all that was holy, she needed these supplies. Out of the corner of her eye, she saw a flash of yellow as the blonde woman slid off her barrel and approached their wagon, clutching her bag.

The Commission agent guided the man back to his place in line, assuring him there was enough for everyone.

"If you'll not give us anything, sir, we'll just go to the Christian Commission headquarters on the other side of the square. Their line is longer, but perhaps that's because they care deeply about relieving the suffering of the wounded, no matter from which section of the country they hail."

"That is all very well and good, but the Sanitary Commission was formed first, and are every bit as generous, if not more so, than our sister commission."

"Even for Confederates?"

He paused. "The women who donate their money and goods to the Sanitary Commission do so with the understanding that they will benefit the Union."

Liberty's face fell. The blonde woman with the carpetbag frowned, too.

"However, we believe that we are still the United States of America." The man's narrow chest puffed up. "Every man is part of the Union, in that sense, whether they like it or not. You shall have what you need." He ordered another volunteer to load into their wagon barrels and crates of items more precious than gold: bread, beef, condensed milk, sponges, combs, tooth powder, eye shades, fans, eggs, jellies, bandages, stockings, mosquito netting, drawers, shirts, and small bags of camphor to sweeten the air around one's person.

As he loaded a crate of slippers into the wagon, he instructed her to give them to one-legged patients, first. "They'll go twice as far that way."

She nodded, relief flooding her. "Yes, of course. Would it be possible for us to bring supplies to the Lutheran Seminary hospital as well?" She still harbored guilt for using their medical supplies on her own Rebel patients. "It's on the way back to our farm, and would be no trouble for us to stop."

The agent consulted a checklist. "They're on the list for distribution. If you'd like to take some items to them, we'd be most grateful. As long as you promise prompt delivery—no keeping these for yourself, now."

She smiled. "You can trust me."

He loaded more supplies in the wagon, wished them good day, and patted their horse before moving to the next in line.

"Excuse me, Miss." The woman who'd been watching the transaction shoved a strand of blonde hair off her flushed face. "My name is Myrtle Henderson, and I've come from Baltimore to help, which was no easy task mind you, with the railroad still being out. Slept nary a wink all night."

Libbie appraised her. She was tall, but her face and figure were childlike. But what did age matter, when one was willing to work in times like this? "Are you with the Sanitary Commission?"

"No."

"Christian Commission?"

"No."

Obviously she was not with the convent from Emmitsburg, Maryland.

"I'm just here with myself, and I want to help."

279

She crowded close to Liberty and whispered. "Only, I got a hankerin' to work with Confederate wounded—seeing as they seem likely to be most neglected. Wouldn't you say that's true?"

Liberty glanced at Bella, who nodded. "Do you have any nursing experience?" Liberty asked.

"Did you, before this battle?"

Liberty raised an eyebrow. "I must warn you, a field hospital can be quite shocking. The smells and sounds are even worse than what you'll see."

"I'm smellin' and hearin' plenty right here in town. Is it worse than this?"

"No. In fact, the open air is a great benefit to us at the farm."

"How are you set for water? Because they are sure running out of it here, folks say."

"We have a water source nearby, Willoughby Run."

"Is it contaminated? By the dead?"

Why had Liberty not considered this before?

"Because if it is, I can boil it. I imagine you're short on time with five hundred patients, but if you ain't got clean water, they ain't gonna get any better, that's sure."

"Fair enough. Would you be willing to make beef tea, too, and muck out straw matted with blood and filth? Would you comb lice out of hair, moisten bandages, disinfect the trench?"

"I can do most anything you put me to do. I just

want to help. Wouldn't you be glad for another set of hands?

Liberty would. "Climb aboard. We've one stop to make before going home."

Atop Seminary Ridge, the red-bricked theological school rose above the trees that flanked it, its gazebo-like cupola gleamed. A yellow flag flailed against the weathervane spiking the sky. Inside, where just weeks ago students prayed, slept, studied, and ate together, rows of patients now rested on rubber blankets on the floor. Swarming about them with food and bandages were Gettysburg women Liberty recognized and volunteer nurses she didn't, including several visiting nuns.

Voices ricocheted between the walls and in the stairwells on either end of the building, but by now, the sound of human suffering did not jar Liberty as it once had. Now, she had the means to relieve it piled high in the wagon just outside.

Before she could bring her supplies in, a boy brushed past Liberty carrying an amputated leg.

"Why, Hugh!" Liberty touched his shoulder. It was Hugh Ziegler, no older than eleven years, and son of the seminary steward and matron.

He turned to her and shrugged, his eyes clouded. "We all do our part, Miss Holloway. Mama cooks. My sisters nurse. I carry limbs out

281

back and pile them up like stove wood." He turned back to his chore and trudged away.

Just then fellow townswoman Sarah Broadhead shot out of one of the stairwells, panting for breath, furrows carved into her brow. "They are drowning down there! One hundred men! What is to be done?"

One of the women bringing food to the men set down her tray and hurried to her. "What did you say? Patients? Downstairs?"

Liberty and Bella looked at each other. It was four days after the battle's end. *How could they not know?*

"They are wounded in three or four places each, they cannot help themselves one mite. They are practically swimming." Nuns and nurses now huddled around Sarah and Margaret. Liberty rushed forward to join them, heard swishing skirts behind her as Bella and Myrtle followed.

"Where are the men to be taken?" Liberty ventured.

"The fourth story."

Sarah gasped. "I fear we cannot accomplish all of it today."

"It must be done without delay. All of it." Margaret's eyes were hard and rimmed with red. "Did you not hear what happened at one of the field hospitals outside of town?"

Dread shuddered through Liberty as she waited for the answer.

"Twenty men were laid on the ground after their amputations. When it rained on July fourth, they were left there. Drowned in two feet of water. All twenty of them."

The horrifying words slid into Liberty. Thank God, thank God she and Isaac had been able to save her own patients at Holloway Farm. But one hundred more lives were now at stake.

"Sarah, you and I will find the most able among the patients to carry the men," Margaret ordered. "The rest of you, please find all the stretchers you can and bring them here."

Bella frowned. "You're asking wounded men to carry wounded men?"

"Some are injured only slightly and are already working as hospital attendants. What else would you have me do, order the weaker sex to do it? Besides, we nurses have our own duties to attend to."

"I'm not as weak as these patients here." But Margaret had already scurried off to find more help.

Liberty sent Myrtle to begin unloading the wagon of its supplies and turned back to Bella, waiting for the words she knew were coming.

"These men are going to wear out fast with this work." Bella's jaw was set. "Delicate ladies and nuns may not be much good for this kind of labor, but my arms are strong for the task. I'm helping."

"Are you certain?" Liberty's muscles ached at the mere thought. A nun swept over to them and dropped off a stretcher.

"These are Union men. If I have been willing to help the Rebel wounded at your farm, Miss Liberty, it should not surprise you that I want to help the patients wearing the same color as my Abraham. You and Myrtle go back to the farm, I'll walk there when I'm done."

Bella picked up one end of the stretcher as a plaintive cry for help floated up the stairwell. Liberty furtively glanced around. Others may be coming to help, but there was no sign of them yet. The patients downstairs had already waited long enough.

"If you're helping, I'm helping." Libbie snatched up the other end of Bella's stretcher. "Let's make sure these men live to enjoy everything we just brought them from the Sanitary Commission." Out of the corner of her eye, she noticed a couple of men slowly coming toward the stairwell to assist. She could read in their gait and posture that though they may not have been seriously injured, they were famished and exhausted. Their help may add to Bella and Liberty's efforts, but not replace them. With every breath she took her spirit hissed. *Make haste. Make haste. Make haste.*

With pairs of men eventually following, Liberty and Bella descended to the basement and waded almost up to their knees into water contaminated with the waste of a hundred helpless men. Breathing fetid air above ground was bad enough —but swimming in liquid stink was far worse. The water soaked through her clothing. The stench was a thick paste in her mouth.

Soiled skirts and aprons floated in circles around each of them like water-logged halos. Each pair worked as quickly as they could. Bella held one end of the stretcher while Liberty guided a patient's body through the water and onto the canvas. Cringing at the sight of the foul water soaking his bandages, she stooped, gripped the wet wooden handles, and lifted until the patient was horizontal. He was of average height and weight, about five feet nine inches tall, she guessed, and perhaps one hundred fifty pounds. Divided the weight by two women, that was only seventy-five pounds to carry. *Only seventy-five pounds! To carry through water, then up four flights of stairs!*

Liberty scanned the dark basement and became overwhelmed at the number of wounded.

"When thou passest through the waters, I will be with thee; and through the rivers, they shall not overflow thee." In a hoarse voice, the patient on her stretcher quoted from the book of Isaiah. "Seems fitting, doesn't it? Just never thought I'd need to be saved from the waters of a theological school!" He closed his eyes as he gripped the edges of the narrow stretcher and whispered, "Thank you, thank you." Whether he was talking to his earthly saviors or his heavenly one, Liberty could not tell.

Slowly, carefully, Liberty and Bella waded through the water toward the stairs, the patient's weight digging into her palms, her heart beating out of her chest. *One patient at a time,* she told herself.

"How long have you been down here, soldier?" She glanced at the bearded face between her hands.

"Don't know what day it is. But we were injured in the first day's fight."

That was last Wednesday. It had been a week. *God have mercy. Mercy!*

Her throat closed up with tears as they neared the shaft of light. Bella went backwards up the stairs, while Liberty was given the luxury of walking face forward. As they emerged from the water, their sodden skirts tangled around their legs. Since they were not wearing hoops under their dresses for their nursing work, their hems hung lower than their heels even without water weighing them down. Now, Liberty felt like she was trying to climb the stairs with a wet bed sheet hanging from her waist, and no hand free to hitch it above her ankles.

With every painstaking step, Bella bent lower and Liberty hoisted her end of the stretcher higher, so the patient stayed as level as possible. Liberty kicked her skirt off her shoe before securing every foothold, then brought the other foot next to it on the same stair, like some sort of Irish jig.

Kick, step, together. Lift the stretcher higher.

Kick, step, together. Lift higher.

Kick, step, together. Lift higher.

The patient groaned as the stretcher rocked its way up the stairs. Her concentration breaking, Liberty took a step without flinging the skirt out of her way first. She teetered backward, then drove her shoulder into the rough brick wall to keep from falling backward. Bella lurched, Liberty jerked, and the patient cried out again. Poor fellow, she would be terrified too if she were him. She seethed at her dirty, soggy skirt.

"Wait," gasped Liberty when they reached the first floor, with more women trudging up behind them with their living cargo. "I cannot stand this a moment longer. May we set you down for just a moment before continuing on?"

They lowered him gently and Liberty pulled the back of her skirt up between her legs and tucked it into the belt at her waist, forming pantaloons.

"Miss Liberty!"

"I don't care what it looks like. I'm completely covered, anyway. There is simply no way I would be able to carry these men up four flights of stairs tripping over this skirt with every step. I'm quite

sure the patients prefer their safety to propriety."
She paused. "Try it!"

Chuckling, Bella came up with her own solution by simply gathering her hem and tying a knot at one side of the skirt, effectively freeing her ankles for movement. "Ready."

They bent at the knees, grasped the handles of the stretcher and hefted the patient up once more. Three more flights of stairs to go.

At the second floor landing, Liberty's arms ached from holding the man's weight above her head while climbing the stairs. They switched places, and Liberty went backwards for the next flight, stooping low while Bella held high.

At the third floor, her muscles quivered with effort.

By the time they reached the fourth floor, they fairly screamed for mercy. Compared to the damp cool of the basement, this top level of the building felt like an oven. Once they moved the patient to a blanket on the floor, Liberty pulled Bella aside. "I don't know how many more times I can do this!"

"Can you do once more?"

Liberty blinked. "Yes."

"Then just think about the one more time. One more patient, one more life saved from drowning in a seminary."

And they did. Again, and again, and again.

After just five patients, they had carried a total

of seven hundred fifty pounds of soldier up twenty *flights* of stairs.

There were many more to carry.

Both women were panting for breath on the first floor before going down for their sixth man. "How on earth did this happen?" Liberty asked a patient not far from where they stood.

The man pulled on some new woolen stockings, then told the story. "Last Wednesday, the wounded men were taken into the seminary for shelter during the heat of battle. On Thursday and Friday, the Rebels planted a battery just behind the seminary. Our boys, attempting to silence it, could not avoid throwing some shells into the building."

Some entered several of the rooms, and injured one of the end walls, and the basement became the only safe place for the patients. The Rebels took control of the town and building on July 1 and captured all medical supplies. Some Union doctors stayed with the wounded in captivity but had no instruments to perform amputations, no medicines to relieve pain, no food or refreshment of any kind.

"Then the rains came after the battle," Liberty prompted.

"Sure enough, and the basement flooded. But the door had been closed over the stairway this whole time, until one of your ladies there heard someone calling out today."

Liberty shuddered. "The poor men. How much they have endured."

"We've many more to fetch." Bella arched her back and rubbed her sore muscles. " 'The LORD is my strength and my shield; my heart trusted in him, and I am helped.' Do you remember that psalm, Miss Liberty?"

She nodded.

"Your turn. Give me a verse with strength."

Liberty smiled. From the time Liberty was a child, whenever Bella wanted to encourage her, she quoted the Bible to her. At some point in her adolescence, Liberty began quoting it back. "The Lord will give strength unto his people; the Lord will bless his people with peace."

Her soft brown skin shining, Bella slid her glance toward the stairs. "Let's take our strength and peace to His people. Ready?"

"I'm sure they are."

The work went slowly, but steadily. Though their muscles still burned, Bella and Liberty volleyed Scriptures up the stairs whenever they could spare the breath, and down the stairs as they passed other laboring women, Catholic and Protestant, all grateful for the reinforcements from God's Word. A few men even joined in with their own favorite verses on God's strength.

God is our refuge and strength, a very present help in trouble.

My flesh and my heart faileth: but God is the

strength of my heart, and my portion for ever.

But they that wait upon the Lord shall renew their strength; they shall mount up with wings as eagles; they shall run, and not be weary; and they shall walk, and not faint.

Fear thou not; for I am with thee: be not dismayed; for I am thy God: I will strengthen thee; yea, I will help thee.

And He did. Though it had taken hours to accomplish, the stretcher bearers had moved one hundred men out of a flooded basement and up to the fourth floor of the seminary. Fifteen thousand pounds of living, breathing cargo, four hundred flights up, and four hundred flights down, covering a total of thirteen thousand stairs. Liberty's muscles felt like rubber, her palms bubbled with blisters, and another dress was ruined.

But not one man had been lost.

Act Four

THE SMOKE CLEARS

"WHAT IN MY GIRLHOOD was a teeming and attractive landscape spread out by the Omnipotent Hand to teach us of His Goodness, has by His direction, become a field for profound thought, where, through coming ages, will be taught lessons of loyalty, patriotism, and sacrifice."
—MATILDA "TILLIE" PIERCE ALLEMAN,
Gettysburg schoolgirl, age 15

"WHILE I WOULD NOT care to live ever that summer again, yet I would not willingly erase that chapter from my life's experience; and I shall always be thankful that I was permitted to minister to the wants and soothe the last hours of some of the brave men who lay suffering and dying for the dear old flag."
—ELIZABETH SALOME "SALLIE" MYERS,
Gettysburg schoolteacher

Chapter Fourteen

Lutheran Theological Seminary,
Gettysburg, Pennsylvania
Wednesday, July 8, 1863

Liberty dredged up a smile as a bandage-wrapped soldier shuffled over to her in red plush–slippered feet, a handkerchief in his hand. She had gotten somewhat used to her own smell, but obviously, her stink was ripe to those who hadn't. Still he approached.

"Hello, beautiful." His tobacco-stained smile looked more like a sneer. Liberty bristled.

"Do I know you?"

"Of course you do. I'm Jonathan Welch. And you're Liberty Holloway."

He looked to be at least forty years old, pale and puffy, with eyes like raisins sunk into a hot cross bun. Shock tremored through Liberty. *No.* "No."

"No? What do you mean, no? Aren't you Liberty Holloway? Widow of a man who fought at First Manassas?"

Confusion fogged her mind. "Yes, but—how do you know that?" She glanced at Bella, whose brown eyes were narrowed on this soldier.

"I told you. I'm Jonathan Welch. We've been writing letters nigh unto two years now—except for when you stopped responding to me about eight months ago. Why was that, anyhow, Libbie? Or did they just get lost in the mail?" He sneered again and snorted. Was that a laugh?

"Her name is *Liberty*." Bella's voice was firm. "But you may call her Miss Holloway."

"Well excuse me, Chocolate! But after so many letters, I do believe I've earned the right of using her first name. Or maybe I'll just call you Gorgeous."

"You? You're Johnny?"

He rolled his eyes. "As in Johnny Reb? No, never. It's Jonathan, only. Or you can call me Handsome."

Johnny Reb. *Just call me Johnny.* Had she been such a fool? The room spun. She fought to maintain her composure.

"When is the last time you wrote me a letter?" She steeled herself for the answer.

"I wrote you one as soon as we got to Gettysburg. Best one I ever wrote, too. Pinned it to the inside of my jacket."

Bella hissed in Liberty's ear. "Miss Liberty, I don't trust this man. We'd best be on our way." She helped Libbie to her feet, and her muscles throbbed in protest.

"Where is that letter now?"

"It's the darnedest thing, Lib. I was wounded in a wheat field, hit my head on the way down," he pointed to his bandage, "and when I came to, my jacket was gone. Thank goodness the scoundrel didn't take my trousers, too."

"He's lying." Bella held Liberty's elbow as her knees threatened to buckle. "Don't listen to him. He's making this up. You know who the real Johnny is. This man is a fool, like Isaac."

Jonathan frowned. "The real Johnny? Have you got a Johnny of your own now?" His eyes popped. "Is he pretending to be me? Did he have my jacket?"

Liberty stared at the man in front of her. Was he an imposter? Or was the man at her home the fraud? The one whose life she'd helped save, the one she'd dressed in her late husband's clothes. The one who had drawn her out of her old grief, then turned her away in his own.

"You're right, Bella. It's time to go." To Jonathan, she added: "Stay away from me."

"Aw, that's not right at all! You've fallen for him, haven't you? He used me! He used my letter to get you! Wait! Listen, listen: 'Never forget how much I love you, and if my last breath escapes me on the battlefield, it will whisper your name.' Did the letter say that? I wrote that!"

"Don't follow me," she threw over her shoulder.

"Suit yourself. You're not the only widow I've set my sights on you know. There's thousands of you out there. You're not so special. Your hair springs every which way, did you know that? I like a woman who knows how to use a comb!

297

Did you hear me? You're nothing special!" His taunts chased after them as they left the building, nipping at her ears. She never cared to see this Jonathan Welch again.

But if this is Jonathan Welch, who is the man who has stolen my heart? Her face burned with mortification.

Outside the seminary, night shrouded the blighted land. But it was nothing compared to the darkness in her heart.

Philadelphia, Pennsylvania
Wednesday, July 8, 1863

The boom sounded so loudly Harrison Caldwell jumped awake and slammed his body to the floor, disoriented, heart racing as his eyes adjusted to the darkness. Slowly, shapes came into focus: newspapers, a bookcase crammed with too many books, a cup of stale coffee, a half-eaten square of gingerbread from his landlady, a book turned upside down on the arm of a chair. His fingers clutched the fibers of a rug, not grass, or mud, or stone.

He was not in battle, but home, in his boarding-house in Philadelphia—and drenched in sweat, though all he wore were his silkaline drawers and undershirt.

Of course. The blast he had heard was only Fort Brown, the cannon sitting at the foot of a flagstaff on Washington Avenue. It was a signal that throngs of hungry men—soldiers or prisoners—would be here before too long. At the sound, no matter the time of day or night, housewives all over the old Southwark neighborhood left their homes and families to prepare coffee, bread, beef, potatoes, and pie at either the Cooper Shop Volunteer Refreshment Saloon or the Union Volunteer Refreshment Saloon. Both were run entirely without help of the government, and between the two of them, seven barrels of coffee and fifteen thousand cooked rations were prepared in the average day.

Now, most likely, more prisoners from Gettysburg were rolling in en route to the prison at Fort Delaware. Or, they could be prisoners from the recent Union victory in Vicksburg, Mississippi, after the forty-seven day siege. The fact that the Rebels had surrendered on Independence Day, the same day that Lee began his withdrawal back across the Potomac, had made the story even grander.

But that was not the story he had fallen asleep thinking about.

Harrison yawned and rubbed his eyes. With a trainload of troops about to invade, there was no use in going to bed. But he could go back to work.

Light flared as he struck a match, removed the glass chimney from the oil lamp, lit the wick, then replaced the smoky chimney. Taking a bite of the dried-out gingerbread, he picked up Fanny Kemble's journal, flipping through it to find the last place he remembered reading. About halfway through, he stopped when he saw a list of names, a partial log of the slave women who had visited Fanny on a particular day. Along with the women's names, Kemble recorded their family details and complaints. He read carefully for clues.

Fanny has had six children, all dead but one. She came to beg to have her work in the field lightened.

Nanny has had three children, two of them are dead; she came to implore that the rule of sending mothers into the field three weeks after their confinement might be altered.

Leah, Caesar's wife, has had six children, three are dead.

Sophy, Lewis's wife, came to beg for some old linen; she is suffering fearfully, has had ten children, five of them are dead. The principal favour she asked was a piece of meat, which I gave her.

Sally, Scipio's wife, has had two mis-carriages and three children born, one of whom is dead. She came complaining of incessant pain and weakness in her back. This woman was a mulatto daughter of a slave called Sophy, by a white man of

300

the name of Walker, who visited the plantation.

Charlotte, Renty's wife, has had two miscarriages, and was with child again. She was almost crippled with rheumatism, and showed me a pair of swollen knees that made my heart ache. I have promised her a pair of flannel trowsers, which I must forthwith set about making. Nearly all the women beg for flannel, and my bolt of red and cream pinstripe is almost gone.

Harrison turned the page to find more names, more miscarriages, dead children, and ailments recorded. *Sarah, Stephen's wife. Sukey, Bush's wife. Molly, Quambo's wife.*

Daphne and Bella, twin sisters.

He stopped. Hunching over the book, he pinned the print with his finger, as if afraid it would flutter off the page. Slowly, he read, committing each line to memory. His bare toes curled into the rug in delight as all the pieces fell into place in his mind.

This was better than he had dared to hope. At last, he had the missing link. Bella Jamison was telling the truth when she said she wasn't at the Weeping Time. It was her twin sister, Daphne, that he had seen. But Bella had most certainly grown up on the Butler plantation, too. The main difference between the sisters, according to Fanny Kemble, was that one of them wanted to learn to read and write, even though it was illegal both for her to learn and for Fanny to teach her.

It didn't stop them.

And it didn't stop there. But the greater part of the story was not printed for public consumption.

Liberty Holloway's face surged in his mind. *The very likeness of Roswell King Jr.,* Lt. Pierce Butler Holmes had said. Liberty had no idea who she was.

But Harrison did. At least, he had a hunch, and if he was right, it wouldn't take long to find evidence. If he could just find Holmes again, and question him . . .

The story just got better.

Holloway Farm
Thursday, July 9, 1863

"Good morning, Silas."

Silas Ford jolted at the sound of his name. His real name.

Dr. Owen O'Leary sat on a squat, three-legged stool beside him and handed him the folded up letter he had written to Liberty before the battle in the wheat field.

"I thought Liberty had this."

"I'm quite sure no one has seen it. Except for me. I burned your trousers soon after your operation, but this must have fallen out on the way to the bonfire. Plucked it out of the mud this morning."

But Liberty said she'd read his letter. That she knew everything. *If this wasn't the letter, then what did she read?*

"Does she know?"

"Does she know, *what?*" Liberty entered the barn, her face dark with anger, and stood above Silas. "Chances are, I don't. I don't know a thing about you. I don't even know your real name. Do I?" A piece of paper was tucked in her folded arms.

"I will come back another time to change your dressing, Silas." Dr. O'Leary slipped out, taking his stool with him.

"Silas," she hissed. Somehow he had dreamed his name would sound sweeter on her lips. She made it sound like it was poison. Maybe he was. "What happened to Johnny? 'Just call me Johnny,' you said. Remember?"

Out of the corner of his eye, he saw Fitz raise a hand in the air. "I'm a Johnny!"

Liberty threw back her head and groaned. "How could I have been so stupid? I can't believe I didn't see it! I saw what I wanted to see, that was all. Stupid! Foolish girl!"

For the first time since she had entered, Silas opened his mouth. "What did you want to see?"

"An honest man, John—Silas. Oh . . . ! I can't believe your name is not Jonathan Welch!"

303

Fitz called out again. "Who's he?"

Silas glared at him, then looked back at Liberty. "Well?"

"Oh, no. I'm not going to say one more word until you tell me exactly who you are and why you're here. Start talking. Go. Right now, Johnny Reb."

"Stop!" Silas raised his hands. "Stop talking and I will. Just give me a minute." He sighed as she twisted her apron in nervous agitation. Her eyes looked larger in her face than before, her collarbones sharper against the thin fabric of her dress. "Would you do me an enormous favor and sit down for this? I'll sprain my neck if I have to talk up to you the whole time."

She thumped herself down on the floor at his feet, her skirt forming a perimeter around her. "Are you Union or Confederacy?"

"It's not that simple."

"Of course it is."

"That mean he a Johnny!" Fitz laughed with glee.

"Is it true?"

Silas rubbed the back of his neck. "I am for the Union."

"A spy?"

"Let me finish! Or I'll never get it out!"

"Do you—did you fight for the Union?"

He narrowed his eyes. "I don't fight at all. I am—I was—a scout. For the Rebels." He patted his stump. "But I'll never be that again, thanks to this."

"A Rebel scout?"

"He mean he tell the Johnnys where the Billys are at. If that's not fightin' too, I don't know what is."

"I've never killed anyone . . . in the war."

Liberty's eyes glittered. "Who did you kill before the war, Silas?" She jumped up again. "You're a *murderer?*"

"Wal!" Fitz slapped his knee. "Ain't you a nasty feller!"

"I'm the son of a slaveholder—"

"What?" Liberty rounded on Silas. "I thought . . ."

"Whatever you thought was wrong, and whatever you think now is guaranteed to be wrong too because you're not letting me talk! This is impossible. I wrote it all out in the right order. I thought you read this!" He held up his letter.

"No Silas, I read *this!*" She speared a letter of her own into the air. "What was I supposed to think? It was pinned to the inside of a Union jacket you were wearing. Should I have assumed you had stolen it, knowing I would find the letter—proof that we'd known each other longer than *just two weeks?*"

Ironically, they had. But she still hadn't put the pieces together.

"I thought you were someone else." Liberty looked away.

Right now, he wished he were. "All right. But I didn't steal the jacket with you in mind. The only thing in my mind at that moment was getting out of that wheat field alive. I had used my shirt as a tourniquet for another soldier, and I took the jacket off of someone else so Union guns wouldn't aim for me."

"Why wouldn' ya just shoot 'em first?"

"I told you, I don't fight. I don't have a weapon. Yes, I used deception to stay alive. But I never lied to you, Liberty."

" 'Just call me Johnny'? Truth in a riddle is not the truth!"

Muffled footsteps on the hay breezed down the row. "Fitz, come with me, let's get you some air." It was Dr. O'Leary.

"No thanks, Doc, this is gettin' real good in here."

"Fitz." The doctor's voice hardened. "Now. Or I'll put you on burial detail."

"I ain't got but the one arm!"

"Then it would take you twice as long."

Fitz muttered out of the barn, followed by Dr. O'Leary.

"I was going to tell you." Silas lowered his voice, as if that would lower his heart rate. "I wanted you to know the truth."

She put her hand to her head. His own was spinning, aching. Finally, she spoke again. "Then tell me."

His letter was gritty in his hand from the granite-flecked soil. He held it out. "My story. From the beginning."

She dropped her arms to her sides. Stepped forward, breaching an invisible chasm between them, and took the letter. "The truth?"

He nodded. *Most of it. Enough of it.*

Liberty lowered herself to the floor and pressed a hand to her heart before opening the grimy paper.

Dear Liberty,

I grew up on a tobacco plantation in central Tennessee, and yes, my father owned slaves. One summer when I was twelve, I became so ill with malaria that my parents sent me to live with my aunt and uncle in the North for the cooler temperatures. The doctor said my constitution was entirely broken down, and for years, every summer I spent with them in Boston. There I dropped my Southern accent and attended abolitionist meetings with my uncle. I heard Frederick Douglass speak, as well as former slaves and free blacks, and it filled me with hatred for both slavery and my father, and for myself, for this was my heritage. Finally, painfully, I realized why there were so many mulatto children running around our plantation. They were my father's children, my half-siblings, born out of his violence and lust for our female Negroes. And Mother did not say a word in protest, at least not in front of me.

I felt God's call on my life to be different, so I decided to become a pastor and preach truth. Maybe that was partly to atone for the sins of my father, I don't know. I do know I wanted to be God's instrument. So I enrolled at Lutheran Theological Seminary. Yes, in Gettysburg.

Liberty looked up at Silas. "Here? You studied here?" She squinted at his face. Silas. Silas. The name was vaguely familiar. Hadn't Levi told her about a former student named Silas?

"Please, just keep reading. Don't stop yet."

She obliged.

One day I heard a woman needed some help around her farm, making repairs, working with wood, that sort of thing. I took the job to earn some extra money. My plan was to buy the freedom of my father's slaves. That woman was your aunt. When I was 22, and you were 14, we met for the first time.

Her breath hitched as she looked up at him. "That was you," she whispered. Aunt Helen had called him simply The Hand, as she had called Liberty The Child, and Bella The Help. My, how he had changed! Strands of silver threaded the dark blond hair above his ears, and faint lines framed his smile and eyes. His face and body were chiseled by army life.

She kept reading.

My first year at the seminary was also my last. When I went home for a break in the summer of '58, we awoke one morning to find that my father's strongest slave, Brutus, escaped in the night. My father interrogated the rest of the slaves for details, and when none came forward, he ordered his overseer to lash a young slave woman, about my age.

I couldn't stand it. My instinct to protect the helpless would not allow me to stay silent. I shouted at him to stop, and in reply, my father told me someone had to pay. That it could be me. He ripped the whip from the overseer's hand, tied me up by my wrists, and flogged me, his own son, in full view of our two dozen slaves. I can still feel the metal beads on the end of those leather braids, raking through my flesh.

It was a week before I could get out of bed, and in that week, I fanned the flame of my loathing for him until it raged as an inferno. God tells us to love our neighbors, but I hated my father, and even my seminary training could not quench that scorching heat. The next time I saw him, he said I had given him no choice but to lash me to a pulp, because I had defied his authority in front of the slaves. He was making a lesson of me, he said. In a torrent of words, I unleashed all my bitterness and anger and frustration upon him. I told him he disgusted me with his abuse of the slave women, in particular, and how that must have hurt my mother. I called him a monster, a tyrant, and worse. He called me a coward, a fool, a disgrace. Rage burned in my veins, curled my hands into trembling fists. "You have tarnished my honor with your words," he said, voice as calm as a lake at sunrise. "Fight like a gentleman." He challenged me to a duel.

Fool that I was, I accepted. Refusing may have been pointless, but I did not resist at all. I jumped at the opportunity to point a loaded gun at my father, and my conscience still torments me for this fact. We were given our walnut-handled pistols, we each took our twenty paces. The next thing I knew, I had fired, but my father had lowered his gun. Did he drop his weapon before I pulled the trigger? Or only after my bullet hit him square in the chest? I will never know. But I see his face, twisted in agony, almost every night in my dreams. "You shot me! You killed your own father!"

How could I live with myself after that?

Somehow I buried my father, with my weeping mother beside me. I also buried my dream of becoming a pastor. How could I be a man of God after what I had done?

My mother banished me from her home, and in truth, I would not have wanted to stay. I bought some land in the eastern part of Tennessee, where slavery was much less prevalent because the land was not suitable for farming. I became a carpenter. For three years, I sent letters to my mother, and never received a reply.

Then war broke out. Tennessee was the last state to join the Confederacy. But the eastern part of the state wanted to secede from the rest of the state and join the Union. That didn't happen of course, but many Tennessee men did sign up for the Union. Suspicions flared over loyalties. I wanted no part of the Confederacy, so decided to start over somewhere else, in the North. But first, I had to say goodbye to my mother.

She turned me away on the doorstep. Heartbroken, and blaming myself for the disintegration of my family, I went to the local saloon and drank more moonshine than I could even look at, until I was right where I wanted to be. Passed out, in sweet oblivion to the miserable reality I created. But when I woke up in a puddle of drool, someone shoved a paper under my nose, pointed to my name and claimed I had enlisted in the Confederate army. It wasn't my signature, Liberty. I couldn't even hold a pen in that state. But they knew me, and they drafted me to fill their ranks. Next thing I knew, they threw some lice-infested uniform and a revolver at me.

I wouldn't touch it. They picked it up by the barrel and struck me with the handle. Still I refused. I would never, I will never, handle a weapon again. This angered the men who signed me up not a little. They reminded me that if I tried to escape my duty, I'd be a deserter, and would be summarily shot.

What was I to do? They could force me to walk with them, but they could not force me to fight. They considered me a waste of space until an officer arranged for me to be a scout for them. Instead of fighting, I could look ahead of them, gather information and report it.

That's what I was doing on June 26. Would to God I had a better story to bring you, but you deserve to know it. I want nothing more in this world than to get beyond this battle, let alone the entire war. I rue my part in it.

I pray God keeps you safe, and gives you peace and happiness. You deserve more than the trials that have come to you.

It was signed, Silas Ford.

Liberty frowned. *Silas Ford. Silas Ford.* She looked at him, eyes wide. "Silas Ford, man of the Lord . . . ?" She could not bring herself to say the rest, but it screamed in her mind. *Took slaves to bed and shot Pa dead!*

Silas shrugged. "You never can tell." His smile fell flat.

"But . . . the rest of the rhyme. Is it all true?" *Did you take slaves to your bed?*

"I have told you the truth, Liberty. I despised my father for what he did to the slaves. Killed him over it! How could you ask whether I abuse the slaves as well? That's not who I am. I want to protect the innocent, not exploit them."

His words rang true. Hadn't he protected Liberty from her intruders? When she was a child, hadn't he found other homes for her kittens

313

instead of following Aunt Helen's instructions to drown them? Hadn't he lost his leg while trying to find help for wounded soldiers? He was more like a shepherd than a wolf.

Before she realized what she was doing, Liberty laid her hand on his good leg. Instantly, inexplicably, his eyes hardened. He flung her hand away.

"I will not have your pity."

She jerked back, as though struck. "If you keep staring at what you've lost, you'll never get over it." She tried to sound clinical, but her hand still tingled from the warmth of his body under her hand. He thought she felt *pity* for him? She would have called it something else. Whatever it was, anger now eclipsed it.

"Pity! Look, Silas." She held up her hands, blistered palms facing him, fingers splayed, before plunging them back on her apron. "Do you know how I spent yesterday? Carrying wounded men up from a basement flooded with rainwater and excrement up sixty-five stairs to the fourth floor. One man nearly drowned before we got to him. He had an arm. One arm. He was a torso, with an arm, and in fairly good spirits! If he didn't need my pity, I won't be giving it to you either!"

Rows of prostrate forms grumbled from beneath their rubber blankets, and she remembered they were not alone. She cut her voice low. "Dr. Stephens killed his own son with an overdose of chloroform in an effort to keep the pain away

314

during the amputation he was about to perform. On his own son. Now the doctor is taking opium that should be used on patients because it numbs his pain. I pity *him*. Twenty men survived the battle, survived amputation, only to drown in two feet of water in a different field hospital! I pity them and the souls who thought they had done them some good by carefully laying them on the ground!"

Though quiet, her voice was sharp, lancing the boil of emotion she had previously kept contained. "We have all lost something, Silas. You know what I have lost. There are barrels of supplies from the Sanitary and Christian Commissions out there, given by people who have suffered, too. Some have lost both husband and sons. Truly, I doubt not that every home in this country has been touched by loss of some kind."

Liberty barely took a breath as the words spilled out of her. "For a little while, I pitied myself. But then I realized, it's only a destroyed farm, it's only my life, I will make a new one later. Other people have it worse than me, and in truth, some even have it worse than you. So you lost a leg." She leaned in. "Look around, Silas. How many men do you see here with all four limbs? How many are in the ground, or rotting on top of it, who would trade places with you if they could?"

Liberty covered her mouth, shocked as she realized that such horror had become ordinary.

This is not normal! her former self whispered in her mind. *It is normal now.* Undeniable truth. Her face was wet with tears.

Silas did not know what to expect from Liberty when she finished reading his letter. But he did not expect this. She stood, practically shaking with emotion in front of him. Black curls, teased free by the wind flowing through the decomposing barn, bobbed beside her flushed face. Sapphire eyes sparkling, her jaw was set, her fists clenched. He could barely believe this strong woman had grown from the orphan girl he had once pitied himself.

"I've said too much," she said quietly, crumpling in her hands the letter she had come with. "I did not intend to make an enemy of you just now."

"Then were we not enemies already, you from North, me from the South?"

Wiping her cheeks, she shook her head. "The lines are not so clearly drawn as they once were. At least, not for me." Fresh tears spilled down her cheeks as she surveyed the patients in the barn. "I hate this war." She lowered herself to sit on her heels in the straw beside him, the fight in her eyes now dwindling.

A long moment passed before either of them spoke again.

"Cease fire?" Silas offered her his hand, and she took it, the blisters on her palm chafing his heart.

A lump shifted in his throat as she smiled through her tears.

"Would you believe I once told myself you were my big brother?" She clasped her hands back in her lap. "Some people have imaginary friends—I tried to have an imaginary family."

Silas drew a deep breath. This was good, safe territory. A big brother. A little sister. Completely innocent. *Make sure it stays that way.* "Another case of mistaken identity. It seems to be a trend." He chuckled. "Come now. I've told you who I really am. It's only fair you tell me who you thought I was." He nodded at the letter in her lap.

"No one special."

He cocked an eyebrow at her, and her face colored.

"That's not what I meant." Liberty pressed her lips into a line before telling the very short tale of Jonathan Welch.

"May I see the letter? The one you thought I wrote?"

She hesitated, but then shrugged and gave it to him. "He means nothing to me, understand. I never kept one of his letters."

Until this one, Silas thought, and scanned the lines. It was a typical war-inspired love letter, full of flowery sentiments, and far too bold for his taste. Silas's face warmed in embarrassment. "You thought I wrote this?" He glanced at her.

"You're the one who said your name was

Johnny." She twisted her apron strings around her fingers.

Silas read on. Good heavens, it was a proposal! And a sappy one at that. Whoever this man was clearly didn't know what real love was. "How could he write this? It's ridiculous. I would never say this to you." He looked up at her, amused by the drivel on the page.

Liberty snatched the letter from him. "I realize you're not the one who proposed, but you don't have to be unkind about it. I wasn't pining for a suitor then, and I'm certainly not now."

"I meant no disrespect to you. He is the fool—"

"For wanting to marry me? Quite."

"That is not at all what I meant."

But she pushed herself up and turned toward the doorway.

It was not how he wanted her to leave. Silas threw the sheet off his legs and struggled to stand, swinging his left leg under him and kneeling on it. "Don't go yet!"

"What are you doing? Sit down! You're not ready for this kind of strain!" Her eyes flashed with alarm. He gripped her arms and pulled himself up, aware that she would not let go of him as long as he remained standing.

"You know that's not fair, walking out when we're talking, when I can't follow you." His head spun, but whether it was from the fire raging in his injured leg, from standing, or from Liberty's nearness, he didn't know. Or care. He would stand as long as he could to keep her close.

"Fair?" She squeezed his upper arms tighter. "What an irrelevant word in a time of war."

"I have no quarrel with you." He pulled her in closer. "I meant only that that Welch fellow was going about his proposal all wrong."

"Is that so?"

"Yes. He wrote of needing you to make him happy. That he could not live without you. Tell me you were not flattered by such selfishness."

She blinked, and he could tell she did not understand. "But how is that selfish?"

How could Liberty, who had once been married, know so little of true love? "You really do need a big brother, don't you?" A smile played on his lips. "Welch wants you to make him happy. But he says nothing of making *you* happy. If a husband loves his wife the way Christ loves the church—as he should do—he will seek to serve her with his life. Die for her, if necessary. And he would do it without complaint. A husband places the utmost importance on his wife's welfare and fulfillment, rather than on his own happiness."

Her eyes filled with tears. "I have seen men willing to live and die for country, even for a symbol of the country, but for a woman? Show me a man who thinks this way."

Silas held her in his gaze, until she looked away. "Welch certainly didn't," he said gently.

319

"That's why I said I would never write such things to you. If I was proposing to a woman, I would have told her that I loved her not for how happy she could make me, but for who she is. That I would be privileged to spend my life caring for her, placing her interests and happiness above my own. If she would give me her hand in marriage, I would devote myself to proving worthy of the honor."

Silas teetered on his left leg while the pain from his right launched fiery darts through his body.

"You'll hurt yourself, Silas." Awkwardly, he let her help him back down to the floor, but he didn't let go of her. "It's too much pressure on the seam. You may have already pulled the flesh apart from putting your entire weight on it."

Silas sighed. "But do you understand me now? Welch didn't deserve you."

Slowly, Liberty released a long breath and nodded. "Thank you." She feathered his back with her fingertips, grazing ridges of scar tissue through his cotton tunic. Her eyes locked with his as her hand froze. Then with a single finger, she tenderly traced the path of the whip down his back, sending shivers down his spine. His muscles flexed beneath her touch. She traced another path, and another, and another, until she had stroked every ribbon of raised flesh on the broad expanse of his back.

"I hate what happened to you," she whispered, and tears slid down her face.

Silas swept his thumb over her cheek. "Please don't cry." *She's like a sister,* he told himself. *A sister.* Liberty leaned her head on his shoulder, and he did not have the strength to push her away. His senses stood at attention as her silky hair pressed against his neck, caught in the scruff on his jaw. The warmth of her petite body melted him like butter on fresh bread.

"I hate what happened to you, too." Voice gravelly, his lips brushed her hair as he spoke. "I'm sorry I'm not who you wanted me to be."

"You're not who I thought you were. There is a difference."

"Would you promise me something, then? Leave me a little dignity and let someone else be my nurse? When we're together, I don't want you inspecting my wound and getting your hands dirty with it."

Her lips pursed, but she nodded. "Fine, I'll send Myrtle if a doctor is not available, but you know I really wouldn't mind tending you myself. My hands have been dirty before."

"Please."

Then the jackal bit his absent leg again, and the cords of his neck pulled taut against the pain. His arm tightened on Liberty as he squeezed his eyes shut. A groan ripped up through his chest until bursting free from his throat.

Liberty slipped out of his arms. "I'll get the doctor."

He nodded, suddenly mute in agony, and her skirt rustled as she hurried away.

Chapter Fifteen

Holloway Farm
Friday, July 10, 1863

With more vigor than the task required, Bella stirred a kettle of milk porridge in the stuffy summer kitchen of Holloway Farm. Swirling steam thickened the air between her and Liberty, who stood, arms crossed, waiting for Bella to respond to the news she had just laid before her. But what could Bella possibly say?

This was not supposed to happen.

Liberty hadn't said as much, but it was plain as day that she was falling in love with a Rebel who'd grown up on a slave-holding plantation. A man whose father, Liberty told her, used black women the same way Pierce Butler's overseer had used Bella's mother. And Liberty's.

Silas Ford, man of the Lord, took slaves to bed and shot Pa dead! Bella had heard the rhyme, too, and shuddered now to think this was the same man with whom Liberty was smitten.

"Is it true?" Bella spoke at length. "Did he help

himself to the slaves too, to satisfy his lust, free of consequences?" Liberty glared at her, though it was a logical question. He was his father's son, after all.

"Of course not." Liberty spat the words. "How dare you? Remember your place, Bella."

"I remember my *place* just fine." Bella's voice was low as she spoke into the steam rising out of the kettle. "I remember teaching you to sew, to quilt, to bake, cook, preserve."

"Yes, as hired help!"

"Hired help. That's right, Miss Liberty. Only, I don't recall what our payment terms have been for the last week, which I have spent helping you, and only you, ever since the battle began. I have jeopardized my relationships with the other women I work for by doing this."

Liberty's eyes grew wide, and Bella could tell she never considered what Bella had risked by staying by her side. "I didn't ask you to stay."

"True enough, Miss Liberty, true enough. Then why did I stay, if you weren't paying me? Why did I help you on Wednesday carry those men out of that flooded basement? Why do I help you run your household when mine sits empty and neglected?" She backed away from the heat of the stove and pinned Liberty with a gaze. It was on the tip of her tongue to say, *You better answer me when I'm talking to you, child.* But Bella bit it back.

"I know you care about my well-being—"

"That's right. I care about you. But I've noticed that you are happy enough to accept my encouragement and help, whether it's paid for or not, but whenever you disagree with me, you put me right back down in my place."

Liberty studied her fingernails rather than meet Bella's gaze again, and Bella turned back to the kettle. Used to be, that was good enough for Bella Jamison. When her last owner had died, the one who had purchased Bella "and her increase" from Pierce Butler, he had willed Liberty to his sister and left Bella a sum of money with which to start her own life, finally, as a free woman. Thank God Fanny Kemble had taught her how to read and write and even arranged for her sale off the plantation after she told her what Roswell King Jr. had done. In Gettysburg, Bella had stayed close enough to watch her daughter grow into womanhood, but far enough removed that Liberty could enjoy the freedom of living as white in a white man's world. Now that Helen Holloway was in the grave, Liberty could do as she pleased with her own life, even though she had been born a slave. She would not have to scrap together an existence, like Bella did. She would not have to keep her head down and take orders from women whose skin shone brighter in the sun. Liberty would never have to wonder if she'd be sold into slavery. She could just . . . live. Without fear. Without apology.

That was fine with Bella, had always been fine. Until now.

"You're playing with fire, Miss Liberty." More like she had jumped into it, heart first.

"I told you, he said he wants to be my friend, nothing more."

"That's how it starts. Would you be willing to hand over your heart to a stranger like him if he asked for it right now?"

Liberty hesitated, and Bella rolled her eyes. "No, of course not. I barely know him."

"And he knows that. You're a Union widow, Liberty. If he approached you any stronger, he knows you'd put a stop to it at once."

"No, that's not true. He doesn't even want me to be his nurse."

"Are you really so blind? Of course he doesn't want you to be his nurse. He wants you to see him as a man, not as your patient."

Color bloomed in Liberty's cheeks and Bella bit back the question burning in her mind: If given the opportunity, would Silas take advantage of a black woman now? A mulatto? A quadroon?

Bella had not detected any malice from him toward her, as a colored woman. But Bella didn't make waves. She did not concern him. If he discovered that Liberty was one-quarter Negro, that would mightily concern him, she felt sure.

"Why are you so willing to condemn him? Just because his father was an abusive slave master?

Silas's back is rippled with scars from taking a lashing in the place of a slave woman!"

As if that was a guarantee of lifelong integrity. But loss and pain and grief and fear changed people. He had lost a leg for the Southern cause, had taken an interest in a woman he thinks is white. *If he finds out she is a quadroon, what will he do?* Just because he does not support slavery does not mean he would be happy knowing Liberty is not pure white.

If Bella wanted to keep Liberty safe from her own identity, she could not share her concerns with her. Secrecy was the only solution. Sweat beaded on her face as she watched the spoon in her brown hand circle the pot. She was going in circles, stewing and sweating for Liberty. But this was what mothers did. *And whether or not she'll ever know it, Liberty will always be my daughter.*

All she could say was, "Be careful. You don't know him yet. I don't trust him. He's Southern." But the label did not carry the weight for Liberty that it did for Bella.

"You are judging him for who his father was. I can only hope he does not do the same for me."

Bella jerked. "What do you know of your father?"

"I know he made a mistake by sleeping with a whore who tried to use me as a bargaining chip with him to secure her own lasting comfort. My father made a mistake in the heat of passion, but my mother was far worse. She was cold, calculated. She would do anything to better her own situation, including having a baby she never intended to love. She never intended to love me."

Shock rippled through Bella. "Who told you these things?"

"My aunt Helen."

"And that's what you believe? That your mother never loved you?"

"Is there a reason to believe otherwise?"

Trapped, Bella's chest heaved with breath. Finally, "Every mother loves her child. Even if they aren't the best at showing it." She looked directly into her daughter's eyes. "Your mother loves you."

"My mother is dead." Liberty's eyes hardened into blue ice.

Bella grabbed her shoulder, the flesh of her flesh. "Hear me, child. Your mother loved you."

She twisted out of Bella's grip. "I am not a child! I am not *your* child, I am no one's child. I am an orphan. And how would you know how every mother feels? You have no children."

Bella stood back as a wall shot up between them, a barricade of deceit and hurt and shame and fear.

"You're right, Miss Liberty. I have no children." After Liberty was born, she had made sure of that.

"And as I cannot pay you for your services of the last week—indeed, I know not how I'll pay for your services forthwith—you are free to go.

I truly hope your staying this long has not cost you your other jobs."

Bella faced her daughter. Liberty's head was held high, jaw set. She had risen up and taken charge of the situation, just as Bella had taught her. She had grown into the self-assured woman Bella had hoped and prayed for. She was giving orders, not taking them.

And now Bella was free to go.

Holloway Farm
Monday, July 13, 1863

Outside the summer kitchen, Myrtle Henderson plunged a broomstick into a kettle of water with lye, agitating the soiled clothing.

She marveled at her good fortune.

Since she had arrived at the Holloway Farm Confederate field hospital last week, she had not had a moment's rest. Though she had expected to stay in the background, need drew her out. Everywhere she went, men called her by name. They needed water, food, bandages, clean clothes, medicine.

They needed her. Hundreds of men wanted Myrtle Henderson. Her lips curved into a shy smile as she stirred the kettle of laundry. *Wouldn't everyone back home be shocked?* But she did not care to dwell on home. Her father's purple handprint on her arm had faded to yellow-grey, but the bruise was still there beneath her shirt-sleeve, a reminder that certainly, she was not missed.

In her twenty-seven years, no one, save the little ragdoll she kept in her pocket, had ever wanted to be around her before. Her face was too wide, her smile too large, her cheeks too ruddy, her figure too shapeless, her hands too rough. She was taller than her peers, and had never understood how to break into those elusive circles of female friendship. Myrtle had always been an outcast, and painfully shy. If anyone called her anything, it was Myrtle the Turtle, for the awkward habit she had of pulling her head down into her neck when she was nervous, a subconscious effort to appear shorter, she supposed, or to disappear altogether. People could be so mean. But not her dolly. Dolly always listened, always smiled at her.

Leaning on her broomstick for a moment, she looked out over the yard, the house, the barn. No one here compared her to a turtle. In fact, many men had called her an angel, especially when they learned she was a Southern-sympathizer. The slightest compliment or words of thanks sent shivers of pleasure through her as she brought dippers of water to their lips, or pulled combs through their hair, looking for vermin. She had never talked to so many men before in her life. Not counting the few times she had defended herself from her father's blows, she had certainly never touched one.

"There you are, Myrtle." Liberty Holloway rounded the corner of the summer kitchen, looking breezy in a coral plaid dress with belted waist and a ruffled hem.

"You headed to church, Miss Libbie?"

Liberty laughed. "I told you, you may call me Liberty or Libbie. No 'Miss' required. And don't poke fun—all my work dresses have been absolutely ruined—soiled beyond redemption, or cut into bandages. Isn't it ironic my Sunday dress is all I have left, and not one church is yet open for services? They're all still crammed full of wounded."

If Myrtle could look that nice in a dress like that, she'd never take it off, Sunday or no. She did not need to look at her own frock to know she looked like a simple peasant next to Liberty. "You wanted to see me?"

"Yes. Silas Ford needs the doctor's attention. Dr. Stephens is available, but he may need an assistant as he changes the plaster strips on his stump. Would you be willing?"

Heat crept up Myrtle's neck, until she could feel the warmth blooming in her cheeks. "Yes, of course." She left the broom where it was and headed to the barn.

Why Silas Ford had been asking for her, Myrtle Henderson, was a mystery to her. No, it was a small miracle. He was easily the most handsome fellow of the entire hospital, and brave, suffering in silence what would have driven other men to screams. And he was asking for her, again.

By the time she reached the barn, Dr. Stephens was already there next to Silas. Straw whispered beneath her feet as she joined them, her heart beating outside her chest at the sight of Silas's body, every muscle taut with pain born from his stump.

"Silas, I have run out of morphia to inject under your skin," the doctor was saying. "But this opium will help. You must take it by mouth. It will numb the pain, relax your muscles. All right?" Silas swallowed the dose, and Myrtle watched his face. The lines in his forehead did not go away.

"How's that for you?" Dr. Stephens asked.

"My stump still burns."

Promptly, Dr. Stephens dipped a sponge in a basin of water, then wrung it out over his bandages. Instant relief shone on Silas's face.

Dr. Stephens cut away the old linen spiraling down the thigh and around the stump and dropped them in a metal bowl on the floor. "Now I need you to drip water from the sponge over these plaster adhesive strips until this entire bowl of water is gone. Do it slowly, carefully, so as not to waste the water. We must soak the strips before we attempt to remove them. I'll be back shortly."

Dr. Stephens left to make his rounds in the barn, while Myrtle followed his instructions.

"I appreciate you doing this, Miss Henderson." Silas smiled.

"Please, call me Myrtle." She slowly squeezed water from the sponge to dribble over the two strips crossing the seam where Dr. O'Leary had brought his flesh back together in a wobbly seam. Crusty threads hung from each end. Her stomach quailed.

"I'm sorry, I know this must be difficult for you."

"Perfectly fine, just fine," she lied. But she would do it for him. She would do anything for Silas Ford, because he needed her. Again, she soaked the sponge in water.

He sighed. "The water feels good."

"You said it burned, and what better way to put out a water than with fire?" She grimaced, horrified at her blunder. "I meant, fire with a water. No! I mean: I'm glad it helps." Myrtle's neck scrunched as she tried to disappear, humiliated.

"Myrtle, I knew exactly what you meant." He smiled, and the world righted itself again. "Believe me, sometimes my mind is so fogged it's all I can do to string two words together. I don't know if it's from the pain or from what they give me for the pain. So don't worry. I understand you fine."

Myrtle lost herself in his kind, green eyes. "I understand you too, Silas. You're from Tennessee? Divided by loyalties, like mine. It's tough, never knowing who's in charge at the time, or who to trust."

"Mmm hmmmm." Silas closed his eyes, and Myrtle's sponge hovered, dry, over his stump. The opium had released pain's grip, and he was finally able to rest. Good. He was so much easier to talk to after he'd had his medicine. His speech slowed, and sometimes slurred, but that was all right with Myrtle. She was far less nervous about trying to impress him then. When he was relaxed, she relaxed. She didn't even mind if he fell asleep while she was with him. Then she could say whatever she wanted, could stare at his face without embarrassment.

"Well, you can trust me, Silas Ford. You can trust Myrtle Henderson. I'll take good care of you. I promise."

She glanced around. Dr. Stephens was at the far end of the barn, he would not be here soon. Emboldened, she reached up and brushed Silas's oak blond hair off his brow.

"You're so easy to talk to, Silas." She knew he did not hear her. "You're almost as easy to talk to as Dolly. And a lot more fun to look at it."

She sat back on her heels and squeezed the dry sponge in her lap for a moment before she resumed soaking his plaster strips. Her stomach was now steeled to both the sight and smell of his undressed stump.

Her heart, on the other hand, felt like jelly. *So this is what it feels like to fall in love.*

Chapter Sixteen

Gettysburg, Pennsylvania
Tuesday, July 14, 1863

Amelia Sanger craned her neck as she gazed at the Italianate cupola atop the two-story blue-bricked railroad depot on Carlisle Street. Morning sun glinted off arched windows and glared into her eyes. She blinked, and inhaled from a small bottle of peppermint oil. Gettysburg still reeked.

It was time to leave.

She should have known it would come to this. It had only been a matter of time. If there had been no battle at all, how different things would have been. Amelia would have made Liberty a cake for her twentieth birthday ten days ago. Liberty would have relished the taste and the attention. She would have embraced Amelia, and they would have set about furnishing the house to be an elegant country inn. They would have been family.

But there had been a battle, and everything changed.

"We just missed the morning train," Liberty said as she emerged from the station. "Do you want me to stay with you in the ladies' waiting room until the next train comes?"

"I can take care of myself from here on out quite well, thank you."

Liberty bit her lip. "Amelia, you know as well as I do that our arrangement simply wasn't working. The farm is still a Confederate field hospital, and it's the last place you want to be. You don't want to help, there is barely enough food to go around, and the place is contaminated. I know you'll be more comfortable in Philadelphia. If you want to come back and visit once this is all over, you're welcome to. But for now—"

"You've had your say. No need to repeat it. You may take your leave."

"But the next train isn't for hours. What will you do in the meantime?"

Amelia looked around. Four disabled cannons were parked near the station, while the land next to the tracks was filled with tents. Beyond the station, Amelia saw only bewildering confusion as the streets thronged with soldiers, nuns, wagons, ambulances, civilians, and sightseers.

"The U.S. Sanitary Commission Lodge," Liberty read off a wooden sign. "Come, let's see if we can learn anything."

They entered through an open tent flap and watched quietly for a moment as women labored over portable cook stoves to bake bread and simmer beef and vegetable stew. Amelia inhaled the divine fragrances, thankful for the respite from the stink of war. Rows of makeshift tables and chairs, now vacant, spoke of useful service to hungry men.

A woman with chestnut hair pulled into a chignon spied Amelia and Liberty, wiped her hands on her stained apron, and approached them.

"Good morning, ladies. Can I help you with anything? Are you looking for a loved one?" Her large, hazel eyes were sincere, kind.

"Charlotte Waverly?" Liberty asked. "I can't believe it's you!"

"Liberty!" Charlotte drew her in a tight embrace. "We've been so inundated with women coming through here looking for their soldiers lately—I'm sorry I didn't recognize you!"

"Two years of war makes quite a difference. Three days of battle on one's doorstep changes . . . everything."

Charlotte nodded. "I had forgotten that you lived in Gettysburg. How do you get on, my dear? Was your farm taken for a hospital?"

Amelia cleared her throat, loudly. How rude of them not to notice her.

Liberty's eyes brightened, and she grasped Amelia's elbow. "Amelia, you are not going to believe this. This is Charlotte Waverly, who nursed Levi in Washington after the First Battle of Bull Run. Charlotte, this is Levi's mother, Amelia Sanger."

For a moment, Amelia's power of speech left her. Then, "You were with my son? When he died? You were the one who wrote to me with news of his death, weren't you?" With trembling hand, she covered her mouth. Tears bit her eyes.

At once, Charlotte threw her arms around her. "I'm so sorry for your loss," she said. "He was a brave young man. You raised a fine son." Charlotte stepped back, but still held Amelia by the shoulders of her black bombazine dress. "You must be very proud. Have you come here to help the wounded, like so many others who have lost a soldier? Of course, I should have known. From what I know of Levi and Liberty, you must be such a caring, giving person. I'm so glad to know you."

"Actually, Charlotte, Amelia was hoping to leave Gettysburg today by rail. Are you feeding the wounded here before they leave?"

Charlotte nodded. "And more. Men straggle in from the hospitals from miles around, at all times of the day, with nothing in their bellies for the tiresome travel ahead of them. So we fix them up with food, fresh clothing and bandages, cologne-scented handkerchiefs, canteens of water, that sort of thing. The ones who arrive after the four o'clock train we provide with cots and bedding for the night, as well. The government has made no provision for these men on their journeys. Can you imagine?"

"Perhaps, if you let me—" Amelia hesitated. But how bad could this be? Surely compared to a field hospital, it would not be so hard to bear. "I could help. Just for a bit, you understand, until my train comes in. I'd love to hear more about what my son's last days were like, if you don't mind."

Charlotte put her fists on her slim hips as she appraised Amelia. "I would like that very much, Mrs. Sanger. I'm happy to share anything I remember about Levi, as long as our hands can keep busy while we visit. And understand, we may have several interruptions."

Amelia nodded. She'd never admit it to Liberty, but refusing to work at Holloway Farm had bored her nearly out of her mind. She hated playing the role of a useless, bitter old woman. She hated disappointing Liberty, too, just when they were starting to get to know each other. But how could she reconcile serving the boys who killed her son? No, she had had no choice but to remain idle and wait out the storm.

Helping Union boys on their journey home though, that would be fine. After all, she had nothing else to do. No one was waiting for her— anywhere.

Almost dazed with shock, Liberty grasped Amelia's hand. "Amelia, I think this will be good for you."

The older woman cocked an eyebrow. "Do you now?"

"Do write to me once you've arrived in Philadelphia. I must get back to the farm."

Charlotte nodded. "Splendid. Amelia, why don't you go see my mother Caroline, just there, and she'll lend you an apron. I'll be right over."

Linking an arm through Liberty's elbow, Charlotte walked her into a different tent, where a surgeon attended patients apparently not quite strong enough yet for the journey. "How are you, Liberty? Truly? Are you forgetting the past, and reaching forth?"

Liberty smiled. "I believe I am."

"Good." Charlotte circled her shoulders with an arm and squeezed lightly. "Dare I ask how your farm withstood the battle storm?"

"It's ruined. Turned into a hospital for Confederate wounded."

Charlotte drew a hand over her mouth. "But it has not ruined *you*. Has it?"

"No. You'd never believe what I am capable of now."

"Oh, yes I would. You do what needs to be done, day after day, until one day, you discover you are doing more than just surviving. Your life has purpose. Am I right?"

Silas's face surged before Liberty, and she beamed.

"Liberty Holloway! I never knew you had

339

dimples!" Charlotte sucked in her breath. "You're not in mourning anymore, are you?" She winked. "Good for you. Amelia may never move past the memory of her son, because she will always be his mother. But widows stop being wives. Widows move on, when the time is right."

The surgeon approached Charlotte and placed his hand on the small of her back. He was younger than the doctors at Holloway Farm—and far more handsome. "I'm sorry to interrupt, darling, but very soon I will need your assistance with these patients."

"Of course, I'll only be a moment, Dr. Lansing." Her face brightened toward him, and he winked at her, his grey eyes twinkling.

"He's more than a doctor, though, isn't he?" Liberty had a feeling that if she had not been standing there, he would not have settled for a wink.

Charlotte smiled. "After the war, he will be my husband."

"Pray God that will be soon."

Charlotte's face grew serious. "Indeed. But in the meantime, we both have work to do. Be well, Liberty. I will do what I can for Amelia. I'll be right here for at least another week, maybe longer, and you can write to me if you need to, after that." She scribbled a Rhode Island address on a scrap of paper and pressed it into Liberty's palm before giving her one more hug. "Remember, you're allowed to move on. Live."

The women parted, and with new breath in her spirit, Liberty climbed back in the wagon she borrowed from Dr. O'Leary. She had one more stop to make before heading back to Holloway Farm.

It was time to say goodbye, for good, to Levi.

Holloway Farm
Tuesday, July 14, 1863

Sunbeams slanted in through the skeletal barn, baking stripes of Silas's body with midsummer heat. Sweat trapped between his back and the India rubber blanket protecting him from the filthy floor. The quilt Libbie had brought for his comfort, he had given to a patient in worse condition.

"Silas?"

He opened his eyes to find Liberty offering him a steaming cup of coffee. He sat up and accepted it with thanks. After months on end of substitute coffee—made from chicory, corn, acorns, beets, okra seeds, or dandelion root—nothing could warm a Southerner's heart like a real cup of coffee.

Shaking off the fog in his brain, he brought the tin cup to his lips and sipped. The first taste burned his tongue, but he didn't even mind, it tasted so good. A subtle smile played on Liberty's lips as she watched him. As he tried not to watch her lips.

He swallowed. "You look . . ." What could he say to her? She looked like an angel, in spite of her careworn dress, fretted at the edges. She looked like all that was fresh and vibrant and lovely. She looked . . . "Well-rested."

"Well, that's a miracle." Eyes crinkling, Liberty laughed out loud, and it sounded like music.

A smiled tugged at the corners of his mouth. "I'm just glad you can say my name without hissing now."

"Of course. We're *friends,* aren't we?" She cocked an eyebrow.

Friends. Right. It's what he had asked for.

Grogginess coated his mind like molasses. He closed his eyes for a moment—and saw his mother's accusing face, jabbing a finger at his chest. *You! You're just like your father. You call it a protective instinct, I call it base desire. No woman is safe around you! I never want to see you again!*

"No!" His eyes popped open again, his chest heaved.

"No?"

Oh no. He shook his head. What did she say? "Oh yes, friends. Yes, we're just friends." His heart thudded as the image of his mother dissolved from his mind.

She knelt by his side, spoke in soft, low tones. "How are you feeling?"

"They've been giving me something for the

pain, which helps. And water. If I pour water on my leg, it helps too. But when my leg is numb to pain, my head aches some, and I have a little nausea, but that's nothing compared to the alternative. But sometimes I also feel . . . It's hard to explain."

"Try."

"Confused."

Liberty pressed her lips into a thin line. "About what?"

"Anything. Everything. I feel a little bit of it right now. But please don't worry. You're not my nurse, remember? That was our arrangement."

"I'm not your nurse. But . . ."

Her voice trailed away, and Silas shook his head. The fog was getting thicker. Oh no. Liberty was frowning. Did he say something wrong? What did she just say? His memory failed him. He shook his head again. Tried to drink his coffee, but it sloshed over the cup's rim.

"Silas, look into my eyes, please."

He tried. But he was getting so sleepy. The cup no longer warmed his hand. She must have taken it from him, and he didn't even notice. *Why* was he so tired? Didn't he just wake up? His eyes started to roll back, he fought against it. He didn't want to sleep, he wanted to see Liberty!

"Your eyes are red, and your breathing is so slow, Silas. I'm worried." She offered him a handkerchief. Was his nose running again?

"Don't be." He eased back onto his rubber blanket. "I'll just rest."

"You need the doctor."

I need you.

But she was already gone.

Myrtle Henderson almost dropped her tray of bread as Liberty stumbled into her right outside the barn.

"Forgive me, Myrtle! I've got to run for the doctor. It's Silas. Could you sit with him? Don't let him fall asleep!" She hitched up her skirt and took off in a blur.

Myrtle's heart raced as her feet carried her to Silas's side. She fumbled the tray onto the ground and gripped Silas's shoulder. "Silas Ford? It's me, Myrtle Henderson. Myrtle is here. Wake up, Silas. It's me, Myrtle."

Squinting, he rolled over and looked at her.

"The doctor is coming." She hoped he would be glad that at least she was here now.

He groaned. "I don't know what's wrong with me, Myrtle."

There was not a single thing wrong with Silas Ford. Everyone who had half a brain knew that. He was perfect. And he needed Myrtle Henderson now.

"Why would you say such a thing?" She licked her dry lips and tucked a strand of blonde hair back into her snood.

"It's Liberty."

Myrtle stared, trying to understand. What did Liberty do to this man?

"I can't talk to her like I want to. I want to protect her from the horror that has become her home."

Myrtle eyebrows knitted together. He was not supposed to think about Liberty like that. He wanted Myrtle. Not Liberty. He said so himself. Silas asked for Myrtle.

"I want to stand between her and everything that could hurt her—but I can't even stand at all. I want her to be happy, but look at all the misery around her. How do I fix this for her? I so desperately want to fix it."

Myrtle picked up a piece of bread from her tray and absently tore at it, letting little pieces of it mound on her apron like snowflakes.

"My mind tells me to leave her alone, that she'd be better off with someone else. But my heart— does not agree." He sighed, looked at Myrtle for a moment before closing his eyes again. "Funny. I can say that to you, but not to her. It's almost like she's cast a spell over me."

A spell. Of course! Myrtle was indignant. "Then I will never let her near you again. You can count on me."

His eyes blazed so hot she felt burned. He looked at her like she was . . . *crazy*. But Myrtle Henderson was not crazy. She plunged her fingers into the bread again, tearing and dropping, tearing and dropping, until her hands were empty and her lap was full of crumbs. With a sweep of her large hand, she sent them scattering to the floor.

"Don't do that, don't keep her away," he said. "I want to see her!"

Was he angry with her? "I'm only trying to help, Silas, and you said she cast a spell on you. Spells aren't good. They're evil."

"It's a figure of speech, Myrtle." Silas rubbed his head and frowned. "She is a very special . . . friend . . . to me."

"I'm your friend."

"You're my nurse. This is different."

Myrtle scrunched into her neck. She knew what he was saying. Liberty was special. Myrtle was not. Myrtle was different. She peeked up at him and saw he was still frowning, a hand covering his eyes as if the light hurt him.

She didn't like it when he frowned. She liked it when he smiled. At her. This was all wrong, all wrong, this was going all wrong. Myrtle slid her hand into her pocket and held Dolly's hand between her thumb and forefinger. Dolly wasn't upset with her. Dolly would never frown at her. Dolly always smiled.

"I just meant to say, I'm shy around her all of a sudden. She's so beautiful, and I have never felt so—exposed. Raw. I can't say or do the things I want to, and it makes me feel embarrassed."

He closed his eyes and covered his forehead with his hand again. "Surely you can understand that."

Myrtle shrank back. He thought Liberty was beautiful? *Of course. She is beautiful,* Dolly whispered to her. Yes, but Silas Ford wasn't supposed to care what Liberty Holloway looked like. He wanted Myrtle. *No, he doesn't, you ninny,* said Dolly. *He's making fun of you.*

Myrtle released Dolly as if she were a burning coal and pounded the pocket closed on top of her, smashing the rag doll within it. Her breath came in short gasps, her vision swayed. *No, no, no. Not Silas.* Dolly was lying. Silas was special. Silas needed Myrtle. Silas needed Myrtle. Silas needed—

Of course. Silas needed medicine. Yes, that was the answer. She looked over her shoulder out the barn door. No sign of Liberty or either doctor yet. It was up to her. Good thing she had slipped a few of those opium pills from Dr. Stephens's kit into her apron pocket. She knew she was smart to do that. Myrtle was smart. Myrtle Henderson knew just what to do.

"This medicine will help."

But he looked like he was asleep. She wiggled the pill between his lips—such beautiful lips—and told him to swallow. Maybe he heard her, or maybe it was a reflex. Either way, he did it.

She did it.

Swelling with pride, she watched him until his muscles relaxed in sleep. Yes. This was the way she liked him. Now she could talk to him and say anything she liked without worrying how she would sound. Without the risk that he would not like what she said.

Myrtle shuddered when she remembered the look on his face when she said she would keep Liberty away. She pressed her rough fingertips to her eyelids, tried to rub out the image of his upside-down mouth.

It didn't work. Another glance over her shoulder. Still no sign of anyone. She reached up, placed an index finger on each corner of his mouth, and pushed up. There. Now he was smiling.

And so was she.

"What's this, what's this?" Dr. Stephens bellowed as he blew in the door, and Myrtle jumped nearly out of her skin.

The doctor knelt down beside Silas. "Was he complaining of the pain again?"

Too flustered to speak, Myrtle just scurried away to let him get a closer look.

"Well, I've got secondary hemorrhages, gangrene, lockjaw, and dysentery out there. I'll not wake him if he's at rest, poor fellow. But if he wakes up in pain, get me immediately, and I'll dispense more opium." Dr. Stephens looked up and down the barn. "It's the least we can do for these chaps." Turning back to Myrtle, "You may resume your other duties now, but check back on him regularly, and as soon as he wakes, you are to find me. He need not suffer in pain. Will you remember?"

Myrtle nodded. She would remember. It was the least she could do.

Gettysburg, Pennsylvania
Tuesday, July 14, 1863

Amelia Sanger thought her heart would burst out of her corset. A young man, perhaps nineteen years of age at the oldest, with black hair that curled on his forehead, arrived at the Sanitary Commission Lodge at the train depot without the slightest hope of recovery. How he had been sent away from his field hospital was a mystery to all at the lodge. The only thing to do now, was make him comfortable.

He had called her *Mama,* eyes glazed with fever, and had clung tight to her hand. He looked just like Levi.

"Don't bother correcting him," whispered Charlotte. "Let him believe his mother has come for him. He will not survive the night." Charlotte asked Amelia to make him a bed with a half sheet and soft straw, and told him his name was Simon.

Amelia could barely tear her gaze from his

beautiful young face. It glistened with sweat, and she mopped his brow with a handkerchief.

"I knew you would come," he said, and she was suddenly struck with the drawl of his words. This was no replica of her son. This was a Rebel boy.

"Charlotte," Amelia called after her. "He is Southern." Surely there had been some mistake.

"Yes. Which means he will never see his mother again. At least the Northern boys stand a chance that a loved one may come for them. But no Southerners will get past the picket lines. You do him a great service by caring for him. You know the Bible, correct, Mrs. Sanger?"

"Yes." Amelia was bewildered by the sudden change of subject. "Of course I do."

"Then you will understand what I mean when I remind you that serving the hungry, the thirsty, the sick, the prisoner—all of this is serving Jesus. Matthew 25. It is what we did for your son after Bull Run, and now you are performing the same service for someone else's son. Yes?" And she left the tent, leaving Amelia speechless with her charge.

"You're not leaving now, Mama, are you? I thought you'd never get here in time." Amelia knelt by Simon and looked at his face again. On closer inspection, he was not as similar to Levi as she had first thought. *But he's someone's son.* Another woman would soon enough know the grief that belonged to a childless mother.

"I'm here," she whispered. "Let me make you a bed to be more comfortable."

After making a mattress on the ground with the sheet and hay, she pulled from a crate a donated quilt, to which was pinned a card. It read: "My son is in the army. Whoever is made warm by this quilt, which I have worked on for six days and most all of six nights, let him remember his own mother's love."

Conviction tightened in Amelia's throat. *Lord, she prayed, I've been so selfish, please give me the attitude of this woman. May I be a conduit of Your love to whomever You place in my path here.*

She helped the boy onto the mattress and gently covered his shivering frame with the quilt. Peace smoothed his brow as he nestled into his fresh new bed.

"I knew you'd come, Mama." His breath slowed, and his color paled, but he slipped his hand into hers, cold and clammy. "Would you sing to me?"

Sing? "Sing what, dear?"

"My favorite hymn. 'Be Still My Soul.'"

Amelia paused. "I—I don't remember the words."

"Me neither. That's why you sent a hymn book with me." Simon smiled and patted his haversack. "Third and fourth verses."

Amelia drew a ragged breath and began, voice quavering at first.

Be still, my soul: when dearest friends
   depart,
And all is darkened in the vale of tears,
Then shalt thou better know His love, His
   heart,
Who comes to soothe thy sorrow and thy
   fears.
Be still, my soul: thy Jesus can repay
From His own fullness all He takes away.

The chug and shriek of a steam engine broke in between the stanzas as a train approached the station. Amelia kept singing, her voice stronger this time, to be heard above the screech of iron slowing on steel.

Be still, my soul: the hour is hastening on
When we shall be forever with the Lord.
When disappointment, grief and fear are
   gone,
Sorrow forgot, love's purest joys restored.
Be still, my soul: when change and tears
   are past
All safe and blessed we shall meet at last.

When she finished, Amelia looked up to find several other faces watching her, not a dry eye among them.

Charlotte was there too. "Your train is here. Thank you so much for your help today."

Simon's eyelids fluttered. He still knew she was there. He would know if she was not.

"Mrs. Sanger?"

"Charlotte, dear, I'm afraid I was mistaken. That's not my train, after all."

"Are you sure? It's headed to Baltimore, where you can transfer to the line to Philadelphia. Isn't that your destination? It's the last civilian passenger car of the day."

"That's not my train," she said again, and smiled as Charlotte's eyebrows raised.

"That's right, Mother," said the boy. "We'll go in the morning, won't we? Home."

The hour is hastening on.

The boy did go home in the morning, but not by rail. Wrapped in a blanket, he was set aside for burial, and Charlotte asked Amelia to write the letter to his mother.

"Please," Charlotte said. "I know it's taxing. But it will mean more coming from you than from me. You were with him in his last moments." She did not need to remind Amelia that Charlotte had been with Levi in his, and had taken up the task of writing to her son's family.

Now it was Amelia's turn. What an agonizing duty. *How do you tell a complete stranger that her son is dead?* Even before she reads a word, the unfamiliar handwriting will give away the message. Her mind will spin back to the first time she held him as a baby to her breast, his first wobbly steps into her arms, the sticky, slobbery kisses on her face, his sweaty arms around her neck after romping about outside. She will long for his scent, just one more time, and will watch him grow into a young man before her eyes. She will crumple to the floor if she has not already fallen and fear she has forgotten how to breathe. Emptiness will rip open inside her and she will expect the void to swallow her whole.

Amelia knew. She remembered it all in vivid detail, when it was her own son who had died. The yellow and white striped summer gown she wore had seemed a garish frame for the letter that had fallen from trembling hands onto her lap. Mad with grief, she had clawed at the silk skirt, knocking over a vase full of daisies, not caring that glass shattered, and water puddled on the walnut table. Hiram, her own husband, accused her of lying. *He is not dead, he cannot be dead.* Over and over again. The loss would destroy the man she had married and replace him with a cruel imposter.

Amelia breathed deeply now. *Today is not about my loss,* she reminded herself. This moment was for someone else. *How do I begin?* Charlotte's letter had begun with a single verse— 2 Corinthians 1:3. She still knew it by heart.

But if Amelia recalled correctly, the verse

ended before the sentence did. Curious, she drew a small black Bible from her satchel and found the passage. "Blessed be God, even the Father of our Lord Jesus Christ, the Father of mercies, and the God of all comfort; Who comforteth us in all our tribulation, that we may be able to comfort them which are in any trouble, by the comfort wherewith we ourselves are comforted of God. For as the sufferings of Christ abound in us, so our consolation also aboundeth by Christ."

Tears dripped on the thin page. God had comforted her, when Hiram certainly couldn't, and now it was Amelia's turn to comfort someone else. She reread the last verse. Had she truly allowed her consolation to abound in Christ? Her heart pinched.

The more Hiram lashed out at her from his own private prison of pain, the more she had dwelled on her loss—not God. She stared at it every day, refused to part with grief, cuddled up to it at night when Hiram left her cold. Mourning had a place, but Amelia Sanger didn't leave it there. She embedded it into her spirit, until the term "survivor" encompassed her being.

Would she advise this woman, about to be plunged into fresh, raw grief, to do the same?

Finally, she knew what to say. She began, not with grief, but with God, "the Father of mercies, and the God of all comfort," following

Charlotte's example. She would end with the lines of Simon's favorite hymn.

> Be still, my soul: the hour is hastening on
> When we shall be forever with the Lord.
> When disappointment, grief and fear are
>   gone,
> Sorrow forgot, love's purest joys restored.

Chapter Seventeen

Holloway Farm
Friday, July 17, 1863

Liberty's tray crashed to the barn floor, draining cups of beef tea into the straw and hard-packed dirt. Steam curled frantically around the steady drips of rain falling from the leaky roof.

"Myrtle!" She called over her shoulder. "Get Dr. O'Leary! Now!"

Myrtle appeared in the doorway, her drenched hair and clothing clinging limply to her body. She took one look at Silas and paled. "Silas wants me," she said. "Not you. I'll stay with him and you go. I know how to make him better."

"Don't argue with me, just get the doctor!" Liberty shouted over the growl of thunder. "Tell him he needs his zinc sulfate! Hurry!"

Liberty watched the awkward girl run away,

tripping on her skirt in the mud, then knelt beside Silas. His skin was cold and clammy, his lips and fingertips tinged an unearthly shade of blue. He opened his eyes, revealing small pupils.

"Liberty?"

"I'm here, Silas. And I'm not leaving."

"Do you see him? My father is just there—how is my father here?" Terror seemed to seize Silas. He shrunk away from the lightning that flashed beyond the door. "So angry, so angry, he's always so angry. I'm sorry, Father!"

Liberty swiveled on her knees, grinding oily straw into her skirt. "No, Silas, you're hallucinating. Don't be afraid."

Please God, don't take him.

Two pairs of footsteps came squelching in. Myrtle dripped on Silas while Dr. O'Leary examined him. He sniffed his breath.

"Does he need more medicine?" Myrtle pulled from her apron pocket a handful of opium pills. "I just gave him some not long ago."

"Good God, girl, what have you done?" Dr. O'Leary snapped at her, and she pulled her head down into her neck.

"He didn't feel good, and this makes him feel better." Her voice wavered. "It makes him sleep."

Comprehension shot through Liberty. The girl she told to take care of Silas had poisoned him. *I should never have let her take my place!*

"Did Dr. Stephens tell you to do that?" Dr.

O'Leary did not look up as he pulled the zinc sulfate solution from his bag. *Just as I suspected. Opium overdose.*

"No, I learned how to do it all by myself. Sometimes Dr. Stephens gives him medicine, and sometimes I do. When the doctor is busy."

Dr. O'Leary's face twitched in anger, as he helped Silas take his first dose of zinc sulfate.

Seething, Liberty stood, grabbed Myrtle by the arm and pulled her outside the barn.

"I trusted you, and so did Silas, and you've nearly killed him." Rain began to soak her clothes.

"What? I gave him medicine! That's what you do for sick people, you give them medicine!"

Was she really that simple? "No, Myrtle, you don't give medicine, the doctors give medicine. If you give too much, or if you give the wrong medicine, you could kill him!"

"Kill Silas Ford? But I don't want to do that, I love—"

Goosebumps covered Libbie's skin, though the summer rain was warm. "You what?"

Myrtle hung her head, slumped her shoulders, rounded her back. "Silas Ford wants Myrtle Henderson. He needs me. He asked for me."

"That's over now." Liberty waved the words away, paced the trampled yard, arms crossed across her chest. She wanted to send her away for good, but with Bella gone . . . she pressed a hand to her aching forehead.

"But I didn't mean to be naughty! I'm a good girl!"

Liberty stared at this childlike creature. She was not malicious. Simple, yes. But mean-spirited and calculating? No.

"Now you listen to me, Myrtle. I believe you meant well. I know you didn't intend to harm Silas—but you have. So if you wish to stay here, you will stick to the duties of laundry, boiling water so we can use it, disinfecting the trench, emptying the chamber pots. Do you understand me?"

Tears filled Myrtle's eyes. "You're angry with me. You yelled at me."

Liberty's fists clenched at her sides. Silas could be on death's doorstep right now. Yet she modulated her tone anyway. "I'm upset that Silas is very, very sick. I need to know that you understand me. You are not to go near Silas ever again. Nor any of the patients."

"But he asked—"

"I am in charge here. I say you will not enter the barn again. If you do, I will personally put you on the train back to Baltimore, for if you cannot be trusted in this hospital, you cannot be trusted in any other. Now tell me that you understand." Shuddering with impatience, she waited for some sign of comprehension.

"Yes," she hissed. "No more Silas." Her eyes flashed. Was she angry now? *Fine. So am I.*

Liberty matched Myrtle's scowl with one of her own before running back into the barn.

Myrtle watched Liberty's lithe form disappear into the gaping barn. She hated that barn with its torn-out doors. It looked like it was laughing at her.

Or yelling at her. She hated it when people yelled at her.

Glowering like the stormy sky, Myrtle plodded back toward the summer kitchen and ducked into its steamy shelter. She sat on a barrel and brought Dolly out of her pocket. At least Dolly was still smiling. Myrtle traced the smile on the rag doll's face with her fingertip, back and forth, back and forth, to reassure her of its permanence.

Myrtle was mortified.

And heartbroken. She brought Dolly to her cheek and sobbed. *No more Silas? No more Silas? But I love him! And he needs me! I helped him feel better whenever he felt any pain!*

Rain splattered against the broken windows, spitting moisture on Myrtle as she sat there. It was as if the sky itself was hissing at her!

"Liberty is mean," she told Dolly.

No, she isn't. She just cares about Silas.

"I care about Silas! I love him!"

So does she.

"What? Who told you that?"

Dolly was lying again. She must be.

I'm not lying, Myrtle. She loves him, and it's plain as your face that Silas loves her, too.

Myrtle's fingers cinched around Dolly's waist and squeezed. "How dare you say that? Maybe she's cast another spell on him. I have to warn him."

You idiot. You simpleton.

Myrtle shook the doll for being so impertinent and rude. How could Dolly be so rude with that wide smile on her face?

"Why else would Silas ask me to be his nurse if he didn't care for me?"

Don't you get it? He wants her to be his sweetheart, not his nurse.

"Shut up." Myrtle jumped to her feet and slammed the doll down on the barrel. Dirt smudged Dolly's face. Myrtle smiled. That felt good.

He loves her. She's beautiful, kind, and smart. You might be kind sometimes, Myrtle, but you sure aren't much to look at, and you definitely could never be accused of intelligence.

"I said, shut up!" Tears watered Myrtle's cheeks, and her face swelled with anger. She hurled Dolly against the opposite wall and sat on the barrel, heaving with emotion.

Lightning split the sky outside, and thunder cracked in her ears, but she did not hear Dolly's voice. Myrtle took a deep breath. She had won. She wiped her face with her hands, then her hands on her apron.

Dumb. Why not just wipe your face with your apron in the first place?

Myrtle jerked. "Why are you so mean to me, Dolly?" She crept over to the doll, lying face down on the jam-stained floor. Hesitantly, she turned her over. Squinted at her.

Faded red dress. Black hair. Pretty, except where the dirt smeared across her face.

Just like Liberty.

Stay away from Silas.

Now even her voice sounded like Liberty.

Myrtle's gaze skittered around her until landing on a silver gleam. So, Myrtle Henderson wasn't smart, was she? A smile curled her lips over her small teeth as she swept a loaf of bread off the cutting board, and put Dolly on it instead. Grasping the knife in her sweaty palm, Myrtle brought the blade down with a whack on Dolly's neck, amputating her head from her body.

"I told you to shut up."

The next day, after Silas had been purged of every last trace of opium in his system, Dr. O'Leary came back to check on him. Sighing, the doctor sat on his three-legged stool and rubbed the back of his neck. "Silas, we need to have a talk."

Silas sat up. He'd already learned the cause for what happened yesterday. Apparently, between a sympathetic doctor and a sympathetic, amateur nurse, he had been given too much opium to

362

numb the pain. It played tricks with his mind, and assaulted his body.

"Your leg is healing as it should, but some pain can be expected. Some patients take opium—or morphia—for the pain in the stump, and some take it for the pain in their hearts. I believe that your overdose yesterday was not by your own design. But now you know what it can do, and you have a choice. Numb the pain and your spirit both, or manage it." He paused.

"Just how much of my letter did you read, Dr. O'Leary?"

"I didn't need to read the letter to be able to read you. You've experienced pain before this that has perhaps never fully healed. I work with sutures and needles and tinctures and sulfates, none of which can fix the human spirit. But I know a Physician who can. Have you consulted the Lord about it?" He glanced heavenward, and a raindrop splattered on his forehead from a leak in the roof.

"He isn't listening."

The doctor frowned and he wiped his face. "Says who? The Bible tells us to pour out our hearts to Him. To pray without ceasing."

" 'If I regard iniquity in my heart, the Lord will not hear me.' I can't help but wonder if losing my leg is punishment for my sin."

"I don't think God works that way. You're quoting Psalm 66:18. But what about the rest of the chapter? You're reading your own fear into that verse."

"Excuse me?"

"To regard iniquity in one's heart, as that verse is written, means to harbor it. To know you have done wrong, but to refuse to confess it and ask for forgiveness. Now let's read the next few verses along with it and see what you think now." He reached into his black leather bag.

"You carry your Bible in your medical kit?"

Dr. O'Leary smiled as he pressed the small black book into Silas's hands. "Several. Don't forget, I'm not just a doctor. I'm a delegate of the Christian Commission, too. But between you and me, even if I wasn't on the commission, I still wouldn't dare leave home without my own Bible. Man does not live by bread alone but by the word of God. Now read."

Silas opened to Psalm 66 and began reading at verse 18. "If I regard iniquity in my heart, the Lord will not hear me: But verily God hath heard me; he hath attended to the voice of my prayer. Blessed be God, which hath not turned away my prayer, nor his mercy from me."

"You see? The chapter ends there. The last word is not despair and isolation, but mercy. If you confess, God will forgive. That's a promise found throughout the Bible. King David mightily made a mess of things, didn't he? He already had wives and concubines a plenty, and yet he had an affair with another man's wife. A soldier in his own army. Then he made sure that soldier was killed in battle by putting him on the front lines."

"Yes, I know the story."

"Then you also may know David repented, thoroughly, and the Bible calls him a man after God's own heart. Flip a few pages back to Psalm 51."

Silas scanned the chapter, recalling the familiar verses as he read them. *Hide thy face from my sins, and blot out all mine iniquities. Create in me a clean heart, O God; and renew a right spirit within me.* But when he reached verse 17, he stopped. Had he ever read this before?

"For thou desirest not sacrifice; else would I give it: thou delightest not in burnt offering. The sacrifices of God are a broken spirit: a broken and a contrite heart, O God, thou wilt not despise." That was Silas. He looked at Dr. O'Leary.

The doctor smiled. "God is close to the broken-hearted. Your father may have been hard to please, but our heavenly Father will not turn you away. Don't push Him away yourself. "

Rain dripped in the quiet space between the two men.

"Keep that," Dr. O'Leary said. "I'm done preaching for now, but you will find more healing within those pages than I can possibly give. Your physical pain will get better with time, you know."

Silas didn't know. What he knew was that his

brain was still unconvinced of the absence of his right leg. But that was crazy. He'd already acted crazy enough.

Dr. O'Leary narrowed his eyes at the suspicion that must have been written on Silas's face. "Is there something you'd like to tell me?"

Silas hesitated.

"You sometimes sense your right leg is still there, don't you? Does it cramp, or itch, or both?"

Silas's jaw dropped.

"Don't worry, old chap. You are not going crazy. These sensations have been documented by countless veterans. In fact, Turner's Lane Hospital in my hometown of Philadelphia is devoted to nervous injuries like those, and Dr. S. W. Mitchell is pioneering the field. Good news, Silas. You will be fine. Those pesky sensations will occur less and less, and eventually your brain catches up to your body. Oh yes, there are those whose nerve damage causes far more severe conse-quences, but I can tell you are not one of those cases."

"How?" A small pinprick of light punctured the dark fog in his mind.

"One example—it's raining. And you're not writhing on the floor."

Silas's face twisted in confusion. "Why would I do that?"

"At Turner's Lane, otherwise called the Stump

Hospital, every time it rains, at least two hundred of our worst cases are thrown into seizures at once. Now, I'm not the nerve expert that Dr. Mitchell is, but I know enough to be able to tell you, you are headed on the path to recovery. In fact, if it weren't for the fact that you'd been sleeping so much this last week and, not to mention our terrible shortage of crutches, you should be up and walking around."

Silas stared at the doctor. Had he heard him right? "I could be walking?"

"With the help of a crutch and for very short spells, yes. But as I said, we don't have any."

"Could I make one?"

Dr. O'Leary smiled. "Miss Holloway thought you might be able to." He held out his hand. "Stand up."

Silas planted his left foot on the floor, clutched the doctor's outstretched hand and pulled himself up. "I thought you were taller than me." The doctor smiled up at him. Hope sparked in Silas's chest. It had felt like a lifetime since he had stood on his own two—since he had stood.

With his arm around the doctor's shoulders, he hopped over to the gaping doorway of that miserable barn and looked out. The world was colored in shades of grey and brown as drizzle pooled in footprints and wagon wheel ruts in the mud. It was beautiful.

Dr. O'Leary pointed to the house. "If you can

make it that far, on the other side is a porch where a young lady has a surprise for you."

"I can make it."

Silas should not have been surprised at how much effort hopping from the barn to the house required, nor at how much strength he had lost since his injury. But when he saw Liberty standing on the porch, waiting for him, new life filled him. Her hand rested on the back of a red velvet armchair she must have dragged out from the parlor. In front of the chair, two barrels supported long planks of wood in a makeshift table.

Silas hopped up the porch steps with Dr. O'Leary supporting him. Liberty beamed up at him as he stood in front of her, dimples twinkling in her cheeks.

"You're much taller when you stand up, aren't you?" she teased. He had forgotten she only came up to his shoulder.

"Now that you know that, would you mind if I sat down?" His left leg began to wobble from the exertion. Silas lowered himself in the armchair and let his gaze roll over the bounty on the boards in front of him. Nails, hammer, screwdrivers, screws, saw, chisel, sandpaper.

"Aunt Helen's old tools," Liberty said. "I've never had much use for them, myself. I thought maybe you might know what to do with them. They seemed so forlorn just sitting in the tool-box, without any purpose."

Silas knew exactly how they felt. He picked up the chisel and relished the feel of the round, smooth wooden handle in his palm.

"Will they work?"

"Just fine," said Silas. "But what of wood?"

Liberty pressed her lips together. "Wood is a rare commodity around here, but I found something I hope will suffice." She pointed to a long slab of mahogany leaning up against the front of the stone house. Dr. O'Leary carried it over and laid it on top of the table for Silas to inspect. "It's the top of the sideboard, from the dining room. Will it do?"

Silas ran his hand across the polished surface. Only a few nicks and scratches marred its sheen. "This is too good to be made into a crutch!"

"But will it work? Will it serve the purpose?" Liberty prodded.

"Yes."

"Then it will be in the greatest service it has ever seen. Far better to hold up a fine man than fine china." She winked.

Silas was itching to get started. To craft something with his hands, to walk again without assistance from another. If skipping medication meant he could think clearly enough to work again—and hold a coherent conversation with Liberty—then he'd gladly put up with the pain.

Dr. O'Leary clapped a hand on Silas's shoulder. "Well then, old chap! I'll leave you to it!"

• • •

Alone in her room, Liberty looked around for something to use as a pad for Silas's new crutch. She had no more dresses to cut up, save her old mourning clothes, and she did not want to use those. Her quilt was ruined. Sheets already stripped into bandages. There was only one thing left to use.

Her baby quilt. Kneeling on the hardwood floor, Libbie opened her cedar chest and pulled it out from the bottom and grazed the odd shapes of wool, flannel, cotton, and silk with her palm. *Why have I been keeping this, anyway?*

But she knew why. As much as she hated the story of how she was born, she could not help but believe that her mother would not have taken the time to create this quilt if she hadn't cared about her well-being, just a little bit. And wasn't it normal to long to be loved by one's own mother? Libbie sighed. *A mother like yours is best forgotten,* her aunt Helen had told her. Maybe she had been right.

She should be past this by now. Liberty had memorized several verses that told her she was God's child, amazing verses that spoke directly to her heart.

Can a woman forget her sucking child, that she should not have compassion on the son of her womb? yea, they may forget, yet will I not forget thee. Isaiah 49:15

370

When my father and my mother forsake me, then the Lord will take me up. Psalm 27:10

A father of the fatherless, and a judge of the widows, is God in his holy habitation. Psalm 68:5

An orphan and a widow—Liberty was both! According to the Bible, she had a special place in God's heart. Shouldn't that be good enough?

Liberty wished it was. She wished, she prayed, she could forget she ever had a mother. Every time she thought or talked about her only brought her pain.

Her thoughts drifted back to her conversation with Bella, who had said her mother had loved her. How could she know? She was just trying to make Liberty feel better. *And then I sent her away.* At least, that was what it had felt like. Guilt lurked in her spirit over their parting, when all Liberty wanted was to be full of joy that Silas had escaped death.

Yes, Silas. She was supposed to be focusing on him now, and his crutch. Liberty dug into her sewing basket, pulled out a ripper, and surgically removed a large patch from the top layer of the quilt. Holding it up, she smiled. No one would ever mistake Silas's crutch now. The pad was a patchwork quilt of four difference pieces of fabric. She would fill it with sawdust from a box of brandy bottles. It would be perfect.

A slight twinge of regret pricked Liberty's heart as she laid the remnant of the baby quilt back in the cedar chest. Slamming the lid shut, she closed her heart to the memory that only hurt her.

Act Five

BEAUTY FROM ASHES

"HAVING BEEN ABLE through Divine help, to pass through all that I [did], I can now say, I would not part with my experience for anything the world can offer. I am proud that I was able to do and to suffer, even so little, during this fearful struggle, 'that this Nation,' in the words of our beloved Lincoln, 'might have a new birth, that the Government of the people, for the people, by the people, should not perish from the earth.'"

—FANNIE BUEHLER,
Gettysburg housewife

Chapter Eighteen

Gettysburg, Pennsylvania
Monday, July 27, 1863

As soon as Harrison Caldwell stepped off the train at the Carlisle Street station, he was assaulted by locomotive fumes and the lingering odor of human waste and decay. The smell of spoiling flesh was not as strong as it had been when he had left, but the telltale ammonia smell still pinched his nose. The town was now overrun with what appeared to be relief workers, loved ones seeking their wounded, and sightseers with a taste for the macabre. The village of twenty-four hundred residents was simply not equipped to sanitize the sewage of the twenty thousand or more visitors that had descended upon them.

Next to the tracks were several tents, one of which was labeled Sanitary Commission Lodge. From this tent, the smell of strong hot coffee and beef stew wafted on the sticky breeze. When a woman in full black mourning slipped out of one and into another of these tents, Harrison did a double take. Amelia Sanger, from Holloway Farm? He followed her into a tent lined on one side with barrels labeled shirts, drawers, dressing gowns, socks, slippers, rags, and bandages. On the others side sat grocer boxes of tea, coffee, soft crackers, tamarinds, and cherry brandy. Tables were likewise stocked with rows of jelly-pots and bottles of black currant and blackberry syrup.

"Pardon me," Harrison ventured, and the widow started.

"Good gracious!" She pressed a hand to her bosom, fingers trapping a hair-work brooch to her high black collar. "Can I help you?"

Of course she wouldn't remember him. It was dark when they met. She was upset. Emptying her own chamber pot, as he recalled. "Aren't you— I believe we met once, at the Holloway Farm."

He waited a moment, until recognition registered on her face. "You're not the reporter, are you?"

"Guilty as charged. But you don't seem to be the same woman I met in the moonlight."

"I'm not." She smiled. "Thank God. Whatever I said to you that night, I hope you've forgotten by now."

Not quite. He tugged his collar away from his neck. "Quite. Are you with the Sanitary Commission?"

"Not officially. I was waiting for a train to Baltimore, to then go on to Philadelphia, when I stumbled upon the good work they are doing here. Lucky for me, they let me help a wee bit. That was a week ago."

"You still haven't caught your train?"

"It wasn't time for me to go. Frankly, the work

376

here is all but done, and the Sanitary Commission Lodge is disbanding. I don't know what I'll do now."

Harrison nodded. "Well, if Philadelphia is your destination, you'll find similar work there that's guaranteed to last until the end of the war."

Her face brightened. "Where?"

He told her about the two refreshment saloons for soldiers and prisoners passing through, and she looked like he had given her the moon. "Now if you'll excuse me, I'm off on a story." He tipped his hat to her, and took his leave. He did not feel compelled to share with her just yet that the story involved Liberty and Bella and would quite possibly scandalize her stockings off her feet.

Back on the street, citizens and soldiers pressed around him, nearly choking him with the competing scents they held near their noses in bags, bottles, or on handkerchiefs. Pennyroyal, peppermint oil, cologne, and camphor cloyed thickly in the air. Sidewalks were blockaded with black coffins stacked high outside embalming parlors. When a passing wagon offered him a ride to the battlefield in the vicinity of the Holloway Farm, Harrison jumped onboard.

Folds of skin hung loosely on the wagon driver's aged face, framing small dark eyes. His German accent flavored his words as he called out the sights through town and countryside. In the fields west of town, Harrison covered his nose and mouth with a handkerchief. For there, where soldiers had hastily buried the dead more than two weeks ago, family members now dug up the graves looking for their loved ones. The land was littered with unburied and half-buried dead.

After they crossed Seminary Ridge, they soon came to Willoughby Run, where Harrison jumped out of the wagon, knapsack swung over his shoulder.

"Four dollars," said the driver.

"Four! You mean for the whole wagon?" Harrison was indignant. When he was an independent reporter, the payment for an entire story had been only five dollars.

"I mean four dollars, from you." The scathing article Lorenzo Ellis had printed in his New York paper flashed back to Harrison's mind. Perhaps there was some truth in it after all.

"Sir, that is a ridiculous amount. Do you charge everyone this much?"

"*Ja*, everyone. I don't play favoritism. Even the soldiers pay this much from here to the station, and are happy for the ride."

"You charge wounded men four dollars for a ride in an uncovered wagon with no springs? Why, you probably bounce them half to death by the time you get there!"

"Four dollars for the ride, two dollars for a loaf of bread if they're hungry."

Madness. A loaf of bread in the country should cost a quarter, no more.

"If you don't pay the fee, you'll drive up the cost even more for the others." His lower lip protruded as he set his wrinkled face in a scowl. Harrison paid the man three dollars, refusing another cent, and vowed to walk all over Gettysburg rather than ever line his pockets again.

At the edge of the lane leading up to Liberty's stone farmhouse, Harrison tripped on a corner of wood sticking up out of the ground. After fishing it up, he ran a finger through the grooves of the chiseled letters, LIBERTY INN. A chuckle escaped him as he scanned the property. Especially for a Union widow, she was quite hospitable indeed.

Liberty's dark hair shone in the noonday sun as she emerged from the gaping barn with a tray of empty cups.

"Excuse me!" he called as he approached. "Hello there, Harrison Caldwell, *Philadelphia Inquirer.* Not sure if you remember me, but I brought Mrs. Jamison here the evening of July 2."

"Oh yes!" Liberty nodded. "I remember. You were present during some of our amputations."

A man joined her side with the help of a crutch, the right leg of his blue wool trousers pinned up.

"Indeed. But I'm afraid I missed meeting this chap. Hello, sir." Harrison shook the man's hand.

"Silas Ford. Pleased to meet you."

A riot of color peeked out from under Silas's arm when he reached out to shake Harrison's hand. "I say, what kind of a crutch have you got there?"

Liberty smiled. "He made it himself, from a mahogany sideboard."

"But she made the pad." Silas pointed the top of his crutch at Harrison. It appeared to be made from a quilt, with one patch made from a red and cream pinstripe flannel. A line from Fanny Kemble's journal washed over him. *Nearly all the women beg for flannel, and my bolt of red and cream pinstripe is almost gone.*

"Where did you get that fabric, Miss Holloway?"

"From an old quilt."

"How old?"

"Quite. Twenty years."

Twenty years. 1843. Four years after Fanny left the Georgia plantation—but not too long for a slave to keep a gift from her master's wife. "A gift from your mother, perhaps?"

Her eyes darkened and she tilted her head at him. "Can I help you with something?"

"Forgive me, yes." Forcing down his excitement, he extended the dirty wooden sign to Silas, since Liberty's hands were full. "Rescued that from certain death by trampling down the lane. Thought you might want to dust it off and hang it up again someday."

Silas studied the board as a sad smile overtook Liberty's face. "I doubt very much that anyone would willingly come to this wasteland. But thank you."

The way Silas looked at her stopped Harrison cold. He was not just a disinterested patient. Oh no, he was *very* interested in Liberty Holloway. His reporter nose sniffed scandal. Was there a budding romance between a Union widow and a Confederate patient? More shocking than that—between the daughter of a slave and the son of a —could he dare to hope—slave owner? Even as he chided himself for leaping to such an unsupported idea, giddiness bubbled inside him.

Liberty raised her eyebrows and cleared her throat. He had made her uncomfortable. She was waiting for him to go.

Recovering himself, he changed the subject. "I'm looking for your—for Mrs. Jamison."

"You'll not find Bella here. She lives at 319 South Washington Street in town. She could be there, or perhaps working for another client at the moment."

Harrison nodded. *Another client.* He searched Liberty's face for the resemblance to Bella that Lt. Holmes had claimed to see. Nose and lips? Possibly.

"Good day, Miss Holloway, Mr. Ford." He tipped his straw hat to them. "You've been most . . . helpful."

• • •

Silas took a deep breath as wind whistled through the apple trees and flirted with wisps of hair around Liberty's face. "That reporter got to you, didn't he?"

Liberty gave him a sideways glance and started walking toward the summer kitchen. He joined her, the crutch digging into his armpit with every hop. "You've never told me about your parents."

"Do I need to?"

"I told you about mine."

"There isn't much to tell." She was walking faster now, and he broke a sweat trying to keep up with her.

"Then it won't take long." He grabbed her elbow. "Please? No more secrets, right?"

Her shoulders slumped with invisible burden, but she nodded. "Let me take this tray back to Myrtle, and I'll meet you on the porch."

When she returned, they sat on the top of the steps, and Silas was grateful to rest his left leg and right arm from his self-imposed rehabilitation exercises. He tired so easily, and his head ached, but Dr. O'Leary told him to expect this as his body adjusted to not having as much opium in his system.

"Now." He focused his attention on Liberty. "Please tell me. I want to know who you are."

It was the wrong thing to say. She whipped her head around to face directly ahead, pressed her lips into a line and stared off into the distance.

Birdsong mocked the tension between them. At long last, she spoke. "I am not who my parents were. Just as you are not who your father was."

His mother did not agree. Her words rang in his ears. *You are no better than your father!* But Silas nodded. "Poor choice of words. I'm sorry. But you can't deny that our parents shape us into who we are, for better or for worse. So. Will you tell me?"

Liberty shared her story in a slow trickle of words, then in a steady stream, until her tale was told. Her eyes were dry, but her unsteady voice betrayed her. This wound was not yet healed, and Silas's heart ached for her.

"My parents were not honorable people, and I was unwanted by everyone." Her voice cracked under the pressure of hurt and shame.

"You can't say that for sure."

She pierced him with her gaze. "I was not loved, because of how I came to be."

His mouth felt like it had been packed with lint. "But your husband loved you."

Liberty broke her gaze with him and looked down at her bare finger. "I was seventeen years old when we married, Silas, and he not much older. He left before we knew what true love meant." She pushed absently at the cuticles on her fingernails. He folded his own hands to keep from covering Liberty's with them.

"Levi said he loved me, but as I look back on

those memories now, it felt like love from a child who was eager to please, but didn't know how." Her cheeks flamed with color, and he struggled to bridle his imagination before it galloped away with him.

She deserves to be loved by a man. Desire swelled in Silas until it melted his iron will to resist her. Her strength, her beauty, her compassion, all of it was intoxicating. "You are loved now, Liberty." His throat closed around the words, but they would not be taken back.

Questions swam in the blue pools of her eyes. He cupped her face in his hand, and breath shuddered on her lips. Heart hammering on his ribs, he slid his fingers into her silky hair, and leaned in, bringing her full, soft lips to his. Any second, she would jerk away from him.

She didn't.

This isn't supposed to happen. Warning clanged in his mind, but his body didn't listen. Liberty leaned into his kiss, pressed her hands against the sandpaper of his jaw before stroking down his neck to his shoulders and circling his neck. With every touch, she sent fire coursing through his veins. His fingers caressed the nape of her neck before sliding down her back and curving around her waist. Her mouth was wine, and he drank deeper, as if he could not get enough of her. This was not brotherly love.

I shouldn't do this. I'm taking advantage of

her. Placing his hands on her shoulders, he pulled back. "Liberty, I—" Her pupils were large as she looked into his eyes, and he felt that she was seeing clear through his soul. The end of her nose was pink, her full lips slightly parted. The passion rising up in him took his breath away—and any words right with it.

"You what?"

He shook his head and drew her closer, inhaling the peppermint oil scent of her skin. "I don't recall," he whispered in her ear.

But he did. If he loved her, he should put her interests above his. And he was not in Liberty's best interests. The old rhyme chanted in his mind: *Silas Ford, man of the Lord, took slaves to bed . . . took slaves to bed . . . took slaves to bed . . .*

He jerked back, and flung her hands away. Groaning, he sunk his head in his hands. What had he done? Was his mother right about him? *You're no better than your father!* She had screamed at him before ordering him to leave her home. *Full of lust, knowing nothing of love!*

Silas couldn't trust himself. The force of his desire frightened him. He wanted more than her lips. He wanted to explore her throat, her ear lobes, her hair. Silas pushed her away to protect her from his own desire. If he was just like his father, then his mother was right. No woman would be safe around him. And the one thing he wanted most was to make sure Liberty Holloway was safe.

He had failed.

"I'm sorry," he whispered.

Liberty's pulse pounded in her ears as she pulled away from Silas, her hands still warm from the heat of his body.

"You're *sorry?*"

Cicadas whirred in her ears, echoing the thrumming of her heart. Whether he was sorry for kissing her, or sorry for pushing her away, she could only guess.

"I lost my head." Silas leaned forward, elbows on his knees. "I don't know what I was thinking."

"You said—"

"I said you are loved." His face was flushed, his lips swollen. "You are. Lots of people care about you. Look how much good you've done here."

Hurt compressed into anger, and she smacked him clean across his face. "Then I better get back to the ones who *care.*"

Liberty jumped to her feet and did not help him do the same. "I have work to do. Don't waste my time again." She hiked up the ruffled hem of her skirt, trotted down the steps and did not look back. Salty tears streamed down her face, tasting of humiliation.

Liberty pressed her fingers to her lips as she hurried toward the summer kitchen. Her mouth still burned from the heat of his kiss. She may have been married once, but she had never felt the fire of passion like that before—from a man, or from herself. She felt like her body would have melted into his like wax under a seal.

And he was sorry. *Well, so am I.* She was sorry she cared about a Southerner so much, sorry she'd deceived herself into believing Silas Ford was trustworthy—and sorry she now knew what it meant to be truly kissed. Most of all, she was sorry that longing awakened inside her. *He's like a brother to me,* she once told Bella. She'd never say that again.

Myrtle Henderson stepped into her path. "What happened?" She swiveled to look past Liberty toward the porch. "What did you do to Silas Ford? He's just sitting there, holding his cheek."

Liberty brushed past her, the sunbaked ruts in the earth punching against the soles of her feet.

"But what did you do to Silas Ford?" Myrtle cried out again, her voice sharper this time.

Liberty had no answer.

And she told me *to stay away from him?* Bewildered, anger boiled in Myrtle until it burst out of her in a shout. "Liberty Holloway, *you* stay away from Silas Ford!"

Liberty whipped around to face her, fire flashing in her eyes. "What did you say?"

A lump bobbed in Myrtle's throat. She knew what it felt like to never have anyone defend her.

She would stand up for Silas. She had to. "I'm not the only one who hurt him, you know."

Liberty stared at her, and Myrtle's skin crawled with the familiar sensation of being thought an idiot. Liberty pressed a hand to her forehead and sighed, her shoulders slumping. Finally, she looked up, eyes rimmed in red. "Myrtle, please go boil the water. You know as well as anyone that if we drink it untreated, we'll grow sick from the contamination from all the corpses near the water source. You have a very important job. A lot of lives depend on you. All right?"

Myrtle watched her walk away, her head held high while her skirt dragged in the dirt like anyone else's. Liberty was not so different from Myrtle.

An idea formed in her mind, and anger crystallized into resolve. She would follow orders. She would boil water. For the patients.

After all, a lot of lives depend on me.

Including Liberty's.

Gettysburg, Pennsylvania
Monday, July 27, 1863

Bella Jamison's house felt like a tomb: hot, dark, and laced with stink. Her windows were closed to keep out the rancid odors lingering in the town, and her shutters were closed to block the sun. But nothing could keep out the blistering heat.

Back aching, and face damp with sweat, Bella

stood over her ironing table and pressed the wrinkles out of a dress. She was lucky, she knew, that her one-week absence had cost her no more than a fierce reprimand from her employer. Truth was, Mrs. Shriver was desperate for help, and would not fire Bella just to make a point. When Mrs. Shriver had returned home, she found it had been used by Rebel sharpshooters. Two ten-inch holes had been punched through the attic walls for their guns. Blood had congealed on the floorboards, and not a crumb of food had been left in the kitchen or garden. Anything valuable—clothing, linens, tools, curtains, money, silver, liquor—was either gone or destroyed. Both the home and the saloon had been used as hospital.

The patients were gone now, either en route to prisons or evacuated to Camp Letterman, a general hospital erected by the Union army a mile north of town. The wounded had been culled from all private homes by now, and the women scrubbed away at the residue of war.

A sharp knock jerked Bella's attention to the door. Setting her iron back on the stovetop, she opened the door, and the gust of hot air, poisoned with the aftermath of battle, nearly knocked her back.

"Mr. Caldwell!" She covered her nose and mouth with her hand, but stepped aside for him to enter. She shut the door quickly behind him.

His red-orange hair splayed up from his head,

evidence he'd been raking his hand through it again. Hat in his hands, the reporter swept a glance over her home.

"You have been spared much, I see."

"My garden suffered the worst. The same is true for most of my neighbors, but many of them still have not come home." Some of them never would. The image of several colored folks being marched out of Gettysburg on July 1 was seared on her memory. Thank God at least Aunt Hester had escaped. She'd hid in the belfry of one of the churches for three nights and two days before coming out again.

Bella smoothed her apron over her dress. "What can I do for you?"

"Please, sit down."

Her hackles raised. "I can stand just fine."

Harrison reached into his knapsack and tossed a book on the kitchen table, the cover of which was soiled, the corners bent and frayed. "Read much?"

She narrowed her eyes at him, then edged closer to the table, read the title of the book. *Journal of a Residence on a Georgian Plantation in 1838–1839.* By Frances Ann Kemble.

Her heart leapt into her throat. Wood scraped on wood as Harrison slid the chair out from the table and gently guided Bella into it.

"I know who you are, Mrs. Jamison." He sat across from her and leaned forward over the red-and-white checked tablecloth.

"You do not know me."

"I know where you came from, which means I know how far you've come to get to where you are today."

She shook her head. He knew nothing.

"You can't deny it. It's right here." He thumped the cover of the book with his finger. "Your mother's abuse at the hands of Roswell King Junior. The way you tried to stop him, but became his special pet instead. Your plea to Fanny to teach you to read and write and speak like her, your twin sister's disinterest in anything but her own babies."

"That proves nothing. You don't know that's me."

"Your name is in the book, Bella. It was your twin, Daphne, I met at the Weeping Time."

Her breath seized. *Was she well? Where did she go?* her heart cried out. But, "There is more than one Bella in the world, you know."

He craned his neck to look past her to the front room. Light sparked in his brown eyes. "Shall we sit somewhere more comfortable?"

He walked directly to the couch and lifted off an old quilt, skimming every patch with his fingertip. Until stopping on the red and cream pinstripe flannel. He looked up at her then, the devil's gleam in his eyes. "I thought so."

Heat crawled up Bella's neck. "You thought *what,* Mr. Caldwell?" He could not know. He could not know anything.

" 'Nearly all the women beg for flannel, and my bolt of red and cream pinstripe is almost gone.' Page one hundred twelve, *Journal of a Residence*."

"Pinstripe flannel is not so very unique." Bella's chest thrust in and out with breath. She pulled at the collar of her dress.

"But red and cream pinstripe of the same shade, aged exactly the same over the last twenty years?"

Perspiration filmed her face, and she dabbed it with the edge of her apron.

"I have seen this fabric one other place. Holloway Farm. Did you know Liberty cut up an old quilt to fashion a pad for the crutch of a Rebel patient? His name is Silas Ford, I believe."

She stared at Harrison's freckle-sprayed face and tried to read it the way he was certainly trying to read hers. He wanted her to admit Liberty was her daughter. But what proof could he have, *real* proof? Perhaps he was even guessing about the piece of flannel. He was a reporter. He hounded up stories for a living.

Bella swallowed hard. "Coincidence." She would not betray her daughter, no matter how her heart was breaking.

Harrison dropped the quilt back on the couch. "I spoke with Lt. Holmes. Pierce Butler Holmes?"

"He was crazy with chloroform, you know."

Harrison crossed back to the kitchen and slacked a hip against the sideboard, hands in his pockets. "No. I mean I found him, at West's

Building Hospital in Baltimore, last week. He's recovering nicely, by the way."

"Stop."

"I asked him about you. Turns out he wasn't just mad with drug, after all."

"Stop talking."

"He remembers you, Bella, because you were about the same age, growing up in very different worlds, but inextricably linked by the physician —his father—who cared for all the Butler slaves. Including your mother, after confinements and the beatings she endured from King's wife. Including you, after your own row with Roswell King Jr., himself."

At the mere mention of the memory, the tangled mass of scar tissue ached on Bella's back. "Leave," she gasped.

He held up his hands. "He told me you were with child, about to give birth, when you 'and your increase' were sold to a man in Virginia named Gideon Holloway. The year was 1843. Liberty Holloway turned twenty this month, didn't she? It's quite a story, to hear him tell it. A story that even I could not make up. And if you're wondering, yes, he went on the record with that. Even better—Pierce Butler himself was there visiting Holmes too, along with his daughter Frances. Butler confirmed the sale."

His words hung in the stifling air, more putrid than the rot that had blown in with him.

"The rest of the story gets a little fuzzy. Gideon died and left Liberty to his sister. Why?"

She glared at him, muscles in her jaw bunching. Gideon loved that girl, wanted her to be raised white for her own sake, even though she was not his daughter. He said he loved Bella too, but she never trusted that. Bella would share none of this with a reporter.

Fear churned and solidified into anger. Bella gritted her teeth. "Don't you have a battle somewhere to cover?"

"We'll get to that. But this is the story I want, Bella. Do you realize what a fantastic tale this is? It could be even better. Why don't you tell Liberty who you are? Don't you think she'd be overjoyed to discover she isn't an orphan after all? Come now, write your own happy ending."

"Oh, I'll tell you how this ends. It ends here. It ends now."

"Surely not yet!"

Bella walked over to him. "Surely I have some say on this. Surely you don't get to tell me what to do just for the sake of a story." Her voice grew quiet. "I sure would like to be you, Mr. Caldwell, running around all over the map to write stories about the bad things that happen to other people."

He opened his mouth to speak, but she raised a hand to stop him. "This is my turn now. I will have my say."

Bella was nearly suffocating. With the windows

shut against the toxic fumes in the street, the heat of summer baked the inside of Bella's house, even with the shutters closed. She unfastened the top two buttons of her collar and paced slowly, to create her own breeze in the dark, steamy room.

"All my life I been bowing to white folks, from yes massa to yes ma'am. Not this time. Now hear me. You covered the battle of Gettysburg, and then you left. The armies left. The surgeons left. And the rest of us stayed, to put life back together again while you're off watching some other big drama unfold. Just don't forget, Mr. Caldwell, that just because you turn in your article doesn't mean the story ends there. See what I mean?"

His flushed face glowed with sweat as he listened. Good.

"Every battle has its aftermath that goes largely unnoticed except by the folks living in it. Right? Well, now you come here saying you know my story, and that gives you the right to share it for me. It's not your story to share. It's not even just mine. It's Liberty's story, too, and you've got no business waltzing in, stirring things up to make a buck for yourself, and then waltzing out again. You want to put a period at the end of our story and move on. It doesn't work that way. Yesterday's news is always somebody's life today. Does it matter to you at all that I don't want her to know where she came from? Did it ever occur to you she might rather believe a lie than the truth? Just leave it a question mark and move on."

"But—"

In two long strides, Bella stood in front of the man and silenced him with a tug down on her collar. Mr. Caldwell's eyes widened at the sight of the scar at the base of her neck.

"You should see the scar I gave the man who gave this to me."

His eyes darted back up to hers.

"I fought to protect my mother. Don't you think I wouldn't fight for my daughter's safety, too. There is no story here, Mr. Caldwell. Just a question mark. Now. Move along."

She released her collar and stood tall.

Harrison rolled the brim of his hat in his hands. "I will. But first, there's something else. About your husband. There's been a battle."

"You're lying. The 54th doesn't fight. They dig ditches. Build breastworks. They don't fight."

"I assure you, they did. They led the assault on Fort Wagner, South Carolina, on July 19. It was, however . . . unsuccessful."

"I haven't heard anything about this."

"News travels slow from South Carolina. Surrounded by Confederate lines, you know, so it had to travel by ship, not telegraph. We only just learned of it at the *Inquirer*'s office ourselves. It will be all over tomorrow's papers. Of the six hundred men, nearly three hundred were killed, missing, or wounded. They fought most nobly, according to witnesses." He retrieved a paper from his knapsack. "Abraham Jamison is on the casualty list. I'm sorry."

Bella eyed the paper as if it were a rattlesnake, ready to strike. She backed away. "You could have typed that page up yourself. If this is some game to get me away from here . . ."

"No game. Your husband has been injured. But it may only be slight. The list doesn't specify. If you want to go to him, I can arrange the passage. I would be willing to accompany you myself."

"If I let you print your story, you mean?"

He shook his head. "I'm not that low, ma'am. No strings attached."

The broken bodies of Gettysburg rolled through her mind, but with Abraham's face on every one of them.

"South Carolina?" The birthplace of the Confederacy, and major port for the slave trade. Just north of Georgia.

"Beaufort, yes. You need not fear, Mrs. Jamison. The area has been controlled by Union troops for more than a year now. You need not fear."

The anger that had fueled her a moment ago fled, taking her strength with it. Her eyes focused on the curtains hanging limply in front of windows shuttered against battle's stench. She had not been able to keep war from her home after all.

Tasting her heartbeat, she turned back to Mr. Caldwell. "When do we go?"

"We can leave Gettysburg tomorrow."

It did not feel soon enough.

Chapter Nineteen

Gettysburg, Pennsylvania
Monday, July 27, 1863

Harrison Caldwell stepped around a pile of old muskets blocking the sidewalk and almost tripped on a four-year-old boy sitting on the other side, pounding with a toy hammer at some percussion caps on the ground. Down the street, another boy launched a used-up shell and called out to his friend, "Hey, you Reb! Don't you hear that grapeshot scream?"

In his mind's eye, Harrison saw all three boys in uniform, perfectly whole until they were ripped apart on the altar of war, the blue-grey smoke of gunpowder consuming their ravaged bodies. He shuddered. The nightmares were bad enough, but these vivid daydreams rattled him to his core.

Loud voices and laughter splashed the night air as it spilled out of the Confectionary and Eating Saloon on West York Street. Though he had not eaten all day, Harrison did not go in. He was in no mood for a crowd.

Instead, he crossed the street and made a bee-line for the Grocery and Provision Store. The wooden sign that swayed, squeaking on its iron rod, was no larger than a foolscap page, yet riddled with six bullet holes. Harrison purchased two boxes of Necco wafers—licorice, of course, and chocolate, which he hoped Bella would enjoy on tomorrow's train ride.

But when he stepped back into the night, and before he could open his package, his nose pinched and his mouth clamped shut against the smell of decay and chloride of lime.

Harrison wasn't all that hungry anyway. But he sure was thirsty.

He checked his pocket watch. Eight o'clock. Still an hour before the sale of beer and liquor would be stopped for the night, thanks to the Union Provost Marshall. With swollen feet and a heavy heart, Harrison Caldwell followed a stream of men into the Eagle Hotel and claimed a stool at the polished cherrywood bar. Oil lamp sconces with soot-rimmed chimneys belied a staff too busy pouring to bother cleaning. Bottles of liquor lined the wall behind the bar in a sparkling glass rainbow of clear, brown, and green.

"Whiskey?" the bartender asked as he wiped down the bar with a terry cloth towel. Cigar smoke clouded above his head. A drunk man at the end wept into his cup, while raucous laughter penetrated the walls from the town square, one block away.

"How'd you guess?"

"Whiskey sales have shot up since you embalmers came to town, threefold. Not that I'm complaining. My business picks up every time yours does." He threw the towel over his shoulder and grinned.

"Oh, I'm not an embalmer." Harrison tugged at the cravat around his neck and scanned the row of pale faces and droopy mustaches lined up at the bar. "I'm a reporter." *A reporter who has just given up one of the best stories I've ever dug up.* He still couldn't believe it.

The man next to him swiveled on his stool to face him. "You don't say. I hate to tell you this, but the battle's over, fella. You missed it. No wonder you need a drink."

The bartender filled Harrison's shot glass, and he threw back the drink. He shivered as the liquid burned all the way down to his stomach. "Yes, well, not all stories ended when the armies left town." Bella's words echoed in his mind. *Just because you turn in your article doesn't mean the story ends there.* He slammed down the glass and asked for another.

"Oh? Go on." The stranger leaned on his elbow, propped up on the sweaty bar, eyes glazed as if he already had a few drinks in his belly.

Harrison tossed down another shot. "I had a

400

great story all lined up, and every bit of it true. Loads of evidence, eyewitness testimonies, the works."

"So what's the problem?"

"Can't print it. Source doesn't want me to." He took a deep breath, tasting the tobacco-fogged air. *Source doesn't want me to?* Since when had that stopped him before?

"Was it really that good of a story?"

Alcohol coursed hotly through his veins. "It was really that good." A shrill, staccato burst of laughter from a corner booth jolted him.

"And it's factual? It all checks out?"

"Most definitely." Harrison wiped his mouth with his sleeve. He had forgotten how good it felt to get drunk.

"Then just run it."

"Oh, no." He wagged his head. "That's not how I work. Wouldn't be right." *At least not in this case.* He could barely hear his own voice—or his conscience—over the buzz of the other patrons.

"Bartender—another drink." The stranger slid the glass, and his stool, closer to Harrison. "This one's on me. Now, don't you hate to let a story like that go to waste? Why don't you just tell me, and I'll let you know what I think of it. Just between us, two bums at the bar. It'll go no further."

Harrison cocked his head at his new friend and clapped him on the shoulder. "I think I will. I think . . . I will. There is a woman in Gettysburg—no two. And they're related. But only one of 'em knowzit, see?"

Whiskey loosened his tongue and untethered him from suspicion. Somehow, between waves of nausea from too much drink, Harrison spilled the story until every last detail had sloshed out.

"Whaddya think?" he asked at the end, now drowsy from the heat and alcohol. "Good story?"

"Very." Smiling, the stranger stood and tugged his bowler hat down on his head.

Harrison fumbled in his pocket for a moment. "Thanks for the drinks, old chap. Here's my card."

The stranger looked at it and smiled broadly. "*Philadelphia Inquirer*! Excellent. And here, good fellow, is mine." Winking, he dropped his card into Harrison's empty glass and disappeared into the crowd.

Harrison leaned over to fish it out, and blinked at his puffy-eyed reflection in the polished cherry wood bar. He should have stopped drinking after the first shot. *Or before it.* Shaking his head, he plucked up the card and squinted at the tiny print swimming before him. *Lorenzo J. Ellis. Reporter, New York Times.*

Suddenly, he was wide awake. Still rubbery with drink, he slammed his cash down on the bar and stumbled toward the door. Harrison was about to be sick.

Holloway Farm
Thursday, July 30, 1863

Pearl-grey mist draped Holloway Farm in muffled quiet as Silas Ford hopped with his crutch to the porch. His mind was just as clouded, but he hoped working with his hands would clear away the haze.

Easing himself into the velvet armchair, he picked up the crutch he had been working on yesterday for another amputee and began sanding the edges. He had barely seen Liberty in the last three days, but that didn't keep her from his mind. Guilt cinched his gut every time he remembered kissing her.

But she kissed back. He sanded the crutch harder, back and forth, until mahogany dust flavored the cool, misty air. Back and forth went his thoughts, from *My mother was right about me* to *I am not my father.* Memories, long stifled, now emerged from the fog.

His father's slave Psyche had come to him, she said, for help. In a surreal twist of the biblical story, she offered herself to him like Potiphar's wife. Only seventeen years old, it took all his strength to look away.

"Please," she had said. "I need to have a baby. Please help me." If she were with child, she told him, his father would give her more food and shorter hours in the field. And, at least for a few months, his father's desire for her would die away. She would have some respite from being his special pet.

Silas had refused, ordered her to put her clothes back on. "Why don't you take a husband?"

"I want a white man's child," she said.

He understood then, that she wanted to bleach her line by him. He would not do it. As he sent her away, he vowed to help in a different way. "I can fix this," he told her.

But he had not locked the door to his chamber. He'd gone to bed earlier than usual that night, and when he awoke, head pounding, in the small hours of the night, Psyche was in his arms.

"Thank you," she whispered.

The encounter remained fogged in his mind even to this day, but even the suggestion of what had taken place choked him with guilt.

Then, after he had been lashed in her place years later by his own father's hand, his mother's words had hurt him even worse. "You're just like your father. I see the way you looked at her. Did you have your way with her too, you and your father both?"

"No!" Her words ripped open new wounds. "I would have done the same for you if it was your back under the lash. I would protect you, Mother."

"But you haven't. Your father has lashed me in so many ways, and you've done nothing. You know nothing of true love, only degraded lust.

404

You fool! Did you not even notice that Psyche is your half-sister?"

Mute with horror, Silas could not respond.

"You are *just* like your father."

She was right. Fear coated him like molasses—dark, sticky, impossible to remove. Perhaps, Silas thought now as he sanded the crutch, he saw the duel as a chance to destroy the part of himself that resembled his father. The part that yearned for what was not his to take.

Silas turned the crutch and sanded another corner. *It didn't work.* Though Silas had sworn off women as penance for his sins, he could not deny that he yearned now for Liberty. *But I'm a reprobate. I don't deserve her.*

"Good morning, Silas." Dr. O'Leary materialized through the fog, freshly shaven and smelling of castile soap and bay rum. "You're going to sand that crutch down to a toothpick if you're not careful. Something on your mind?"

Silas glanced up. "Do you believe people can change, doctor?"

"Quite a question for six-thirty in the morning." He yawned as he leaned against the railing. "But yes, I do. People can change, because God can change us. 'Remember ye not the former things, neither consider the things of old. Behold, I will do a new thing; now it shall spring forth; shall ye not know it? I will even make a way in the wilderness, and rivers in the desert.' From the book of Isaiah."

Silas's hand stilled on the crutch as the words settled into his spirit. He was listening.

Dr. O'Leary bent over the railing and looked at the thornbush that once shone bright with Liberty's yellow roses. "Do you see this bush? It looks like a briar patch now, without the blooms and leaves. Just thorns. But when I look carefully, I can see new growth. Little buds of green are starting to appear, and that tells me that no matter what happened to this bush on the outside, it is still the same on the inside. In a matter of time, we'll be smelling the roses once more. That's what God does for us, too. Where we think there is a wasteland, He will bring new life. Now sometimes, He prunes us back Himself."

"If God is in the business of pruning, I've been lopped off at the ground."

Dr. O'Leary chuckled. "Maybe. But He only cuts off what is dead so we can grow with more vibrancy and bear more fruit. Allowing the diseased part of us to remain would only infect our entire being with spiritual poison. He cares too much about our souls to let that happen. Make sense?"

Silas looked at his stump and nodded. Yes, it made perfect sense.

"Remember not the former things. God is doing a new thing in you."

"I hope you're right, doctor. I've been running from 'the former things' for years. But I can't run anymore." He rapped his knuckles on the crutch.

Dr. O'Leary smiled. "Have you considered that you are, at this very moment, right where God wants you to be? It's time to stop running, Silas, and watch as God paves a new path for you. I'm done preaching now, I promise." He winked.

Silas chuckled. "I always did like a good sermon."

"I know. "

"Ah, so you did read my letter, didn't you?"

Dr. O'Leary shrugged. "Not every word, but my gaze did catch on mention of the seminary. It's none of my business, son, but you don't have to abandon that dream."

"After what I've done? I beg to differ."

"Oh come now. God's instruments are never perfect. If we experienced no pain in our own lives, had no need for healing, we would be tragically irrelevant to the rest of the world. Preaching grace and forgiveness falls flat if we are not desperate for it ourselves."

Silas received his words like parched earth receives the rain. *God, do a new thing in me, he prayed. Make rivers in the desert of my soul.* He studied the doctor before him. "What about you? Didn't you ever want to be a pastor?"

"I considered it strongly, yes. But the call to medicine was stronger. And lucky for all of us, no matter our occupation, we can still minister to God's people." Dr. O'Leary walked over to Silas and squeezed his shoulder. "And now, I best begin my rounds."

"Yes, of course." He looked east toward Seminary Ridge. "The sun will be up soon."

"Oh, the sun has been there for some time." The doctor smiled. "You just couldn't see it through the fog."

A bitter aroma twisted into Liberty's nose, yanking her out of her sleep.

"Rise and shine." Her blonde hair almost white in the sunshine, Myrtle offered a steaming cup of coffee, as she had every morning this week since Tuesday.

It never tasted quite right when Myrtle made it, but she was grateful for the gesture, and always forced it down, knowing it pleased Myrtle. She would hate to waste the coffee no matter how it tasted, considering it was donated by the Sanitary Commission. The patients, she knew, were incredibly grateful to have it.

The tin cup nearly burned Liberty's hands as she sipped the brew and tried not to wince. It really did taste awful. But at least Myrtle was trying.

One more timid sip, and Liberty didn't think she could choke it down. Her stomach revolted.

"I'll finish it later, thank you." She handed it back to Myrtle, expecting to see disappointment written on her face. It wasn't there.

"Not feeling well this morning?"

She didn't. "It's nothing." Liberty clenched her jaw against the rising swell of bile and waited until it subsided. "You may go."

Myrtle stayed and watched her.

"Do you mind?" Liberty still needed to use the chamber pot. "A little privacy would be nice."

With Myrtle now gone, Libbie attended to her meager toilette routine and left the hollowed out shell of her bedroom.

She clutched the banister at the top of the stairs while Major paced a flight beneath her, his claws tapping incessantly on the hardwood floor. With his one good eye, he looked up at her, as if to ask if she was coming.

She wasn't. Pain radiated from her middle to the ends of her arms and legs until she sat on the stairs and waited for it to pass. She was so tired. But the sun was up, she had work to do. She did not have time to be tired.

A fist slammed in the front door. "Liberty Holloway! Miss Holloway? Are you in there? Open up, please."

She glanced at the grandfather clock in the hallway and gasped. Nine-thirty in the morning! Had she really slept that long? She forced herself down the steps.

Swinging wide the door, Liberty found herself confronted by Henry Stahle, editor of the *Gettysburg Compiler*, and Geraldine Bennett, from the Ladies Union Relief Society, her arms folded across her chest, and face folded into a scowl.

"Is it true?" asked Mr. Stahle. He waved a paper in her face, and she pressed a hand to her head.

"Is what true?" In the edges of her vision, she saw Dr. O'Leary, Myrtle, Isaac, and Silas approaching.

"What's all the hubbub?" asked Dr. O'Leary.

"Liberty Holloway, that's what," said Geraldine, her voice triumphant. "Or is that even your real name?"

"What? I don't understand." Her vision swayed.

"Then maybe you should catch up on the news!"

The *New York Times* waved under her nose then. "I get all the major papers. It's how I know what to print in ours," said Stahle. "Imagine my surprise, however, to find a local girl and her mother as a big story on page three! Why didn't you let us have the story first?"

"You know I don't have a mother." Liberty's knees buckled. Dr. O'Leary caught her arm and guided her to sit in the armchair at Silas's workbench.

"What are they talking about?" she whispered, holding her head in her hands. Their voices clanged against her ears, hammered on her skull.

Dr. O'Leary took her pulse, felt her forehead, studied her eyes. "You're not well."

Mr. Stahle pressed closer, but Silas blocked his

path. "The lady isn't well, sir." His voice was low, but firm.

"Aha, let me see, you must be . . ." Stahle skimmed his finger over the newsprint. "Silas Ford, Rebel wounded, romantic suitor to the Union widow. Tell us, Miss Liberty, which man better tickles your fancy—Yankee or Rebel?" Liberty gasped, unable to believe her ears.

Silas snatched the paper from him and hurled it to the ground, pinning it there with his crutch. "Leave!"

"I need a comment from the Widow of Gettysburg for my story!"

"You don't." Silas's right hand held fast to his crutch, but his left hand clenched into a rock-hard weapon. A semicircle of patients, many of them one-armed, formed around the pair of intruders.

"Y'all bothering Miss Liberty here?" It was Fitz. "Well, this here is our hospital, and that gal there done been takin' good care of us. We surely would take offense if you was bothering her."

"We don't want any trouble," said Mr. Stahle.

The patients pressed in around the editor and a wide-eyed Geraldine. "Good! Then you won't mind leaving. Otherwise I just might mistake you for a nurse and ask you to change my bandages." Fitz began unwrapping his stump below his shoulder. "Mmmm . . . do you smell that? What do you think, gangrene? Tasty! Hope it's not contagious!" Cackling mercilessly, he sidled up to Geraldine, sending her shrieking back to the horse and buggy. Mr. Stahle followed, so as not to lose his ride.

Dust billowed up from the lane as they pounded back to the road. "We will be back, Miss Holloway!" Mr. Stahle shouted. "And you can bet your buttons we won't be the only paper after you, either!"

Liberty's head pounded. "Can someone please tell me what this is all about?"

The doctor urged everyone away, except for Silas, who leaned on the railing in front of her, his eyes holding hers.

"Dr. O'Leary, would you tell me what the article says?" There was no way she could focus her eyes on the print right now.

He picked up the *Times*, dusted it off and skimmed it, brow furrowing. He cleared his throat, pulled his collar away from his neck. "It says that Bella Jamison is the mulatto daughter of her slave mother and the mother's white overseer."

"Why would they print that in the *New York Times*?"

"Apparently, the plantation on which she was born and raised was outside Darien, Georgia. The town the 54th Massachusetts regiment raided in June. Did you know her husband is in the 54th?"

Liberty nodded. "Well, that's interesting, but I don't see why it's in a New York paper."

"There was a battle at Fort Wagner on Saturday, and her husband was wounded."

"Is it serious?"

"Doesn't say. The focus really isn't on him, Miss Holloway." He licked his lips and swallowed. Liberty glanced at Silas, whose gaze was fixed on the doctor. "Apparently there was a patient here on which Dr. Stephens operated, a Lt. Pierce Butler Holmes. He recognized Bella as she held the light. Is that correct?"

"He did say something like that, but he was raving mad with chloroform at the time."

"And is it also true that he said something about you?" He winced.

And she remembered. "He said I was the very likeness of Ross someone."

"Roswell King Jr.?"

"That's it." Goosebumps pimpled her flesh. "But he said that about Bella, too. That we were twins or something. I tell you, he was not in his right mind."

"Yes, well . . . One can't believe everything one reads in the paper, now can one?"

He wasn't telling her something. She extended her hand for the paper, and he reluctantly gave it to her. She scanned.

Liberty Holloway . . . daughter of Bella Jamison . . .

"What?" Liberty's headache sharpened, but she read further.

Liberty Holloway . . . Union widow . . . offered home as a Confederate field hospital at Gettysburg "Offered? Sacrificed would be more like it."

. . . developing romance with Rebel soldier . . . "Where is this coming from?"

. . . even though she is one-quarter black and the illegitimate daughter of a former slave and her overseer.

She let the paper fall and looked at Silas. His chiseled face was taut with suspense, his green eyes piercing hers. "It says," her voice squeaked, "that Bella is my mother. But I have no mother. And Bella has no children."

You're right, Miss Liberty. I have no children.

"Is it possible, you could be mistaken?" the doctor asked quietly. "Wouldn't it be grand to have a mother after all?"

"But I don't! My mother didn't want me, didn't love me. And now she's dead."

Your mother loves you.

"Could it be that she loved you more than you could possibly fathom? That she would rather be assured of your comfort than of your affection toward her?"

Hear me, child. Your mother loved you.

"My comfort? Growing up as an orphan was anything but comfortable!"

Silas's face paled. His knuckles were as white as the railing he gripped. "Do you know what it means to live in fear of being enslaved?"

"No."

"Then you were comfortable." Silas raised his eyes to meet hers. "You are free."

"So is she."

He shook his head. "Trust me. It isn't the same."

A horrible idea seized her, then. "Aunt Helen said my mother used me to try to gain security from my father. Did Bella try to use my father to gain her own freedom? Is that why she had me?"

Silas pinched the bridge of his nose before rubbing his hand over his jaw. "I don't know, Liberty. Not necessarily. It could be that your father used her. And that's the fate she wanted to protect you from."

Liberty reeled as Bella's words played back to her: *What about Silas? Did he help himself to the slaves too, to satisfy his lust, free of consequences?*

It had made no sense at the time. Bella's tears, her accusations, her conclusions. But what if . . . God help her . . . what if it was all true? Though Silas and Dr. O'Leary remained with her, the magnitude of this revelation crowded them from her mind. Her head sank into her hands as she waded through her tangled thoughts. *Me. One-quarter Negro. I'm colored?* The fact that her skin was golden white did not negate the term. *My grandmother was a slave,* she told herself, but her brain struggled to comprehend. *My mother was a slave!*

415

She had always hated slavery, always believed Negroes should be free. But did she truly believe they were equal to whites? In value, intelligence, moral capacity? If she had, surely it would not bother her so much to now learn of her heritage. *Remember your place.* Her own voice rang in her ears. *But I said that only as an employer to the hired help, nothing more or less than that.* The logic did not satisfy her conscience. *Was I also reminding her of the shade of her skin?*

Liberty's head swam. Her father wasn't who she thought he was, either. He wasn't just a slave owner, as she once believed—although that had been hard enough to accept. He was a plantation overseer, and one who bedded and abused women who stood no chance against him, however hard they may have tried. Women like Bella. *Women like me.* This was also her heritage. Did her father's blood war against her mother's blood within her? Was her father's inheritance to her the conviction that colored skin was a mark of inferiority? That she herself was inferior, too?

Liberty lifted her head and met Silas's gaze. His features were stony, and she could feel her own hardening to match. If the story was true, they had more in common than they had known. The sins of their fathers. But while Silas was merely witness to his father's wickedness, Liberty was the fruit of sin itself, a mix of master and slave, power and bondage, white and black. In this, they were as far apart as east from west.

She broke from his gaze and pushed herself up to stand. "I have to find Bella."

"You are not well enough." Dr. O'Leary laid a hand on her shoulder. "Rest first, and then I'll let you borrow my horse and wagon."

"Rest? After this? I don't think I'll be able to sleep for days!"

"I'll not allow you to leave in this condition. Come, I'll give you some laudanum, and you can rest. Just for a spell. Then you can go find Bella."

Silas Ford was upset. Liberty upset him again. Myrtle saw it from where she stood behind a hickory tree. She knew it was right to hide there, within earshot, when Dr. O'Leary ordered everyone away. She had heard almost everything.

Then, right after the doctor led Liberty upstairs to her room, she saw Silas sniff and rub his eyes as he left the porch. That's what men did when they were sad. Myrtle thought she could hear her own heart breaking into pieces for him. She knew what it was like to be sad, to cry quietly when no one else was watching.

Myrtle Henderson was watching. It was Liberty's fault, she knew it. She cast a spell on him. Then she slapped him. *And now we learn she isn't such a high and mighty mistress after all. She isn't even all white, like me.* Yet Liberty

417

had talked down to Myrtle, had embarrassed her and ordered her around like she was a mistress to be reckoned with.

She wasn't. She was black. Like her papa always said, one drop of mud will taint the whole pail of milk. The article said Bella was a mulatto woman—that meant half black. And Liberty was her daughter, so that made Liberty colored, too. Might as well be black as pitch. And black folks did not order white folks around the way Liberty bossed Myrtle. They certainly did not marry white folks. That was against the law.

Was that what her mama had tried to do? Myrtle wasn't close enough to the porch to hear every word of the conversation, but from what she gathered, Liberty came from a line of slaves who used their masters to lighten their babies' skin colors. *How did they do that?* Maybe they cast spells.

Like Liberty had done to Silas. Slowly, comprehension spread through Myrtle until her whole being was awakened to the danger. Myrtle Henderson had been put in charge of Silas Ford's care once. She would not abandon him in his hour of need now. She had to break the spell, herself. But how?

So far, making Liberty's coffee with unboiled, contaminated water had not entirely solved her problem. Though perhaps a little sick, Liberty was still alive, and still hurting Silas Ford. Poisoning her was not working fast enough. She had to find another way.

Myrtle plunged her hand into her apron pocket and fondled the headless Dolly. That was it. That was the answer. *I have to break Liberty.*

She knew exactly how.

Myrtle had not intended to eavesdrop the other day when she was collecting soiled linens at the barn. The doctors were amputating on a patient whose stump had turned gangrenous. Dr. Stephens shouted at Dr. O'Leary to take away the chloroform, that too much would kill, and she could not help hearing. She had stood by while they discussed the matter, Dr. Stephens showing Dr. O'Leary how to use his small metal device instead of the towel folded into a cone that Dr. O'Leary's manual said to use. She watched and she learned.

Now Dr. O'Leary was upstairs putting Liberty to sleep. Myrtle smiled when she spied his leather bag still on the porch. *Perfect.* It was time for Liberty to go to sleep, and never wake up. They would blame it on the laudanum, like they blamed Silas's sickness on the opium. *Too much medicine can kill.* Someone might even call it tragic, but Myrtle knew the truth. She was doing Silas a favor. He would thank her for saving him. He might even kiss her.

Myrtle slinked up to the bag, fished out a tin canister of chloroform and the small towel, and stuffed them in her apron pockets. Dr. O'Leary emerged from the house, walked off with his kit without so much as a how-do-you-do, and Myrtle climbed the stairs.

She poked her head in the room and found Liberty sitting up on her bed, doing needlework. Her heart sank.

"I heard you were supposed to take a nap," she said.

Liberty looked up. "From whom?"

Myrtle blinked. "The doctor, on his way out." It was not a very big lie.

"Yes, well, it will take a few minutes before the laudanum takes effect. I can't just lie here, or I'll go crazy. Stitching calms me down. The only problem is, my hands are shaking so my stitches aren't all perfect." She reached into the basket for her scissors. "Can't find my ripper . . ."

Myrtle nodded, bit her lip.

"Myrtle, would you mind reading to me? To help take my mind off . . ." her voice trailed away. "Here, sit on the edge of the bed." There was no other chair on the room.

Liberty handed her a book. *Les Miserables.* "I've marked the page where I left off reading, a lifetime ago, it seems."

Myrtle opened it and began reading. "You thought me ugly, didn't you?" She stopped. The words seemed to come straight from her heart, but they were there, printed on the page. "What's this about?"

Liberty's needle dove in and out of a piece of fabric as she explained. "A girl named Éponine— that's who just spoke—loves a man named Marius, but Marius loves a woman named Cosette." Myrtle listened closely as Liberty explained. "It's quite heartbreaking, really. And at this point in the story, there is a battle, and Marius was in danger, so Éponine blocked the bullet with her own body. I love this character."

"Why?"

Liberty yawned. "Éponine had a rough life, but she is softened by love. You wonder, as you read, whether that love will end in jealousy that destroys, or sacrifice that heals. Go on, please."

Myrtle read on, not quite understanding everything, but fully comprehending one thing. Éponine was a hero. Though she was not loved, she had sacrificed for the man she loved.

She turned the page and continued. " 'Promise to give me a kiss on my brow when I am dead.— I shall feel it.' She dropped her head again on Marius' knees, and her eyelids closed. He thought the poor soul had departed. Éponine remained motionless. All at once, at the very moment when Marius fancied her asleep forever, she slowly opened her eyes in which appeared the somber profundity of death, and said to him in a tone whose sweetness seemed already to proceed from another world:—'And by the way, Monsieur Marius, I believe that I was a little bit in love with you.' She tried to smile once more and expired."

Tears filled Myrtle's eyes as she finished the chapter. Liberty's hands stilled, and her eyelids fluttered as she lay down. Myrtle took the needle, cloth, and scissors from her lap and placed them back in the sewing basket. *Soon,* she thought as she wiped her runny nose, *soon Liberty will sleep forever.*

But first—Myrtle turned one more page in the book and read: "Marius kept his promise. He dropped a kiss on that livid brow, where the icy perspiration stood in beads."

He kissed her.

Would Silas kiss Myrtle if he knew she had killed Liberty? The whisper of her conscience told her no. *But Liberty deceived him! Liberty is colored, and Silas is a Southern white man.* They couldn't be together, it wasn't allowed! Removing Liberty from Silas's life would be helping him, even if he didn't realize it.

But would he kiss her for it?

Don't keep her away, I want to see her! Silas's voice sounded in her ears. But that was before he knew the truth about who she was.

Myrtle would help Silas. This was the help he needed now.

A faint snore wheezed through Liberty's nose. Myrtle's heart beat faster. She licked her lips as she uncorked the chloroform tin and rolled the towel into a cone shape. *But how much chloroform did they put on?* She hadn't seen. Myrtle tipped the tin and let the clear liquid flow out in a braided trickle, soaking the towel with two or three ounces. She hoped it was enough. Her heartbeat pounded in her ears as she corked the tin.

Footsteps thumped on the staircase, and Myrtle jolted. Could she chloroform Liberty and flee the room before anyone entered?

She couldn't. She needed more time.

"Myrtle?" A whispered call, from Dr. O'Leary. "Are you up here?"

Her large hands fumbling, Myrtle tucked the chloroform and towel in Liberty's sewing basket and shoved it under the bed with her foot.

The door squeaked open. "There you are. I'm looking for my chloroform. Have you seen it?"

Myrtle's tongue cleaved to the roof of her mouth. Her head twitched.

Dr. O'Leary rubbed the back of his neck and muttered something to himself. "Well, come now. Let her rest."

Myrtle hesitated.

But Dr. O'Leary was frowning at her. She didn't like it when people frowned at her. "Come, Myrtle. Now."

She scuttled after him out the door, and he closed it on her opportunity.

Nerves buzzing like the flies near her patients, Liberty rapped her knuckles on the door at 319

South Washington Street, and tried to imagine what she would say when Bella opened the door. Soggy heat wrapped around her like a used towel, until sweat soaked her already soiled dress. She knocked again, and looked down at her Sunday best, now her everyday worst. Rumpled, stained, limp. She looked like a wilted tulip trampled in the mud, and felt like it too.

Still no answer. Liberty opened one of the shutters and peered in through the window. There was a book lying on the kitchen table. She could just read the title on the cover. *Journal of a Residence on a Georgian Plantation.*

She went back to the door and pounded harder. "Bella? Please let me in, if you're in there!"

An older woman Liberty recognized as the Fosters' washerwoman came up to her then. "Bella's gone, baby. Left four days ago with some gentleman from Philadelphia."

The reporter from Philadelphia? "I need to get in, I need to see that book."

"Why?" Her tone was not sharp. Why indeed?

"I think there may be some information in it about my—my—Bella." Her head still ached.

"Your Bella?" She smiled. "And who are you?"

"Liberty Holloway. Bella is my—" *Hired help. Mother?* Somehow, she could not bring herself to complete the sentence.

"I know who Bella is, child. And I know who you are too."

"You do?"

She nodded, dark eyes twinkling. "You are special to Bella. And somehow I know, that if she were home, she would fling open that door to you and welcome you in to her table for a cup of tea, like she always does for me."

Remembering her manners, Liberty extended a hand. "I don't believe we've properly met."

The woman grasped it with her gnarled hand. "You can call me Aunt Hester. Everyone does. Now. Let me see if I can help you out, baby."

She walked around to the back of the house and felt around a window until her fingers pulled a key from a deep notch in a sill. Liberty stood back while Aunt Hester jiggled the key in the back door and swung it wide for Liberty.

"I'll come by and check on you in a little bit to see how you're getting along. But for now I best get back to my laundry while the sun still shines."

And Liberty stood in Bella's house for the first time in her life, alone. It was tidy, but not clean at the moment. Dust swirled in the sunbeams and layered the furniture, confirming that Bella had not been here in days.

Fatigue settled on Liberty. She sagged into a chair at the small kitchen table and opened Fanny Kemble's *Journal*, ashamed that she had never wondered much about Bella's life prior to Gettysburg.

As she began reading the book, she was transported to a time and place completely foreign to her. Deeper and deeper she sunk into the text. Then she saw it—the first mention of Bella, marked by the presence of Harrison's card.

Daphne and Bella, twin sisters. Mulatto, about twelve years old, although neither of them know their birthday. The only living children of Judy. Five siblings in the grave. Bella asked me to teach her to read. It is illegal for her to read, and just as illegal for me to teach her. But I believe I shall do it. They also begged for flannel, the red and cream pinstripe being an especial favorite.

Liberty stopped. The flannel patch of her baby quilt, now part of Silas's crutch, grew bright in her mind. She pressed a hand to her forehead and flipped through a few more pages.

Judy told me a miserable story of her former experiences on the plantation under Mr. K—'s overseership. It seems that Bella and Daphne were born of Mr. K—, who forced her, flogged her severely for having resisted him, and then sent her off, as a further punishment, to Five Pound—a horrible swamp in a remote corner of the estate, to which the slaves are sometimes banished for such offences as are not sufficiently atoned for by the lash.

Liberty put down the book. Was this Judy her own grandmother? She could not fathom such an experience, and slowly, Bella's resistance to Silas fell into place.

Later in the journal, Liberty read that not only was Judy forced and flogged by Roswell King Jr., but that after she bore his children, his wife came to the hospital, flogged her again, and sent her back to Five Pound. Could such horrific accounts be believed?

As if in anticipation of Liberty's reaction, Fanny Kemble had written: *I make no comment on these terrible stories, and tell them to you as nearly as possible in the perfectly plain unvarnished manner in which they are told to me. I do not wish to add to, or perhaps I ought to say take away from, the effect of such narrations by amplifying the simple horror and misery of their bare details.*

This was the life Bella had escaped. Chills swept over Liberty's skin.

But when she read the beginning of the next chapter, she thought she was going to be sick.

Found Bella, Judy's girl, near death on the floor of the hospital today. She had taken a knife with which she sought to defend her mother against Mr. K— last week, and he had used it to gash her neck instead, then flogged her to within an inch of life. I have sent for Mr. Holmes, the Darien town physician immediately. Keep in mind, the girl is twelve years old. I fear that by next year, Mr. K— will drag her into his bed as well.

He had gashed Bella's neck? But Liberty had never seen a scar.

She had never seen her neck.

In an entry dated some months later: *Young Bella is not safe from Mr. K—. He has taken her, though she fights, to his bed. She bears new scars for every time. Thank goodness her menses has not yet begun. I have seen girls of fourteen with babies of their ow—*

Enough! Liberty shoved the book away from her and let it thud to the floor. She buried her face in her arms as the voices of Aunt Helen and Bella clashed together in her mind, along with the words of Lt. Pierce Butler Holmes, who had called Liberty the very likeness of Roswell King Jr. Her heart bled as the lines of the *Journal* resounded in her spirit. She wept for Bella, for Judy, for untold numbers of women whose stories had never been recorded. She wept because she had never once asked Bella what her life was like before she knew her, had not fully considered the agony the last month's ordeal must have meant to her.

She wept.

The door creaked on its hinges, and Liberty looked up to find Aunt Hester standing over her. In an instant, Aunt Hester wrapped her arms around Libbie, in a lye soap-scented squeeze. Liberty melted into it, wet Aunt Hester's shoulder with her tears.

"There, there, honey child," she cooed. "You

found what you was lookin' for, didn't you now? There, there. You can tell me about it."

Liberty did. Aunt Hester's face crinkled as she nodded throughout the story, peppering it with "That's just so," and "That's the way it was, too."

"But Aunt Hester, could Bella be my mother? Is this my heritage, too?"

A sad smile pushed the wrinkles back on Aunt Liz's face. "She's never told me so. But if Bella Jamison is your mama, you can be sure of one thing. She would have to love you more than life itself to do what she did for you. Don't you see that, child? This—" She thumped her knuckles on the journal. "This is what she protected you from. The child of a slave is born a slave, even if the father is free and white. Bella didn't want any child of hers to have any kind of life like she knew. So she gave you up, like Moses's mama in the Bible. She thought it was better you didn't know."

Liberty's head spun. *Born a slave?* She pushed back from the table and began to rise. Her legs didn't hold her, and she stumbled over the table.

"You sick? Lie down, child." Aunt Hester ushered her over to the couch in the front room.

"I'm s-s-so cold." Liberty's teeth chattered. "I'm freezing." Aunt Hester covered her with a quilt while mumbling about the sweltering heat. "Can I just wait here for a little bit? Maybe Bella will come home."

429

Aunt Hester left, and Bella did not come. Chilled with fever, Liberty clutched at the quilt to pull it tighter around her shoulders—and froze when her fingers felt a familiar patch of flannel. Holding the quilt up to the light that slanted through the shutters, a piece of red and cream pinstripe shone back at her. At that moment, Liberty knew. This patch, and the one on her own quilt, had been cut from the same cloth.

Just like her and Bella.

Chapter Twenty

Beaufort, South Carolina
Friday, July 31, 1863

A grove of live oaks, dripping with moss and shadow, crowded down a grassy bank as if to dip their giant toes in the river that curved around Beaufort in a watery embrace. Waves of wet heat washed over Bella as she and Harrison turned onto Church Street, each one triggering memories of her childhood in the South.

"Are you ready?" Harrison mopped his damp forehead with his handkerchief and nodded toward the Episcopal Church, now serving as hospital for the 54th Massachussetts. The white building was nearly blinding in its sunlit brilliance, while in the cemetery before it, amputations were carried out on tables made from tombstones. Fanning herself with a palmetto branch, Bella averted her gaze from the pile of black limbs as Harrison escorted her through the front door.

Inside, chandeliers hung high over pews packed with men. It was a better hospital than the barn at Holloway Farm, but wooden benches did not make soft beds. Moans bounced between the walls and high ceiling of the sanctuary like discordant organ notes. Though the air was heavy with the smell of injury, Bella's senses had mercifully dulled to it. A sidelong glance at Harrison told her he was not so lucky.

"I can find him on my own." She waved Harrison away. "I'll find you outside when I'm done." With a tug on his collar and weak smile, he stepped outside again.

Slowly, Bella walked down the center aisle, craning her neck as she turned right and left in search of her husband, until she found him. Heart in her throat, she squeezed between the pews and sidled closer, finally kneeling by his side.

"Abraham? It's me, Bella." After so many weeks without communication, she felt like reintro-ducing herself.

He awoke. "Bella? You're here?" He reached out and grasped her hand, brought it to his cracked lips and kissed it. "I heard about the battle at Gettysburg. You're all right?"

She fanned him with the palmetto branch. "I'm

all right." It was such a relative term. But a crowded church hospital in South Carolina was not the place to share the details of her recent ordeal. Anyone who overheard her say she worked at a Confederate field hospital would not be likely to be sympathetic. "How do you fare?"

"It's nothing, a wound in the thigh, but it will heal. How did you know, how did you get here?"

"It was in the papers, of course. A reporter brought me here to find you. Will you come home now?" Cicadas thrummed through the open windows as she waited for his answer.

"No. I can still fight."

"For pay?" She had not intended to sound so shrill. But she had been without his support for months, and it wasn't getting any easier to live on the income from her employers. She may not even have any left by the time she got home after this trip.

"For honor."

Her hand stilled for a moment. "What does that even mean, Abraham? The army feeds you, but it doesn't feed me. I'm hungry. Do you hear me?"

Surprise—disappointment in Bella, she guessed —played across his features, and she was ashamed that their reunion had grown bitter so quickly. "They offered us pay, but it wasn't what we agreed to. They said they'd pay us thirteen dollars a month, same as the white soldiers. Now they say they'll give us ten, but they'll take three dollars out for uniforms. Seven dollars—it's almost half-pay."

"And seven dollars more than nothing! Take the money, Abraham, I would take it if I could."

His face knotted in frustration. "Don't you get it? We gotta fight on equal terms with the white soldiers or they'll only think of us as hired labor. We have to help win this war or we'll never be granted full citizenship. We're going to hold out and keep fighting until they give us what they promised us. Equal pay."

Tears choked Bella. "How many men did the 54th lose at Fort Wagner, Abraham?"

He looked away.

"Two hundred ninety-seven casualties out of six hundred men. You were cut to pieces, Abraham, and now you're telling me not only did you do it for free once, but you'd do it for free again. Now tell me how that makes a lick of sense to you."

"We did more than just lose men, Bella," he growled, and her heart ached that they spent their time arguing. "We proved that black men fight. Black men have honor. We lost men because we threw ourselves into the fray, willing to sacrifice all for our country, and for the freedom of colored folks everywhere. After the raid at Darien, people thought colored troops were common looters, undeserving of any respect. And I can see why. But now we've shown them we deserve a place in this country alongside the white men. Do you see?"

She saw. But she was still hungry. "I didn't come here to fight, Abe. I came because I thought you might want me here."

"You know I'm glad to see you. But I'm not coming home yet, if that's what you're after. Go home, Bella."

Bella pressed her lips into a line, felt her nostrils flare as she stood up and looked out over the pews. "Abraham, is that a woman I see?"

"Rosalie, yes."

"What happened to her?"

"She was shot in the shoulder by a white Union officer for getting between him and her daughter."

Bella's hackles rose. "What did you say?"

"Rosalie and her daughter are former slaves and serve with the colored nurses and laundresses at the Union general hospital. An officer tried to take her daughter to his bed, and she fought him. He shot her for it, and she is still recovering."

"A Yankee did that," she repeated, as much to herself as to Abraham.

"Just so."

"Were there no consequences for the man?"

"Not one. Other officers have the same idea. Do you see now, Bella, why we fight? Not just to defeat the South, but to defeat the idea everywhere that colored people are less valuable and less worthy of respect than whites."

Bella was still looking at Rosalie, motionless in

434

her bed, shot for trying to protect her daughter. That was a story fit for a newspaper.

And what had Bella done to protect Liberty? Dressed down a reporter. But Liberty was still alone in a sea of Southern men, when even the Northern ones could not be trusted.

Bella lingered by Abraham's side a while longer, forcing herself to speak of pleasant things when the very unpleasant clamored for her attention. When she could see he needed to rest, they said goodbye, and Bella stepped back outside, squinting into the sunshine.

Harrison approached her, his brown eyes dark, his carrot-colored hair matted to his head from wearing his hat. She joined him, and they left the cemetery together.

"Mr. Caldwell, I've got a story for you."

"Well, I am sorry to say, I have no paper."

Bella stopped walking. "What?"

"There was a letter from my editor at the Union headquarters at the Verdier House, probably arrived here about the same time we did. I've been sacked."

"Why?"

He cleared his throat. "Apparently, I've been scooped. That means someone else printed a story I was working on." He winced, and she knew.

"Take me home, Mr. Caldwell. On the next steamer north."

Holloway Farm
Friday, July 31, 1863

Silas sat in the armchair on the porch and stared blankly toward the road, barely noticing the crickets' song. Darkness coated him, inside and out.

He had fallen in love with a quadroon? *I don't know that for certain yet.* But his gut told him it was the truth. Psyche's face surged in his mind, the slave who wanted to carry a white man's child. His child. Silas rubbed his eyes with the heels of his hands. *No, no, Liberty would never do that. She had no idea what her heritage was. She wasn't even looking for a suitor.* Still, he could not shake the feeling that his developing relationship with Libbie had been wrong. According to the law, it was. Marriage between whites and Negroes was illegal. It couldn't be done. So whatever affection he might harbor for Liberty Holloway, he couldn't do a thing about it. He would not court her, because he could not marry her. The decision was out of his hands. Leaning back in his chair, he waited for the relief of conclusion to wash over him.

It didn't. Was it in his blood, this desire for a woman he couldn't have? It hadn't stopped his father, but Silas would not follow in those footsteps. He would respect the law. *But the law also sanctions slavery, and you don't support that.* His conscience pricked. *This is different,* he told himself. But how? The same principles drive both slavery and the law forbidding inter-racial marriage. *No, it's different. Somehow it's different.* Hoofbeats sounded on the road to Holloway Farm, and something told him that was the sound of his own heart, running away, again.

But these hoofbeats grew louder. The covered wagon turned into the lane, the horse ambled slowly toward the dooryard. It was Liberty. He had no idea how to behave around her now, and he guessed she felt the same about him. For now, it was enough for Silas to know she was safely home. Dawn was beginning to break over the ridge. In the pale grey light, he took up his crutch, ducked into the house, and nearly tripped over Isaac.

"Watch it!"

Silas had little patience for this fool. "Have you seen Dr. O'Leary yet this morning?"

"No." Isaac stretched and pushed himself up to his feet.

Silas looked over his shoulder. The wagon was nearly at the house. "Just tell him Liberty's back with his horse and wagon. She wasn't well when she left. I was hoping he could see to her, make sure she's all right."

"Suddenly not interested in her yourself anymore, are you, Silas?" His name sounded ridiculous on Isaac's lisping tongue. "Don't look

437

so shocked. Myrtle told me all about it. She heard the whole thing."

Silas's face grew warm. "Who else knows?"

Isaac shrugged. "Only everybody." He flashed a gap-toothed grin. "Looks like you weren't the only one trying to hide who you really were. But cheer up! Just because she's not good enough for the main course don't mean you can't have a little on the side!" He licked his lips.

In an instant, Silas's hand was clutching Isaac's puny throat, his fingers itching to squeeze ever tighter. Isaac's face grew red, tiny guttural noises escaping his mutilated mouth. Rage boiled in Silas like a long-dormant geyser blasting up through the surface, against all the men who thought women of any color were fair game for their own desires—against Isaac, against his father . . . against himself, for not being able to stop it.

Isaac sputtered in Silas's grip, the lump of his throat probing his sweaty palm. Then with a single well-placed kick, he knocked the crutch from under Silas. As Silas jerked to balance himself, Isaac twisted out of his grasp and rubbed his throat, coughing.

"You could have killed me!" he wheezed.

Shaken at how close he had come to killing another man, Silas picked up his crutch and threaded his way through the house to exit at the back door.

• • •

Crickets chirped all around Liberty as Isaac helped her out of the wagon. She had never meant to sleep so long at Bella's house, and had ridden straight home as soon as she awoke early that morning.

"Feeling better, Miss Holloway?" Isaac held her elbow as he guided her into the house.

"Not completely, to be honest. Do you think the doctors would mind if I just rest awhile longer in my own bed? Maybe just an hour or so."

"That would be just fine, I reckon. Most are still sleeping themselves. It would be a shame to wake them just yet, wouldn't it?"

Liberty nodded, but paused at the bottom of the stairs. She was worn out at the mere sight of them.

"Would you let me help you to your room?"

Normally she'd say no. But this time she was relieved to make an exception. With an arm around her waist, he helped support her to the top of the stairs. To her surprise, Major followed, his nails clicking on the hardwood stairs. He never followed her up the stairs, ever since Levi had died. A dart of pain shot up her neck as she looked over her shoulder at him. He whined.

At the top of the stairs, Liberty thanked Isaac and knelt to wrap her arms around Major's furry neck. "What is it, boy?" His good eye was clouded. He did not wag his tail.

"Come on, Miss Holloway, let's get you to bed."

"I can take it from here, Isaac, thank you. Your job is done."

He yanked her up by her arm. "Not quite."

Though he smiled at her, the look in his eyes turned Liberty's blood cold as he turned her toward her bedroom.

"Not you." Isaac shoved Major back with his boot before closing and locking the door.

The click of the latch blasted in Libbie's ears like cannon fire. Her mouth went dry, her knees weak, and she reached for the bedpost for support.

"That's right, Lib, just ease on back onto that bed." His lisping voice raked her skin.

Her heart pulsed in her throat as he approached.

"Now. We got ourselves a score to settle, don't we? You been ordering me around for weeks, making me call you Miss, acting like you own the place." Major whined from the other side of the door as he slid his paws beneath it.

"I do own this place, Isaac."

He sneered. "Where I come from, colored folks don't own property. And now I know, you got colored blood in you. Ain't that so? The whole world knows it now, too."

The hair on the back of her neck raised on end. Bella's face swam before her. *Rise up, Miss Liberty.* "This is my farm. I am the mistress here, and I order you to leave immediately." She lifted her chin, but her voice was less convincing than her words.

Isaac laughed. "A colored mistress!" He closed the distance between them, and she leaned back, pinned against the bedpost. Heat radiated in the mere inches separating their bodies. "You don't look colored, Lib. But I am only too happy to take that paper's word for it. It makes this all the more pleasant for me."

He reached for her collar button. She knocked his hand away, but he caught both her wrists and squeezed.

"Oh no, you don't. This has been a long time coming."

Rise up, Miss Liberty.

Her arms still held fast in Isaac's grip, she thrust her knee up sharply into his groin. His pain released her as a growl rumbled up out of his chest. Heart beating wildly against its cage, Liberty rolled over the bed and off the other side, then scrambled toward the door, her dress dragging on the floor behind her without the support of her hoops.

Isaac whirled around and stomped on the hem of her skirt. Her body jerked backwards, and he lunged for her waist.

"Stop!" she gasped. Weak from sickness, she had no spare strength to scream.

He ground her body against his, his eyes smoldering. "We're done talking. It's time to put you in your place." A feral smile curled his lips. "And to put me in mine."

Remember your place. How many times had Liberty said that to Bella?

Liberty shuddered as she saw her reflection in his eyes. She found Bella there too.

In a fraction of a second, understanding flashed through her as she saw what Bella must have seen in Roswell King Jr., what Judy had seen, right before they were taken. Three generations of fear surged through Liberty.

This was what Bella had wanted Liberty to be spared.

But I won't be, will I? Liberty felt herself weaken in Isaac's hold. She looked away from his flushed face as he pulled her back toward the naked mattress, the quilt and sheets being long gone. Dawn's light now streamed in through the open window. Without even the cover of darkness, Liberty already felt shamefully exposed.

Isaac thrust her onto the bed and began unbuckling his trousers. Tears slid down her face and filled her ears. This was the legacy she was born into. *Like mother, like daughter.*

No. Like the sun breaking through the fog, the truth dissolved the lie. *What did the journal say?* Bella never took this lying down. Neither did Judy. They fought it. Every single time.

Rise up.

Chest heaving with breath, she clenched her teeth and eyed again the distance to the door.

Lord, give me the strength!

• • •

Sun-sparked water streamed over Silas as he pulled himself up out of Willoughby Run. A month after the battle, he wasn't convinced it was safe to drink, but he couldn't help but take a dip in the water to cool down after he had nearly choked Isaac to death. It had been years since he had allowed his anger to overpower his will.

Scrubbing his body and hair with a towel, he put his clothes back on and planned his departure from Holloway Farm. *It's the right thing to do.* He could get around on his crutch as well as the doctor could hope. It was time to carve out a new life for himself. One that didn't involve the war. *Or Liberty.* He was sure she would not tolerate him now.

As Silas began making his way back to the farm, an odd-shaped patch of lush green grass caught his eye. He looked at the farm again, and memory locked into place. This was the spot where he had fallen, with the wound that changed his life forever. On one knee, he knelt, and grazed his palm over the silky blades. The blood he had spilled had fertilized the ground.

He closed his eyes to sift the profound from the ordinary, his ears filling with birdsong.

And barking.

Barking? But Major was deaf, and hadn't barked the entire time Silas had known him. Suspicion drew Silas toward the sound, all the way back to the farm.

In the dooryard, Major hurled himself against Silas and howled, pitifully. Silas bent to scratch him behind the ears, but Major wasn't interested.

Silas jerked his head toward Liberty's second story window in time to see Isaac slam her by the shoulders against her bedroom door. His heart nearly stopped. Her dress was ripped at the neckline, and her dark hair curled wildly about her shoulders.

Just because she's not good enough for the main course don't mean you can't have a little on the side!

They stumbled out of view. *I should never have let Isaac out of my sight! What have I done?* Silas's pulse throbbed in his head, his mind grappled for a solution. *I have to get there!* With one leg, by the time he made it up to the house and up the stairs, Isaac could have ravaged Liberty already. He slammed his crutch into the ground and yelled in frustration against his own impotence.

Fitz came trotting out from the barn. "What's the racket?"

"Isaac's got Liberty." He pointed to the window. "Fitz, I need a gun. Do you have one? Can you get me one?"

Fitz raised his eyebrows. "You fixin' to fire into the window? What if you miss?"

"Get me a gun! Now!" His voice was laced with rage meant for Isaac and all other men like him. Fitz ran off and in moments, brought back an Enfield rifle.

Without being told, Fitz held the crutch steady under Silas's arm as Silas ripped the top off the cartridge and poured powder and bullet into the barrel.

"You know you got one shot, don't you? You miss, we'll never see him through the window again."

He knew. He also knew that if he missed Isaac, he could very likely hit Liberty. "That's why I won't miss." He glanced up and saw a flash of her black hair again before it disappeared.

Silas drew the rammer and slammed it down the barrel.

Another thud sounded from the bedroom.

Metal rang on metal as he whipped the rammer out of the barrel and returned it to its holder.

"It don't look good, Silas. I don't see 'em."

Liberty cried out.

Silas primed the gun with a percussion cap and shouldered it, squinting down the barrel through the front site. Sweat and stream water stung his eyes. He blinked the moisture away and prayed for a good clean shot. Just one clean shot.

He waited.

And heard nothing.

• • •

It's over. I can't fight anymore.

Liberty squeezed her eyes shut against Isaac's face as he straddled her on the floor.

"Liberty!"

Her eyes popped open at the sound of Silas's voice.

"Rise up!"

Isaac looked up, and Liberty punched him in the jaw. He dropped on top of her. Her spine dug into the hardwood floor as she writhed and wormed to wiggle out from beneath him. She lunged toward the window, clawed at the window-sill, but he pulled her backwards across the floor.

Liberty kicked at his face, then spied the chamber pot she had never emptied from yester-day morning. She flung off the lid, grabbed it by the handles and sloshed her waste all over Isaac's face.

He shrieked and covered his eyes as she scrambled to her feet.

Dripping and reeking with stink, Isaac leapt up and slammed his body against hers, pinning her to the door once more. "Even if you'd blinded me, it wouldn't stop me. I know my way around in the dark." He planted both hands on the door, trapping her between them. "When will you just stop fighting, woman? You will never win!"

A rifle shot cracked the air and smashed into Isaac's arm. He screeched and crumbled to his knees as Liberty ran to the other side of the room. His arm bloomed with scarlet, and blood seeped into the floor, brightening the grain of the wood.

Liberty looked out the window but saw only the blue-grey fog of gunpowder dissolving in the air.

"They'll cut off my arm," Isaac moaned. "Please, please don't let them chop my arm off! I don't want to live like a freak for the rest of my life!" Holding his arm, he curled up into a fetal position near the bed.

Too late. Liberty slowly stepped back to the door, unlocked it, and turned the latch, expelling a sigh of relief.

Too soon. Isaac lashed out a leg and kicked the door closed. "You did this to me!" He plunged his hand in her sewing basket and whipped out the scissors, holding them like a knife.

Myrtle had seen the wagon return with Liberty this morning and hurried to make her coffee. Now that coffee spilled down the stairs as Myrtle hiked up her skirts and ran toward the bedroom. Something was wrong. Isaac was yelling. She could tell from his lisp.

Bursting into the room, she took in the scene in a second that seemed to last minutes. Liberty's hair curling about her shoulders, her dress ripped at the neckline, her face bruised, lip bleeding. Isaac with his trousers off, raising the scissors in the air, stumbling but mad with fury.

Isaac had attacked Liberty, perhaps just to have his way with her.

Let him.

"Help me!" Liberty breathed. The floor, slippery with blood, Isaac's arm soaked with crimson. Someone had shot Isaac through the window. *It had to be Silas.* But it hadn't stopped Isaac.

Myrtle would help Silas. In a span of time no longer than a breath, Myrtle decided to be a hero.

From behind, she punched Isaac where the bullet had entered his arm, then knocked the scissors out of his hand as he reeled in pain. She slammed him down on the floor and straddled him, pinning his arms across his chest.

"The chloroform." She nodded to the basket, and Liberty rushed to it, her eyes wide with surprise as she found the chloroform and cloth towel. Liberty knew exactly what to do with them. Folding the towel into a cone, she doused it with chloroform and scrambled back to Isaac. Myrtle snatched it from her and pressed it over his face.

Myrtle wanted to kill him herself. She wanted Silas to thank her, even if it was for saving Liberty.

Isaac's shrill cry turned rabid as he screamed into the cloth, kicking at nothing, then fell silent and limp beneath the drug.

"It's over," whispered Liberty.

But it wasn't. Not yet. Myrtle gazed calmly at

the towel beneath her white-knuckled hand. She had to be sure he couldn't hurt Liberty anymore.

Myrtle knew what it was like to be hurt.

Liberty backed away from the body on the floor in shock. When Myrtle finally took her hand away, she left the towel on Isaac like a burial face cloth.

Footsteps—and a crutch—pounded on the staircase and in the hallway before Silas, Fitz, and Dr. Stephens spilled into the room, followed by Major. Self-consciously she stood and pushed her hair back away from her face while the men huddled over Isaac.

"He's dead." The doctor pronounced and smelled the cloth.

"W–we were j–just trying to subdue him—" Liberty covered her mouth with her hand.

"I did it," Myrtle said proudly. "Myrtle Henderson killed Isaac Tucker. I saved Liberty for you, Silas."

The men exchanged stupefied glances.

"He attacked Liberty. He was going to hurt her. So I stopped him."

Myrtle's confession hung in the air, all eyes on her simple, smiling face. At length, Dr. Stephens said, "As far as I'm concerned, this man is a casualty of the battle at Gettysburg."

Silas approached Liberty and scanned her battered face. Part of her wanted to reach for him and burrow into his chest and feel his arms wrapped around her. Another part of her couldn't help but wonder. If Bella had been right about Isaac, could she be right about Silas, too?

Silas reached out to touch her face, and she flinched away from him.

"Liberty." His voice was gravelly with unchecked emotion. "I swear I would never hurt you. If anything had happened to you, I don't know what I would have done—" His voice cracked, and a lump bobbed in his throat. "Forgive me for not getting here faster—I came as soon as I could . . ." He drew a breath before turning to Myrtle. "Thank you for helping Liberty. I will always be grateful."

Myrtle beamed at him, and Liberty saw in her eyes the childlike devotion that drove her. Stepping over to him, Myrtle closed her eyes and lifted her face to him like a sunflower leaning toward the light.

And jolted awkwardly at the sound of Dr. Stephens calling her. "Could you fetch Dr. O'Leary for me, please? We need to move the body downstairs and I could use some help. Fitz is somewhat at a loss and Silas . . . well, I'd like to let him have some time with Miss Holloway alone."

For Myrtle, the spell had been broken. Heartbreak was written on her face as she tucked her chin into her neck. "Why don't I just help you myself?" She returned to Isaac, picked up his feet, and followed the doctor and Fitz out of the room.

Liberty's knees gave way in utter exhaustion, and Silas circled her waist with his arm before she could slide to the floor next to her bureau. He guided her to the edge of her bed, where they sat. "Are you going to be all right?" he whispered, and she nodded, aware that his hand still rested on the small of her back. Major sat on the hem of her skirt and looked up at her. She buried her fingers in the fur behind his ears.

"I was so close to not being all right. I was sure I couldn't fight him off anymore . . ." Tears stole her voice as Bella's face surged in her mind. Bella had fought, too, but no one came to rescue her. *Where is she now?* "I miss my mother," she whispered.

"Then it's true? You are certain?" His face was tight. She nodded. He looked away for a long moment after she nodded, and slowly withdrew his hand from her. "She will come back for you."

"How do you know?" Her voice trembled with uncertainty.

"She loves you too much to stay away. She always has."

Liberty nodded. Her eyes burned.

"Silas Ford?" A Union officer stood in the doorway, Dr. O'Leary at his side, a sponge and bristle brush in his hands.

"I'm sorry, Silas," Dr. O'Leary muttered. "I had to bring him up."

The officer cleared his throat. "I read all about

you in the paper. As you no longer require medical attention, you are hereby arrested as a prisoner of war."

Liberty's breath grew ragged in her chest as she and Silas stood. She locked eyes with him. "Will I see you again?"

"For what purpose?" He cut his voice low and wrapped her hand in his. "Whatever we felt—or feel—for one another, it has to end here. Now. Surely you must know that we cannot be together. Not now."

"Move it, Ford." The officer frowned, and Silas began to draw his hand away from Liberty.

"Don't stay away," she breathed.

"Don't you see?" He swallowed. "It's the only way. Don't wait for me, Liberty. Live your life, and be happy. You deserve nothing less. And you deserve far more than me." Silas tucked her hair behind her ear and slid his hand to the back of her head, his fingers deep in her unpinned hair. She closed her eyes and lifted her face to his as he leaned in, smelling of sawdust and sun. Gently, he tilted her head down and pressed a kiss to her hair, the scruff of his chin grazing her forehead. She should not have yearned for him to draw her close, to burn her lips with his once more, when he chose to part as a brother might leave a sister.

A sob trapped in her throat as he whispered, "Be well," and followed the officer out of the room.

Though her heart kicked and screamed, her tears had all run dry. No words formed with which she could call him back, or call him out. Liberty was utterly spent.

Dr. O'Leary crossed the room to her side, his eyes tired. "I do apologize, Miss Holloway. They're taking everyone. All those who are well enough to travel are being rounded up for prison. Those who are not are being evacuated to Camp Letterman, a general hospital a mile outside of Gettysburg along York Pike."

"Where will he go?"

"Fort Delaware, most likely, along with about six thousand other Confederate prisoners from Gettysburg. That's in addition to the thousands already there."

Her throat ached with dread. "Will he be all right?"

Dr. O'Leary sighed. "I don't know. The prisons are lousy with disease, and there's never enough food or clothing. Some of the Christian Commission's most important work is getting supplies into prisons to ease their existence a little bit. Of course, our focus is on Union prisoners. But Confederate prisoners fare poorly too, I'm sorry to say."

Of course they did. This was war.

"I came to help clean up in here, since my work with the patients is done." The floor was sticky with the sour residue of the struggle. Dr. O'Leary crossed to the window and leaned out. "Amazing that Silas hit his mark from that distance and angle."

Liberty jolted. How could she have forgotten to ask who shot Isaac? "Are you telling me he's the one who fired into the bedroom?

"Indeed." He straightened and turned to face her, rolling up his sleeves.

"You must be mistaken. He refuses to use a weapon. It could not have been him. He only came up after the struggle was over."

Dr. O'Leary shook his head. "No, Miss Holloway. He helped end it."

"You're certain?"

"Fitz handed him the gun and watched him do it. He's a crack-shot. He didn't want to kill him, just disable him, to protect you. I know he said he'd never handle a gun again, but love is a powerful thing." He knelt to scrub the floor. "That was the difference between Silas and Isaac, you know. Love gives, lust takes. Love is about the other person. Lust is about self. Love gives birth to passion as an expression of a couple's love and commitment. But lust gives vent only to greed for satisfying one's own appetites. Love cares about who you are. Lust cares only about what you can do for him."

Dr. O'Leary sat back on his heels and looked into her eyes. "Silas Ford, as far as I can tell, is a man who knows how to love."

Liberty broke his gaze, turning away. Silas was gone now, and there was nothing to be done about it.

A long moment later, Liberty found her voice again, willed it to remain steady. "I do appreciate your help cleaning in here, Dr. O'Leary. But first, would you mind if I change my dress?"

The doctor left her in privacy while she peeled off her ruined dress and replaced it with all she had left.

Wilted crepe from neck to toe, faded from fresh black to worn rust, cloaked her. It was not the dress of one in fresh grief, but of one who had lived with it, day in and day out, until it had become a second skin. Somehow, her mourning clothes suited her now. She was surrounded and filled by loss.

Chapter Twenty-One

A heavy breeze stirred the branches of the apple tree above Myrtle, rustling the lacey canopy of leaves. Sitting cross-legged next to the mound of earth where Isaac now slept, her hands shook as she threaded the slippery, silver needle. Hunched over her work, she cursed her large fingers as they fumbled with Dolly's head and body. She needed to talk to someone, and Dolly wasn't talking back anymore. Maybe she shouldn't have chopped her head off.

Maybe she shouldn't have killed Isaac.

Myrtle pinched Dolly's head and body together and stabbed the needle through the fabric, pulling the thread until the knot tugged from one side. She made another stitch, and other, carefully turning Dolly until the head was secured back onto the body. Myrtle tied a knot and snipped the thread, gazing at her handiwork.

Dolly didn't remind her of Liberty anymore. Her neck had shrunk with the stitches so she looked a little more like Frankenstein's monster.

No, said Dolly. *I look like you. Myrtle the Turtle.*

Myrtle moaned. She wasn't in the mood for Dolly's attitude today. She needed a friend who would listen, that was all.

"I didn't mean to kill him."

Yes you did. You meant to kill me, and you meant to kill Isaac. Only, you can't put him back together again.

Myrtle pinched the stitches of Dolly's throat between her thumb and forefinger. "I wanted to help Silas. I heard him outside, as I was bringing the coffee up to Liberty. He said, 'Help me.' That's always been my job. Take care of Silas Ford." She eased her hold on Dolly's neck.

Even though it meant keeping Liberty alive?

Tears bit Myrtle's eyes. "I said I would help him. And I did. Myrtle Henderson helped Silas Ford."

Because you wanted a kiss. But he didn't, did he?

Myrtle didn't respond. The truth was too bitter to taste on her tongue.

"I was a hero. To both of them."

Yes. Dolly nodded between Myrtle's fingers. *Like Éponine.*

Myrtle froze. She was exactly like Éponine.

You're forgetting one little thing. Marius kissed Éponine only after she was dead. The smile on Dolly's face turned into a sneer. *Is that what you want? Because if you do, you know exactly how to—*

"No!" Myrtle yelled at the doll in her fist. "You're not my friend if you say things like that to me. I don't need a friend like you." Tears slid down her broad cheeks. "You're just a doll. You aren't even real."

Dolly said nothing.

"I made a good decision to help Liberty and Silas, and I made it without you telling me what to do." Myrtle drew a fortifying breath. "I don't need a friend like you." Myrtle stared at the doll, daring it to talk back. To sneer. To so much as twitch. It didn't.

With a glance over her shoulder, Myrtle dug a small hole in the soil, placed the doll inside, and replaced the patch of earth on top of it. "That's more like it," Myrtle said, but only to herself.

Silas was gone along with the rest of the

patients. Myrtle Henderson had helped him the best she could. Now it was time for Myrtle Henderson to leave.

Holloway Farm
Thursday, August 6, 1863

Dear Liberty,
I arrived in Philadelphia on Tuesday, having spent the interim working out of the Sanitary Commission Lodge at the Gettysburg Railroad Depot. I have found a pleasantly situated boardinghouse for myself, but keep busy during the day at the Union Volunteer Hospital, next to the Union Refreshment Saloon . . .

Liberty laid Amelia's letter on the black crepe of her lap and looked out from her armchair on the porch. So much had changed in just a few weeks' time. Now Amelia was working with the wounded, and Holloway Farm was barren. Liberty had lived on this farm by herself before, but she had never felt such emptiness crushing around her as she did now.

Wind groaned through the barn, which was so hopelessly laced with vermin and the floor soaked with blood she dared not go near it. Her gardens were completely obliterated. Fences gone, the beds looked no different from the dirt dooryard.

Dr. O'Leary had raked out and burned the soiled straw before leaving, but the floors of her home were stained and infused with the odor of a hospital. Her house was a shell of what it once had been. Most of the furniture had been destroyed. Or used for crutches.

Everything had been hollowed out and used up.

Including Liberty. True to Mr. Stahle's word, more papers had come to find out if the story in the *New York Times* about her and Bella and Silas was true. She had told them it was, and they had sold their papers with her story.

Hunger clawed at her stomach, but she had no food. She had no money. All she had was memory, and even that did not serve her well.

Silas's parting words still haunted her. *Surely you must know that we cannot be together. Not now.* He told her to live her life. He might as well have added, *without me.* Was it because he was being sent away to prison, or because of the news that she was one-quarter Negro? If prison was the only obstacle, why did he tell her not to wait for him? If her heritage was the problem for him, why would she want a man like that anyway?

Though the discovery of her parentage had rocked Liberty, it also served to prove to her that the color of one's skin, or the composition of one's blood, did not define a person. It did not make people better or worse, more or less valuable than anyone else. If Libbie had not fully believed that before the issue became a personal one, she was convinced of the truth now.

As for what others thought of her—she had not the energy to care. Before Dr. O'Leary escorted Myrtle to Baltimore on his way home to Philadelphia, he reminded her where to anchor herself. "Above all else," he had said, "you are a child of God, and the bride of Christ. Love Him above all else. Serve Him. When you do that, you'll begin to see yourself as God sees you, and your relationships to everyone else will fall into place."

Lord, make me into the woman you want me to be. Major grunted as he rolled on to his side at her feet, and she bent down to pet him. When Liberty sat up again, she saw a lone figure coming up the lane, carrying a package.

A dark figure.

Bella.

Liberty jumped to her feet, hiked up her skirts and flew down the steps to meet her. Bella set her package on the ground.

"It's you." Nearly breathless, Liberty flung her arms around Bella's neck. "I missed you." Tears tightened her throat as Bella wrapped her arms around Liberty and squeezed. "I missed my mother."

Bella inhaled sharply and pulled back to look Liberty in the eyes. "You know?"

"I know. And I'm sorry, I'm so sorry, for

everything. Thank you for trying to protect me. I understand now why you did it."

Bella touched the yellow bruise on Liberty's face, and a fire lit behind her eyes. "Somebody hurt you?" Her voice was low. "Jesus," she whispered, not in blasphemy, but prayer.

"Not like they hurt you." Liberty swallowed. "I read the *Journal*. I fought back, just like you did. And I won."

Bella's mouth trembled, and tears traced her cheeks. "Sweet Jesus," she whispered. "Thank You, Jesus." Then, "Where is he?"

"Dead. It was Isaac."

"You—you killed him?"

Liberty shook her head. "No. Myrtle did, with chloroform. After Silas shot him through the bedroom window."

Bella's eyebrows curved high in her forehead. "And where is Silas?"

"Gone, too. Prison camp." She managed to say it without crying as she studied Bella's face for her reaction.

"Just as well," Bella said. But it wasn't. Liberty looked away. There was no use arguing, anyway. "I brought you something." Bella picked up her bundle and began walking to the house.

Sitting on the porch, she drew a cheesecloth off the package.

"A birthday cake?" Liberty laughed. "Did you carry a birthday cake three miles?"

Bella smiled. "Happy birthday, Liberty."

Libbie frowned. "But my birthday is—"

"Today."

"Not the Fourth of July?" Confusion rippled Libbie's brow. "But I thought I was named for our country's birthday."

"You were named for yourself. I named you Liberty, because even though you were born in bondage, a slave by birthright, you were given an inheritance of freedom by my master, Gideon Holloway. You need to know this. You were not named because your birth fell on Independence Day. You were named for your own freedom."

Liberty's brows knitted together as she looked into the depths of Bella's eyes. "I need to ask you something. Do I really look like him? Like my father?"

Bella laid a hand on her shoulder. "You look like you. You are your own person. You are not who your father was, and you are not even me. You and God get to decide who you are—nobody else."

"I understand that. But don't you see the face of your attacker when you look at me? Lt. Holmes said I was the very likeness of him. I need to know if—do you look at me and see tragedy?"

Tears glossed Bella's eyes. "No, child." She placed a hand on Liberty's cheek. "You are my triumph." She sliced a piece of cake and handed it to Liberty. "Happy birthday, Liberty. You've got a lot to celebrate. And so do I."

Liberty thanked her and bit into the cake, savoring the sweetness as it melted on her tongue. A comfortable silence filled several moments as they ate. Then, "Did you see Abraham? Is he all right?"

Bella swallowed her bite, nodding. "He'll do fine. Not very seriously injured, and definitely not ready to come home."

"Did he say anything about being paid?"

"He did. Turns out they offered the colored troops some money, but less than they're giving the white soldiers by almost half. So they refused to take it."

"He's still going to fight? For free?"

"Yes. They'd rather fight for free, as volunteers, than accept half-pay and be seen as hired mercenaries. They mean to hold out until they are paid on equal terms with the white soldiers."

"Will you be able to hold out, without his income?"

"I mean to try. And what will you do?"

The wind fretted loose tendrils of Liberty's hair as she looked around. The house would never be an inn now, and the wheat field she meant to sell was now trampled into oblivion. The dead slept beneath the apple trees. "I don't know. But I know I can't stay here."

Camp Letterman
Monday, August 10, 1863

Whispers followed Liberty wherever she went. "There goes the Widow of Gettysburg," they said as she swished by in her mourning clothes. She did not care. She mourned no longer for Levi, but for the loss of Silas, wherever he was, and for Gettysburg itself, the town that hemorrhaged innocence. The men who fought and died here, and those who were wounded, or imprisoned. For every man who was lost to death, disease, or injury, Liberty imagined a group of women who mourned—sisters, wife, mother, daughters—until her mind's eye formed an endless parade of darkly veiled forms on the horizon.

Liberty did not care that Camp Letterman had not asked for her help, had certainly not demanded it of her. She arranged for Major to stay with Bella, pitched a small tent and camped outside the nurses' quarters anyway. There was nothing for her at home.

This place was nothing like Holloway Farm had been in its hospital days. Skirted by woods on the northeast and southwest, the camp was laid out on a gentle slope, supported by a good spring with all the clean water they could ask for. Five hundred tents were laid out in six long avenues, their great fluttering pairs of white wings brooding peace-fully over the eight to ten men inside each tent. When Liberty arrived, there were sixteen hundred patients, half of them Confederate.

A mind-numbing monotony filled Liberty's days, for which she was grateful. The day she arrived, a line of stretchers a mile and a half long made its slow procession into the camp, and she set about her work at once. She washed agonized faces, combed out matted hair, bandaged slight wounds, and tipped drinks of raspberry vinegar and lemon syrup into parched mouths. She wrote letters to Rebel mothers and Union wives.

Hunger gnawed at her vitals until the new camp kitchen was erected and filled with monstrous stoves and huge caldrons with which to cook thousands of meals. Nurses darted in and out of the Sanitary Commission and the Christian Commission tents just west of the graveyard and embalmers tent, and then to the general cook-house, each one eager for the greatest amount of luxuries for her patients.

After the grisly work at the field hospital, Liberty's duties at Camp Letterman felt more like methodical housekeeping. Beef tea was passed three times a day, stimulants three times, and extra diet three times—making nine visits which each woman nurse made a day to each of the two hundred men under her charge. This was done besides washing the faces and combing the hair of those who were still unable to perform these services for themselves, preparing the extra drinks

465

ordered by the surgeons, and seeing that the bedding and clothing of every man was kept clean by the men nurses.

Liberty's feet swelled in her shoes, and when she removed them, found the skin rubbed off her toes. She felt immune to the pain of physical exertion, but when women came looking for their loved ones, her heart was cut to the quick.

There was no time for leisure at Camp Letterman, and no room for selfish regrets. From waking till sleeping, Liberty's day was spent in the service of others, from both North and South. If she was lucky, her slumber would be dreamless.

As long as Camp Letterman remained open, she would not go back to Holloway Farm.

Camp Letterman
Wednesday, August 26, 1863

Against her will, a lump formed in Liberty's throat as soon as she spotted them. Two bedraggled women and two small children poked their heads in every tent on their way down the lane, looking lost and forlorn. By the time they got to Liberty, their errand was no secret.

"Hello." The younger of the two women spoke first. "My name is Carrie Daws. This is my mother-in-law, Betty, and my daughter Virginia and son Samuel. We received a letter from a Liberty Holloway that my husband was here."

"Jeremiah Daws?" A Virginia man.

"Yes!"

"But how did you get through the picket lines?"

Betty and Carrie exchanged a glance. "We took the Oath of Allegiance to the Union." Carrie twisted her hands together. "It was the only way. My father-in-law turned back, but I would have said anything to be able to see Jeremiah again."

Liberty nodded. Thank God Jeremiah was not dead yet. There had been too many near misses, each one heartrending. "I'm Liberty. I'm so pleased to see you."

"Is he—" Betty covered her trembling mouth with her hand.

"Alive. Follow me, I'll take you to him."

Inside the northwest tent of Ward M, Jeremiah lay on his cot, insensible due to the merciful morphine. He had never recovered from the amputation of his arms. Beneath his bandages, gangrene crawled ever farther. Liberty was glad his dressings had just been changed.

"Daddy?" Virginia laid a small hand on his sallow face.

"Does he know we're here?"

The pleading in Carrie's eyes sliced through Liberty's heart. She shook her head. "The morphine keeps him comfortable, but he's not aware of his surroundings." She read the sorrow in their faces, and guessed at how much they had endured to arrive here. The travel must have been torturous, and very likely, at least some friends and family would shun them for taking the oath to the North, when their own land was ravaged by the Yankees. And now Jeremiah was so far gone he couldn't enjoy their comfort.

Dr. Stephens ducked into the tent and seemed to surmise the situation in a single glance. "You are Jeremiah's family?"

Four heads bobbed.

Dr. Stephens rubbed a hand over his face. "He's not long for this world, I'm afraid. I can let the morphine wear off so he can recognize you before he goes, if you like. You may get a conversation with him, albeit brief."

After a heartbeat's hesitation, Carrie nodded, and at a gesture from the doctor, she, Betty, and the children sat on the wooden floor of the tent next to his cot, waiting, while the doctor continued his rounds with the other nine patients in the tent.

Liberty left them there, and stepped back out into the sunshine, but did not feel its warmth as her black crepe absorbed it. *How long will it be before Carrie and Betty dye their own clothes black?* she wondered.

The rest of the afternoon passed as usual, and Liberty made her rounds bringing beef tea, milk toast, and reading materials from the Christian Commission to the two hundred patients in her ward. No sight or smell could bother her now.

But when the telltale wails arose from a tent in Ward M, her heart could not help but bleed with tears in empathy.

The sojourners' mourning filled Liberty's tent that night, and Liberty slept under the stars. Fresh grief like theirs needed a place to unfurl in relative privacy.

Philadelphia, Pennsylvania
Monday, September 14, 1863

The crisp autumn wind cooled Amelia Sanger's warm face as she hustled into the Union Refreshment Saloon. The cannon they called Fort Brown had fired minutes ago, signaling another crowd of troops would be arriving shortly. She adored the thirty patients at the hospital—they all called her Mamamelia—but when time allowed, as it did today, she was eager to help slice the beef or bread, or better yet, serve the food onto the plates of the grateful soldiers.

Of course, sometimes, they weren't soldiers at all, but prisoners on their way to camp, or just released from it, or refugees from the South. All of them had their fill of food and drink here, all of them were welcome to use the washing center for a shave and a haircut, and as many as possible were given paper, envelopes, and stamps to write home. It was work Amelia believed in. Now if she could only convince her tired feet to keep up with her spirit.

"Good afternoon, Mamamelia!" Amelia's friend and fellow volunteer Phoebe Bilbow smiled as she tucked her grey hair back into her snood. "Would you like to work the line today?"

"How did you know?" Amelia laughed. She had made sure that everyone knew she loved interacting with the soldiers more than anything else. She probably whined more than most when she was stuck washing dishes in the back.

Tying an apron on over her black bombazine dress, she took her post behind the tray of slightly pink, succulent beef, and inhaled the divine aroma. After a diet of hardtack and desiccated vegetables, fresh beef was always a big hit with the men.

Here they come. Amelia watched in eager anticipation as the men rushed the line. Oh, these men looked hungry. One after another, she placed a slice of juicy beef on their trays as they went by, and each one thanked her in his own way.

"Fresh beef!"

"Thank you!"

"Oh, I've dreamed about this day."

"Amelia."

With a slice of beef suspended in the air, Amelia looked up in surprise.

"Amelia Sanger."

Her metal tongs clattered into the pan of beef

as she covered her mouth with her hands. "Silas Ford." The man Liberty had clothed in Levi's shirt, who had sat in Levi's vacant chair. The man Liberty fell in love with, though she never admitted it to anyone.

"Hey, you're holding up the line, Johnny."

Silas looked back over his shoulder. "Nope. I'm a Billy now, remember?" He turned back to Amelia and grinned. "Took the Oath of Allegiance. They let me go."

She hadn't even known he'd been taken prisoner. Suddenly, Liberty's silence began to fall into place. *The poor girl.* Amelia fumbled to fish the tongs out of the pan juices. "Please, find a seat. I will join you as soon as everyone has been served."

For the rest of the line, Amelia's mind was back at Holloway Farm, reliving the darkness of those battle days, and tasting again a hint of bitterness that Liberty had replaced Levi in her heart. She sighed and reminded herself of all that God had taught her in the last two and a half months. Not the least of which was that Liberty was quite capable of making her own decisions, and should not be held hostage to grief.

When the last man had received his meat, Amelia wiped her hands on her apron and found Silas at the end of a long table. He had lost weight in prison, but his face was as handsome as ever.

"How's Liberty?" His first words, without preamble.

"I don't know. I don't even know where she is."

His green eyes bore into hers. "What do you mean?"

"She hasn't returned a single letter I've written her. I haven't heard a word from her since I left in July."

Silas wadded up his napkin and tossed it on the table. "Does she think you're upset about—well, do you have much time to read the news?"

"I told her I didn't think any differently of her after learning that Bella is her mother. I've done nothing to turn her away that I'm aware of." She paused, and watched him stew. "The question is, does she know where you are?"

"Of course not." He sipped his coffee. "There is no point in pursuing . . . anything. Not now."

Understanding glimmered in Amelia. As of two years ago, marriage between whites and blacks was illegal in Ohio, too. "I see. Such a shame." His eyes raised to meet hers. "I've seen Liberty with Levi, and I've seen her with you. She loved you. I don't know what she's feeling now, or even where she is, but I know she loved you once, and she very likely still does. In fact, I have a hunch that the reason she isn't answering my letters is due in large part to your absence."

"Really? Why?"

"Grief isolates. She lost you, you know. She lost everything."

"Except her mother. And I don't think Bella wants me around her daughter, regardless of what the law says."

Amelia leaned back in her chair, said nothing. It was a moot point anyhow.

"I wish I could help her." Silas sighed.

"Even though you'd receive no promises in return? Whatever you have in mind, she'll not be able to repay you with anything. Not with money, not with her heart, not with a future."

"What I'd get in return is of no account to me. I just want to clean up the mess I left, so to speak, and let her live her life." He propped his head in his hands, elbows on the table in front of him. "Never mind that I have no idea how to go about it fresh from prison. . . ."

"I don't believe it."

Amelia and Silas looked up to see Harrison Caldwell standing at the end of the table. He shook Silas's hand vigorously and slid onto a chair across from him.

"What are you doing here, Silas?"

He told him. "What about you?"

"Oh, I live in the neighborhood. I come here fairly frequently to talk to the men passing through. Always on the lookout for a story, especially since I was sacked from the *Inquirer*. I'm working on my own now."

"You were dismissed?"

He rubbed a hand over his freckled face. "Yeah. I was. The upshot of it is that I can write any story I want now. No more battles for me. Downside is finding the stories I can sell."

"How do you like happy endings, Harrison?" Amelia smiled at the bewildered look on his face.

"Love them. Have you got one for me?"

"Almost. But first, it may be none of my business, but Silas could use a little help getting back on his feet, after just being released from prison."

If Amelia Sanger was good at anything, it was meddling in other people's business.

Camp Letterman
Wednesday, September 23, 1863

A violent gust of wind shook hickory and oak leaves from their branches, sent them dancing in the air before fluttering to the ground like golden confetti. The smoky autumn air of Camp Letterman was spiced with the aroma of cooking chickens and hams. More than four thousand of the birds had been brought in for today's picnic and festivities, a much-needed break from the monotony of hospital life for both patients and workers alike. A band from York trumpeted popular tunes while each patient who could be moved was brought to open-air banqueting tables and had his fill of meat, pies, ice cream, and other delicacies brought by the citizens of Gettysburg and the surrounding area. Patients and attendants competed in foot races, greased pole and gander-pulling contests. For one glorious day, there was more laughter and jesting than moans and sighs.

Laughter bubbled up out of Liberty to see Virginia and Samuel tripping over each other in the three-legged race. A pair of convalescent soldiers deliberately stayed behind them to make sure they didn't come in last place.

"This has been so good for the children." Carrie Daws approached Liberty. "I haven't heard them laugh this much in months."

Smiling, Liberty nodded, still watching the ridiculous antics of the patients. "It's been good for everyone. Thank you for your help in getting everything ready."

Carrie waved the gratitude away. "You know I could not have left right after Jeremiah died anyway. Staying and helping has been a way to work out my grief. So many of these Confederate patients didn't have family to come tend to their sides—it was my pleasure to represent Southern sympathy to them."

Virginia and Samuel crossed the finish line, and both Liberty and Carrie erupted into cheers, along with the rest of the crowd.

"Walk with me?" Carrie led the way to the graveyard and found Jeremiah's marker. Unable to afford the cost of a coffin and shipment back home, his body would remain here, at least until Carrie could come back for it later.

A cool breeze feathered Libbie's face with the faint scent of evergreens from the wreaths adorning every tent in the camp. Reverently, she knelt with Carrie between rows of the dead. Carrie kissed the earth that covered Jeremiah's body, then dabbed the corners of her eyes with a handkerchief she had trimmed with black ribbon on her first day here.

At length, she turned to Liberty, tears brimming in her eyes. "I can't thank you enough for letting us stay in your tent and help with the patients. You know, some of my friends lost their men in this battle too, but they all refused to come. I don't judge them for their loyalty to the Confederacy. But I pity them that they will not have a tangible way of closing this chapter of their lives—at least see for themselves the final resting place of their dead. It cost me dearly to make this trip, but I'm glad I did it. And now, it's time for us to go home." She tilted her head. "What about you, Widow of Gettysburg? When will you go home?"

"I'll stay as long as I'm needed."

Carrie nodded. "You have your own grief to work out, I see. You work harder than any other nurse here, and you are the only one not attached to the government or a commission. One day,

Camp Letterman will close. I pray that by then, your heart will let you rest."

Rest? No, thank you. Still, she smiled and thanked Carrie as they stood and headed back to the festivities.

When they reached the edge of the crowd, Carrie hugged Liberty and rejoined Betty and her children, while Liberty remained a spectator. The band from York now played a melancholy tune, but one that had become the most popular song on both sides of the Mason and Dixon line: "When This Cruel War Is Over." As the notes floated on the breeze, men and women joined in the chorus:

Weeping, sad and lonely, hopes and fears how vain!

When this cruel war is over, praying that we meet again.

Crows squawked against the blue and gold autumn sky, as another woman with red-rimmed eyes wandered in and among the crowd, looking for husband, brother, or son.

This cruel war was not over yet.

Campus of Lutheran Theological Seminary
Thursday, September 24, 1863

Unease roiling his stomach, Silas climbed the steps of Dr. Samuel Simon Schmucker's house—*mansion was more like it*—and noted the damage the Rebels had caused to his former professor's home. Window frames had been shattered, sashes broken, the greater part of the glass destroyed. Several shells had knocked through the brick walls.

He rapped his knuckles on the front door and waited, hat in his hands, until the white-haired reverend answered it.

"Can I help you, son?"

Silas's new suit grew warm on his body. "You may not remember me, but I was a student of yours once. Silas Ford."

Dr. Schmucker's eyes widened in his pale face as he reached out and grasped Silas's hand with a hearty shake. "I don't believe it. Silas Ford, man of the Lord, here again at last!"

Silas winced as the rest of the rhyme sounded in his mind. *Took slaves to bed and shot Pa dead!* "Actually, sir, I wouldn't mind if I never hear that mocking phrase again."

"I'm not mocking you, Silas. Come in, come in." He stepped back and closed the door after Silas entered his home. "You were one of my most promising students."

A short laugh escaped Silas as he followed Dr. Schmucker down a hall. "I had to study harder than most to get the same marks."

"I'm not speaking of academics. I'm speaking of your heart." He paused in a doorway. "Here, let us visit in my study." Silas could not help but notice how sparse his bookshelves were as they sat in wooden chairs. "The place was ransacked by the Rebels. So many of my books, papers, sermons—destroyed. An oil painting of my father—slashed with a bayonet. But let us not speak of it. I'm far more interested in you. You had such a shepherd's spirit. I was so sorry when you discontinued your courses."

"I understand my mother told you why."

Dr. Schmucker nodded, peering down his hawklike nose. "She did. In a letter. I'm sorry to say one of my student assistants found it, came up with the rhyme you referred to earlier, and it spread like wildfire. Something in our human nature loves to watch another man fall from grace, you know. That's not to excuse it. I'm sorry you had to hear it."

"I'm sorry it was born from the truth." Silas rubbed his jaw. "Something has been troubling me, though. I understand my mother would have told you I shot my father in a duel, hence the 'shot Pa dead' line. But where did the phrase 'took slaves to bed' come from? Did she say something about me taking advantage of slaves in her letter too? I can think of only one incident, but I never told her about it." He focused on the pleats in his trousers, unable to meet his gaze.

"She did mention it. This I found strange, as well—quite unbelievable, actually. Until I received another letter from her. Last month."

Silas's head flew up. "You can't be serious."

Dr. Schmucker went to his bookcase, pulled from it a small personal Bible, and withdrew a folded sheet of foolscap from within its pages. "It's for you."

Silas stood to accept the letter, and opened it immediately.

July 18, 1863

Dear Dr. Schmucker,

I once wrote to you that my son Silas Ford was as likely to become a pastor as Lucifer was to become God Himself.

Silas returned to his chair, hands growing clammy. He loosened the cravat around his neck.

I wrote to you in anger. I did many things in anger that I now regret more than words can say. Chief among them was turning my son away rather than making peace with him before he went to war. As months turned to years, my anger faded. My loneliness sharpened, and I wanted—I want—more than anything to set things right with my son. I've had no letter from him since he joined the army, and I wouldn't know how to reach him either.

But now I hear tell of the battle of

Gettysburg, and I suspect if my Silas isn't dead yet, he was there for that great contest along with the rest of Lee's army. And if he was, I suspect he might try to visit you and make amends, or a confession, whichever his state of mind. It is in this hope I write to you now. I have my own confession to make. You not being a priest, this is not for you. This is for my boy.

Silas, you must forgive me. In my own pain, I tried to do you wrong. Your father used slave women for his own pleasure for years. I tricked myself into thinking it did not bother me as long as it was lust that drove him. I knew he loved me, and took his animal passions out on the Negro women to keep our love and marriage more pure. Then Psyche came along, and she was different. To my horror, he developed an affection for her that made her special. He singled her out, and meantime, our marriage bed went cold.

My jealousy knew no bounds. All I could think of was how to drive a wedge between Psyche and your father. And I'm ashamed to say it now, but I used you.

"Go to Silas," I told Psyche. "Offer yourself to him and make sure he does not refuse. He likes to help—make him think you need this from him for some reason." She said you didn't take her, and I just went crazy thinking that you had a stronger will than your father, and you a young man not yet married. My plan was that you would taste the forbidden fruit, get drunk on the pleasure of it, and find a way to keep her for yourself. Then my husband would come back to me. Maybe your father would just sell Psyche off the plantation so neither of you could have her.

It was not a well-conceived plan, I know. But it was all I had in my desperation. So one night at dinner I put something in your drink to make you sleep deeply. I told Psyche to slide in between the sheets with you and get you to give into temptation in your drunkenness.

Psyche followed my instructions—what choice did she have? But Silas, you never did a thing. She told me you were so dead asleep you snored like a bear for hours. That she tucked herself in your arms, but nothing roused you. You did nothing wrong, Silas. You were completely inno-cent.

Even if I never see you or hear from you again, I hope this sets you free. You were always such a good boy, Silas. You must forgive me for my wrongdoing in this, and for blaming you for your father's death. Do not forget, he is the one who invited death by suggesting a duel. Be at peace with yourself.

The letters blurred together on the page until Silas rubbed the moisture out of his eyes. Silas remembered going to bed early that night, and waking up, still groggy, with Psyche in his arms. As she left, she had said "Thank you." All this time, he had imagined she was thanking him for granting her request. *She was thanking me for leaving her alone!*

"I'm sorry you did not learn the truth sooner, son. But thank God she found you here at Gettysburg. God works in mysterious ways, does He not?"

Silas nodded mutely, unable to find his voice. Shock at his mother's ruse sliced through him. Her own guilt was punishment enough, Silas felt sure of that. He could not leave her in those shackles he knew so well, not when she was offering him the olive branch. He would write to her. And soon.

For now, he relished in the absolution contained on a single sheet of foolscap. "I'm not like my father," he whispered as relief washed over him.

"I would argue that you are." Smiling, Dr. Schmucker pointed to the heavens outside the broken window, and a fresh breeze rustled the letter in his hand.

Closing his eyes, Silas breathed a silent prayer. "I'm trying to be," he said at length.

Dr. Schmucker tented his fingers together and nodded. "That's what matters. Now tell me. Why did you come?"

"I never did like unfinished business." He leaned forward to measure his former professor's reaction. "I am considering, perhaps—that is to say, would you allow me to resume my studies here?"

Dr. Schmucker beamed. "Nothing would give me greater pleasure than to see you back at the seminary. Classes were supposed to resume today, but the last patient only left the seminary building eight days ago. We need a bit more time to prepare the building for students again, but yes, there is room for one more! Several of our students have enlisted, you see, so our numbers are already down."

Silas stood, straightened his jacket over his trousers. "It would have to be next fall for me. I'm afraid I can't be ready to enroll this fall just yet."

"More unfinished business?"

"You could say that, yes."

"Well, if there is anything Dr. Krauth or I can do for you, you just say the word, won't you?"

Silas shook the reverend's hand as he stood. "As a matter of fact, I believe there is."

Gettysburg, Pennsylvania
Thursday, September 24, 1863

With applesauce simmering on Bella Jamison's stove, she opened her windows and breathed in deeply. When cooler weather had finally swept away the persistent stink of battle's aftermath, she realized she had not taken a deep breath in months. Now autumn ushered in the smell of fermenting apples instead of flesh, and decaying fallen leaves instead bodies.

A year ago, she had taught Liberty how to make applesauce at Holloway Farm. Now, she could not get Liberty to come home for anything. That girl was stuck, in more ways than one. Life goes on after loss, Bella had tried to tell her. But Liberty was wrapped up in loss, still wearing her mourning clothes, and walking the graveyard at Camp Letterman every night with the other nurses to weep over those who had been buried that day.

Major bumped into Bella's leg as he sprawled out on the kitchen floor and watched the door. *That poor beast is always waiting for someone to come back for him.* Sighing, Bella dashed some cinnamon in the pot of applesauce, stirred, and tasted it. *Just about perfect.* A knock sounded on the door as she was adding kindling to the stove.

"Come on in!" She was expecting Aunt Hester.

When she turned around, however, it was Silas Ford standing in her kitchen in a camel-colored suit almost the same shade as his hair, rolling the brim of his bowler in his hands. Lines of anxiety framed his eyes.

"Hello, ma'am," he said, and she noticed for the first time that he was standing without a crutch. He smiled and without being asked, hiked his right pant leg up to show a well-formed prosthetic leg wearing a shoe. He dropped the trouser leg.

Major ambled over to Silas for attention, and the color drained from the man's face as he bent to greet the dog. "Is Liberty—gone?"

Bella nodded. "But not that kind of gone. She's nursing at Camp Letterman, the general hospital outside of town. Haven't been able to get her to come home for anything. Not that there's much of a home for her to come back to . . ." She wiped her hands on her apron. "Please have a seat, Mr. Ford." Regaining his composure, he pulled a chair out for her at the kitchen table before lowering himself into his own.

"Please call me Silas. I heard your husband was injured at Fort Wagner. I pray he is well?"

"He is, thank you."

"And how are you? After, um, everything here? Things settling back down to normal?"

Bella chuckled as she folded the copy of *The Christian Recorder* lying on the table between them. In nearly every issue now, letters decried the unequal pay for black soldiers. There was still no resolution. She was still scraping by. "There's nothing normal about it. But I expect you're here about Liberty."

"Actually, Mrs. Jamison, first of all, I'm here about you."

Bella fingered the edge of the newspaper. And waited.

"You have every reason to dislike me. I know what I represent to you. My father did to other women what Roswell King Jr. did to you."

Her blood simmered. "I know he did." She clenched her teeth.

"Please forgive me."

An admission of guilt? "Forgive you for what? If you hurt Liberty, so help me—"

"I didn't. I'm asking you to forgive me for the sins of my father."

Bella snorted. "That's ridiculous."

"Then forgive me for not being able to stop him, or for not trying hard enough. Forgive me for being white, for being Southern, for being raised on a slave-holding plantation, for being a Rebel scout. Forgive me for not being who you wanted for your daughter. Forgive me for whatever it is you hold against me."

Bella's cheeks grew warm. She did hold his father's sins against him. She had placed him in the same category as her worst nightmare, out of fear. Wasn't that what other people had done to her time and again? They had judged her for the group they placed her in, not for who she was as an individual.

Lord, have mercy. She ought to know better.

"The truth is—" Silas swallowed. "I need to be forgiven. If I could find the women my father abused, I would fall at their feet and beg them outright for it. They deserved protection, just as you did, just as your mother did. Just as Liberty did." His voice broke, and he pinched the bridge of his nose for a moment before continuing. "I've asked God for forgiveness, and He says in His word that He's given it to me. But I would really like to hear it from you, too. I can't live under the weight of this anymore."

The barricade Bella had erected around her heart began to crumble. If this man was in earnest, and she believed he was, how could she in good conscience deny his request?

"I forgive you, Silas." She grasped his white hand in her light brown one and squeezed until his eyes showed her he believed it "Now. Speak the rest of your mind in peace. You want to court her. Don't you?" She rose from the table and returned to the stove.

He frowned. "You know I can't do that."

"And why not, young man?" Her spoon stilled in the pot.

"Why, because she's colored, and I'm white." Lines etched his forehead, but Bella could feel her own headache coming on.

"Do you love her or not?"

"That's not fair, Mrs. Jamison. It's beside the point."

"That is the entire point. People have married for far less than that." Her spoon was clenched in her left hand, both fists propped on her hips. She could smack this man at her table if she let her irritation get the best of her.

"I don't understa—"

"You have got some nerve waltzing in here, asking me for forgiveness and then shunning my daughter on account of her being mine. Where in God's great earth does that make any lick of sense?"

"It's not my choice!"

"The devil it isn't." Burning with anger, Bella turned her back to him and lowered her voice as she stirred. "You know where the door is. Get out of my home."

She heard him push away from the table, walk to the door, and stop. "If it wasn't for the law, I'd be here asking for your permission—and blessing."

Bella spun around. "What law?"

"The law that says white and blacks can't marry, of course. Nothing else could keep me from her."

Bella closed her eyes for a moment. "You mean to tell me you came here to ask my forgiveness even though you thought you couldn't pursue Liberty?"

His blank expression was answer enough.

"Sit down. Sit down." She left her spoon at the

stovetop and guided him back to the table. "There is no such law."

The words did not seem to register. "What did you say?"

"There is no such law in Pennsylvania. Not anymore. Not in a long while. I know all the Southern states make interracial marriage illegal, and plenty of Northern ones too. But you're not in those states. You're here."

"No such law," he whispered. "Then . . ." Silas stood, nearly knocked his chair over backwards and Major scrambled out of his way.

"You know if you ever harm a hair on her head, I'll come after you, don't you?"

"Does that mean I have your blessing to court her?"

Bella chuckled. "It means you have my blessing to try. I don't know what she'll say, but she can speak for herself. You got a plan to bring her back to the land of the living?"

His eyes twinkled as he grinned.

"Well, are you going to tell me?" she prodded.

"I plan to make her dreams come true. But I sure could use your help."

Holloway Farm
Tuesday, November 17, 1863

With her hands covering her eyes as per Bella's instructions, Liberty Holloway nearly fell asleep on the ride from Camp Letterman to wherever Bella was taking her in the leather-lined carriage. The steady rhythm of the horses' hooves and the smoke-scented wind teased her senses just enough to keep her upright. Only when her hands stopped working did she realize how exhausted she was. Her strength seemed to dwindle along with the patients at Camp Letterman.

Two days ago, Camp Letterman only had sixty patients. Today, the last one left for his home in Cincinnati. The five hundred tents would soon be filled with thousands of visitors for the dedication ceremony of the National Soldiers' Cemetery.

"Open your eyes."

Liberty obeyed, and squinted for a moment against the brightness of the lowering sun as her eyes adjusted. The first thing she saw was her old sign for Liberty Inn, but cleaned, touched up, and polished. The oak gleamed in the sun, reminding her of . . . she shook her head and bit her lip. *This is exactly why I didn't want to come here!*

As the carriage turned into the lane, Liberty leaned out over the edge in disbelief. Little green blades were poking up through the dirt, where before it had been a vast sea of endless dirt. She turned to Bella. "You seeded the yard?"

Bella only laughed and clucked her tongue to the horses. They slowed in front of the porch, and Liberty climbed down while Bella tied the reins to the hitching post. Bright yellow and orange chrysanthemums consumed the porch, while pumpkins lined the steps and perimeter of the floor.

The porch no longer sagged, or cracked, or splintered. The floor and railings were made of all new wood, painted white. But these railings were not the straight slats of her former porch. They were curved and tooled like miniature bedposts. *Beautiful!* On one side of the porch, two rockers sat with cushions in their seats, while on the other side, a porch swing swayed in the breeze.

"What did you do?"

"There's more."

Liberty's pulse quickened as she stepped through the front door and almost stumbled into Major, who was wagging his entire rear end in greeting. In truth, the dog was the only thing familiar about this place. *Where am I?* she wondered as she wrapped her arms around her clumsy Newfoundland's neck. She was surrounded by new floorboards, freshly painted walls, new varnished crown molding. Even the banister and railing of the staircase were new, carved in the same beautiful pattern as the porch railings had been.

But it wasn't just the structure that was new. The four bedrooms on the first floor each had new beds with handmade quilts, wash stands, writing desks, bureaus and lamps. The dining room had a mahogany sideboard again, and matching table and chairs. The kitchen, too, was entirely refurbished.

Liberty ran upstairs to the room that had once been hers. It was repainted a warm butter color, and new curtains sashayed in the autumn air. But when she came to her bed, she stopped. For there across the mattress, was her old baby quilt sewn into a larger one. Somehow, Bella had turned a remnant into a masterpiece, matching odd shapes together until it was a perfect fit, old and new together.

"Perfect," she whispered, and Bella joined her side.

"Now," Bella said as she circled her waist with her arm. "Don't you think it's time to cast off these mourning clothes?"

Liberty's eyes widened as Bella threw open the doors of her bureau to reveal four new dresses. None of them were black. Bella pulled out a corn-flower blue light wool with black velvet edging.

"Let's see if I got the measurements right." Bella unfastened Liberty's buttons for her and helped her out of the rusty black gown. "Don't forget your hoops." She smiled. It had been more than four months since Liberty had worn hoops under her skirts. She had forgotten what it felt like to look—and feel—like a lady. Liberty stepped into them and Bella tied them over her drawers and camisole. Next was the dress. It skimmed her curves in all the right places.

Hoofbeats grew louder on the dirt lane outside her house.

"Someone's coming." Liberty leaned out the window to look. A single horseman trotted up the lane. Looking up at her from beneath the brim of his hat, he grinned and winked.

Liberty sucked in her breath and jumped away from the window. "Bella." She grabbed her hands. "Bella." Her heart pounded against her corset. "Am I seeing things that are not there?"

"Go on and see for yourself."

Slowly, Liberty glided down the staircase, afraid that every step brought her closer to having her wild hope crushed with some practical reality. *It's a salesman. Or a traveler arriving for the dedication ceremony.*

With her heart in her throat, she pushed open the door and swept out onto the porch. The man dismounted, a little stiffly, but successfully, and walked toward her.

Standing in front of her, he removed his hat and looked down into her eyes. A strand of her hair blew across her face, and he tucked it behind her ear, his thumb resting on her cheek for a heartbeat.

"You don't look like a Rebel," she whispered.

Silas laughed out loud. "And you, my dear, don't look like a widow."

She flung her arms around his neck and felt her feet leave the earth as he held her tightly in an embrace. Her tears wet his neck as she whispered, "I thought I'd never see you again."

His lips found hers, and he kissed her tenderly, as if unsure of her reaction. She deepened the kiss and felt his fingers in her hair.

"I have a feeling we're being watched." She turned and pointed to her bedroom window, where the curtain fell quickly back into place.

"I have a feeling she wouldn't mind."

"Do you mean you two were in on this together?" Liberty was stunned.

Silas nodded. "But I had help. Bella and some women from her church made the quilts and curtains for the entire house. I hear a few women from the Ladies Union Relief Society pitched in, too. Can you guess who helped me make the furniture and repair the damage to the house and outbuildings?"

She shook her head. Who would have helped him?

His smile warmed her. "Wood-working students from Pennsylvania College and the Lutheran Theological Seminary." Silas laughed at the shock that must have been written on her face. "I met with my old professor, Dr. Schmucker, in September. I wanted to tell him my story, vindicate myself from that little rhyme his students love to chant. And I—" he licked his lips. "I asked if I could come back. Complete my training at the seminary."

Liberty clutched his arms. "And?"

"And he said yes. Next fall, I'll begin. In the meantime, I have other business to attend to here."

"So you're staying? Another year in Gettysburg?"

"Oh, at least." He winked. "Then when Rev. Schmucker asked about you—he reads the papers like anyone else—I told him about my project here to fix up your place. That's when he recruited more than a dozen of his students to pitch in and help. They were only too eager to meet the legendary 'Silas Ford, man of the Lord,' especially after Rev. Schmucker reclaimed my reputation. I couldn't have done all this without them."

"But how did you pay for it all? I don't have any money to pay anything back!"

"You happen to have a benefactor."

"What?"

"Come with me." He led her by the hand to where the barn once stood. "We razed the old building to the ground and rebuilt this carriage house, big enough to accommodate a full house at Liberty Inn."

She shook her head in disbelief. "But who's we?"

Liberty gasped as Harrison Caldwell and Amelia Sanger emerged from the new structure.

Amelia wrapped her in an embrace. "I wrote you letters!"

"I'm sorry I didn't get them, Amelia—I left for Camp Letterman and never came back until now."

Harrison toed the ground with his shoe. "Hi, Miss Holloway."

"Don't you have a newspaper to write for?"

"I'm on my own now. I go where I want to, write the stories I want to. But this time, I took a break to help pick up the pieces from a mess I had a hand in creating." He smiled past Liberty's shoulder and she turned to see Bella smiling back at him. Had the entire world changed in the few months she was at Camp Letterman?

"There's one more surprise," Silas said. "The carriage and horses that Bella used to bring you home in? They're yours."

Liberty's knees weakened, and she leaned against Silas. "How?"

"I'm getting old, Liberty," said Amelia. "And I've got gobs of money. Levi would have wanted some of it to go to you. I told you that."

Silas drew Liberty in and kissed her again before tucking her against his chest. "Welcome home, Liberty. This is where you belong."

"Thousands of visitors will soon descend upon you for the dedication ceremony, and you'll be able to charge whatever you like," said Amelia. "Put two in a room, put them on the parlor floor, charge them just the same. Gettysburg style." She laughed. "You've already got your first customers right here."

Liberty looked around. "All of you?" Silas, Harrison, and Amelia all nodded.

"Just name your price."

The November wind scraped Liberty's face, as Carrie Daws appeared in her mind, along with Betty, Virginia, and Samuel. They were gone now, but there would be other widows and orphans making the pilgrimage to Gettysburg, especially now that the Federal government no longer required them to pledge allegiance to the Union in order to retrieve the bodies. Each fallen soldier had a mother, father, siblings, perhaps a wife and children. Wouldn't they long to visit the final resting place of their loved one?

Weeping may endure for a night, but joy cometh in the morning. Let them spend their night at Liberty Inn.

"So what will you charge?" Harrison buried his hands in his pockets.

"Nothing." She paused. "That is, widows and children of the men buried here can stay free of charge, whether they hail from Minnesota or Alabama. Liberty Inn can be much more than just a livelihood for me. It can be respite for the grieving. Other visitors will come and go and pay a normal fare. But widows and orphans who lack the means can stay at Liberty Inn for free."

Silas wrapped his arm around her shoulders, but Harrison frowned. "So they'll twiddle their thumbs while they stay for free."

Bella caught Liberty's eyes. "No, that wouldn't help them at all," she said. "They're going to keep their hands busy, aren't they, Liberty? While they stay, they can help in the garden and kitchen. They can make jams and jellies, needlework and quilts. We can sell their work at the Fahnestock Brothers Store as products made by the widows of Gettysburg. All proceeds will go to the maintenance of Liberty Inn."

"It's perfect." Amelia's pale face creased into a smile. "'. . . we may be able to comfort them which are in any trouble, by the comfort where-with we ourselves are comforted of God.'"

The war had not ended with Gettysburg, as both North and South had hoped, but it was no longer a time to hate. *At least not here, at Liberty Inn.*

Liberty blinked away the moisture in her eyes and looked down at her hand, her fingers entwined with Silas's. A Union widow and a Rebel veteran. The daughter of a slave, the son of a slave holder. Children of God. Where prejudice and hatred and fear had sought to unravel them, love and forgiveness had bound them together. "It's time to heal."

Epilogue

Gettysburg, Pennsylvania
Thursday, November 19, 1863

The weather was unseasonably mild for the dedication of the Soldiers' National Cemetery on Cemetery Hill, and warmth flooded Liberty as the crowd pressed her closer to Silas. Twenty thousand people had descended upon Gettysburg for the occasion. The sea of faces, fevered with patriotic zeal during the parade this morning, were now cloaked in solemnity. But none were as sober as the people who had lived through the ordeal personally. Liberty caught Evergreen Cemetery keeper Elizabeth Thorn's eye and offered a smile for the one-month-old baby in her arms.

As the honorable Edward Everett, former secretary of state, took the platform now for the dedication ceremony, Silas wrapped his arm around Liberty's shoulders, and she nestled into his chest, inhaling his bay rum scent as the orator began. Amelia and Bella stood just in front of them.

"Standing beneath this serene sky, overlooking these broad fields now reposing from the labors of the waning year, the mighty Alleghenies dimly towering before us, the graves of our brethren beneath our feet, it is with hesitation that I raise my poor voice to break the eloquent silence of God and Nature. But the duty to which you have called me must be performed;—grant me, I pray you, your indulgence and your sympathy."

For the next hour, Everett held the crowd captive, and Liberty noticed Harrison Caldwell scribbling notes on his pad of paper. Everett spoke of Roman, Italian, French, and British governments, took the audience through the events of the American Revolution, the definition of rebellion, the birth and plan of the Confederacy, and the movements of both armies from the days of late June until the glorious Fourth of July when victory was secured for the Union.

Then, it was the women's turn. Liberty leaned in to listen as Everett spoke several sentences to commend matrons and maidens for delighting in their labors and serving the "least of these."

Liberty kept her gaze on the speaker, but her thoughts wrapped themselves around the man standing next to her. She had considered him the "least of these," and God had rewarded her with love and belonging she had never known before. She could never have imagined where loving her enemy would lead.

Everett went on for another hour after that, and the people punctuated his conclusion with thunderous applause. Then, President Abraham Lincoln traded places with him, and the contrast could not have been starker. Everett, of average height and whose head was framed by such fuzzy white hair it looked like a thick layer of lint was stuck to it, his face that of a victor. Lincoln, taller than anyone else in the crowd, whose stovepipe hat matched his dark hair and beard, his face, that of a sufferer. He looked so sad, so tired. He was not celebrating victory, but still solemnly in the fight. His voice was higher pitched than she had imagined it would be for a man of his stature, but his words, though simpler and far fewer than Everett's, captured the essence of the occasion.

Not even the wind stirred as the president spoke. "It is rather for us to be here dedicated to the great task remaining before us—that from these honored dead we take increased devotion to that cause for which they gave the last full measure of devotion—that we here highly resolve that these dead shall not have died in vain—that this nation, under God, shall have a new birth of freedom—and that government of the people, by the people, for the people, shall not perish from the earth."

Mr. Lincoln left the stage. Liberty, along with the rest of the crowd, was stunned at the brevity of his remarks. An awkward moment passed as twenty thousand people came to the realization that Lincoln's speech was over almost as soon as it had begun, then erupted into a delayed cheer for their burdened commander in chief.

Harrison Caldwell jostled his way next to Silas, Liberty, Amelia, and Bella. "So." He tucked his pencil and paper into his knapsack. "Two hours and two minutes later, the Soldiers' National Cemetery is dedicated."

"How did you rate our speakers?" Silas asked.

Harrison straightened the slouch hat on his head. "I preferred Lincoln."

"A newsman would. Shorter is better, right?"

The reporter chuckled. "Usually, yes. But a little clarification would have been appropriate. Lincoln said that the men who died here gave their last full measure of devotion in doing so. But I believe the fullest measure of our devotion to the cause is not just dying for it, but living for it. From where I'm standing, each one of you is giving your full measures of devotion in your own ways."

"Let me guess," said Bella. "You want to write a story about it."

"It's a great story." A smile brightened his face. "But you should be the ones to tell it. Write your story. The world needs to hear your voice, not just the voices of the reporters."

"Women don't publish," said Amelia. "It isn't ladylike."

Harrison shook his head and pulled a package of wafers from his pocket. "I'm telling you, just write it." He popped a wafer in his mouth and tucked it in his cheek. "If you don't, no one else is going to do it for you."

503

"And what will you do?" Liberty asked.

"Me? Oh, I'll keep writing stories, but my battle days are behind me." He tilted his head toward the platform. "I should at least try to get an interview with the president." Harrison shook hands with Silas, Amelia, Bella, and Liberty. "I deeply regret any sorrow or pain I may have caused you all."

Liberty squeezed his hand. "God used it for good, Mr. Caldwell." If Harrison hadn't dug up their story—and leaked it to the *New York Times* —she might have lived her entire life not knowing what a strong, respectable mother she had in Bella.

Smiling, Harrison nodded, tipped his hat, and melted into the crowd encircling the president. For a long moment, Liberty watched the throng of people that had come for this momentous day.

"Who could have believed that all of this would have unfolded in Gettysburg?" Amelia scanned the red-brick homes and gleaming white steeples in the distance. "Several months ago, if people had heard of Gettysburg, it would have been because of the seminary or college. From now on, the name will be synonymous with death."

"For now, yes." Liberty sighed. "But perhaps, not always. We can let tragedy define us, or we can refuse to let the story end there. Wouldn't it be wonderful if Gettysburg came to be known not just for the incredible loss that hallowed this ground, but for the devotion of those of us who survived? Or as the turning point of the war?"

Silas smiled into Liberty's eyes. "Look around, Liberty. For Amelia, Bella, Harrison, you, and me—it has been a turning point, indeed. Each of us has suffered, but each has risen above it. When I look at you, I see triumph, not trial, written on your face."

The warmth of his gaze burned her cheeks. Bella cleared her throat and told Libbie she and Amelia would meet them back at the house.

With people teeming around them, Silas stood still and cupped Liberty's face in his hands. "But that isn't all I see. Is it?"

Liberty's breath hitched. "What do you see?"

"Hope." His voice was low as he enveloped her hands with his. "Liberty, I was going to wait to say this until I had more to offer you. But I don't want you to have to wonder one more moment about my intentions. You need to know you are loved. You are . . ." A lump shifted in his throat. "My beloved. I love you. Your heritage does not change that, nor should it."

Liberty's heart grew wings, but as he drew a deep breath, she knew he was not done.

"I would fight for you. I would die for you. But more than that, I would live for you with the full measure of my devotion. I would sacrifice all to win you, fight for your heart after it has already been won. That I might pursue you, with the heart of a lion, that I might be all you have dreamed of and make you feel loved . . . protected . . . cherished—That is my desire and my passion and my delight."

Silas pulled from his pocket a gold and sapphire ring. "Would you do me the honor of becoming my wife?"

Heart in her throat, Liberty slid her finger into the ring and smiled through her tears. "Nothing would make me happier," she whispered. She wrapped her arms around Silas, felt the strength of his shoulders beneath her palms before clasping his neck. She kissed the smile on his face, inhaling his scent as though she were breathing him in. His hands curved around her waist and neck as he held her close.

Silas leaned back to look at her, the November wind blowing between them. "That I might have both the Lord and you—it is too great a gift to fully comprehend. Are you ready, Beloved?"

He offered his hand, and she squeezed it in response. Together, they walked away from Cemetery Hill.

In just one week, they would be celebrating Thanksgiving Day as a nation for the first time, by proclamation of the president. But Liberty did not need an order from the White House to be grateful for what God had done in her life.

Weeping had endured for a night. But joy came in the morning.

Abraham Lincoln's Gettysburg Address

Four score and seven years ago our fathers brought forth on this continent a new nation, conceived in liberty, and dedicated to the proposition that all men are created equal.

Now we are engaged in a great civil war, testing whether that nation, or any nation, so conceived and so dedicated, can long endure. We are met on a great battle-field of that war. We have come to dedicate a portion of that field, as a final resting place for those who here gave their lives that that nation might live. It is altogether fitting and proper that we should do this.

But, in a larger sense, we can not dedicate, we can not consecrate, we can not hallow this ground. The brave men, living and dead, who struggled here, have consecrated it, far above our poor power to add or detract. The world will little note, nor long remember what we say here, but it can never forget what they did here. It is for us the living, rather, to be dedicated here to the unfinished work which they who fought here have thus far so nobly advanced. It is rather for us to be here dedicated to the great task remaining before us—that from these honored dead we take increased devotion to that cause for which they gave the last full measure of devotion—that we here highly resolve that these dead shall not have died in vain—that this nation, under God, shall have a new birth of freedom—and that govern-ment of the people, by the people, for the people, shall not perish from the earth.

The History behind the Story

Widow of Gettysburg was inspired by the letters, diaries, and first-person accounts of Gettysburg civilians who I had the pleasure of meeting in the archives of the Adams County Historical Society in Gettysburg, Pennsylvania, a few years ago. Perhaps like you, my knowledge of Gettysburg up until that time was limited to what I knew of the battle itself. But once I discovered the forgotten work of the women of Gettysburg, their stories came to life for me, and I hope it came to life for you too, through this novel.

Although her name is inspired by a Gettysburg teenager named Liberty Hollinger, Liberty Holloway is a purely fictional character. But she did what real women were called upon to do. They watched their homes and farms become ruined, they assisted surgeons, even with amputations. Women discovered one hundred men in the flooded basement of the Lutheran Theological Seminary and arranged for their rescue. They learned to show love to their enemy as they cared for Rebel wounded. Several women from Gettysburg actually did marry men who they or their mothers helped nurse back to life, whether the soldiers had worn blue or grey. One Gettysburg woman pitched her tent at Camp

Letterman (also a real place) and stayed there for four months, which inspired Liberty's action to do the same. The Holloway Farm's location was based on the position of the real farm belonging to J. E. Plank, on the west bank of Willoughby Run.

The major events preceding and during the three-day battle were depicted as historically as possible, including the Rebels passing through Gettysburg on June 26, General Buford's cavalry coming through on June 30, the locations of Lee's and Meade's headquarters, the late arrival of General Stuart, the battles at Little Round Top and the Wheat Field, and Pickett's, Trimble's and Pettigrew's Charge on the third day. The Confederate capture of Union medical supplies from the seminary is also true to history. The minor character Theodore Hopkins who died from loading too many charges in his musket before firing at Little Round Top represented a real danger and cause of death. Among the 35,000 muskets recovered from the fields of Gettysburg, 6,000 were found to have between 3 and 10 charges in its barrel, and one musket held 22 charges.

The wake of battle rocked the town long after the last soldier had been buried. There are several records of women who worked so hard during and after the battle that their health broke down, a few to the point of death. While six months pregnant, Elizabeth Thorn buried 105 bodies in her cemetery, and complained of ill health from it for the rest of her life. At least one girl was orphaned when her mother died from drinking polluted water from a well which had been used as a burial pit for corpses without her knowledge. Several young men and boys were killed from trying to harvest lead from unexploded shells they had found on the fields. Some residents moved away from town, unable to cope with the memories. Many in the black community of Gettysburg simply did not return. The fictional Aunt Hester was based on the historical Elizabeth Butler, Aunt Liz, a washerwoman for the McCreary family, who was captured on July 1 but hid in the bell tower of Christ Lutheran Church until danger passed, three nights and two days later.

Silas Ford represents a portion of Confederate soldiers who were conscripted into the army against their will. The phantom pain he experienced is well-understood now, but at the time, a Philadelphia doctor named Silas Weir Mitchell was pioneering the field of nerve injuries, and just beginning to learn about the phenomenon. After the Civil War, the presence of 35,000 amputee veterans prompted profound developments in prosthetic limbs. The use of opium and morphine did translate into abuse for tens of thousands of soldiers during the Civil War.

Country doctors from the South, like the fictional Dr. Stephens, were one of the demographics most likely to suffer opium addiction.

The Sanitary and Christian Commissions performed critical work at Gettysburg, and the efforts depicted in this novel were true to history. Though most delegates of the Christian Commission volunteered to minister to the spiritual needs of the soldiers, those who could serve the physical needs, like the fictional Dr. O'Leary, willingly did all they could in medical capacities as well.

Bella's husband Abraham Jamison is a fictional character, but the events the 54th Massachusetts regiment experienced in the novel are true to history, including the raid on Darien, the battle at Fort Wagner, and the struggle for equal pay. It is also true, unfortunately, that black women who served as nurses in a hospital in the Sea Islands were used by Union officers, and that at least one black woman was shot in the shoulder while trying to protect her daughter from sexual assault. Congress finally passed a bill granting black soldiers equal pay in June 1864.

By 1863, most states had laws against interracial marriage. Of the states that did, Pennsylvania was the first to repeal the law in 1780, as part of a gradual process toward the abolition of slavery in that state. It would be sixty-three years until the next state (Massachusetts) would follow suit.

The Loving V. Virginia case in 1967 forced the last sixteen states with anti-miscegenation laws (including Tennessee) to repeal them.

Pierce Butler and Fanny Kemble were well-known not only in their native city of Philadelphia, but around the country, for Fanny was a famous British actress before marrying Pierce. Their tumultuous marriage and divorce, due largely to their opposite views on slavery, was common knowledge. Fanny's *Journal of a Residence on a Georgian Plantation* was published in the United States just before the battle of Gettysburg. All the excerpts from the journal are verbatim, except for the ones mentioning Bella, who is a fictional character. Roswell King Jr., the Butler overseer, is a historical figure who sired countless children by force with slave women. The Weeping Time, too, was a historical event. Lt. Pierce Butler Holmes, the godson of Pierce Butler, was also a historical figure who fought and was wounded at Gettysburg, and most likely taken to a Confederate field hospital along Willoughby Run before he was moved to a prison in Baltimore.

Gettysburg residents Elizabeth Thorn, Hettie Shriver, Tillie Pierce, Jennie Wade, Sarah Broadhead (the Sarah who helped rescue men from the seminary basement), Hugh Ziegler and Dr. Samuel Simon Schmucker are also historical figures who appear in the novel. The baby

Elizabeth carried during and after the battle, Rose, was born sick and weak, and the child died at age fourteen. Elizabeth believed it was due to the physical and psychological stress of the battle and its aftermath. Her husband Peter survived the war, as did Hettie Shriver's husband George. Visitors to Gettysburg are able to stay at the Tillie Pierce House Inn, tour the Shriver House Museum, the Jennie Wade House (which was her sister's home, but where she was killed), and see the Evergreen Cemetery gatehouse, where Elizabeth Thorn and her family lived. More about all of these can be found at www.heroinesbehindthelines.com. Other historic landmarks mentioned in this novel that can still be seen today include the Soldiers' National Cemetery, Lutheran Theological Seminary (which now hosts the Seminary Ridge Museum), the Samuel Simon Schmucker House, Christ Lutheran Church, the Gettysburg Depot, and Gettysburg College (formerly Pennsylvania College). The Soldiers' National Cemetery has approximately 3,500 soldiers buried on its grounds. In the 1870s, Southern veterans' societies relocated 3,200 Confederate remains to cemeteries in Virginia, Georgia, and the Carolinas, such as Hollywood Cemetery in Richmond, Virginia. A few Confederates do remain interred at Gettysburg National Cemetery.

The signs and symptoms of combat fatigue that

Harrison Caldwell experienced were very real to war correspondents—and soldiers—of the day. I replaced Uriah Painter, the real reporter from the *Philadelphia Inquirer* who was on the scene, with Harrison, but Charles Carleton Coffin, Whitelaw Reid, and Sam Wilkeson were all real war correspondents. After the war, Coffin, who was a devout Christian and considered one of the best war correspondents of his time, went on to author fifteen books. Whitelaw Reid's coverage of the Civil War prompted Horace Greely to make him managing editor of the *New York Tribune* in 1868. Eventually, he controlled the paper himself, and went on to serve as minister to France and ambassador to Great Britain.

Readers of *Wedded to War* will recognize Charlotte Waverly from the first book in the Heroines Behind the Lines series. The nurse Charlotte's character was inspired by Georgeanne Woolsey, who did indeed nurse for three weeks at the Sanitary Commission Lodge at Gettysburg.

The text from the newspaper articles, General Lee's General Orders No. 73, as well as the addresses by Edward Everett and Abraham Lincoln, are also verbatim.

It was considered crass and unladylike for women to write and publish, so many civilian accounts were not recorded for decades. Sarah Broadhead did print her diary from June 15–July 11, 1863, to help raise money at the Sanitary

Commission Fair in Philadelphia in June 1864. Consulting the bibliography will show you when the other first-person narratives were recorded. Monuments have since been raised to honor Gettysburg civilian women Jennie Wade, the only civilian killed in battle, and Elizabeth Thorn, the pregnant gravedigger.

Primary source material, maps, photos, and other resources can be found at www.heroines behindthelines.com.

Selected Bibliography

Alleman, Tillie Pierce. *At Gettysburg: Or, What a Girl Saw and Heard of the Battle.* New York: W. Lake Borland, 1889.

Aughinbaugh, Nellie. *Personal Experiences of a Young Girl during the Battle of Gettysburg.* Privately printed, circa 1926–1938. Adams County Historical Society, Gettysburg, Pennsylvania.

Bearss, Edwin, and Anthony Waskie. *Philadelphia and the Civil War: Arsenal of the Union.* Charleston, South Carolina: The History Press, 2011.

Bell, Malcolm Jr. *Major Butler's Legacy: Five Generations of a Slaveholding Family.* Athens, Georgia: The University of Georgia Press, 1987.

Bennett, Gerald R. *Days of "Uncertainty and Dread": The Ordeal Endured by the Citizens at Gettysburg.* Gettysburg: The Gettysburg Foundation, 1994.

Broadhead, Sarah. *The Diary of a Lady of Gettysburg, Pennsylvania.* Privately printed, 1864. Adams County Historical Society, Gettysburg, Pennsylvania.

Buehler, Fannie. *Recollections of the Rebel Invasion and One Woman's Experience during the Battle of Gettysburg.* Gettysburg: Star and Sentinel, 1896.

Coco, Gregory A. *A Strange and Blighted Land: Gettysburg: The Aftermath of a Battle.* Gettysburg, Pennsylvania: Thomas Publications, 1995.

_____. *A Vast Sea of Misery: A History and Guide to the Union and Confederate Field Hospitals at Gettysburg, July 1–November 20, 1863.* Gettysburg, Pennsylvania: Thomas Publications, 1988.

_____. *Waster Valor: The Confederate Dead at Gettysburg.* Gettysburg, Pennsylvania: Thomas Publications, 1990.

Coffin, Charles Carleton. *Marching to Victory: The Second Half of the War of the Rebellion.* New York: Harper and Brothers Publishers, 1888.

Conklin, Eileen F. *Women at Gettysburg 1863.* Gettysburg, Pennsylvania: Thomas Publications, 1993.

Cooper, Samuel. *The Practice of Surgery.* London: A and R Spottiswoode, 1820.

Creighton, Margaret S. *The Colors of Courage: Gettysburg's Forgotten History: Immigrants, Women, and African Americans in the Civil War's Defining Battle.* New York: Perseus Books Group, 2005.

Dreese, Michael A. *The Hospital on Seminary Ridge at the Battle of Gettysburg.* Jefferson,

North Carolina: McFarland & Company, Inc., Publishers, 2002.

Duncan, Russell, ed. *Blue-Eyed Child of Fortune: The Civil War Letters of Colonel Robert Gould Shaw.* Athens, Georgia: The University of Georgia Press, 1992.

Foote, Shelby. *Stars in Their Courses: The Gettysburg Campaign.* New York: Random House, 1994.

Griffis, William Elliot. *Charles Carleton Coffin: War Correspondent, Traveller, Author, and Statesman.* Boston: Estes and Lauriat, 1898.

Hoisington, Daniel J. *Gettysburg and the Christian Commission.* Roseville, Minnesota: Edinborough Press, 2002.

Holmes, James. *Dr. Bullie's Notes: Reminiscences of Early Georgia and of Philadelphia and New Haven in the 1800s.* Atlanta: Cherokee Publishing Company, 1976.

Jones, Bernie D. *Fathers of Conscience: Mixed-Race Inheritance in the Antebellum South.* Athens, Georgia: The University of Georgia Press, 2009.

Kemble, Frances Anne. *Journal of a Residence on a Georgian Plantation 1838–1839.* New York: Harper Brothers Publishers, 1863.

Koontz, Hilda C., ed. *A Sanctuary for the Wounded: The Civil War Hospital at Christ Lutheran Church, Gettysburg, Pennsylvania.*

Gettysburg, Pennsylvania: Christ Evangelical Lutheran Church, 2009.

Letterman, Jonathan. *Medical Recollections of the Army of the Potomac.* New York: D. Appleton and Company, 1866.

Perry, James M. *A Bohemian Brigade: The Civil War Correspondents.* New York: John Wiley & Sons, Inc., 2000.

Sheldon, George. *When the Smoke Cleared at Gettysburg: The Tragic Aftermath of the Bloodiest Battle of the Civil War.* Nashville: Cumberland House, 2003.

Taylor, Frank H. *Philadelphia in the Civil War 1861–1865.* Philadelphia: Dunlap Printing Company, 1913.

Woolsey, Georgeanna. *Three Weeks at Gettysburg.* New York: Anson D. F. Randolph, 1863.

Discussion Guide

1. In June 1863, before the governor's official call to arms, the people of Gettysburg didn't take threats of invasion seriously. When has there been a time in your own life when you did not, for whatever reason, heed warning signs of danger? Has there ever been a time when your own community (local or broader) ignored red flags of impending disaster?

2. Bella made a choice to protect her daughter by keeping her heritage a secret, a deception that lasted twenty years. Do you believe there are ever good reasons to deceive someone else? If so, what would those be?

3. Abraham Jamison and the rest of the 54th Massachusetts regiment decided to fight for free rather than take unequal pay, causing great hardships for their families who depended on income. When have you had to take a stand on principle that required personal sacrifice, or sacrifice on the part of your family?

4. For a time, both Liberty and Amelia cloaked themselves in grief until it eclipsed their

individual identities. Has loss ever threatened to define you? What did you do about it?

5. Bella valued Liberty's protection above all else, which is something all parents can relate to. How do we know when to let our children experience danger?

6. Liberty's guilt over her response to Levi's wounds haunted her for two years. How does one break free of guilt?

7. One of the verses that helped Liberty move on was Philippians 3:13–14. In the NIV, the verses read: "But one thing I do: Forgetting what is behind and straining toward what is ahead, I press on toward the goal to win the prize for which God has called me heavenward in Christ Jesus." What do those verses mean to you?

8. What Bible verses have helped pull you through a difficult time?

9. During the course of the book, Liberty's hatred for Rebels transformed into compassion for wounded men, no matter where they hailed from. When and how has your perspective on an enemy changed?

10. Dr. Stephens used opium to deaden his senses to emotional pain, even though he knew it harmed his body. How do people do this in our culture today? Other than drugs, what else do we do when we want to numb our own heartaches?

11. At one point in the story, Silas asked Dr. O'Leary if he believed people could really change. How would you have answered him? What evidence of change have you seen in people's lives? What caused it?

12. Silas was held captive by the idea that God would not listen to him because of wrongs he committed in the past, or for neglecting to do what he knew was right. Do you believe there is anything that God cannot forgive?

13. One of the greatest heartaches at Gettysburg was all the unidentified bodies buried in unmarked locations. This was especially grievous for Southern family members who hated the fact that their soldiers were buried on what was then "foreign soil." What would you do if you did not have a gravesite for a loved one and could not recover his or her remains? How would that affect your grief?

14. Liberty, Silas, and Bella all felt categorized at some points in the novel. When have you felt like you were lumped in with a group and not given value as an individual?

15. Liberty's change of heart toward Southern wounded earned her disdain from others. When have your loyalties or perspectives shifted, causing surprise or disapproval from those in your life?

16. At one point, Dr. Stephens tells Liberty, "You don't know what you can do until you are required to do it." When has this proven to be true in your own life?

17. Amelia finally found solace from her grief by being able to comfort others who walked in the valley she had trod. When have you been able to use your life experiences to guide or comfort others?

18. Liberty had no choice when her farm was taken for a hospital, but no one forced her to pitch her tent at Camp Letterman and fill her days with more nursing. Why did she do that? Do we do the same thing to avoid painful realities in our own lives?

19. Some Gettysburg citizens became ill from pollution they were not aware of, such as corpses contaminating their drinking water. How do our spirits become polluted without us recognizing it? What are the warning signs, and how do we recover from that?

20. At the end of the book, Harrison Caldwell urged Bella and Liberty to write their own stories of their experiences during and after the battle. Why is it important to record our personal histories, even if it may not be significant on a national scale? How can writing be a form of therapy?

Acknowledgments

No book is written without the help of many others, so I have plenty of people on my list to thank. I am indebted to:

Moody Publishers/River North Fiction, for being committed to sharing these important stories in the Heroines Behind the Lines series.

My agent, Tim Beals of Credo Communications, for his continual support.

Rachel Hauck, author and consultant with My Book Therapy, for helping me brainstorm some key plot elements.

My husband, Rob, for allowing me to devote so much time to this project while he made memories with the kids, and for putting up with seeing me in frumpy elastic-waistband writing pants for most of every day for nearly two months straight. Good thing you married me for my mind. Thanks also for creating the beautiful map at the front of this book!

My children, Elsa and Ethan, for doing their best to let me write whenever they saw me wearing my writing pants.

My parents, Peter and Pixie Falck, for watching my kids so I could write, and to my dad specifically for his help researching some details of the battle.

Scott Hancock, associate professor of history and Africana studies at Gettysburg College, for pointing me to several valuable resources that helped me understand the climate of Gettysburg toward the black community.

A slew of historical consultants, including Benjamin Neely, Tim Smith, and Mavis Starner, Adams County Historical Society in Gettysburg; Roberta Brent, A. R. Wentz Library, Lutheran Theological Seminary in Gettysburg; Denise Doyle, Seminary Ridge Museum in Gettysburg; Terry Reimer, National Museum of Civil War Medicine in Frederick, Maryland; Peter Leavell, historian and award-winning author of *Gideon's Call*.

Jordyn Redwood, author and pediatric emergency room nurse, for being my medical consultant.

My dear friend Bettina Dowell, for invaluable research done on-site in Philadelphia.

The Civil War History writers group, for invariably having answers for my every question, whether it had to do with ammunition, pollution, or fashion: in particular, Debbie Lynne Costello, Loree Huebner, Kathleen Maher, Roland Mann, Tina Pinson, Patrick G. Whalen, Rachel Wilder. Special thanks to Debbie Lynne Costello and Kathleen Maher for being my beta-readers!

My friends Star Henderson and Kristy Brown,

for volunteering as impromptu research assistants when I needed it most.

All my reader friends, who have given me so much encouragement after my debut novel, *Wedded to War*, was released.

Keurig and the makers of K-cups for energizing my inspiration at the touch of a button.

Above all, I thank Jesus, for His use of parables to teach us profound truths, for His presence in my life, and for His presence, I hope, between the pages of my books.

Center Point Large Print
600 Brooks Road / PO Box 1
Thorndike, ME 04986-0001 USA

(207) 568-3717

US & Canada:
1 800 929-9108
www.centerpointlargeprint.com